Prince of Rhodes

Pine Trees

Prince of Rhodes

Pine Trees

R A Usher

SigmaDelta Books

First published 2022 by SigmaDelta Books

ISBN 979-8-4852-5662-3

Copyright © by R A Usher 2022

First Printing, 2022

Please address all enquiries to
SigmaDelta Books
21 Malbank, Cheshire CW5 5LU
www.sigmadeltabooks.com

Cover Illustration Credit

Cats Eys Photo 11438231 © Elena Varenik
Dreamstime.com

I would like to draw the reader's attention to the plight of hospitality workers on the island of Rhodes, indeed anyone that works in hospitality anywhere in Greece. While I have been writing this sequel, the world has suffered wave after wave of the pandemic.

The effect of the pandemic in Greece has resulted in two short summer seasons. In an ordinary year, a hospitality worker will expect employment from March to the end of October.

During this time, they must earn enough income to keep themselves and their families through November, December, January and February. In 2020 the tourist season was reduced to just four months. And a similar situation has arisen in 2021. It is tough for them, yet they still manage to smile and ensure that we (the tourists) have a fantastic time.

Through my visits to Rhodes, I have come across a lady that I call Saint Sophia. And she truly is a saint. This lady uses her own time and money to help those in need throughout the island.

Every day, Sophia and all tourism workers hide their struggles, worries and concerns to benefit others.

I dedicate this book to St Sophia and every hospitality worker in Greece.

Contents

Preface

Over the last three years, I have travelled a peculiar journey filled with fantasy in an imaginary world. In March 2019, I decided to write a non-fiction textbook on customer service and hospitality. I intended to use my Greek experiences as a shining example of what good customer service is.

Those who have read the Prince of Rhodes will have read how that textbook morphed into a novel. The premise of book one was that there was a band of renegade Olympians that were determined to undermine tourism on the island and return Rhodes to its agricultural roots.

Since its publication in March 2020, I have received many requests for a sequel. And the object in your hands is that sequel. Producing the story Prince of Rhodes – Pine Trees has allowed Rod to fill my head with a new journey. This journey is a little darker, and I claim no responsibility for the story. Rod Prince has driven everything in the story.

I have often read that a character tells the author what to write, and now I have experienced it first-hand. My fingers were merely transferring to the computer what Rod was telling me to type. Once again, I must thank my wife, Kim, for her patience and for allowing me time to adjust back to the real world after a writing session. She is also my greatest critic, and her honesty, though sometimes painful, has been invaluable when my storytelling gets too fanciful.

I must also thank Heather Cadwallader for offering to proofread my writing. I owe a lot to my editor, Paul Usher, without whose encouragement this story would still be stuck in the darkest recesses of my mind. It is probably also appropriate to thank those readers that have asked for a sequel.

My most immense thank you must go to Rod Prince, the character, and his constant fretting about what to do next. Without his continuous badgering, this story would be stuck in the first chapter. I hope you enjoy Rod's story and recognise elements of it when you visit Greece, Rhodes or Pefkos.

I want to say that the names of characters and locations are entirely fictional, but this is only partly true because several bar and taverna owners answered my plea when I asked for permission to include them and their establishment in the story. As a result of winning a prize in a charity raffle, two other people stepped up and let me use their names in the book. Debbie Webster and Suzanne Jones, I thank you. Although real names and establishments have been included, the actions of these volunteers in the book are entirely fictional. They are, after all, words dictated to me by a fictional character.

It is probably a good time to warn the reader that Rod has shown me a darker side to his life. As a result of his frustrations, his use of profanities has increased. I can only apologise on his behalf if this offends any readers.

Istoriko

"Can't you at least be honest with me?" I asked. Kam continued chucking her belongings into her flower-covered, carry-on case. She always went for the flashy colours. Me? I'd always had a less conspicuous approach.

"I am... I am being honest. I'll be back. I'm hardly likely just to use hand luggage if I'm going for good. Why don't you listen to me for once?" She slammed the lid of the case shut, frustrated at my doubt. Her reasoning was flawed, given that we were both still getting a generous income from D80 Ltd, our reward for overcoming the renegade gods.

"Of course, you will only need hand luggage. You can restock your wardrobe as soon as you get to the UK. Skimpy tops and shorts aren't going to be much good in England. You could've invited her here. You know the climate makes her feel better."

"Rich says he wants to treat her in the UK where the climate is colder."

I'd had my suspicions about her relationship with bloody Richard for a long time. Odd weekends away in Thessaloniki.

Late-night meetings to help with his medical research into fibromyalgia.

Another bloody lie.

"Oh, it's Rich now, is it? Why can't you just tell the truth for once? You've changed so much since we won the battle for Helios Hotel."

"I've changed? Have you looked at yourself recently? You aren't the man I married." She screamed, "You have become arrogant. You have become Mister Untouchable. You spend all your time with Zeus, and now you are becoming just like him. You've stopped involving me in decisions that affect me. We were always equal partners in this marriage. And my relationship with Rich is purely platonic. We are just friends."

At that claim, my adrenaline rose, and I launched her case across the room, its neatly packed contents now a crumpled mess across the floor. A trail of multi-coloured material. Lingerie that I had never seen before outlining the path to the truth. The truth was screaming in all its sordid glory in the form of a box of a dozen condoms. "Equal partners! Bullshit. I was always the mild-mannered one. I let you walk all over me. My life was only peaceful if I agreed with you. And what the fuck do you need johnnies for? Don't bother. I'll tell you what. He's welcome to you."

She clearly hadn't realised that I'd exposed the truth until I mentioned the play balloons. She gazed out of the window; her mouth firmly closed as if forcing herself not to spew forth any more lies. Tears ran down her face. These were tears of hurt; she was grieving. We were both grieving as we accelerated the final death throes of our once happy marriage.

Immortality doesn't give you eternal happiness.

Her anger returned, but her voice didn't. She scooped up her belongings and started to repack her case.

I just sneered at her as I walked out, making sure that I stepped on the box of condoms.

I hope I've punctured them all.

I uttered the final words of my marriage, "Have a good life." And I slammed the door shut behind me as I headed for my sanctuary that was the beach.

≈≈≈

I gazed out to sea and pondered where it had all gone wrong. Today was supposed to be the day that I kissed Kam goodbye at the airport as she departed for the UK. Her mission was to tend to Mags whose health had deteriorated since winning the battle for the Helios Hotel Resort. Kam's travelling companion was a Greek doctor who was a specialist in fibromyalgia which had crippled Mag's movement for years. And it was becoming more and more unmanageable.

We both knew he was the God of the Healing Arts, Asclepius. It was he that had the snake entwined staff that is now the symbol of medicine today. You will see it on the badges of ambulance paramedics in the UK. In the States, it appears on the star of life. In contemporary times he existed under the name Richard Bates or Rich to Kam. He was, in fact, the specialist that oversaw the blood swaps that kept us all immortal. He was based in Thessaloniki and was the son of Apollo. It was our link with Apollo that led to an introduction. The contradiction was that his appearance made him appear nearer the age of Zeus. He looked more like Zeus' younger brother than his grandson.

Kam had fallen for him big time. Richard this, Richard that, and Richard every bloody thing. To fill the boredom of our eternal life, she started to work for him in his medical facility. I'd suspected for about six months that there was more to it than she was telling me. I should have put a stop to it and nipped it in the bud. It suited me to have Kam occupied; it gave me time to manage the Olympian gods. She would say I'd taken her for granted. I would say I was busy.

For the first time since the war, I was truly alone. Alyss was in Athens, running a blog about the vegan lifestyle. Clearly, Athena's idea because Alyss always hated vegetables.

Lindon, meanwhile, had become a filmmaker. He was into making natural history films, and he was touring the world with Artemis. It was all logged on YouTube, and they had quite a following. He'd listened to me when I said that he needed followers if he wanted to become a god. They aimed to photograph nature and illustrate how many parts of the world were untouched by humans. With Artemis' help, he showed how some parts of the world had remained unchanged for 3000 years. It is no coincidence that these were the very places modern man hadn't exploited.

I shuddered and shook the lump from my throat. I had to stay on the island to stop the bloody god's fucking things up again. Without me, they wouldn't exist.

The power I'd gained had crept up on me. It wasn't an overnight change, but it became clear over time. It grew more evident that without me, the Olympian Dreams board of directors couldn't function. Not one of them had an IQ of any value. I even tested them.

"Hey Zeus, why don't we organise a quiz night for the staff? We can take part too."

"No. That is getting too close to the staff. Next thing you know, they will want to be our friends. They will expect us to be nice to them. They are mere mortals."

"No, they aren't. You know as well as I do that you are using them."

"I give them work, and I pay them well. That is not using them."

"Have you told them that they are immortal and that their only use to you is as a living blood bank?"

Zeus looked at me. He didn't show any guilt. His look was full of resentment because I had my own blood bank. He also knew that I didn't need to farm ex-mortals to maintain the freshness of the blood.

"You show me another way of storing the blood, and I will do it."

"No. If I do that, you will kill your livestock."

"Well then. There is your answer."

You don't want to do the quiz because you are stupid.

He'd taken part in our first staff quiz. It wasn't difficult to turn the quiz results into an IQ test, given that the quotient is a result of mental age divided by chronological age. Dividing any number by 3000 will give a pretty small result. I was confident when I told any of them that I had a far higher IQ than all of them put together. The cruellest part was that I even illustrated the point to Zeus, but he didn't have the intelligence to figure out why my IQ was 148, and his IQ was only 1.2. He just had to accept that I was over a hundred times more intelligent than him. He didn't see the disadvantage of having such a large denominator in his division. Poor sod just couldn't figure it out. Having documentary evidence took away any argument that he was more intelligent than I was. And that is why he didn't want to take part in another staff quiz. So many lies still surrounded me.

Because I had all the power, he made no decisions without consulting me first. He'd even started referring to me as the Prince of Rhodes.

"Rod Prince, you truly are the Prince of Rhodes," had become his new catchphrase as I doled out some meaningless advice to him on how to run Olympian.

Inside, my mind was telling me a different story. With Kam and the kids gone, my support had gone. I was alone, and all I had in my armoury was bluster and bravado. We'd decided that we were strongest together, and that was how we won the war. Now they'd all gone to do their own thing and left me to my fears and doubts.

I'd become bored with the power, often just galling Zeus just for the sheer hell of it. If our interactions had been online, I would have been called a troll, and he would be my victim. He and I both knew there was fuck all he could do to me. As Kam said, "Mister Invincible."

Monos

I sat shivering in the boardroom of Olympian dreams. All my senses stood to attention. They were telling me that something was wrong. I could hear my pulse, taste my fear, and I could see the panic in the face of Helios. The wall clock behind me, counting the seconds with a disapproving tut-tut-tut.

It reminded me of when my headmaster, Mr Whitehouse, had called my parents and me to a meeting. That time I deserved six of the best and took it like a grown-up. My crime? I'd discovered the word twat. I thought it would be good to call my form teacher a twat. But this time, I hadn't done anything wrong and didn't expect it to finish with a bamboo cane across my arse. Despite my self-reassurance, I was still filled with dread. It was the abruptness of the invite to the meeting that concerned me. Our relationship had changed, and Zeus hadn't made any demands on me since the war. But his text message demanded:

'Meeting boardroom 30 minutes come alone Z'.

And there I was, ten minutes of sitting in silence with Helios, Hades and Hera just contemplating their navels. The only communication was via Helios' look of terror. The gods hadn't even acknowledged my presence in the room. My greeting and questions just met with silence and fidgeting. I also tried trolling them, "Tick-tock clock on the wall, which is cleverest of us all?" Before anyone could react, the boardroom door finally swung open with a crash as it banged against a chair.

Zeus didn't even sit; the door slammed shut, broke the silence, and made everyone sit up straight. Tut-tut-tut, the clock continued, and it started to snow dust that the shockwave of the slamming door had dislodged from the ceiling. And all eyes were suddenly on me.

"What?" I queried, looking at them all in turn. Christ. Anyone would think I'd just farted out loud.

Finally, Zeus spoke. "Rod, you have a problem."

"Why do you do that?" I asked, and he looked at me as if I had just spoken in a language he'd never met. "You tell me I have a problem. When in fact you have a problem, and you want me to solve it."

"This time is different." And he stared right through me. He was waiting for a reaction. I just raised my right eyebrow. "The problem is Demeter has fallen out with Hades and Persephone. She has left the underworld. She is angry, and she is blaming you."

I laughed, "Is that all. I can deal with Demeter. I've done it before, and I can do it again."

"I know that, so does she. The problem is she has recruited help. The entire pantheon now knows you are immortal and worse still that you know how to remove immortality."

"But the whole pantheon knows how to remove immortality."

"No, they don't. It is only you and the Olympian gods that know that secret. You are perceived as the weakest link."

"Weakest link? That's a joke. I am the intelligent one."

I stared blankly through him as I tried to permutate the possibilities of my next move. He continued, "You are a wanted man. You are a threat to every immortal that lives."

"Of course. I know they're all fakes with the good fortune to have amber blood. Amber blood that I can remove. But you're still on my side, right?"

"I am afraid not, Rod," was his stark response. "We like you, and we are grateful for everything you have done for us. That is why I am warning you. But you are now the enemy, and I can't have anything else to do with you."

I looked at each of the deities in the room, "What the fuck. I helped you save the island. I've virtually been your leader since the war. You wouldn't have been able to function without me. I am the brains behind your board."

"No, Rod, you helped us find Apollo. And he is the reason for your predicament. He told you the secret that will now lead to your death."

"So why haven't you had me killed already?"

"As I said, we like you and perceive you as our brother. As family. We wanted to warn you, but that is all." He gestured around the room, "None of us here is safe as long as you are alive."

The room took on an instant chill. The atmosphere was frosted by the sorrowful group of deities.

"What about the rest of my family? Are they seen as a threat too?"

"We can't be sure, the word on Olympus is that you need to be silenced and Apollo punished. While we cannot help you, we will not help your assailants, either. We have made a set of komboloi for you. It is made up of the amulets of everyone in this room. That is the only protection we can offer you. It guarantees that none of us can do you harm."

"For fuck's sake, you are the king of the Gods, and you should overrule them."

"And that is the problem. I am the King, but Demeter has let it be known that you are the kingmaker. So, no, I cannot overrule them. That is out of the question. I am in the middle of a power struggle. I cannot be seen as weak by your enemy. If I am seen to be helping you, I will inevitably be overthrown. The only thing that has stopped it happening already is that they are fearful of my strength.... "

I interrupted him right there. "Hang on. This sounds too familiar. You mean you have a problem. You are under threat, and you want to use me as a weapon to help you solve it. Next, you will bring out a contract for me to sign."

Helios looked edgy at my statement, and still, he wouldn't look me in the eye. "What about you? My great ancestor, where do you stand in this power struggle?" He didn't respond, but he did glance across at Zeus.

"There is no contract. It is more of an agreement. You retain the protection of our amulets, and in return, you agree not to harm anyone in this room."

"Why would you even think I would harm any of you?"

"It is not that we think you would, the issue is that you could, and you do. You have become arrogant and continually erode my authority."

"Let me get this right. Politically your leadership is being challenged. To be able to repel your challengers, you are turning me, and Apollo, into your enemies so that you can give an example of your power and authority."

"I wouldn't put it quite like that, but if I am to remain as King of the Gods, I must distance myself from the threat you pose. To remain in contact with you is too dangerous. I would have a conflict of interest."

"Oh. And using us to assassinate your opponents isn't dangerous."

"What does Apollo think of your scheme?"

I could have guessed Zeus' response. "Um, I haven't told him yet. I hoped you would do that."

"What about wanting to be a better father? The one thing you always longed for and you abandon it in favour of your other job. King of the Gods."

The rest of the board sat silent. They were witnessing a mere human challenge the authority of Zeus, and he was just sitting and taking it.

Hades chipped in at this point. "Rod. I have a lot of respect for you, but this is a perfect illustration of the problem. For 3000 years, no other being has dared to speak to Zeus the way you do. They would be cast into the underworld. Our opponents see this and think Zeus has become too soft to be King. He needs to be seen to assert himself. As he said, you have become arrogant."

"Me arrogant? I am the nicest bloke you would ever meet. Everything I have done has been for the betterment of you guys. And if he is that assertive, why is he using me to do the asserting."

"Using you as his agent is better than the proof our opponents want. They want him to destroy you and Apollo."

"You guys do realise that Apollo and I are the keepers of a blood bank?"

"Of course," acknowledged Zeus.

Fortunately, since winning the war, everyone on the board of Olympian Dreams had worked together on blood storage. We had calculated that all the guys could donate four times a year and the girls three times a year. The harvested blood was frozen to increase its shelf-life. We'd recruited the help of Asclepius and christened him Richard Bates. That was my idea. I referred to him as Dick Master of the Blood Bates. We paid him a handsome fee for harvesting the blood and doing transfusions, as necessary. It was stored at the sanctuary in the mountains.

"How long have we been considered a threat?"

"For many months, we have tried to protect you. But the threat is now imminent."

"For fuck's sake. If you had let me know as soon as you knew, I would have had time to prepare."

"We are sure you are prepared enough. We have thought long and hard about letting you know at all."

"No, what you have done is to make sure the family are separated. Lindon is fuck knows where with Artemis. Alyss is a vegan in Athens with…" And then I paused as the light bulb went on in my head. "You crafty bastard. Not only have you separated us, but we are all stuck with a divine escort. Why would you do that?"

"Relax, Rod. Think about who the chaperones are. They are allies, not enemies."

"Yes, your bloody allies. I thought you were an ally and not an enemy. But here you are. Casting me out."

"Well, we wouldn't put it quite like that, but yes, you must leave. Besides, if what I hear is correct, you have driven them away."

Helios finally chipped in, "Where will you go, my friend?"

One thing I'd learnt early in my relationship with the gods was to keep my cards close to my chest. I looked at him and raised an eyebrow, "Friend? You're nothing but an imposter. Anyway, what are you doing here? If I recall, you are a Titan, not an Olympian. Where the true god of the sun and I go is none of your bloody business." That shut you up, didn't it? *Twat.*

He had no comeback. I didn't feel in the least bit cruel. Maybe I shouldn't have been so blunt. Zeus wore a wry smile. In the past, we'd often discussed Helios' lack of intellect. But the joke was on Zeus because no one in the room had any intelligence.

"Now, now Rod, be gentle with poor Helios. He is just concerned for you."

"I'm still not telling any of you where I am going. It'll just leave me open to more treachery."

"Ok, this is the deal. I am not signing your agreement. I will take your amulets. But be warned. I promise you that if anything happens to any of my family. You will be all be made mortal, and then I will kill each of you. Your political opponents will be the least of your problems." And I spat at Zeus. Not as an insult but as a seal on the promise.

Not one of them spat back. They just stared at me. They had gone silent on me the way that Kam had before I stormed out.

"Remember this. You guys will need me long before I need you." This was a lie because, at that point, I felt lonelier than I'd ever felt before. I snatched up the komboloi, barging past Zeus and flung the door open. I enjoyed the noise he made as it connected with his elbow.

≈≈≈

"Rod, my brother, how are you? And what news of your family?" said Giannis.

We hugged and did the cheek kiss.

"Giannis, I have a load to tell you. Kam has buggered off with your grandson…" and I proceeded to tell him all that had happened at Olympian.

"Well, Rod, it seems this sanctuary is no longer safe," lamented Apollo, "We should find somewhere together."

"I have already been thinking about my options. I considered returning to the UK. But Kam would think I was chasing after her. And part of me wants to stay and fight. Besides, going back doesn't guarantee they won't trace me there."

Apollo contributed, "I think you will be safer here. We will be stronger together here on Rhodes. We have access to the blood bank, and the weather is better." And he smiled to lighten the mood.

I wasn't in the spirit of lightening the mood, "Giannis, this is serious. We don't know how long we have. We need to find somewhere that we wouldn't expect to be seen and still somewhere that gives us complete solitude when we need it. We have to move the blood, and its location must be our secret."

"The solitude will be easy. The Pine Tree forest around Monolithos will allow us to hide from anyone. And Monolithos means lonely rock."

"Perfect, I guess there is no electricity, so that won't be where we store the blood. That will need to be in a more populated location."

Then Giannis pointed out, "Anywhere which is more public will need to have a large British population. Otherwise, you will stand out."

"Unfortunately, the places where I blend in best are where the Olympians blend in best."

"I think I know just the place. It is over towards Lindos. You will have heard of it. It is called Pine Trees. You may know it as Pefki or Pefkos."

"Perfect, I've always liked visiting Pefkos. I have Greek and British friends there."

"Do any of them know of your relationship with the gods? Do they know of your immortality?"

"No. Of course not."

"Perfect. Pefkos will be our new home."

Pefki

Sat in the sanctuary among all the old farm implements. I thought back to the day Giannis revealed they were all gold-tipped weapons. I was woken from my imaginings by a sudden loud bang. The auctioneer had banged his gavel onto the sound block., "Πωλούνται" shouted the sales agent, and Giannis jabbered in Greek before hanging up the speakerphone. My heart was in my mouth and choked on every pulse of its thumping beat. Less than one million euros for a 20-room hotel and we hadn't even looked it over.

"That's it, Rod, we are now the proud owners of the Pefko Dentro Spiti Xenodocheio."

"Pefko, what Hotel? Bloody hell, that's a bit of a mouthful," I said, picking up on the two words I'd managed to understand. "More like a tongue twister."

Giannis looked at me with a frown. I'm not sure if he even knew what a tongue twister was.

"No, No, in English, it is Pine Trees House Hotel. Pefko is a pine tree, and Spiti is a house. Therefore, it is the Pine Trees House. The good news is that they are leaving all the fixtures, so we get to use the big chiller units in the basement under the kitchen."

"And that is the perfect storage for the blood. When do we get to see it?"

"We get the keys tomorrow; they are being couriered to Helios Hotel. Filipos will have them by 9:00 am. So far as anyone is concerned, I was the agent acting for him, and he has bought the Pefkos House to add to his portfolio of hotels."

≈≈≈

"Ah Vangeli, my friend, I believe you have a package for me?"

"Of course, unless you want to sell me its contents for two million euros," and he roared with laughter."

"Mr Filipos, you are ever the businessman," I responded with a much quieter laugh.

"No, that was my way of saying you have an excellent deal. That hotel and location are worth twice what you paid for it. Congratulations, I will make you into a Greek businessman yet."

The hotel was surprisingly spacious and yet had a warm feel to it. Every room had been prepared before the auction. All rooms were perfect in every way, and they were ready to be occupied by guests. You know that feeling when you buy or rent somewhere, and it needs nothing doing to it. The hotel had been closed for a year for refurbishment. And as the previous owners had wanted to leave Greece, they hadn't pursued any bookings or even attached themselves to a tour operator. It was a clean slate, or should I say clean marble. Everywhere was white. The ground floor housed reception and a sizeable bar-cum-dining area, reminiscent of a UK pub-chain pub, just not so cramped. The first and second floor rooms either had views of the sea or the pool backed by the mountainous area inland. The roof space had the potential for a roof garden or a penthouse. All bedrooms had en suite bathrooms of black and white marble, and each of the veranda windows was full-length sliding glass. The entire wall between the front and back walls were completely mirrored, which helped to make the rooms appear larger than they were. I am confident that it was a deliberate act to have the mirrored wall facing the bed. At that point, my thoughts strayed to Kam and whether or not she would ever come back.

"OK, Giannis, what's the catch."

"There is no catch. We won it at an auction fair and square. It just so happens no other bidder was willing to bid against us."

"Not willing to bid against us. You mean they'd been warned off." The rat I could smell was worse than a bush tucker trial of fish guts.

"Why do you think we were posing as agents for Filipos? No local on Rhodes would ever want to upset him. Just about every household has at least one member of the family that works for him."

"I've seen that in action. He can be an angry man."

"Yes, and if you upset him, someone in your family will suffer. He is ruthless. You are a fortunate man because he likes you."

"Extra lucky, because I am hoping he can help us staff the hotel when we eventually open for business. Have you thought any more about the date to open?"

"For this first season, we will be taking over-bookers. Mostly in July and August."

"Over-bookers?"

"Yes, remember your first visit to the island. The hotel hadn't heard of you, so they sent you to another hotel, Helios. Well, we will be Helios for hotels on this side of the island.

"Genius, why didn't I think of that?"

"It was Filipos' idea, don't forget he is the expert at hotels, and we should use him for as much as he is willing to give."

"True. But he is still shit at customer service, and we won't be seeking his help with that." And we both laughed out loud.

With the noise we were making, we didn't see the intruder enter the reception. Without warning, it launched itself at Giannis, hissing, growling, and scratching at his face. If he hadn't been immortal, I am sure it would have killed him. I picked up a fire extinguisher, pulled the pin, squeezed the trigger and fired foam directly at the beast. It screamed, scrambled down Giannis' body, and fled the scene.

"Fucking cats," roared Giannis. That wasn't the first time I had heard a Greek say that.

I could have laughed about it any other time, but at that moment, I could have crapped myself. I've never disliked animals. I tended to just accept them, never fussing over them. I just ignored them. Unfortunately, this had the effect of drawing them to me, Kam who loves to fuss over animals, says my nonchalance is read as being a pack leader, so they strive to obtain my approval. That theory wasn't working at that point because Giannis wasn't paying the cat any attention. It was as if the cat had sought him out. I was closer to the cat, and it completely ignored me to get to him.

"Thanks, Rod. I hate cats. Should we put poison down to kill them?"

"No. No way. I'm not a great fan of animals, but I'm not cruel. I could only kill it if I thought it was a god sent to kill us."

"Maybe it was trying to kill us."

"No, it wasn't. Remember that the gods are ordinary people with immortality, and they have manufactured a myth to give them a godship. They can't transform into animals. It just took a dislike to you, probably sensed you hated cats, so it hated you back."

It was directly after this event that I discovered we'd bought a hotel whose nearest neighbour was a charity called Nine-Lives. Nine-Lives mission was to protect, feed, and neuter stray cats. Giannis needed to change his attitude to cats; otherwise, we were in for a lot of trouble with our neighbour. Battles we could do without, we had more significant battles to fight.

≈≈≈

"Your best option is to manage it yourself. I know you could do it. You have virtually done it for me at Helios."

"Yes, I know, but I won't be there all the time. I need someone to run it while I am not there."

"You need an assistant. First, you must find someone you

can trust," said Filipos, returning the advice I'd given him when we first met. He continued, "I can put one of my managers on secondment to you. I will offer the opportunity to all of them and see who wants to work for the strange Englishman," he laughed. "You should interview them and pick which one you like."

Aphrodite

I probably didn't pick the best day to conduct the interviews given what happened to Caesar on the ides of March. Giannis had assisted by sifting through the applications allowing us to come up with a shortlist of four. His was a significant contribution given that a Greek CV is typically over five pages long. I sat in reception, reviewing the sea of paper before me, waiting for the first candidate to arrive. I glanced out of the glass front of reception in time to see a battered old Fiat appear in a cloud of dust. It let out a loud backfire which sounded more like a fart. It clattered to a stop, the engine rattling like a bag of bolts. It reminded me of that stormy day when my Eos died back in 2012. I was sure that the pink beast before me was once gleaming blood red. It had obviously lived a long life in the sun. The car's body was flecked with irregular brown spots, which gave it the appearance of a leopard with mange. It had stopped before it crashed through the glass front, but the cloud of fumes and dust didn't. The fumes preceded the driver announcing his arrival. I was now a teary-eyed spectator as the exhaust pollution stung my eyes. The drivers dented door opened with a noise louder than the fart that had emitted earlier, and like an echo, it clattered loudly as it was slammed shut. As the driver appeared through the cloud of dust and smoke, his face looked familiar. I glanced down at his application, and sure enough, the photograph on his CV confirmed that the first candidate had arrived.

Lefteris Afroudakis, his resume announced loudly with an over large font. I don't know which was the loudest, the car, the CV, or Lefteris' voice as he boomed, "Yassas, Mister Prince."

I reached out to shake his hand, "Yassas, Mister Afroudakis. Come through," and I pushed the door open to my office, "Please, call me Rod."

"Lefteris," he said. He entered the room and got off to a flying start as he sat in my chair. The smell of exhaust fumes was replaced by an aroma that I can only describe as cat piss.

"Would you like coffee, Lefteris?" He loudly declined. The percolator was on a shelf behind my now occupied seat. I made myself a coffee, and this allowed me to look him over without him realising. I was not sure if his hair was greasy from hair gel or if he had just got out of the shower. He was dressed smart enough but hadn't shaved. The light blue shirt he was wearing was wet all down the back. I thought to myself, *please don't lean back. You're sitting in my chair.*

I put my coffee down on the desk in front of him, and he waved his hand. "Oh, I said no to coffee."

"Lefteris, it is my coffee. Your chair is there," and I gestured to the other chair in the office. At which he sidled around the desk.

"I apologise. Nervous." He announced.

Nervous or not, I'd made up my mind. Mister Lefteris Loud and I weren't going to get along. I couldn't cope with a daily assault on my olfactory nerves. I had to go through the process of asking him questions. The nadir of the whole process came with his answer to one of the questions.

"Lefteris, tell me about the last time you had to deal with an angry guest."

"Ah, I have had to deal with this a lot."

I interrupted, "In Mister Filipos' hotel?" Knowing full well that angry guests were a thing of the past at Helios.

"No, at Prometheus."

"You haven't mentioned Prometheus on your application."

"I didn't want people to know I worked at Prometheus. It is a bad hotel."

Minus one for massaging the truth in your application. Minus a second point for slagging off a previous employer.

"OK, please continue. Tell me about the last time you had to deal with an upset guest at the Prometheus hotel. How did you deal with them?"

"It was a guest that complained about the quality of the food. They wanted vegetables only. They didn't eat meat."

"Vegetarians."

"Yes, and that is ridiculous. People can't survive without meat."

He paused and looked at me for affirmation. I winced.

"I told them that the website doesn't say we cater for such people. I told them they were only staying for two weeks. I was sure that it wouldn't hurt them for such a short time."

"And did that calm them down?"

"I don't know because they left the hotel." And he laughed, he bloody laughed.

God help me if this is the best we've got.

The sad part was that he couldn't see anything wrong with his answer.

I made some notes on his CV. *Should include Loud, Liar, Discriminatory, Intolerant, Not self-aware and, No empathy.*

I couldn't get him out of the office quick enough. I didn't even bother asking him if he had any questions.

I stood and reached to shake his hand, "thank you for your time and for showing an interest in the position. We will be in touch."

Then I had to stand in reception and watch as he struggled to get his Fiat to start. Fortunately, I'd remembered to close the door before the second fart of thick black exhaust exploded from the arse of the pink leopard.

≈≈≈

"No, trust me, Giannis. He can't be the best of the four candidates. I hope the other three are an improvement. I am worried that we aren't going to find a manager." And I closed the call on my mobile before throwing it down onto the desk. The whole Lefteris interview reminded me why Filipos always used to get so angry.

No one cares about the guests, so long as they are earning a wage.

Candidates two and three weren't any better. Number two stank worse than Lefteris and the farting leopard. And three answered every question with a question. He also kicked a stray cat on the way in. I wondered where the famous Greek filoxenia had gone. The fourth candidate didn't even show up.

I called Filipos. "Vangelis, please help. I had four of your managers in for an interview, and none of them was anywhere near suitable. I am surprised they work for you."

His reply was stark, "Give me their names, and I will fire them."

"No, I don't mean for that to happen. I am just surprised that they managed to survive an interview with you."

"They would have been interviewed by one of my General Managers."

"Can I have one of those guys?" I can't believe I asked, given the candidates they had passed to work for Filipos.

"I'm afraid not, my friend."

I ended the call and threw the phone down onto my desk again. I reached across to the percolator; I needed an extra-strong black coffee.

"Hello," shouted a female voice from reception.

If that's number four, they've blown it. Punctuality is key.

I opened my office door and froze. The woman before me was dressed like a businesswoman, casual blazer, white blouse, and a pencil skirt cut tastefully above the knee. *Christ, look at the height of those stilettos.* Her hair was held up in a ponytail. But this pony had such a long tail that it was able to cascade down over the front of her left shoulder. It appropriately formed a directional arrow as it signalled to the location of her left breast.

I was roused from my imagination, "I am sorry to startle you, and I seem to have let a cat in through the front door."

I stammered, "That's OK, it's a hotel cat."

"How sweet. Does it have a name?"

"Not yet. It's only been the hotel cat for a week." I lied, trying to conceal the fact I'd dumped it in Kremasti the previous day.

I looked down at the cat as it rubbed itself against the visitor's bare legs, able to weave between them as the woman stood with her feet apart. *God, I've got so many puns in my head.*

"I'm sorry, is the cat bothering you?"

"No, I love cats, and this is such a sweet little kitten."

It was pure black and must have had some Persian history because it was long-haired and had copper coloured eye's which shone like a brand new one-cent piece.

"No, it's fine. It is so sweet. I am sorry for just dropping in, but I understand you are looking for a hotel manager."

Well, that got my attention. "Um, yes, we are."

"We?" she questioned.

"Yes, I have a partner that owns the hotel with me."

"I see. I was going to ask if I could apply for the role. Do I apply to you or your partner?" she asked as she offered her CV to me.

"Me. Please come through to my office, and I opened the door for her. I inhaled as she passed me. *Oh my god, what a beautiful smell.*

"Please sit. Would you like a coffee?"

As she sat in the correct chair, she flashed her white teeth from between her bright red lipstick. "Coffee would be lovely."

I turned to hand her the coffee just as she crossed her legs.

The cup started to rattle on the saucer as my mind flashed back to Sharon Stone in Basic Instinct. I hurriedly collapsed down into my chair before I could be accused of staring.

I cleared my throat and started to read her CV, "What hotels have you managed?"

"Unfortunately, my experience is limited to placements while I was studying for my degree in Hospitality and Tourism Management. But the placements include some prestigious hotels on the island. I worked at Olympian Dream on a six-month placement in my final year."

This rang more than a few alarm bells. It meant that she would have been at the god's lair for six months. "How did you hear about our vacancy?"

"I have a college friend that works at Helios Hotel, and she told me about it."

"Do you know why she didn't apply for the position herself?"

She looked disappointed that I was asking about her friend. "She is happy at Helios and prefers that side of the island."

"What about you? Why are you interested in the role?"

"Honestly?"

"Of course."

"I understand that you wish to employ a manager that can run the hotel in your absence. A twenty-room hotel would be perfect for me to make a success and grow my CV." She flashed her teeth at me again. This time running her tongue along her upper lip. "And it is on the side of the island I wish to work." As if pulling out all the stops, she went in for the kill. "I love British people, and the thought of working for an

Englishman excites me." And she uncrossed her legs and lent forward, revealing a hint of cleavage. To be honest, the confidence of this woman terrified me to the point I hadn't even introduced myself or asked for her name.

"Please forgive my rudeness, I'm …"

"Rod Prince, owner of Pefkos House Hotel. I have done my research. I am Aphrodite… Aphrodite Koutos." she interrupted.

"You have put in some preparation to get an interview, haven't you?"

"No, I have put a lot of preparation to succeed in getting the role." And she flashed those pearly white teeth again. I was half expecting to see a starburst flash from the corner of her mouth, reminiscent of a particular toothpaste advert.

I bet that makeup took more than a minute or two to apply as well. This girl is trying to impress.

Then I felt my hackles rise as my body went on full alert, ready to fight or flight. There was only one kind of being that would put that much effort into their preparation to get close to me. I went into full detection mode, and I stared deep into her eyes. I was waiting for her to do the squinty god thing.

"When you were at Olympian Dreams, did you meet with the board?"

"No, I didn't. I saw them from a distance, of course. They were a pretty strange group. One of them used to drive a taxi everywhere. I could hear him shouting all the time. My mentor was the operations manager, and he never let me anywhere near the boardroom." The whole time she was talking, I stared directly into her eyes. I was looking for tell-tale signs of the honesty of her reply.

Inside I breathed a sigh of relief. She appeared ignorant of the fact that the entire board were gods. More importantly, she won't have seen me coming and going.

She must have misread my intention because she raised her right eyebrow and licked that bloody top lip again. Oh well, she passed that test. My hackles subsided, and I found myself asking when she could start.

"I graduated last summer and spent last season, on placement at a hotel in Rhodes new town. I have had a relaxing winter, and I can start as soon as you wish."

"We have no immediate bookings. The plan is to take walk-ins and overbookers in July and August. The key part of the role will be to recruit staff between now and the start of June. We can discuss some of the detail once you are in the role. I will employ you from 1st April until 30th November. At the end of the season, we could potentially discuss a winter retainer. Are those terms agreeable to you?"

"Yes, perfectly agreeable. Would you like me to start looking for suitable staff right away?"

"No, not while I'm not paying you."

"I don't mind. Why don't I come in next Monday, and we can talk about your needs?" And she paused, raised her eyebrow and wore a devilish grin. "I mean your staffing needs."

I stammered, "That sounds good to me."

She smiled, "That's a date, 9:00 Monday. Thank you so much for giving me a chance. I promise I won't let you down." She stood, shook my hand and then she was gone. She'd disappeared as suddenly as she'd appeared. All that was left was the traces of that beautiful scent. I inhaled deeply through my nostrils to savour the aroma.

The cat remained, jumping up on my desk, as it settled down and started to purr quietly. "Looks like you've got a job as well. You've been promoted to hotel cat. But what are we going to call you?" I started to rattle out names of famous cats, "Felix, Corky, Lenny, Leo, Clarence, Elsa …" *God, I don't even know if you are male or female.*

In the blink of an eye, the cat's mood changed. It growled, hissed, and spat. Standing with its body rigid, it faced the door to the office. As it was between me and the door, its tail pointed towards me like an arrow. The scene reminded me of some Attenborough video of big cats about to commence a battle. My office door swung open, and in one movement, the cat launched at the person entering. "Rod. Get it off me. Help."

Giannis was squealing like a cat. "Bloody hell Giannis, it's only a kitten."

"Come on, kitty, Giannis is a friend," I spoke in a soothing voice and put my hands around its chest to try and extricate it from Giannis' clothing. My touch seemed to do the trick, as the cat seemed to take that as a signal that it would be safe.

"That bloody cat has got to go," said Giannis in a stern voice.

"How? I've already tried taking it to the cat hotel in Kremasti, and that has got to be over 50 kilometres away. It reappeared this morning."

"I can't cope with being attacked when I visit."

"We will just have to teach it to like you, or you could stop coming here," I smirked at him; he didn't notice. He was too busy counting the scratches.

I moved back towards him, and the cat growled, "This is Giannis. He is a friend," I whispered as I stroked the cat to calm it. The feline fur devil was having none of it and continued to growl. Giannis backed off, and the cat finally shut up.

Giannis stayed safely in the doorway, "What news of the interviews?"

"We have a manager," I beamed.

"Why do you smile?"

"It's a manageress, professionally qualified, some experience. And most importantly, she passed the god test. She isn't one, and that's why I'm grinning."

"Which one of the four did you select?"

"None of them. This was a lady that had heard we were looking for a manager. She has worked at Olympian and Helios, but I will check her credentials with Filipos. She is coming here on Monday at 9:00. You can meet her then. But please don't abuse the kitten in front of her because she likes cats. Here, have a look at her CV." And I handed him the written path of her life. I was seeking reassurance that I had made the correct choice.

"Aphrodite? You are hiding from every god alive, and you employ someone called Aphrodite."

"What's in a name? None of the deities uses their given names. Hold your judgement until you've met her and had a chance to talk to her."

≈≈≈

Filipos had spoken to one of his general managers, and it turns out that Aphrodite had indeed spent a period at Helios, and she'd impressed. The manager would have employed her, but she was adamant that she wanted to work on the island's East side. Something to do with wanting to be near her parents.

My phone buzzed, warning me that Aphrodite was due in 30 minutes. The kitten had been playing gently on my lap. I knew Giannis was near because the cat stood rigidly upright and started to hiss. I hugged it close and whispered to it, trying to calm it. Giannis walked into the office, and I tightened my grip on the cat. This eventually calmed her down, but it didn't quiet Giannis. He was terrified of the tiny fur ball. I gradually released my grip on her.

"Hello," shouted Aphrodite. The cat recognised her voice because it leapt from my lap. It ran past Giannis. In seconds, it came back into the room, escorting Aphrodite safely past Giannis.

I stood, held out my hand, "Aphrodite, good to see you again. This is my business partner Giannis." I nodded in his general direction without taking my eyes off of the vision before me.

"Giannis, this is Aphrodite."

He held out his hand but didn't speak. He simply acknowledged Aphrodite with a slight nod in her direction. While it was their turn to shake hands, I took the opportunity to raise my hand to my face, inhaling deeply as I did. My hand was carrying her scent and delighted my nostrils.

"Have we met?" she queried.

He stammered, "I don't think so. Most of my time is spent up in the mountain, in Apollona. I have a taverna there." I wondered if she was aware that she is the reason that men stammer in her presence.

"That might be it. I have been to Apollona."

Giannis looked at me and raised both eyebrows. His body language confirmed that he approved of Aphrodite. I knew he would because he always did have an eye for a pretty picture.

We spent the rest of the day discussing what we were looking for in the team that she would build. She warned that financially we should employ staff for one month at a time. We decided that we would give her a staffing budget, and she could allocate that as she saw fit. We also agreed that we wouldn't accept any guests until June at the earliest. As a business, she was targeting a packed hotel in July and August. I wasn't happy because I'd told Filipos many times that we should factor in two empty rooms each week to accommodate running repairs. If we filled the hotel with guests, we were setting ourselves up for guest complaints. But Aphrodite saw that as wasted income, and Giannis agreed with her. He'd been seduced by her beauty and assertiveness. The discussion ended with me declaring, "We'll see."

Giannis' mobile rang, "Parakalo? Nai... uhu... fuck...OK...Parakalo." And he dropped the phone on the table. "Aphrodite, I apologise, but Rod and I need to be somewhere. Rod, give her the spare key."

I looked at him, thinking to myself, *what the fuck.*

I gave her the key, "Can the kitten stay with you? When you go, just let it out. It won't go far."

"Of course. Is there anything I can do to help?"

Giannis snapped the way Greeks do, "No. Use the office and find us some staff. We will be gone for a few days."

I was as puzzled as Aphrodite. The cat wasn't puzzled. I followed Giannis through the door, and the cat meowed before following me through the door. "Sorry, Giannis. It looks like the cat's coming with us."

Bastet

In a voice taut with stress, Giannis said, "We will go in my car. I will drive, and you can keep that bloody cat from attacking me."

"Why? Where are we going? What's wrong?"

"There are gods in Apollona. The call was from the box keeper."

"If there are gods there, why are we going there?"

"Because I've got paperwork there, and they will find out we have a place in Pefkos. We are supposed to be disappearing, not leaving a trail."

"For fuck's sake, Giannis, we discussed this before. You were to leave Apollona and not leave anything to connect your old life with the new you. Do we know who the gods are?"

"No. The box keeper says that two strangers have been asking questions about me."

"We can hardly go to Apollona in broad daylight."

"I'll park the car between Apollona and Eleousa. It's March, so it will be dark by six, and we can walk into the village unseen." I smiled to myself as he'd started to use contractions in his speech.

"I think the cat has got used to you. Stroke it and see."

Giannis looked at me with squinted eyes. It was as if I was talking in a foreign tongue. Another godly habit he hadn't managed to shrug off. "You are still a crazy Englishman."

His right hand reached over to stroke the cat. It stiffened, and its long fur rose to attention, but it didn't growl or hiss and spit. The bonus was that Giannis got to keep his skin intact. It was the weirdest of sights, a three-thousand-year-old man terrified of a tiny kitten. "There you go. It's accepted you." He wasn't convinced, but at least he'd stopped squinting.

≈≈≈

Six o clock approached, and the air chilled, and the stars twinkled as if sending a coded message. The shadow of the earth on the moon, displaying the thinnest of crescents. Giannis glanced up, "It's a young moon."

There was no way I was leaving the cat in the car, not knowing when or if we might make it back. Phones on silent, Giannis shivered visibly.

I looked at him, and through chattering teeth, I stuttered, "Are you scared?"

"No. I am Greek, and it is bloody freezing."

This reassured me, but he did have a point it was a bit nippy. I pulled the zip up on my black bomber jacket. I still shivered. I guessed I was terrified. I whispered, "N-n-no. You are G-G-G-Greek, and you are talking loud."

We started the ten-minute walk into Apollona. We took the

kitten with us. The cat led the way, I had no idea how it knew where we were heading, but it stayed in front of us all the way to the taverna. Occasionally, it glanced over its shoulder at us to make sure we were still following it. The walk warmed me up, but my body continued to tremble. It was almost a relief when we approached the street lighting of Apollona until Giannis pointed out, "We are visible now."

"Shush," I whispered. I put my hand in my jacket pocket to confirm I had my lucky gold-tipped dart to hand. It was still safely sheathed by the tip cover. My mind darted back to when Giannis revealed the damage that gold could do to the amber blood of an immortal. "Do you remember the time we first met?"

"Of course. I told you of the Olympians secrets." And he'd finally turned his volume down.

"Yes. And that is how we have found ourselves in this mess."

"No. This is the same mess you were in before. You wouldn't have survived then without the secrets. This is a completely different mess. This is down to your arrogance."

I wanted to tell him it was my intelligence that saved my family. His last comment made me shut up. *Christ. Don't pull any punches, will you?*

It wasn't long before I realised the street lighting wasn't our only problem. Most of the houses we passed hadn't closed their blinds. And lit windows from numerous homes stretched ahead of us like the landing lights of a runway. We were no longer hidden by the darkness. "Why don't Greeks close their blinds when night falls?"

"How else do we know what our neighbours are up to? Close the shutters, and Yiayia is sightless."

Again he tried to call the keeper of the boxes. No reply.

"We have to assume the worst because he always answers my call," said Giannis.

As we neared the taverna, the cat slowed and crouched as if it was stalking a sparrow or some other small prey. Its tail pointed towards where Giannis and I were stood. It started to let out a low-pitched growl. We could see a dance of light and shadow in the taverners living quarters.

"Someone is in my bedroom. Should we leave it for now?" Whispered Giannis.

"No, we can't. We can't risk them finding anything that gives our new location away. If they've already found it, they would be gone already. It is now or never."

I unsheathed my dart. "We have surprise on our side. We can get into your room without going through the taverna."

"But if we go through the taverna, everyone in there will be a friend of mine. They will help us," reassured Giannis.

"Exactly, you walk into the taverna, and they will all greet you in their booming voices. That would be a perfect way to announce our arrival. We'll go through the side door."

Giannis handed me his keys. *Oh, I guess I'm going in first then.*

I went to put the key in the lock, and I felt the door give. The lock had already been broken. As I pushed the door open, the kitten took the lead and dashed up the stairs. What followed can only be described as a cacophony of screams, growling, and hissing. It was a catfight. Before I'd even figured out what was happening, a massive shadowy figure came dashing down the stairs, leaping 2 steps at a time. The sinister being was closely followed by the cat. The figure barged past me, and my dart snagged on the visitor's clothing. I later examined the dart, and sure enough, it had traces of red blood on it. If the intruder was a god, they were now mortal. In the meantime, the commotion had alerted the entire taverna as they joined us from the bar. My first thought was that there should be a second intruder if the box keeper was correct.

Giannis' phone vibrated, "Yes, are you OK? And they have gone now? OK, pack away the boxes and go to the address I gave you yesterday. We will see you there."

"They have gone. They were seen speeding away in a car. The keeper couldn't answer the phone when I called because he had one of the strangers with him. His boxes are still safe."

He addressed the locals, "All is good. Drinks are on the house."

We went upstairs and managed to retrieve the papers that so nearly gave our whereabouts away. Giannis reassured me that they hadn't been disturbed. They were still under the rug in his bedroom.

I tried to phone Zeus, but the number didn't exist. *The bastard has changed his number.*

From some stupid sense of misguided loyalty, I thought I should warn him that there were new gods on the island.

Sod him if he is going to fuck about deleting his number.

I was more interested in trying to figure out which gods we'd just encountered. I couldn't give a description, but the box keeper could. We returned to Pine Trees to debrief what had just happened and who we were dealing with.

≈≈≈

"You only need to call me the box keeper when there is someone around, I am Petros, or you can call me Pete," *Who'd have thought it. Bloody Pete.*

"Did you see the cat move?" Queried Giannis.

"More to the point, it completely bypassed you. It must be getting used to you," and I laughed.

"I'm bloody glad it has got used to me too."

"This might seem a strange question, but is Petros a god?"

"No. He is my crony. Like yourself, he has immortality, but he is just a servant of a god. You see?"

"Yes, but don't you see? The cat likes me. It also likes Aphrodite, and it isn't freaking out about Pete." I nodded towards Petros as if asking for permission to call him Pete. "It hated the intruder, and it used to hate you. Do you reckon there's a chance it can sense gods?"

"Take it to Zeus and find out," and all three of us laughed.

"Can you imagine that? Zeus with a ball of fluff scratching at him," They both laughed.

I was more interested in trying to prove my theory. If I was correct, it meant we had an early warning system that didn't involve getting close enough to do the squinty eye test.

"Does Zeus know who Pete is?"

"I don't know," answered Giannis.

"I'd be up for it," said Pete anticipating what was coming next.

Giannis warned, "Athena and Artemis will know who Pete is."

"It doesn't matter. Athena is in Athens with Alyss, and Artemis is with Lindon somewhere that isn't Greece."

"You don't need to confront anyone. Just watch the cat and see how it behaves when you go to Olympian Dreams."

Pete raised the question we hadn't even been thinking about. "What is the cat called?"

"Christ, we don't even know if it's male or female," I lamented.

Pete hoisted the kitten up by its tail before announcing, "It is female, and she has been spayed."

"What do you guys reckon to calling her Jet? It reflects the speed at which she shot upstairs at the taverna."

Giannis said, "I don't care. It is only a bloody cat."

Pete voted. "Yes, that is a good name."

"No. She is more than just a cat, and she just saved our secret. OK Jet, welcome to the war."

≈≈≈

Pete relayed his visit to Olympian Dreams. "Before we got anywhere near the boardroom, Jet was hissing and growling like she was possessed by the devil himself. Oh, by the way, we have Zeus' new phone number. Look. It has been painted over the old one on his taxi." And he showed us an image on his phone.

"What a dick. I knew he wouldn't figure out the stupidity of changing his number when he needs it displayed on his taxi. Great work, Pete." I think the direction of that interaction was lost on Giannis.

"I don't get it," was all he said.

"Don't worry, it's a human thing," Pete and I both laughed. Giannis didn't look happy. He resented that he was outnumbered. Even though he'd been outnumbered for three thousand years.

"Can you not do that. And who gave Petros a say in anything?"

"Given that he's in as much danger as us, I think he's entitled to a say."

"But he is only a crony."

I sniped back, "If it comes to it, I'm a crony too."

"No, you are arrogant. You are showing off in front of another human. Maybe Zeus is right, and you are a threat to all deities."

"Awww, come on, Giannis. It was a laugh at Zeus' expense. Remember him? The same guy that you didn't talk to for hundreds of years."

"Yes? Well, it was a bit close to home, given that I don't get the joke and he is my father."

"OK, let's clear this up. I call you Giannis because we are brothers. I don't see you as a deity. If I did, I would call you Apollo. It is you that told me that the gods don't have any powers beyond immortality. You don't consider yourself a god, and I don't consider you a god. You are just a human. Zeus is stupid, and you are not stupid. Zeus has cast us both out of his inner circle. Given our power over immortality, that should tell you how stupid he is. There is no difference between you and me." Then I paused a little so he could digest the logic that proved I wasn't arrogant.

"How does that prove you are not arrogant?"

"Because the people that don't understand that logic are the same people that would think I was arrogant. That's how I know you understand the logic." That confused him more, but he knew that if he called me arrogant again, it would be admitting he was stupid. "What about you, Pete? Did you follow the logic?"

"I'm not sure I did, Rod." He bemused.

"I did. I understood," bragged Giannis as if proving he wasn't another dumb deity.

"Good. Because you need to be on the ball and bright as a star if we are to defeat our enemy. And don't forget if I am arrogant, then you must be too. We are brothers. We are the same. Anyway, let's have no more in-fighting and put it behind us." I'd started to confuse myself by that point. "I think we all have a date with a bottle of ouzo. Who's up for it?"

By the time we'd downed our third shot, the conversation had returned to normal.

"Do you think I'm right that Jet can sense when a god is nearby?"

"Maybe," said Pete.

"More importantly, who were the gods that went to Apollona?" Said Giannis.

"We're going to have to do a bit more research," I concluded.

Phobos and Deimos

It didn't take long for the research to be completed. I was in Rhodes new town, buying clothes from Pull & Bear. Some formal trousers and a couple of shirts. It then hit me how much I missed Kam. I felt loneliness wash over me. Triggered by her not being there to tell me I was buying something that looked shit on me. I started to ponder on the last time we were together, my anger, the row. I thought the shirts were fine, white with thin blue stripes. Very business-like. They complimented the navy tapered-leg trousers. I guessed she would say it looked too formal. That was the look I was after. I wanted to be dressed like a leader, like a boss. Internally I questioned, *like Zeus?*

I was crossing the road by the central taxi rank when I almost got run down by a taxi, and I had the green light. *What the fuck,* "Malaka."

The taxi driver dropped his window. I could feel the flow of cooled air emanate from the open window. "What the fuck are you doing," said Zeus.

"And who the hell do you think you are talking to," I

replied.

He got out of the taxi, slammed the door shut, with the engine still running. "You mortalised a god."

"Of course I did. He was a threat to me and Giann ... Apollo. I guessed he was trying to find where we'd relocated to. Anyway, it has nothing to do with you since you cast us out. I see you have a new phone number."

"How do you know that?" He queried.

"Duh, stupid, it's written on your taxi."

He sheepishly glanced at the altered phone number, which was clearly on display, "Oh."

"And that proves my point. You aren't fit to be king of the gods. I might as well walk away and let them overthrow you. I might as well just return to the UK and leave you to your destiny."

"No, please. Please don't do that."

"Then get back into your cab and sod off," I commanded.

"OK, I am going, but please don't abandon me. I need you to see this through."

"One thing. Before you go, who were the gods that came?"

"The god you mortalised was Phobos. God of fear. The one that you left unharmed was his brother. The god of terror, Deimos."

"In that case, get lost and leave me to it."

Zeus jumped back into his taxi. True to form, there was a screech of spinning rubber as he jumped the lights, which had now turned red.

As soon as I'd returned to Pine Trees, the three of us started our monthly blood donation. Moving to a monthly rather than a quarterly donation was a risk. Asclepius assured us that it was the easiest way to increase the stock level. The procedure was to take in by transfusion a single bag of blood that was approaching its expiry date. We then spent 20 minutes on a treadmill merging the old and new blood. This was to refresh and enrich the blood. We then donated two bags back to storage. It always took about 15 minutes per bag. By the time we added a recovery period, it was always a good couple of hours. It was an opportunity to just chill in the cold of the walk-in fridge. Given the heat outside, it was always a pleasurable experience. It was also an opportunity to just sit and talk. I told Pete and Giannis of my run-in with Zeus and his naming of the intruders.

"Phobos and Deimos gods of fear and terror? Sent to frighten us off," said Giannis.

"And discover our whereabouts," added Pete.

"We just have to hope that we disturbed them before they found what they were looking for," I said, voicing my concern out loud.

"It matters not. They have achieved their goal," added Pete.

With a puzzled look on his face, Giannis queried, "What do you mean?"

"Are you frightened? I know I am. If they were sent to frighten us and make us fearful, then they've succeeded," I said.

And Pete nodded in agreement.

"When I told Zeus, I was thinking of walking away and leaving them to it, he went into a real panic."

"Of course, he did because he has so much to lose. He has had it all his own way for thousands of years, and now he is being challenged. He knows there is a big battle on its way. I know my father and trust me, he is terrified."

I pointed out, "I guess that's why Phobos and Deimos have been sent."

Pete added his contribution, and it sent a chill down my already cooled spine, "We don't know where they were sent from or even if they were sent. Maybe there are a hundred gods on the island. Just because we only encountered two of them, it doesn't mean they are the only ones here."

"That's a sobering thought. And we have no way of finding out," I added, looking at Giannis, hoping he knew of a way.

It was Pete that offered a possible solution, "What if we lured them to come out into the open again and took one or both of them, prisoner?"

"Why? Do you fancy capturing fear and terror? I know I bloody don't. A cornered beast is at its most dangerous. If we found ourselves in that position, it would be a fight to the death. Like I said to Zeus, I have half a mind to walk away."

"That is exactly what Phobos and Deimos want. That is why they were selected to reveal themselves first," said Giannis in his first meaningful contribution.

"More to the point. How does Zeus know it was them?"

"I also wonder if we would be better separating. Imagine if they walked into the hotel and we were all here. If we separated, then they could only capture one of us at a time.

Then there would be two of us to mount a rescue," advised Pete.

I raised my voice, "Right. This conversation stops right now. This is a conversation filled with fear about what might happen. We've let fear and terror get under our skin, but we can't let that happen. We need a plan to capture one of them and get answers. The only way we can achieve that is by working together. No more talk of giving up or separating. Agreed?"

They both replied together, "Agreed."

All for one and one for all. Thank God I didn't say that thought out loud. When I look back, we were a motley crew. Our team consisted of a three-thousand-year-old Greek god with no powers and little understanding of modern-day technology. A three-thousand-year-old Greek human who had some knowledge of modern-day technology and some knowledge of the gods. His greatest strength was that he was a critical thinker. And then there was me, little understanding of Greek gods, an adequate understanding of modern technology. My strength? The brain power of many Greek gods put together. I'd been accused by the gods at Olympian Dreams of being arrogant, but it wasn't arrogance. It was superiority, but it was the only power I had. It was a bit like the story of the Kings new clothes. The perceived arrogance was my means of making the deities believe that I was more powerful than them.

"By the way, Giannis, Aphrodite is coming in tomorrow at nine. Will you be here? We can talk to her about the features we want our new staff to exhibit."

"Of course. We also need to make sure we have a security system down here."

Pete chipped in, "I can arrange that. I will go into town tomorrow and organise something."

≈≈≈

I put on my new clothes hoping that they would make me appear to be a confident hotel owner. Aphrodite was due in an hour, and she was bound to be dressed for a board room meeting. My uniform was the navy pinstriped pants, a gleaming white shirt with thin blue pinstripes, and a scarlet tie. And I polished my shoes. I was relieved when Giannis turned up in jeans and a t-shirt. I knew he was coming because Jet went on full alert. She did relax once she saw it was only Giannis.

"Bloody hell, Rod. What's the occasion? You look like you are heading to a bloody wedding. You look like Zeus. I guess you're trying to impress someone." And he laughed at me.

The embarrassment caused my volume to go up to Greek levels, "Well, it isn't to impress you."

"Does Kam know you have appointed a manageress?"

"No. She doesn't. She doesn't even know I've purchased a hotel and probably doesn't even care. More to the point, I don't care either. We have a communications embargo.

Giannis just grinned. I couldn't tell him that she had buggered off with his son.

Before I knew it, nine o'clock loomed, and Aphrodite arrived. Jet greeted her in her usual manner, walking figures of eight between Aphrodite's naked calves and slender ankles.

Jesus, those heels certainly accentuate your calves.

As I raised my eyes, I realised that Aphrodite had caught me staring at her legs. I could feel myself blush. She just smiled and licked that top lip again.

Giannis broke the moment, "OK. We have much to discuss. We need to decide exactly what we want from our staff."

I sat at my desk. Giannis sat opposite me. Aphrodite squeezed behind my chair and sat at the edge of the desk immediately to my right. It reminded me of the brainstorming sessions with my family. *God, how I miss you all.* Then my inner thoughts were distracted. *Did she just brush her breasts against my head?*

Giannis just wanted to employ Greeks. Aphrodite was insistent that ability in hospitality was of greater importance. Because we were in Pefkos, I was adamant that the ability to speak English was a priority. Gradually, we honed the requirements to the point that I thought we were all in agreement.

"That's it then, hospitality or customer service experience is the greatest priority above nationality. The second priority should be a good command of the English language …"

Before I could finish, Giannis interrupted, "We haven't decided on men or women."

I looked at Aphrodite, then we both looked at Giannis. I was about to respond to him when Aphrodite placed her slender hand on mine. I trembled, and she spoke, "Giannis, if we select someone that meets the first two requirements, their gender is irrelevant. Haven't you been paying attention?"

He growled, "Bloody humans, ganging up on me again."

Uh-oh. You idiot. Aphrodite looked at me puzzled, and I glared at Giannis, "What are you talking about, man? Have you been on the ouzo again?"

"I meant um ... um ... cat lovers. I was thinking of that bloody cat you both like so much."

We might just recover this. "You mean Jet?" And with perfect timing, Jet jumped up onto the desk and changed the topic of conversation.

Aphrodite interrupted, "Oh. You have given her a name. Jet, what a pretty name, so sweet." And she squeezed my hand.

My heart was pounding as I slid my hand from under hers and petted Jet.

"Yes, Giannis is sore because Jet doesn't like him. But she adores our friend Pete, and we keep teasing him about it. Don't we, Giannis?" And I raised an eyebrow inviting an affirmative response from him.

He replied as directed, but he was still irate, "Yes, and I am sick of it. You both always try to make me look stupid."

"Oh Giannis, come on, we don't try to do anything."

Aphrodite took over. She leant forward, and this caused her leg to encounter mine. I moved it away, but her leg followed. I trembled again and swallowed deeply.

"Giannis," she said in a sultry voice and Greek accent. She smiled at him and licked her top lip. "I admire you as my employer, and you are special to me because you are Greek. Just because I like Jet and you don't, it doesn't mean I think any less of you." Then I felt her foot move up my leg. I could have stood up, but I would have fallen over.

"Yes, come on, Giannis. You know Pete, and I love you like a brother."

Aphrodite spoke in Greek. I didn't catch much of what was said. She used words that were new to me. But I did notice one phrase, "S'agapo."

This caused me to relax a little, now that she was flirting with him. She had just told him she loved him too.

He blushed, and his brashness was gone, "Ignore me. I am just a little touchy at the moment, what with moving out of Apollona."

My heart rate was just starting to subside when Aphrodite squeezed my leg. *Shit, I can't deal with this.*

I could barely speak, "OK, to recap the priorities. Customer service, English and sex doesn't matter."

"Surely you mean gender doesn't matter. Because sex does," and those full red lips smiled, and that tongue darted across that top lip again.

Shit, I'm going to pass out in a minute. "M-M-Meeting adjourned, you guys go and get lunch. I have some paperwork to tie up."

Giannis smiled, "Yes. Come, Aphrodite, I know just the place."

As much as I tried, all I could do was stare at Aphrodite's rear as they left the office. The cat stayed with me. "Bloody hell, Jet, what am I going to do? How can I stop the bloody flirting? She bloody terrifies me more than any god." Jet just purred and rubbed herself up against me. "Don't you bloody start."

My immediate task was to get a bigger desk. It needed to have sufficient length and width to all sit around it without being too close. I didn't want another meeting like that.

Paranoia

Pete had done well. He'd found a builder that reworked the layout of the back office in just three days. Our office expanded to accommodate access to the cold store in the basement. It now resembled a board room. The cold basement had been divided into two storage areas, one of which could be used by the kitchen. The other became the owner's wine store. The door to access the cold store was digitally coded to stay locked, and a signal could be sent from our phones to unlock it. It was the same as having a home hub. The system was as secure as our phones.

Surprisingly, Giannis was the first to voice my concerns, "What happens if we all lose our phones?"

Pete moved to the door, "Athanasia." The door clicked and swung open.

"That's not very secure. Anyone could say immortality in Greek and do that," queried Giannis. As he finished talking, the door slammed shut.

"OK, you try it, Rod," invited Pete.

I moved towards the door, "Athanasia," the device just let

out a single ping.

"See, it is secure. I had to stand in front of the door and say Athanasia." I was still in front of the door, so it just pinged again.

"Oh, I get it," I said, revealing my enlightenment.

Before I could elaborate, Giannis went off on one again, "You are both doing it to me again."

Pete and I chorused, "Doing what?"

"Making me look stupid."

"Come on, Giannis, we aren't. It is just that I realised how the system works. It uses voice recognition and iris recognition together. You know about many things that I have no understanding of. Don't get cranky when I understand the technology, and you don't. It's just one of those things."

He grunted, "Well, it doesn't feel good when you show how clever you are."

"For god's sake, you are starting to sound like your dad. What happened to the chilled-out Giannis?"

"He got crushed by the new Rod," and he glared at me. "There was a time when you consulted with me about things because you were lost in your new world. Now, look at you, the big man that knows it all."

He had just used a phrase that I used to use with Lindon as he was maturing. *Maybe he is right. I'm getting too big for my boots.* I just replied the same way Lindon used to with me, "Whatever you say, I am sorry if I have upset you." It was always Lindon's way of saying, 'sorry you are upset, but I am not changing.' This seemed to placate Giannis.

"You are right though, there is a floor in the security," I

said as if to confirm that Giannis wasn't stupid.

It was Pete's turn to express confusion, "How so?"

"The codeword is too commonly used by us. Can you imagine being here with a god present, and I start arguing with them about immortality …" and the door swung open.

Giannis re-joined the conversation, "We need a word that isn't used very often."

Isn't that what I just said? "Exactly, Giannis. See, you aren't stupid," And I winked at him.

He beamed a Cheshire-Cat type grin of pride.

Pete looked at me because he knew exactly what I had just done. He winked at me, and I beamed a Cheshire-Cat grin of arrogance.

The space created by the modifications meant we could get a more extensive desk. The old desk was put in a room behind reception. This would be Aphrodite's office. The new desk of polished black oak almost created problems with Giannis, but I steered him into which seat was to be his.

I opened the bidding, "I think I like that end of the table, it has its back to the cold store, and I can't be distracted by the cats at the charity next door."

Giannis countered, "I was hoping that would be my end of the desk."

"OK, if it means that much to you, you can have it. I will just have to put up with the distractions of facing the cold store and the view out of the window." Of course, I had to feign disappointment that I hadn't got what I wanted.

We spent the morning organising our relative ends of the desk, placing two chairs on both long sides. We now had a proper boardroom. Of course, it was nowhere near as lavish as the one at Olympian dreams. But it did allow space for other people to join discussions without sitting on our laps or playing footsy.

≈≈≈

We were able to hold our first meeting with Aphrodite, and we included Pete.

"Aphrodite, can we introduce Pete? We have appointed him as director of security. You are still our general manager. But in our absence, you will need to clear your decisions with him. The way you would with us."

She pouted those red lips, relaying her disappointment. "Does that mean I won't be dealing directly with you and Giannis?"

"When we are around, of course, you will deal with us. When we're away, you will answer to Pete."

Changing the layout of the room changed the dynamics of all our relationships. For the first time, I felt like I was the boss. I pulled out a chair gestured for her to sit. It was closer to me than Giannis, but still too far for her to play footsy with me. Pete sat at my right hand.

I lowered the lid on my laptop, and it disappeared into a hidden compartment in the desk. Giannis spotted this and looked amazed. He closed his computer, which he hadn't even used yet, and looked open-mouthed as it too disappeared into the desk. "With the modifications, you now have an office of your own just off reception. You can use the boardroom if you need more space. Giannis, would you show Aphrodite to her office?"

I watched that exquisite rear as it disappeared through the doorway.

"Pete, I need you to make it your business to know what she is up to every second of the day. You must check all her staff. We cannot afford to employ any gods."

Pete knew how to manage me, "OK, boss." And he smiled.

"Don't let Giannis hear you calling me that." And I smiled back.

≈≈≈

"Aphrodite, how do you like your office? Is it to your liking?" I asked, knowing that she would say she loved it, even if she didn't.

"I love it."

"How is the search for staff going?" Opened Giannis.

"Slowly, but I have shortlisted, and I am confident that we will be able to fill all positions with reliable staff that know customer service and speak a good level of English."

"Excellent," I beamed before adding, "Can you pass your shortlist to Pete before you proceed. We need to do a security clearance on them."

She looked puzzled, "Why all the security?"

Giannis, true to form, jumped in with the wrong answer, "We can't tell you it is a secret."

I buried my head in my hands. *You are becoming a damned liability.*

"Giannis is partly correct. The truth is that I have a mental health condition that makes me paranoid about people trying to harm me. I didn't want you to know about it." *For god's sake, now she'll think I'm paranoid.*

"Ah, that explains why you have been pushing me away then."

"Yep, I'm afraid so."

She just looked straight into my eyes and said, "I will just have to show you that I mean you no harm." Then she winked and blew a kiss.

I blushed, Pete laughed, and Giannis roared. Aphrodite just licked her top lip again

"What's so funny?"

Aphrodite provided the answer, "Being paranoid is a Greek thing. We trust no one, not even our own government. You are turning Greek. That's what is funny."

I thought to myself, *Oh, what the hell.* And I blew a kiss back at her.

Everyone roared. Giannis said, "He is already Greek. Look at him, flirting with the staff."

Back in the UK, I could have been charged with sexual harassment. Probably got a black eye from Kam too. But here, it was a milestone. I was no longer the dumb Englishman. I was a clever Greek. For the first time in my life. Greece felt like home. Something I'd yearned for since that first visit in 2013.

≈≈≈

I had spent much of my time ensuring the hotel was set up to my liking. As the modifications neared completion, I spent more time searching for information on the remaining three hundred Greek gods.

Pete entered the boardroom. "Rod, we have a problem."

"Don't tell me. The builders want more money."

"No. If that was it, I could deal with it. I haven't been able to contact Giannis since yesterday's meeting with Aphrodite."

"Have you tried his mobile?"

"Of course. My name is Pete. I am not Giannis." That was the first time I'd heard Pete voice a hint of disloyalty to Giannis.

I moved toward the basement security door. "Maybe he is giving blood - Athanasia." And the door swung open."

Pete followed me down to the cold store. "That knocks that theory on the head." I unlocked and opened the chest freezer, which was sat in the corner of the room. It was still humming to itself. "How much blood should we have?"

"Twenty-six bags." He said as he scanned the donation log.

"And when was the last entry?"

"March 24th. It is dated for the other day, when we all came down to switch blood, just after our run-in with the gods in Apollona."

"Then why do we have twenty-seven bags?"

Pete looked at me as if I was wrong. "There can't be. We keep meticulous records. Check again."

"No, you check for me. I will try and find him. He may be at Monolithos. You know what the mobile signal is like down there. He is probably there. If you need me, send a text, and I will pick it up when I get back in range. I'm going to take Jet with me."

≈≈≈

Monolithos was our other sanctuary. The one that was out of the public gaze. We were in the process of setting up the location. We'd found a well-hidden cave deep in the pine forest. We had christened it Big Pefkos. I parked up at The Castle Café at Monolithos. I had a frappe and spent some time playing with the parrot. I looked at my phone, and the signal strength was on one bar. I messaged Pete.

'I'm at the café. What news of the bags?'

The message came back quickly.

'We have an extra bag. It has yesterday's date on it.'

I pondered to myself. *What are you up to, Giannis?*

I left my coffee half-drunk and made my way into the forest. To big Pefkos.

It was a bit of a trek, but I hoped that it would lead me to Giannis. As we neared the cave, Jet went into hyper detection mode. Hissing, crying, tail pointing. There was a god nearby. I guessed it was going to be Giannis. Once I could see the cave, Jet was still snarling and growling. The difference was that she was looking in the opposite direction.

I left her to it and entered the cave. I flicked my phone torch on. What I saw made my spine freeze. A feeling I hadn't felt since Poseidon had tried to kill me at Apollona. Only a few days earlier, Giannis and I had cleared any evidence of habitation. Our efforts had all been undone. Remnants of a fire were still smouldering. It was clear that someone had been staying in our sanctuary. I wanted to shout for Giannis but didn't dare.

I was startled as Jet joined me. Her blackness acting as camouflage against the lack of light in the cave. She was calm, telling me there was no god in the cave. I extinguished the torch and let my eyes adjust to the blackness. I fumbled my way to the back of the darkness and felt for the solid rock in front of me. I turned to my right and inched my way forward. My eye's straining to make anything out in the darkness. It was a delay until I managed to make out the super black that was the narrow passage. The passage that would lead to the upper chamber. Jets constant purring, a reassurance that we may be alone. As I continued forward up the inclined gap in the cave wall, my eyes detected the almost imperceptible flicker of light ahead.

I entered the upper chamber, and it was deserted except for the flickering of a candle. Its flame dancing in the draught created by the natural flow of air from the mouth of the cave. The air continuing its journey through the fissure in the roof above the candle. I flicked my torch back on. I scanned the chamber, looking for any differences from my last visit. Save for the flickering candle, everything was just as we'd left it. *What are you playing at Giannis? And, where are you?*

I turned to make my exit along the narrow corridor. The harsh light of my phone ignited a bright reflection from the wall by the portal to the main cave. I inspected the source of the reflected light; it was the amulet that Giannis gave me during the first war. It was the amulet of Apollo. It had been wedged into a small cleft in the rock. A one-word message was etched on the wall above the split in the rock. 'SORRY', was its stark message. I extracted the amulet and placed it into my pocket along with the komboloi that the board had given me.

≈≈≈

"You are the one that has known him the longest, and you are his crony. What is he up to?"

"I don't know, Rod," said Pete.

"Why would he give me his amulet?"

"You know the answer to that. It is your protection from him."

"Yes. But why do I need to be protected from him?"

"We can only guess at the possibilities."

"And all of the possibilities are out of character. He is loyal and considers himself my brother. He even agreed we are stronger together. I think he's had a breakdown."

"I don't. He has a strong character, and Greeks are too laid back to have breakdowns."

"So does Filipos, but he had a breakdown when the Argonists destroyed his hotel. I hope he has had a breakdown. It is the only answer that doesn't put us at great risk."

"How so?"

"He may have switched to the other side. He may have been captured. He has deserted the combat. He may betray the secret of Pine Trees. We just don't know."

"Do not assume the worst. To do so will mean you have lost the race before it has started."

"You are right. I suspect that if he's betrayed us or

changed sides, we would already know about it. I think we should change the password to the blood chamber. Just in case."

"Quite!"

The loss of Giannis hit me hard. I was now even more alone than before Zeus evicted me. *Maybe it is time to throw in the towel and walk away.*

Nemesis

Aphrodite was a welcome distraction, but she had to be told something about Giannis' absence. "Mister Rod, where is Mister Giannis?"

"He has some business in Athens. He won't be joining us for the meeting today."

She smiled. Most likely because she now only had one boss to flirt with. "What is his business in Athens? Is it business or personal?"

Pete interjected before I could reply. "It is business and not of your concern." Being brash isn't a Greek quality I have mastered yet. *Thanks, Pete.*

I had taken to playing with my worry beads. It eased the stresses I'd felt since Giannis had disappeared. I pulled them out and started playing with them. Something I immediately regretted.

"Oh, what a beautiful komboloi," said Aphrodite. And she rolled her office chair in my direction and grabbed my hand.

I glanced at Pete. He was smirking at me.

"The medallions are so pretty. What do they represent?"

"They are just old coins I got from a souvenir shop in Rhodes Old Town. Each one represents a person that has had an impact on my life."

"Ooooh. Have you got one that represents your favourite hotel manager?" And she winked at me.

I blushed. "Er. Um. Aphrodite…"

"Oh, Mr Rod. Please call me Affi; all my friends do." She had broken a Greek tradition. As the more senior, in age and position, it was up to me to introduce familiarity.

Pete came to my rescue. "Aphrodite. That is inappropriate. Please leave the meeting now."

Affi exited the room, and I thought to myself, *don't look at her bum.* But I decided to ignore myself, and I looked anyway. Jet followed her.

"Rod, be careful. I know she isn't a goddess. But I fear she is playing you for her own advantage. In Greece, it is highly inappropriate for an employee to ask their boss to be informal. If you want informality, it must be you that initiates it. Please be careful."

"Don't be silly. It's a British thing, and she has picked up on it. That's all. You worry too much."

"No. Now Giannis has gone. I want to be your crony and swear my allegiance and loyalty to you. I am not worrying too much. I am just doing my job as a crony."

"I must be the first crony to have their own crony." And we both laughed.

"I have seen the way she looks at you. She did it with Giannis, too and look what happened to him. Might it be a good idea to get Kam back to Rhodes?"

"No. that's impossible. She is staying in the UK. I don't even want her to know about me being cast out by Zeus."

"Are you sure that is the only reason?" And he nodded towards the door that Affi had left through.

"We need to sort a new password for the lock to downstairs," I said, completely changing the subject.

"Very well, One last word on the subject of Aphrodite. A Greek proverb – 'An open enemy is better than a false friend.' Now the password."

"I'm sorry to say that I have been trying to identify English words that Greek's find difficult to pronounce. Once we have chosen a word. You must practice saying it with an English accent. At least it will give us an additional layer of security."

He laughed. "Did you have any words in mind?"

"Yes, anything that has Q and H in it. I was thinking something like Hungry Squirrel."

I then spent ten minutes trying to teach the poor sod how to pronounce the phrase. And it still sounded like Xungeree skeerel. It needed a lot more work. His 'h' was too harsh, and the 'qui' was stuck at 'kee'. At least it reassured me that no Greek would be able to access the blood. I just had to get Pete to be able to do it.

"We will stop there. I might pick another phrase yet." And I chuckled at him. It was nice that he could laugh back. "Can you checkout the names on Affi's, I mean Aphrodite's list? I am popping to town for some shopping." And I slid the list of names of applicants to him.

Aphrodite was at her desk. "Affi, I am going to town for some shopping. I will be gone for the rest of the day. And by the way, you can call me Rod."

She gave an uncharacteristic squeal. "Can I come? I need to buy some office supplies. It would be better for the environment to use only one car."

She had covered all the bases and rendered my potential excuses impotent. I swallowed deeply and said, "Of course. But Jet stays here. I don't want her getting lost in town." *What else could I say?*

Being a gentleman, I opened the passenger door for her. She put her left foot into the car and slid her bottom into the seat. Her right leg was still on the ground. The angle created between her legs was too great to protect anyone's modesty. I had just discovered when an obtuse angle could be a cute angle. Doing the gentlemanly thing, I had a quick glance, and then I looked away. I looked at her face, and she had been watching me, watching her. She smiled and licked her upper lip again. *Bugger, she's caught me looking.* After what seemed an eternity, she placed both feet in the car, and I could finally shut the door.

I slipped the car into first gear, and I felt cool, smooth flesh against the back of my hand. Aphrodite squealed, "Ooooh, Rod. You naughty boy, you touched my knee."

No, I didn't. You're sitting with your legs apart, and your knee is where first gear should be. "Sorry. It was an accident. I was just trying to change gear."

"I could always change gears for you. That is if you don't mind me handling your gear stick." *For god's sake, why me?*

Trying to pull off at the next junction without using first gear was fun. "Don't be afraid to use first gear. I don't mind, and I won't tell anyone that you keep touching my knee." And she laughed.

I didn't relish that we had the best part of an hours journey ahead of us without using first gear. The whole sixty kilometres became me trying to either speed across junctions to beat a red light or crawling along, waiting for red lights to go green without stopping.

The conversation was as erratic as my driving. We must have spoken about a new topic every kilometre.

"Why has Giannis gone to Athens? When will he be back? How long have you lived in Rhodes?" You would think she was interviewing me. The trouble is she interspersed these interview questions with a range of inappropriate questions. "Have you ever been to the nudist beach in Faliraki? Would you like to go there someday? These closed questions were easy to answer with a blunt no. It was the open questions that were most difficult. These started off quite gentle at first. "What do men find most attractive in a woman? What do you find attractive in a woman? How would you describe me to someone? Do you think I am attractive? What do you like best about my body?"

"Stop. You are asking questions I cannot answer. I am married, and I love and miss my wife and family. You cannot ask me these questions. It isn't fair."

"Oh, don't be so stuffy. It's just fun. All you have to do is say no comment." She laughed again. "What was your most erotic moment?"

"No comment."

"Who is the most beautiful woman you've ever met?"

"That's easy. The goddess, Athena." And I was left silent as I realised what I'd said.

Aphrodite broke the silence. "Silly, I meant a real live woman."

If only you knew how real Athena was.

"Who is the most beautiful living woman you have ever met?"

"My wife."

"OK. Who is the most beautiful Greek woman you have ever met?"

"No comment."

Then she started to narrow it down. Really putting the pressure on. "Try this one. Who is the most beautiful hotel manager you have ever met?"

I tried to evade her. "Do you mean in efficiency or looks?"

"Looks."

"No comment."

It was a relief when we arrived at the car park in Mandraki. "I have some shopping to do. I am then meeting with friends. You can get your office supplies. Here is some money for you to get something to eat. I will meet you back here in two hours." And I handed her a fifty euro note. She looked disappointed, but I couldn't put up with any more of her interrogation.

"Well, I can at least walk along the harbour and into town with you. Then we can separate."

I sighed. "OK. So long as you promise me, no more questions."

"I swear on my heart." She placed her right hand over her

heart. Well, it was actually her left breast, and I'm sure she squeezed it. I didn't look at her face. But I knew that her top lip was being licked again.

The walk along Mandraki was enjoyable. Early April is my favourite time of year on Rhodes. The sun is starting to warm everything up. On the drive from Pefkos to Rhodes, the air was full of the scent of blossoms and blooms coming into season. The deep blue of the Mediterranean stretched away to our right. On the left, so much green was visible, vegetation making the most of the winter irrigation. Before the baking heat of the summer dried everything out.

"Do you mind if I ask one more question?"

"So long as it isn't sexual."

"Oh, I love the way English people say sexual." I glared at her.

She looked sheepish. "What do you miss most about your wife being in England?"

"The easier answer is everything. But I miss her support. She is someone I can bounce ideas off. She is the one that stops me from making stupid mistakes. She is the one that makes me feel whole. I miss things like her holding my hand when we walk along the harbour."

"I can do all those things for you while she isn't here. I can be her caretaker." She seemed to really care. And she reached across the gap between us, and she took hold of my hand. I didn't pull my hand away. Instead, I looked skywards. *Oh, Kam, I miss you so much.*

We reached the point of Mandraki just across from the taxi rank. It was time to go our separate ways. Aphrodite to New

Town and me to Old Town. "I will see you back at the car in two hours. Don't forget to get yourself something to eat."

She turned to kiss me. This time I did pull away, "It is only a kiss." And she sighed.

"I appreciate your support, but we cannot go there. Just friends. Nothing more."

I couldn't tell her that I didn't want Zeus to know of her existence and that we were in the most popular area of Rhodes.

≈≈≈

I entered Irene's and the guys were pleased to see me. "How is the trident? We hope you are keeping it polished."

"Yes, Christos. It is polished daily, Filipos has promised me. And yes, the plaque advertising Irene's Gold is polished as well."

"What are you looking for? For you, there is fifty per cent off everything."

"It is a special order. Top secret just between you guys and me."

"Mystery and intrigue, we like that," said Lazaros.

"I want a silver coin made. I want relief showing my head on one side, and the back side is to have the island on it. Two words on it. With the head, the English word, protection. On the island side, I would like the Greek version of the word. Prostasia, but in Greek letters, Προστασία. Can you do that?"

"Of course. You know we can. Is it a surprise for Kam?"

"No. She is in the UK now looking after Mama. It is for a special friend."

"That's a relief. I thought you were going to say it was a present to the island. You were offering to protect it."

The guys then had a conversation about me. "He really is turning Greek if he thinks he is capable of protecting the island," said Lazaros.

"He has already turned Greek if he has a special friend. What is her name?" And they both laughed. I just ignored them.

"Do you want stamps, wax cast, or use dies?"

"What's the difference?"

"Time and quality. How detailed do you want your head?"

"Something like these," and I pulled my komboloi out of my pocket.

"Stamps. When would you like it? Once the stamps are made, you can make as many as you like. The stamp is the most complex part of the process," said Lazaros.

Christos chipped in, "We can probably have the stamps inside two weeks."

"Stamps it is then."

"We will start the process. It will be two hundred euros."

"You guys are too good to me."

"Nothing is too good for the Prince of Rhodes." And they laughed again.

I still had time to waste before meeting Aphrodite back at the car. I crossed over into New Town and went to Trianon Café. It is run by a good friend of Kam's. I felt that being close to her would bring me closer to Kam.

Trianon is on the corner of Grigori Lampraki Street and 25th March, just up from McDonald's. Though they are only yards apart, the food and service are worlds apart. You can often see locals in there pawing over statistics and predictions before going next door to place bets on the Opap and lottery. In the UK, it would be like having a pub next door to a bookmaker. I'm sure that it is no coincidence that on the opposite side of the café, the neighbour is a bank. Trianon is fronted by a wooden framed conservatory that is opened or closed according to the season.

"Just a cheese toastie, please, Katerina."

"Where is Kam?"

"In the UK looking after her mum."

"That's why I want a cheese toastie. It's her favourite."

"And to drink?"

"Her favourite again. Mythos, please."

She disappeared to place my order. I felt the familiar rub against my legs. "Jet. What the hell are you doing here?" She just purred and continued to rub up against me.

Katerina returned with my Mythos. "Shoo," she said.

"No. She's OK. She's my cat. I left her in Pefkos, and she must have got out and managed to make her way here and found me. Isn't that amazing?"

"Wow. Better than a dog."

"She is my crutch while Kam is away."

"Bless you. If you need anything while you are on your own, you know where I am."

"Thank you. But I have all the bases covered, and I do know how to use a washing machine." And I laughed.

"Your food will be ready shortly."

"Ok. Maybe we'll see you later, won't we Jet?" By now, Jet

was on my lap, but she already knew better than to get on the table.

Without any warning, she put an end to my petting and launched from my lap. I heard a familiar voice from behind. "Oh, Jet baby. Have you come all this way to see me? How did you know I would be here?"

I didn't need to turn around to know that Aphrodite was behind me, but I swung around anyway. *And how did you know I would be here.*

"What a coincidence, Rod. We both chose the same place to eat."

I hoped it was a coincidence. I was more concerned that I was too easy to locate. If Aphrodite could find me, who else could?

Before my cheese toastie could even make its appearance, my question was answered. Jet knew before any of us that something was wrong. Arched back, rigid tail, growling, hissing, and spitting. I looked in the direction that the cat was pointing. At that exact moment, Jet launched and latched onto the server, bringing my food towards me.

The toastie somersaulted across the bar. The server screamed. Aphrodite squealed. Katerina shouted. The regulars cheered. I just said, "Oh shit."

There was no doubting the server was a god. But was I prey, or was it an unfortunate coincidence? I needed to make a swift decision. *Am I just an embarrassed cat owner, or am I a killer of gods? Do I remain secret like Clarke Kent, or do I go public like Superman?*

Superman it was. Though, of course, I could hardly stop to

put my underpants outside my pinstriped trousers. I unsheathed my dart and lunged forward to grab Jet. The dart was between my knuckles. It couldn't fail to puncture the skin of the goddess. I pulled Jet from her, and I could see amber spots on her white shirt where Jet's claws had pierced her skin. It confirmed she was a deity. Amongst the amber stains, there was one spec of red. It proved she was now mortal. I reverted to being an embarrassed cat owner. "I am so sorry. She is usually such a placid kitten. Katerina, I am so sorry. Can your server join me so that I may recompense her for the horror my cat has just put her through?"

"Of course, I was going to send her home anyway. I can't expect her to work after that."

The place was full of locals that were scowling at Jet and me. Aphrodite didn't have a clue what was going on. Several Greeks spoke out loud. "Malaka." It was clearly aimed at me.

"Rod, what came over her. That was worse than how she reacts when Giannis is about."

"I don't know. Could you do me a favour and go back to the car and take Jet with you. I want to apologise to the server. It will be better if Jet isn't around just in case she has another fit." And I handed her the keys to the car.

"Of course. But don't be long."

"I will be as long as it takes. You shouldn't forget who your boss is." She looked crestfallen that I would speak to her like that.

"Oh. Ok. I will see you when you are done then." She scooped up Jet and stormed off.

"I am so sorry. Please sit. Katerina, another Mythos for me

and whatever this young lady wants."

The newly mortalised goddess sat and smiled. "Portokalatha for me please, Katerina. Thank you. Mister?" And she paused for me to introduce myself.

"I am Rod Prince." Her facial expression changed instantly, but I'd expected that.

"Well, this is embarrassing," she proclaimed.

"Yes, given that you are on the island to kill me. I have introduced myself. Would you care to return the favour?"

She looked about us, checking that nobody was close enough to hear. She whispered, "You will know me as Nemesis, the Goddess of retribution. I punish beings for having a hubristic nature. You are accused of being arrogant, overconfident. With your foolish pride, you dare to belittle the powerful gods. And yet you have no power."

She doesn't know. She doesn't have a bloody clue that I have just mortalised her. "I have powers, I have intelligence, and I know the secret of the gods."

"Nonsense. I have the power of balance. Zeus has been too generous with you, and that is why you are feeling sadness now. I am balancing your good fortune with bad fortune. The more that Zeus favours you. The more I can introduce misery into your life."

"Idle threats. That is pure coincidence. I can destroy you. My powers are hidden and have not been written about by ancient Greek poets. My powers are unknown. I am…" and I stopped because I saw our drinks being brought to the table.

The server spoke to Nemesis in Greek. I caught the gist. It was along the lines, "Are you OK, child?"

"Nai," said Nemesis. And we were alone again.

I finished my sentence, "… Your worst nightmare."

She laughed. "You are a mere mortal. I am an immortal goddess. What nightmare can you bring to me?"

"If I told you, that would spoil my fun. But I will tell you this. And I bid you to heed my warnings well. I mean the gods no harm. But if you continue to hunt me down and put my life at risk. I will put an end to every god that still walks this earth." *Fuck me. I'm even talking like I'm three thousand years old now.* "I can bring upon every god more devastation than the rise in Christianity inflicted on your world."

Now she was listening. "Tell me what you know."

"No. I will not tell you, but I will warn you. We are going to finish our drinks and go our separate ways. If our paths cross again at any time, your world as you know it will end."

"You can't kill me." And she looked at me, doing the squinty eye thing. I just stared at her. She sank her orangeade and walked off in the direction of the kitchen.

I necked the best part of my pint and decided to leave the rest. I put twenty euros in the pot on the table and shouted across the bar. "Katerina, I will see you soon."

I strolled back to Mandraki. My mind was filled with thoughts of how I could have handled things differently. *I couldn't have killed her there and then. There were too many witnesses. What story do I give Aphrodite? Will Nemesis find out she has lost her immortality.*

≈≈≈

"Mister Rod, did you manage to sort the problem out?"

"Why am I suddenly, Mister Rod?"

"You made it clear that you are the boss, and I am your employee," she said. She was having a sulk.

"No, I didn't. I made it clear that I don't take orders from you or anyone."

"It wasn't an order. I was suggesting you get the incident sorted out quickly. I could hear what the Greeks were saying about you. I was worried for you and wanted you out of there as soon as possible."

"Oh. I didn't know that. You sounded like a wife, and I was reacting to that." *Why do women do that to me? It's always my fault somehow.* "Jesus Rod, you can destroy gods, but you can't argue with mortal women ..." *Oh shit.*

"Sorry. What did you say about gods?" Aphrodite's interest piqued at what I'd just said out loud.

"I think you are a goddess, And I don't want to argue with you."

"Awww, that is sweet. We aren't arguing, silly. I am sorry you thought I was acting like a wife." She leant forward with her bright red lips pursed. To avoid the incoming threat, I swayed back onto my heels. I found myself leant against the car with my retreat blocked. The red danger that was her lips landed square on their target - my mouth.

I tried to talk. But I was always told not to speak with my mouth full. I managed to extricate myself from her grip. "Where is Jet?"

"She is in the car." And she came in for a second helping of my face.

I rushed to get the words out. "No, plutonic, remember?"

"Plutonic? Surely you mean platonic. Plutonic relates to the god of the underworld, Pluto. He is also known as Hades."

A shiver ran down my spine, and it killed any risk of passion. It was a built-in cold shower. "What? How do you know these things?"

"You are so sweet and innocent. I am Greek and studied it as a subsidiary subject as part of my degree."

"Yes. I did mean platonic. Right. We are heading back to the hotel. And no questions. I need to concentrate on my driving."

"Αμφιταλαντεύσμαι."

"What is that word?"

"It doesn't matter." She sighed out loud, clearly frustrated.

For the journey back, my mind was racing. I was analysing every interaction I'd had with Aphrodite. *She can't be a goddess. Can she?*

"Can you teach me about the gods?"

"ζεστό και κρύο."

"Hot and cold?"

"The word you asked about. Αμφιταλαντεύσμαι. It means wavering. In English, you say hot and cold. It comes from a fable by Aesop. The Man and the Satyr."

"What as that got to do with anything?"

"You wanted to learn about the gods. Satyrs are gods."

"Oh. I thought you were saying I was blowing hot and cold."

"I was. One moment you appear to want affection. The next, you are pushing me away."

"What was Nemesis goddess of?

She is the goddess of retribution. She punishes those that exhibit hubris. Those that have shown arrogance against the gods. She balances good and bad – justice. Her most famous victim was Narcissus. He fell in love with himself." She laughed. "Just like you."

"I'm not a narcissist."

"Are you sure?"

"I told you. No questions."

She grunted. "ζεστό και κρύο."

For the rest of the journey, we both remained silent. I had a lot more to think about than the battle with the gods.

Harpocrates

The debrief session with Pete was an experience. He was like a bloody headmaster telling off a naughty Kid. "Why didn't you finish her off?"

"Because she didn't try to finish me off. I guess she didn't realise I'd pricked her. I suspect she will come for me when she eventually realises."

"She will not realise until she is mortally injured and fails to reincarnate. You should have finished her off."

"I was surrounded by angry locals. They were angry that my cat had savaged their server. Most of them don't like cats anyway. Jet gave them a reason to dislike cats even more."

"You could have laid in wait and got her at the end of the night."

"No, I couldn't. I had to get back to Aphrodite at the car."

"And that is another stupid mistake. You are getting too close to that girl."

"It is a platonic relationship, no sex. We've already had that conversation."

"Exactly. Did that conversation come out of the blue, or

did Aphrodite try to seduce you? Forcing you to have that conversation?"

"The motive doesn't matter. We have had that conversation."

"Then tell me, has she made an advance towards you since you had the conversation."

"OK, point taken. But don't forget you are only my advisor, not my keeper."

"And that is what I am doing. Giving you advice."

"Anyway, enough of Aphrodite. I can handle her. Nemesis is the main issue. Why didn't she attack me? And why didn't she react to the red blood on her shirt?"

"I think you are missing a link, Rod. It is only the gods of the house of Olympia that know that particular secret."

"What secret?"

"The amber blood to red blood secret."

"What? Something doesn't make sense. Zeus has cast me out because the wider gods feel threatened by me. But other than the gold thing, I have no threat. If they don't know I can convert their blood, why do they see me as a threat."

Pete then said something that chilled me to my core. "The house of Olympian is the house of secrets. Nothing is what it seems. You can be sure that whatever reason Zeus has given you. It is a lie. Unlock that secret, and you will have a superior hand."

"So, what secrets are you holding, Pete."

"I can hold no secrets from you. You are my master, and I have sworn my loyalty to you since Giannis disappeared."

"Yes. That's another bloody secret. Where the hell is he?"

Pete brought me up to speed on all the checks he'd carried out on Aphrodite's applicants. There weren't any deities among them. That was a relief anyway. I couldn't wait to see his face when I gave him the amulet that Lazaros and Christos were making.

I found myself in the position of trying to find out the secrets that stood in my way. At the same time, I had my own secrets. I was keeping my godly link a secret from Aphrodite. My feelings for Aphrodite were secret from both Pete and Aphrodite. *Secrets, bloody secrets.* I mused to myself a dozen times a day. Then there was the secret that Pete and I were keeping from every other being on the planet.

"Fish and Chips."

"What about fees and hips," he responded.

"That will be the new password to the blood vault. You need to start practising it with an English accent." And I laughed.

"Why fees and heeps?"

"Because I have been told that it is one of the most difficult phrases for a Greek to say correctly. You don't have an 'eff'. Your 'i' is always an 'ee'. Also, you don't have a 'chu'. A friend told me I would have a lot of fun trying to teach you to say it.

"Oh, that's nice. What do you English call it? Taking the piss?"

"Sorry, but it has to be something that a Greek god wouldn't be able to say. Even if they found out what it was."

"Well, I better go and start practising then," he said sarcastically, and he skulked off.

≈≈≈

I picked up the handset off my desk, "Affi, can you come in for a minute, please?"

It took less than 5 seconds for her to enter the room. I could have told her over the handset. But then, I would have denied myself the opportunity of watching her beautiful calves. Those naked calves were always accentuated by her high heels. "Pete says all of your candidates have passed the security checks. You can go ahead and start the interviews."

"You could have told me that over the phone."

In a moment of brazenness, I replied. "But then I wouldn't have got to see your beautiful legs."

"So today it is hot Rod."

She couldn't understand why I pissed myself laughing. I got her to google 'what is a hot rod'. It reported back 'a motor vehicle or device that is modified to give it extra power or speed.' I think that being called Hot Rod was rather fitting. Given the extra power I'd gained. At least she saw why I laughed at her.

She said, "Malaka!"

I should have pulled rank on her and bollocked her for calling her boss that. Instead, I pulled her boardroom chair closer to mine and asked her to take a seat. Her red-lipped smile beamed at me. She looked straight into my eyes. She was watching to see where I looked. I glanced down at her knees and back into her eyes. She knew what I was asking of her. I knew she was still watching my gaze. My eyes travelled down her body, and then time stood still as she slowly and deliberately crossed her legs. She gave me my own Sharon Stone moment. I looked back at her face and was hypnotised by her as she very, very slowly ran her tongue across her top lip. *Jesus, she knows how to play me.*

She kicked off her red high heels and ran her bare foot up my leg. *Oh shit.* I needed to break the spell. To escape the chains that shackled me to the path I didn't want to travel. I closed my eyes for a second. When I opened them again, the image I saw was the photograph on my desk. It was Kam. "No. Stop. We cannot do this."

"Krio, uh? Μάρμαρο." I recognised that word - Marble

She rose without uncrossing her legs. *There'll be no more Sharon Stone for me.* She didn't even slip her shoes back on. She scooped them up in one movement as she stormed out of the boardroom.

More secrets. Secrets from Kam, secrets from Aphrodite. I couldn't tell Kam what just happened, and I couldn't tell Affi what I really wanted to do at that moment.

My mobile vibrated on my desk where it was charging. It flashed into life. 'SECRETS' was the solitary word in the notification. I opened the message to read more, and there was no more. Just that one word, in uppercase:

'SECRETS.'

It wasn't a number in my contacts list. The number started with +3069, so it was from a Greek mobile.

'Who is this?'

'Secret.'

'Well, if you aren't going to share it, why bother texting?'
It must be Aphrodite or Giannis. There was a long pause before

a response came back.

'Trade secrets.'

'What trade secrets. Hotel trade?'

This reply came instantly.

'No. Let us trade secrets.'

Giannis was never strong at writing texts, and his punctuation was shit. I surmised that he wasn't sending the messages. I shouted through to Aphrodite. "Affi, can you come into the boardroom? Please."

I pushed her chair a little further away. "Please, sit."

"Are you a modified car or marble?" And she smiled.

I'd taken too long to reply to the last text. Almost with impatience, my phone lit up again.

'Are you ready to trade secrets?'

'I need to know who you are.'

And I swung the phone around on the desk and placed it in front of Aphrodite.

She was in the process of reading the messages when another text came in. I stood up and read it over her shoulder.

'My identity must remain a secret.'

That answers the question. It isn't Aphrodite. I looked down at her, and she half turned and looked up at me. "Is that from your wife?"

"Kam? I don't think so. We aren't in contact with each other, and it is a Greek number."

"What secrets are they talking about?"

"I don't know. I am worried someone has found out about you and me."

"What is there to find out. We haven't done anything. You

have made it clear there is no you and me. Our relationship is platonic."

"The kiss, the bare legs, playing footsie."

"You are seeing too much in these messages. If it is from a Greek, they have a different meaning to what you are thinking. This sounds like they have a secret they will tell you. In return, they want you to tell them a secret. This isn't a blackmail attempt. They want to know a secret that you hold."

I just looked at her, and my mind was in a whirl. I had so many secrets to tell. Which one did they want? I picked up the phone and started to type.

'I need something.'

'My secrets are complex.'

'What are your secrets?'

I sat back on my chair, pondering. I threw the phone down on the desk. The same way that Filipos always did. Aphrodite swung the phone towards her so she could read the text.

The phone buzzed as a reply came in. She read it and looked at me with a puzzled expression. She swung it back towards me. Maintaining her observation of my face.

'I hold a secret that will be of interest to you.'

'It is about Zeus and the Olympian Gods.'

Fuck.

Aphrodite asked a one-word question, "Rod?"

"It's complicated."

"I know a lot about the Gods. From the myths. What secrets could there be?"

"Umm. I don't know, but I will handle it from here. You can go now."

"No. I can help you. Let me stay. I am interested to know where this is going. I can keep your secret."

"I don't know. I want to tell you. But I can't."

"Of course, you can. It can be our secret. Who will know that you have told me? Who will know what we have shared?"

"Telling you could affect a lot of other people. I would have to live with the guilt of knowing I'd shared something with you. It would become another secret."

"Yes. But a shared secret."

All the while, the phone was buzzing underneath my hand. Normally an exhibitionist, I didn't want to lift my hand for fear of what I would reveal.

"Oh, please let me look at it. I find it exciting. Aren't you intrigued?"

"Trust me. We're at a crossroads. To the left is normality and the life you are living. To the right is the unknown and a life forever changed. Once I have told you, it cannot be undone. No matter what happens in the future, there will be no going back." The phone continued to buzz under my hand.

She looked into my eyes and licked her top lip.

"No. Stop that. This is too serious for your flirtations."

"I'm sorry. I really want you to trust me. To give me your secrets. You once told me you wanted a manager you could trust. I thought you told me I was that manager."

"Like I said. If we share a secret, it will impact others. Not least my family, my wife. If they find out I had revealed the secrets, then my deceit would be revealed. They will be betrayed."

"Then tell them that you are going to share your secrets

with me. Then you won't be deceiving them."

"No. I would then have to explain why I decided to share the greatest secret of my family. I could hardly say it was because you tempted me with your mouth and flashes up your skirt. That is a secret in itself."

"That is my point. We already share a secret."

"Yes, but not a secret you could die for." The phone buzzed again. "If you knew something could lead to your death, would you still want to know it?"

Then she tried to inject some humour. "I drive on Greek roads, don't I?"

"We need to trust each other completely. We need to share full loyalty. We will need to be prepared to die for what we know."

For the first time, she was showing some alarm. "You are serious, aren't you?"

"Yes. Deadly serious. The texts that are coming in will change your life forever. And I literally mean forever, for eternity. We are at the point of no return. It is your last chance to pull out. To preserve your status quo."

She looked straight into my eyes. I looked deep into hers. It was probably the only time since we met that I didn't let my eyes wander to other parts of her anatomy. "OK. I want to do it. Let us see where this adventure takes us."

She pulled her chair alongside mine, and I slid the phone towards her and lifted my hand. There were nine notifications. I opened the app.

'I can reveal a secret about Zeus and his family.'
'In return, I want to know your secret.'

'The secret you spoke of with Nemesis.'

That one made Aphrodite look at me with a quizzed look on her face.

'You are the victim of a deception.'

'I think you may be immortal.'

'I have spoken with Apollo.'

Another quizzical look.

'You have a secret. I want to know what it is.'

'I offer you three secrets for your one!'

'Trade secrets.'

I sent a two-word reply.

'Speak later.'

Aphrodite broke the stunned silence. "I have many questions."

"Welcome to my world. There are always more questions than answers. We can't talk here. There is a risk of Pete hearing."

"I know where we can go." She stood up and led me out of the boardroom.

I was glad that the non-disclosure contract I'd signed with Zeus in 2013 no longer applied.

≈≈≈

She'd led me to the furthest room from the boardroom. Beautiful view out of the window. Looking out over the rooftops of the hotels below. I could see the deep blue of the Mediterranean glistening under the lighter blue of the sky. *So many shades of blue.*

I grabbed the tv remote and flicked through the radio

channels. I found a Greek station that was playing a soft ballad. Aphrodite clicked the lock on the door. I sat on the chair by the white desk in the room. Aphrodite approached and grabbed my hand, leading me to the bed.

"Platonic!" I said but still climbed onto the bed alongside her. I felt disarmed as we were side by side, facing the TV. I couldn't look into her eyes to judge her reactions. I eased myself up onto my left elbow. Affi mirroring my movement. I was no longer disarmed. Her face was no more than a foot from mine. I could feel her breath on my face and smell the scent she was wearing. It was intoxicating. My pulse had quickened, and the noise from it filled my ears. Her eyes smiled at me, and mine smiled back.

I opened my mouth to speak and break the tension. She licked her top lip seductively, and no words came out of my mouth. I readied myself to jump out of reach of her charms. She tutted, "Alright. Yes, platonic." I was able to relax again.

I took a deep breath through my nose. *I love that scent.* "We could be here a while. Are you sure you want to do this? Once we start, we must finish. There will be no going back."

"Yes. I want it."

"How much do you want it? Would you be ready to die for it?"

"Now you are making me nervous."

"Answer my question. Would you be ready to die to find the secrets behind the texts? Behind Giannis and Pete? Olympian Dreams? And that woman the other night?"

She thought for a moment. "Can you hold me?"

I looked at her quizzically, "Why?"

"I am thinking about what you said about trusting each other and loyalty. I want to feel your protection. Can you offer me protection?"

"Yes, I can offer you protection. But there are no guarantees in life… or death."

I shuffled along the bed and put my right arm around her waist. She responded and lowered herself onto the bed. My arm was now cradling her close, and I could feel her breast pushing against my body. "Thank you."

"Take your time. The decision you are about to make is the greatest decision you will ever make. And I promise you total loyalty, the same loyalty I give my family. I will try to protect you… with my life if it is necessary." I didn't know if that promise would lose its punch once she knew I was immortal.

"Yes. I am prepared to die for the secret. I want it, and I don't care about the cost. Give it to me."

"No, I need you to prove to me how badly you want it."

She pushed me onto my back and straddled me. She pulled at my tie and removed it over my head without undoing it. I couldn't process what was happening quick enough or take evasive action. I shouted, "Platonic."

She replied, "Secret."

In my distraction, I missed that she'd slipped the noose that was my tie over my right wrist. I only caught up as she twisted the two ends around my left wrist. With the speed of the magician doing the vanishing knot trick, my hands were welded together as one.

She ripped my shirt open and demanded, "Secret. Give it to me. I am yours, and you have my trust and loyalty. Change my life. I want it now." She slid her hands over my chest and twisted my nipples. *Ouch, that hurt, bitch.*

Once again, I shouted, "Platonic!" I was using it as if it was a safe word.

"Take my life. I am yours. I would die for you." The tune on the radio played a faster beat, and the pace of her movements quickened to match the tempo.

She licked her top lip, tasting her own lipstick. She leant forward as if to transfer the flavour to me. I turned my face away to maintain my faithfulness to Kam. "I would do anything to have your secret. And she took my earlobe into her mouth."

"Platonic," I shouted in vain.

She whispered into my ear, "Take me, take my soul. I am yours."

I thrust upwards. I needed to get her off me. My earlobe was still in her mouth, and she bit it hard as she ground her crotch down on me to counter my thrust." *Ouch, double ouch. That bloody hurt more.* But at least it stopped my nipple from hurting. I could feel her breath in my ear as she panted between her clenched teeth. I could feel her heartbeat in tune with mine as her breasts rubbed against my chest. I could feel the warmth of her groin as it pinned me to the bed.

Her bite loosened on my earlobe. "Yes, platonic. Now give me your secret."

"Jesus Christ, woman. What the hell was that?"

"That was me proving to you how much I want to know the secret you hold."

"But you scared the shit out of me. Didn't you hear me

shout platonic?"

"Of course, but you wanted me to show you how much I wanted to know the secret."

"Now untie my hands; otherwise, you will hear no secrets from me."

I pushed her off me, and we resumed to our original positions. Except, of course, I was warier of her.

"Would you hug me again?" She asked.

"Yes, so long as you don't try that shit again. I'm bloody knackered. I need to recover before I go through that again."

"Knackered?"

"Yes, it's an English phrase for tired."

"Why are you tired?" I couldn't tell her that I felt like we'd just had sex.

"All that struggling to keep it platonic."

"Why? Did you want it to be more?"

"No! That's not what I meant. I meant the physical effort. Did you want it to be more?"

"That's my secret. Will you hug me again?" And she fucking licked her top lip. *How do I keep walking into it?*

"First, I tell you the secret, and you agree to keep it platonic and trust everything I do. Deal? I hope you know what this means." And I spat at her.

"Oh yes, I know what it means," And she spat back at me.

I embraced her and kissed her on her forehead. "OK. Let's begin our journey into the unknown."

She sighed and said, "Yes, please."

"The Greek gods are still alive."

She broke loose from my arms and pushed me onto my

back. *Oh God, not again.*

She didn't straddle me this time. She just laughed, then punched me on the chest. "Stop teasing. I want to know the secret."

"Aphrodite. Look into my eyes. Do I look like I'm teasing? That is the biggest secret of all. The Greek gods are still around, and there are many of them on Rhodes."

Her face changed as she processed what I was saying. She knew I was telling the truth. "You are serious, aren't you?"

"Yes, and that is why you are now in as much danger as I am."

"How do you know they are still alive?"

"It is a long story. But in short, they are immortal. Why wouldn't they still be alive?"

"But… they are myths. They are just stories. They aren't real."

"How do you know? What evidence do you have that proves they aren't real?"

"We were taught it at school. It is all about morality and living a fair and just life."

"But where did the stories come from? The imagination of poets and storytellers or from real people committing real deeds."

"I could say the same to you. What evidence do you have that the gods are real?"

"Do you know what Giannis' real name is? It's Apollo."

"Don't be silly. He is a human."

"No, he is a god, and he is immortal."

"How do you know this? How is that proof?" *She's got a*

point. I can hardly say because Athena told me.

Over the next few hours, I told her every anecdote from my interactions with the gods. I was making no progress. She had an answer for everything. The sun had started to set, and the light in the room had all but disappeared. Just the glow from the TV playing the radio station.

"OK ... Do you trust me?"

"Yes. Didn't I prove that earlier?"

"I am going to ask you to do something that goes against everything you know and believe." She looked into my eyes and frowned. "It is something you probably have never thought you could do. But you must trust me."

"What is it?"

"I want you to come to the kitchen with me. I want you to stab me through the heart. I want you to kill me."

"No, I won't do that. You are a crazy Englishman."

"You said you trusted me. Believe me, I don't want to die. But we need to do this to prove to you that I'm not crazy. I'm immortal. It's about trust, and we spat on the deal, remember?"

"I don't know. If you die, I will go to jail for murder."

"Trust me," I repeated, and it was my turn to push her down on the bed. My hands gripped her wrist and held them on either side of her head. I pushed them tightly into the pillow, and I leant in and kissed her hard. So hard that I pinched my lips between her teeth and mine. *Ouch, that bloody hurt again.*

Her tongue started to dance with mine to the music still playing from the TV. I broke off the dance. "Now, trust me.

You swore you would trust me."

"Oh, yes, I trust you."

I was astride her, the way she had pinned me down earlier. I released her hands and ripped her blouse open. *Bitch, you ruined my shirt. Now I'm going to ruin yours.* "If you trust me, then kill me!" Then I climbed off the bed, and I spat at her. "That's the fucking deal. You spat on it. If you don't kill me, I will kill myself."

She started to cry and sob. "Why are you being like this? I love you."

"Don't say that. It's platonic. Yes, I want to fuck you, but I can't ... I can't love you. I still love Kam. You have to trust me. You must kill me so that I won't die. Then you will know I am being true. You will believe. Then I can trust you, protect you. You will be killed by the gods if we don't do this."

"I'm scared." And she continued to sob.

"I warned you. Your life will never be the same."

She was a pitiful sight. I felt like a real shit, but it was for her own good. She couldn't wander around Rhodes with the information I had given her and not know the secrets she held.

"Why are you being like this. I love you. Please hold me."

"Oh, sweetheart. It is for the best. It can't be love, but it's the nearest thing to it. It has to stay platonic."

"Please hug me again."

I climbed back on the bed and pulled her into my arms. Her body quivered as she sobbed. I could feel the roughness of the lace of her bra scratching against my chest. *Oh, in a different life.*

I whispered in her ear, "Please trust me. I won't die, but it is the only way you can see that everything I have said is true. Now get dressed. We must go to the kitchen."

≈≈≈

I took a deep breath. She was still sobbing as she plunged the thin blade of the filleting knife between my ribs. I felt the sharp pain as it penetrated my flesh and entered my heart. My mind went blank for a moment. As I returned to consciousness, I was able to see the light reflecting from the blade as she removed it from my chest. Her tear-stained eyes blinked. She stood there open-mouthed and speechless.

I broke the silence and eased the tension, "See. I told you I wouldn't die." I looked at the mascara stains on her face.

She stared at the knife blade and then at the still open wound on my chest. I was unsure if she found it funny or if she was relieved, but she started to laugh. "Where is the blood?"

"That amber-coloured liquid is my blood."

Even though I had proved my immortality, she still wore a frown of disbelief. "But…but…"

"Yes. It is hard to believe, but everything I have told you this afternoon is true. The gods still live, and many of them are on Rhodes."

"If you are immortal, why are you in danger?"

"Because I know how to remove immortality. I know how to turn every god into a mortal."

"How?"

I took a deep breath and pondered on the events of the afternoon. I'd demanded complete trust and loyalty. I had offered her the same commitment, but I'd also told her I would try to protect her. "That's one secret, I will not tell you."

"What about our deal?"

"I promised to protect you. Your protection will be your ignorance of that secret."

"Does Kam know the secret?"

"Of course, because she is my wife. We don't have secrets from each other." I paused for a moment and thought about Kam's secret, *Richard bloody Bates*.

The look she gave me was that of a jealous mistress that couldn't prise her lover away from his family. "That's a lie. I am your secret, your dirty little secret. Your bit on the side."

"Rubbish. We have a platonic friendship. It isn't sexual, and it must never be sexual."

"And if you keep telling yourself that, then maybe you will continue to believe it. If we are so innocent, why don't you tell her?"

"Because we aren't in contact with each other."

"Who decided you cannot communicate?" That was another secret I wasn't prepared to reveal at that time. If she knew my marriage had fallen apart, she would be motivated to keep trying to seduce me.

I didn't answer. How could I? It'd been my decision all along. *I don't care what she says. I know it is platonic.* She accepted and understood my silence.

"Where do we go from here?"

"I don't know, but you mustn't reveal anything of today's events to Pete."

In a complete change of direction, she asked, "Can I stab

you again?"

"No. Because it stings like hell," and I tried to lighten the mood by smiling at her.

"One more question. Are you actually a God, and you are just pretending that you aren't?"

"Definitely not."

Nymph

I had to share the events of the revelation with Pete. It wasn't my choice, I kind of just stumbled into it. "Pete, before Aphrodite gets in, I have something to tell you. I don't think you're going to like it."

"I already know because you left the mess in the kitchen. You could have at least cleaned up. Who was it anyway?"

"What?"

"I suppose we need to sell up and move on now they know where we are. Whose amber did you spill?"

"No, we don't need to move on. It was my amber."

He looked at me. But I couldn't read his face. "Have you been playing silly buggers again?"

"No. I have given Aphrodite the secret."

"Jesus, Rod. I warned you about her. You let her get too close."

"It wasn't like that. I had some texts come in asking me about the episode at Trianon Café. They were from someone that knew of the interaction with Nemesis. The sender wanted to trade secrets about Zeus in return for our ultimate secret."

"And you thought the best way to keep our secret was to share it all with your nymph."

"She isn't a nymph." *More like a bloody nympho.*

"Rod, do you even know what a nymph is?"

I didn't have a bloody clue what a nymph was. In my mind, the image of a nymph was a fairy that played and danced in the water. "No. I don't."

"A nymph is the consort of a god. Zeus had a predilection for nymphs, and it led to all manner of trouble for him. They are supposed to be guardians of a person or place. You selected her to take care of this place in your absence. And you are consorting with her. Now tell me she isn't a nymph. You have created her. I bet you even got her to promise to protect you."

"Tell me, Pete, have you ever played poker? Because you would be bloody good at it."

"No. I haven't, but I will tell you this. You are turning into Zeus. I have sworn my loyalty to you, and I am happy to work for you. But I could never work for Zeus."

Christ, he's the one being cryptic now.

You have left us no choice. You know what we have to do now, don't you?"

I didn't have time to answer before we heard Aphrodite arrive for work. I thought he was going to say we had to kill her.

"We will talk later."

Her voice shouted from reception, "Mister Rod, Mister Pete, are you at work today?"

"We are in the boardroom. Come through, please,"

responded Pete.

She didn't take her eyes off mine. I tried to signal to her that Pete knew of the previous day's events.

Pete, no longer being cryptic, came right out and laid the cards on the table. "Aphrodite, I know that you know some secrets. I understand you have a knowledge of the myths. Do you know what a nymph is?"

"Of course I do."

"Then you will understand the consequences of what I am about to say," and he paused.

I felt uncomfortable with Aphrodite standing while I was sitting. It reminded me of the dominant attitude she displayed when she had pinned me to the bed. "Affi, please sit." And I gestured toward her usual chair.

She gave me a nervous smile and then looked at Pete. She had a tremble in her voice as she spoke. "What do you want to tell me?"

"Rod has turned you into a nymph. His consort, his protector of Pine Trees and his personal protector. It has left us with a predicament."

Fuck me, he's going to come right out with it and tell her she must die.

"Hang on, Pete, we haven't discussed it yet."

"There is no discussion to be had. I am sworn to protect you."

"But you can't kill her just because she knows the secrets."

They both looked at me. Aphrodite had a look of horror because I had broken the news of what Pete had in mind.

Pete looked at me like I'd gone mad. "What are you on

about Rod? I didn't say anything about me killing her. She is in danger, and you must protect her. There is only one thing you can do."

"Well. I'm not killing her either."

And he ignored me, returned his gaze to Aphrodite. "A decision must be made. Only Rod can make that decision. You are his nymph, and I am his crony. We cannot make the decision. If Rod is a decent man, he will make the right decision." *Hold on, I'm still in the room, you know.* And then Pete looked at me. "Are you a decent man Rod?"

I frowned as I looked at him. "Yes. Of Course,"

"Then make the decision."

I didn't have a clue what he was talking about. Aphrodite didn't either. She looked like the accused in a dock waiting for a jury to give a guilty verdict and pass the death sentence.

"For fucks sake, Pete, stop being cryptic. I don't know what decision I'm supposed to make."

"I can't tell you. If I tell you, it will be my decision. It must be yours and yours alone."

"We will leave you to it; you need to think. Think about your journey to where you are now. But first, reassure your nymph you aren't going to kill her."

"Affi. I swear I will protect you and that whatever the decision is, it won't involve you dying."

And they left me to my own confusion. My mind was filled with all the possible decisions I might have to make. My mobile announcing the arrival of a text message soon disrupted my contemplation. *Bugger, not the trade secrets again.* It was a pleasant surprise to see it was from Lazaros.

'ur amulet is ready.'

At least it provided me with an excuse to escape the solitude of the boardroom. As I passed through reception. I looked at Aphrodite and smiled. "I haven't decided yet. I am going to Rhodes for the rest of the day." She forced a smile back at me."

"Pete, you can have the boardroom back."

"See you later, hopefully with a decision." He sounded like he had the hump with me, but I didn't care.

≈≈≈

As I strolled along Mandraki, I had plenty of time to ponder on what decision I had to make. As I was in no hurry to get to Irene's Gold, it was a perfect opportunity to sit on one of the harbourside seats. The warmth of the sun, the noise of early-season tourists speaking their differing tongues. Watching some woman with an Australian accent trying to sell a RIB riding experience to the tourists. *Probably fell in love with the island and found a Greek guy to marry.*

But all this noise and activity was only serving as a distraction, a delaying tactic. *What did Pete mean? Make the decision? He told me to think about my journey to where I am now.* I glanced across at an empty birth, recalling that was where we boarded the Poseidon on that fateful day when we were all drowned. It reminded me that I had to be thankful to Zeus that he had made us all immortal. As if the cogs in my head had been lubricated, it became clear what Pete was talking about. I had to be the one to decide to bestow immortality on Aphrodite. She was my nymph, and I was responsible for her welfare. The best way I could protect her was to give her immortality.

Boosted by my realisation, I made my way to Irene's and my amulet. It was stunning, although you couldn't tell who the image was meant to be, like all good amulets. The wording on the front and back was sharp and readable, and the island's outline was obviously Rhodes. But the profile of my head could have been anybody.

"Wow. It is beautiful, everything I'd hoped it would be."

"Do you want to take the die or leave it with us in case you need another one made?"

"You guys look after it for me, please. But I will take a strong chain and mount for it, though."

"Is that a man chain or a lady's chain?"

"Mans…, no forget the mount and chain. I will let them decide when I give it to them."

Christos polished it up and carefully placed it into its presentation box.

Amulet

On the drive back to Pine trees, I had another decision to make. I'd initially intended to give the amulet to Pete. But while I was at Irene's, I'd started to consider that perhaps a better home for it would be Aphrodite.

"Have you made your decision?" Said Pete as forthright as ever.

"I have indeed. Though you could have been a bit more helpful pointing out what I was deciding about."

"You appear a bit more cheerful," said Aphrodite.

"Oh, I am. I have an announcement to make. Something that will bind you and me together for all time. To mark the occasion, I have a present for you." And I handed her the presentation box.

Pete looked at me and raised an eyebrow. Aphrodite looked like she was about to burst into tears as she said, "But you are already married."

It took a moment for me to figure out the misunderstanding that was happening. "No. It isn't a ring. Open it and see."

Aphrodite blushed at her mistake. Pete's airborne eyebrow settled back on his face where it belonged. "Oh, it is lovely," and she examined it, "protection. This is an amulet, isn't it?"

"Yes, it is my amulet, and it is my way of showing you that I will protect you. A promise that I will never harm you."

Pete, clearly unaware that it was intended as a gift for him, displayed the widest grin you could imagine. "Are you going to actually announce your decision to the poor girl?"

I turned to Aphrodite, got on one knee, and held her hand. "I have promised to protect you from harm. But when I am not near you, and I cannot fulfil that promise, I will give you your own protection. Tomorrow morning you will be made immortal."

Pete breathed an audible sigh of relief, "Bloody hell, I thought you were going to propose to her for a minute."

Aphrodite said, "Am I supposed to be happy or sad?"

"Happy, of course. It means you will stay as you are forever."

"Does it hurt?"

"Don't worry, you won't feel anything. You will be unconscious."

"What? Why will I be unconscious?"

I looked at Pete for help.

Pete looked at Aphrodite, "Don't worry. I will be carrying out the procedure. You will need to be unconscious because we need to drain your normal blood from your body. It will then be replaced by the amber blood of immortality."

The amount of detail he was giving made her withdraw her hand from mine. "I am frightened."

"Don't be afraid, child. I will give you a sleeping draught. It will give you pleasant dreams, and when you awake, you will be immortal. You will have no recollection beyond drinking the potion."

I reached for her hand again and squeezed it. "Remember my promise, I will never harm you. Trust me, trust the amulet. Give us your consent."

"What if I don't agree?"

"Then you won't be made immortal. You won't be Rod's nymph. And you won't be the manager of Pine Trees anymore. You will have your old life back."

"But I still know the secrets. Won't that put me in danger?"

I interrupted their conversation. "Yes, it will put you in danger. That is why I want to make you immortal, but you must agree to it. You must give me your consent."

"I want to, but I am still scared. Promise me it won't hurt."

"I promise. The draught you drink is very pleasant, and it tastes sweet. It doesn't even make you drowsy. You go off into a sweet dream."

"Ok. I give you consent."

"Good," said Pete. And it was time for me to breathe a sigh of relief. Protecting her would be so much easier if she had the protection of immortality.

"What if I change my mind?" *She is still bloody wavering.*

Then Pete became sinister. "You cannot change your mind. The decision has been made, and your consent is given. By midday tomorrow, you will be immortal. Tonight, you will sleep at the hotel, and you aren't to be left alone. Rod?"

"Yes. Stay here tonight, and I can protect you. I can answer any questions you might have. We can have Jet with us, and she will ensure no gods get near my room. We will have a celebratory drink this evening." And I winked at her.

≈≈≈

"Ha-ha. The first time I resurrected, I didn't know I was immortal. I bent down to wash my hair in the private pool. Alyss pushed me in headfirst, and I drowned."

Aphrodite laughed at the image I'd painted. "Alyss sounds like fun. I would love to meet her."

"Well, she is immortal too, so there is every chance you will meet."

Aphrodite held up her glass. "Can I have a top-up, please?"

"Of course, madam. Same again? Or would you like something else?"

"I would like the same drink, but I would also like something else."

"You aren't flirting with me by any chance, are you?" And I flirted back.

Jet did her figure of eight around Aphrodite's legs before jumping onto an armchair, near the door, and settling down.

"Me? I don't flirt," she teased.

I handed her the glass of Merlot and sat on the sofa beside her. "That's a pity because I enjoy a beautiful woman flirting with me." And I laughed to try and hide my comment as if it was a joke.

"I'm not allowed to flirt. You said we must stay platonic, and you are my master. I have to do what you say."

"Ha-ha. No, I am not your master. You are my nymph."

"Well, maybe I should dress like a nymph."

"You can't. You don't have a long white gown here."

"I have obviously seen different images of nymphs …" And she started to undo her blouse.

She'd already unbuttoned the top three buttons before I recollected other images I had seen of nymphs. *Bloody hell, she's going to get naked.* "No. Platonic!"

She just said, "Hot and Cold." And continued to remove her blouse.

I took a massive swig from my glass of Merlot. As she undid her bra, I gulped and nearly choked on the red wine still in my mouth. Through my spluttering, I managed to say, "Stop! We can't do this. It's time you went to bed."

She pouted, scooped up her blouse and staggered off to the bedroom. I was left to my thoughts on the sofa. *Be careful, Rod. She's going to be more trouble than all the gods put together.* I was alone with my thoughts as I drifted off in my drunken state.

≈≈≈

I stirred early as the sun was rising and starting to stream through the open blinds. As my brain cleared its fuzz. I realised I wasn't alone on the sofa. I needed to figure out how to extricate myself from Aphrodite. The semi-naked Aphrodite. My regular biological clock had kicked in, and I was thankful that I was still fully clothed. She could have misread what the lower part of my body was doing. I managed to lift a leg over her and place it on the floor as I stood up. She rolled into the vacant space created by my leaving.

I headed straight for the bathroom, shedding my clothes

on the way. I needed a cold shower. I caught my breath as the chilled water cascaded down on me. I smiled with pride that I had been a good husband and resisted temptation. My thoughts stung as I wondered what Kam was up to and how much she had resisted temptation. I shut the water off and turned to grab a towel, only to be met by a completely naked Aphrodite. *Oh Shit.* "No breakfast for you, young lady. You have a medical procedure to get ready for." As I walked past her, I slapped her naked arse cheek. My thinking was if I didn't mention the previous evening, she might not remember it.

"I am still scared. Can you hold me?"

"No. Not while we're both naked. Hurry up, shower, and get dressed. Pete will be here in fifteen minutes. I'll wait in the lounge."

≈≈≈

We were to join Pete in the cool of the blood store. Unfortunately, he hadn't quite perfected the accent needed to speak the password.

"Fish and Chips," I commanded, and the door swung open.

Pete said, "OK child, go down the stairs, put this gown on and sit on either of the reclined chairs. Shout when you are ready, and Rod and I will join you."

Ever protective, Jet followed Aphrodite down the stairs.

"She is still nervous, Pete. The sooner we start the process, the better."

"We should have just done it without telling her. We have given her too much time to worry about it."

Aphrodite signalled her readiness. When we joined her, she was in tears. Jet was sat on the empty recliner, clearly concerned. "Hold me, please, Rod."

I'll be in the way, but I'm right here and held her outstretched hand. "Relax, take deep breaths. I'll stay for the whole procedure."

Before handing it to Aphrodite, Pete shook the corked flask and decanted the draught into a shot glass. "You must drink it as if it is a shot. Straight down in one."

She took the glass from him and looked at me. I nodded at her and threw my head back, demonstrating the way I took a shot of ouzo. She gave one last sob as she downed the potion. Her eyes glazed over but didn't close. It was disconcerting that she continued to sob.

"That's it, she's gone. Let's get to work," said Pete as he reconfigured the chair so that it now resembled a bed.

He lifted the cover from the surgical tray by his side. He handed me a catheter for her left arm while he inserted one in her right arm. "Here, you better have this. She was holding it," and he passed me the amulet. I placed it in my pocket and inserted the catheter. By the time I'd pissed about trying to find a vein in her forearm, Pete had already finished his side and connected it to the modified plasmapheresis machine. Richard had provided it because it was easier than doing it manually. The way he'd done for centuries. I didn't know how it worked. I was more amazed that no hygiene procedures were followed. As we were inserting amber blood for immortality, the body couldn't die. The crucial aspect was the pace of the process. Twenty-five per cent of the exchange had to take place in the first ten minutes.

Pete, frustrated at my incompetence, came to my side of Aphrodite. "Here, let me do it. We will be here all day otherwise."

I stepped back and let him do his work. He expertly located a vein and inserted the catheter. It took a fraction of a second. He returned to Aphrodite's right side, and by opening the drain valve, he gradually let his tube fill with the amber. He closed the valve just as it started to trickle out onto the floor, signifying the line was full.

"Right, that's it. Fully open your valve and watch for any seepage on your side. I trembled as the tube turned from a milky plastic to a stream of red. As it reached the machine, the gentle hum emanating from it changed its tone. Then I heard it start to fill the reservoir at the base of the device. I always thought it was something we could donate to the local hospital. But it was contaminated with amber, so we just had to discard it illegally.

"Here we go," said Pete as he fully opened the main valve on his catheter. He adjusted the machine to maximise the rate it was pushing amber into Aphrodite.

"I have got blood seeping out of my catheter," I shouted urgently. I was alarmed.

"It will do. I have put a lot of pressure onto the amber to get it in quickly. I want to put the poor girl out of her misery. She is still sobbing."

"Have you seen that before?"

"Nope, not as long as I have been doing this. She is supposed to be dreaming of nice things.

I mopped the tears from her cheeks and looked at the timer on the machine. Five minutes. Pete was watching the information closely.

"Her blood pressure is sky-high. I just need a few more seconds." Now it was his turn to change the pitch of his voice, expressing concern.

"Pete, you're going to kill her."

"That's it." He spun around to adjust the machine. And still, Aphrodite sobbed.

"What did you do?

"I pushed three pints of amber into her in just over five minutes. That's what I did. I saved us twenty-five minutes. I want her conscious as soon as possible. She will be immortal within the hour... I hope!"

And still, she was crying, with her eyes wide open.

"What do you mean you hope?"

"Her reaction to the draught is different from anything I have seen before. She should be babbling on about happy things. I am worried she is having a psychedelic crisis, what you moderns know as a bad trip."

"Shit. She isn't going to believe anything I tell her again," I held her hand, and finally, her sobs started to subside. Jet appeared less concerned as she jumped up onto Aphrodite's stomach.

"All we can do now is wait. It should all be over in forty-five minutes."

"Jesus, that wasn't good." I gradually let go of her hand. The way a parent would when they have just got a baby off to sleep and don't want to disturb it. The sobs didn't return.

"I think we should stay with her until it is complete."

I agreed with him. My mobile buzzed in my pocket. I had a bad feeling as I looked at it. *Shit.* "Trade secrets," it read.

I passed the phone to Pete, "What do you make of this?"

"You want my advice?"

"Umm, yeah. That's why I passed it to you." By the look on his face, I could tell that he was disappointed I'd spoken to him like that. "I'm sorry, Pete. I'm just stressed with this lot." Waving my hands in Aphrodite's direction.

"It's OK. I am just as worried as you are. Now, about the text. I wager it is most likely from a god. Given that you are a fugitive from them anyway, you can't upset them anymore, can you? You should agree to share secrets, see how much you can get from them, and not tell them what they want to know.

"That's the sort of thing Zeus would do."

"Exactly. You are growing to be more like Zeus every day. Why not act as if you were him?"

"They wouldn't fall for such a simple con."

"Yes, they would. How many times have you suggested that they aren't as clever as you? The whole pantheon is after you because of your arrogance before the gods. So be arrogant with them. They will expect it. That is another reason you should have destroyed Nemesis when you had the chance. Zeus would have done it properly."

"Bloody hell, you're going to turn me into a monster."

"No, Rod. You are doing that all by yourself. I am just hurrying you along a bit."

"You're a proper speedy Gonzalez today, aren't you."

Aphrodite made us both jump as she took a huge gasp of

air. Pete looked at the dials. "That's it, job done. She is starting to come around help me get her unplugged from the machine. Leave the catheters in, for now. She may need them."

"Bloody hell, Pete, you aren't exactly filling me with confidence."

For the first time since taking the draught, Aphrodite closed her eyes as she blinked. She had a smile on her face as Jet licked her cheeks. "Mmmmm," she groaned. She looked at me, "I love you, Rod."

Fuck me, Pete. What have you done? I looked at Pete as if trying to send my thought to him. He must have received them loud and clear because he looked at me and shrugged.

"Good afternoon Miss Immortal." That was all I could think to say.

"Don't tease. I am Mrs Prince."

Pete came to the rescue. "No, child. That was your happy dream from the draught."

"But it was so real, I couldn't stop crying. I was so happy. I married Rod."

Pete looked at me. This time I read his thoughts. *You are to blame for this. It's your fault. Stop flirting with the poor girl.*

"Remember, we are in a platonic relationship. I am in love with my wife and wouldn't be unfaithful to her."

I could see tears welling up in Aphrodite's eyes.

"Please hold me," she pleaded.

"I can't."

I handed her the amulet. Then I turned, and I left the basement. I was heartbroken that I'd caused so much hurt to her. I'd wilfully played with her emotions like a game of cat and mouse. I was ashamed of myself.

Themis

I took Jet to Monolithos. I wanted solitude and time to think. Of course, it meant I wouldn't see Aphrodite for a few days, which I needed. I'd left her in the care of Pete. It was heaven. No mobile signal, just me and nature. I didn't eat. I just wasn't hungry. Jet fed herself using mother nature's pantry.

Being in self-isolation really helps to focus the mind. I knew what I had to do about the gods. And I knew what I had to do about Aphrodite. With clarity of mind, I returned to Pefkos.

I wasn't expecting the reception I got. I walked into Pine Trees, and Aphrodite had her head down messing with paperwork. As the door swung behind me, it made her look up. She did a double-take and squealed. She ran around her desk, kicking off her high heels, and launched herself at me. "I have been worried about you." And she kissed me full on the lips.

"Whoa, platonic remember?"

"I know, but this is special. I have been missing you."

"Don't you remember our last conversation? In the

basement?"

"Yes. Of course, I do. Silly. I know you love your wife, and you will always be faithful to her. But I enjoyed our fun times, and we did make promises to each other. Besides, I am your nymph. Please can we go back to how it was?"

I know I'm going to regret this. "OK, but you will have to work harder at keeping it platonic."

"Of course. You are my master, whether I like it or not. I have to do what you command."

"The boardroom door opened at the same time as Pete spoke, "Aphrodite, what is all the shrieking about? … Ah, Rod. I was beginning to think you had done a Giannis on us."

"No, I just needed to clear my head and get my strategies sorted. Have you tested her immortality yet?"

Aphrodite answered before Pete could even open his mouth. "No, he hasn't. I wouldn't let him. I want you to be my first." And the cheeky cow licked her lips. *There she goes with the bloody double entendres again.*

I looked at her and raised my eyebrow. She just giggled.

Pete left us to it.

"If you let me stay here tonight, we could do it then. Please say yes."

"God, Aphrodite, your immortalisation has left you acting like a teenager."

"That is because I am your nymph." She giggled again.

"Very well. Yes, you can stay in my apartment tonight. But I command you not to try anything sexual. Do you understand? I'm commanding you. You cannot refuse."

"I know what a command is, silly. What will you do if I am

naughty and disobey you?" She licked her lip and giggled again.

I put on my best commanding voice. "Come on up when you finish down here. Order a couple of Pizzas and bring them with you. We have a lot to do and plans to make."

I didn't wait for her to reply. I shouted out to Pete through the boardroom door. "See you in the morning, Pete."

≈≈≈

"Seriously, why wouldn't you let Pete test your immortality?"

"Because you and I have already tested each other for trust. I have your amulet. And you swore to protect me."

"OK, choose your method. How would you like to die?" I stressed the word die because I needed her to know that you first had to die to be able to resurrect. The look on her face reminded me of how scared she was the morning we immortalised her.

"Will you hold me?"

"No, sorry. I need you to be able to face this without that comfort. If you are attacked by a god, I might not always be with you. Do you understand? This is to make sure you know what to expect when you resurrect. Choose your method. It's probably better not to choose anything to do with fire. The smell of singed hair and burnt skin clings to the walls."

"What would you choose?"

"You know what I would choose. What method did I ask you to use to kill me?"

"I am so scared; I wish you would hold me."

"Awww, sweetheart, don't be scared." I held out my arms to hug her, and she nestled into my left shoulder, embracing me back. She placed her arms on my shoulders as f we were about to do an end of the evening dance. She lifted her face towards mine and kissed me with passion. Her eyes were closed, and she couldn't see it coming. I plunged the knife through her rib cage. Her eyes opened with shock as she felt the tip puncture her heart. I could feel it beating erratically through the handle of the knife. I knew it was stinging her because it was a pain I'd felt several times myself. She gulped for air as her resurrecting body demanded oxygen. I withdrew the knife to allow the resurrection to progress. She had stopped kissing me and stepped back. Looking down to examine her white blouse. The tear in the material evidence of where the knife had penetrated. The amber staining showing that she had been cut. She looked up at me, laughed and then she started to cry. The look on her face told me she was shedding tears of joy and that she was immortal.

We consumed cold pizza for the next few hours, drank lots of red wine, and discussed secrets.

"I want you to suspend staff recruitment. I will inform Filipos that I am unable to take overflow guests. If Pine Trees is going to be a place of secrets, the fewer strangers we have here, the better. Can you spread the word that we are having trouble with Greek bureaucracy? Everyone will understand the reason that we haven't opened yet."

"Of course. But what do I do? My job is to manage the

hotel."

"I think you have risen above being a hotel manager. You are now part of the inner circle. Your key role now is to support me. I want you to help me understand the gods. Who my enemies are? You are key to my planning."

"Is that why you made me immortal?"

"No. I made you immortal to keep you alive. I had revealed too much to you, and you had to die. The only way my heart would let me do that was if you were immortalised."

I could hear the rising excitement in her tone. "You did it because you love me?"

"No comment. Now back to secrets."

She smiled at me. "But that is now another secret."

Ignoring her response, I ploughed on with the conversation. "I want to restart the text conversation with Trade Secrets. Who could the sender be?"

"Who already knows the secret? Because it won't be one of them."

"I understand that. But I need to know which secret they are trying to get me to reveal. Take yourself, for example. You know many of the secrets of the Olympians. But you don't know them all. The only people that know everything is the Olympians and my family. Oh, and Pete."

"Then you must do what you said. Restart the conversation with Trade Secrets."

I looked at the time. It was still early. "There is no time like the present. Pour the wine down the drain. We won't drink any more tonight."

While Affi tidied away the evidence of our drinking, I cast

my phone screen to the TV.

Just as she sat by my side on the sofa, I launched the opening message:

'Who are you?'

Back came an instant reply.

'Secret.'

'Cut it out. Do you want to talk or not?'

'Trade secrets.'

'I need to know who I am trading with.'

'I am a friend of a friend.'

'No, you're not. Name the friend.'

'Nemesis.'

'She isn't a friend.'

'She wants to be your friend.'

'No, she doesn't. She wants to kill me.'

'No, she wants retribution. I want justice.'

Affi interrupted at this point. "Stop sending for a minute. Nemesis is the goddess of retribution. You said she is punishing you because of your arrogance before Zeus. Suppose she is doubting the evidence she is working with."

"OK, let's say you are right. Who would partner Nemesis? Who would be on the side of the innocent?

A light went on in Affi's head as she squealed. "I've got it! You are talking to Themis. She worked closely with Nemesis. Themis makes the rules, Nemesis enacts them. Themis is justice, Nemesis is retribution.

"OK. I can see that. I fired off another text:

'Hello Themis'

There was silence. We waited, and still, there was no reply.

Affi said, "I think we took too long replying to their last message. They have given up."

"No. Think about it. Why did we take a long time to reply?"

"Because I told you to stop."

"Yes. But that was because we needed to discuss the text conversation. Themis is doing the same thing. She must be discussing my response with someone. I have also unwittingly given them a hint that I am not alone." I sent another message:

'Are you there?'

'Yes. Don't go away. Be patient.'

And we were back to waiting again. Affi said, "This is so exciting."

I looked at her like she had two heads. "No, it isn't. It's frightening. They know who I am. They have managed to get my mobile number. How much else do they know? You might be excited, but I'm not. I am worried. We could be walking into a trap." At last, a message came back to us:

'OK. Yes, I am Themis.'

'Well, that took a long time.'

'I had to consult.'

'Who with? Nemesis?'

And with that, we were stuck waiting again. So now she obviously had to get permission to answer that question as well.

'It's a straightforward question.'

'Yes. Nemesis. She wants to meet with you.'

'What guarantees do I have for my safety?'

'We will both be there.'

'How does that guarantee my safety?'

'I am only interested in justice.'

'That sounds like a threat to me.'

'It is… if you are guilty.'

'Then there will be no meeting. Bye'

'Wait'

And we waited. "Affi, we can open the wine again. This conversation is going nowhere." I sent the last message:

'Come back with guarantees. Bye'

'No, wait'

I'd had enough of waiting. Affi might be excited by the prospect of continuing. But I shut my phone off. She returned with the wine just as I was throwing my lifeless phone onto the coffee table. "What did you do that for?"

"They told me to wait. I'm not doing what they say without any guarantees. During the last war, I learnt very quickly that we need to be in control. By walking away from the discussion, I retain control. Surely you learnt that on your management course."

"Yes, but they might have come back with a guarantee."

"In which case, it will be a stronger guarantee tomorrow. Now let's relax and enjoy the rest of the evening."

"Will you tell me more secrets. The ones that I don't know yet."

"I have revealed them in the stories I have told you."

"But you haven't told me how you destroyed the gods in the war you talk of."

"There is only one more secret to reveal, and the time isn't right. Instead, I want you to tell me about Nemesis and Themis. I want you to tell me everything that you know about them."

I poured us each glass of cheap red. Like an idiot, I'd got Affi to throw the wine down the drain, and she'd emptied an almost full bottle of Merlot down the sink. "Start with Themis."

"Let me see how much I can remember. She was a Titan. When the Olympians overthrew the Titans, they let the female Titans keep their positions. Themis became the Goddess of Justice on Mount Olympus."

"Hang on. She became an Olympian?"

"Yes. Why?"

"I thought all of the Olympians knew all of the secrets. Sorry. Carry on."

"Prometheus was her nephew."

"That's not good. I arranged the destruction of Prometheus."

"How?"

"Doesn't matter. Carry on."

"Save your interruptions until the end, please.

"Themis was Zeus's second wife."

I just sat there open-mouthed. I put my hand up because I had a burning question to ask, although I didn't want to interrupt. Affi nodded, permitting me to ask my question. "Did they have any children?"

"Stories vary, but it is thought they were parents of …" She stopped suddenly and gasped.

"What? What is it?"

"They were parents of the nymphs."

"That's just a coincidence. You weren't born a nymph. You

are only my nymph because of your actions. It is just how Pete described you. Don't worry. I won't hold it against you." And we both laughed.

"There isn't much more to say about Themis other than it was her and Zeus that plotted the trojan war. It was aimed at bringing an end to the age of heroes."

"Fuck. That's a major worry. If they think that the Rhodes war was some kind of heroic act. Where does Nemesis fit in with all of this?"

While she readied her response. I poured us both a second glass of plonk. The cat flap clattered in the door. Jet had arrived home. I had a cat flap installed because it meant if a god came to the door, Jet would see them off even before I managed to open it. She jumped up on the sofa and settled between Affi and me.

"Where was I?"

"Nemesis."

"Oh yes. Nemesis, the Goddess of Retribution and Revenge. That is most of what she is known for. She was the mother to Helen of Troy. So there is the trojan war link again. But basically, she was the executioner to rules of justice laid down by Themis."

"So, what you are saying is that Themis is the boss. And it is probably Themis that sent Nemesis to punish me. I am starting to understand now. Themis is investigating me. Trying to find out if I am guilty of the charges against me."

"Why don't you turn on your phone? Find out what they want?"

"Nope. I think it is time you booked a taxi to take you

home."

"I want to stay. You said I should stay here tonight. Please don't make me go."

"Alright, but no funny business."

"Whatever do you mean?"

She poured us both another drink, and she settled back on the sofa. "Do I need to know the last secret to be able to protect you better?"

The wine was doing the trick because I almost relented. Instead, I concentrated hard on not letting it slip while I related more of the events from the war. I relayed to her that I thought the secret that Themis and Nemesis were after was how to remove immortality. I didn't explain how gold and amber blood don't mix well. I told her how we'd used the secret to mortalise most of the Olympians. Her inquisitiveness did mean I had to explain my motivations for immortalising them again. I just couldn't bring myself to tell her exactly how I mortalised the gods. She assumed, and I let her believe, that it was just a reverse blood exchange.

"Wow. Now I know why they want you dead."

"Yes. They know I can kill them. But they don't know how to kill me. The puzzle is that Zeus knows, so if he is in cahoots with them, why hasn't he told them?"

"Maybe he is telling the truth when he told you why they were after you. Because you are arrogant."

"Well. Do you think I am arrogant?"

"Sometimes you are. Especially when you are cold marble. You're not arrogant when you are hot Rod."

"Anyway. It's time for bed. I do all my best thinking when

I'm asleep. You take the bedroom. I'll have the sofa again."

"Why don't we share the bed?"

"You know why!"

"Yes. I know we are just platonic friends, and I understand we can't have a sexual relationship. Think of me as your new Giannis. Tomorrow I will show you how much I understand that we are just friends."

I uttered one word before making my way to the bedroom. "Platonic."

Prostasia

It was a restless night. Hot and humid, and I was craving the feel of soft cold flesh. I woke many times and sensed bodily contact with Affi's chilled skin. Despite the temptation to savour the coolness, I adjusted to keep a respectable distance between us. I guessed she was trying hard to be my new Giannis because I heard her fart many times during the night. On the plus side, my constant stirring into a half-sleep meant I could recollect the vivid dreams I was having. I sensed they might provide a solution to the questions filling my head.

I woke first because I was cold. Affi had kicked the covers off and was completely naked. Her pale skin reflecting the moonlight that shone through the open blinds. It was a weird experience because I was able to look at her nakedness and not have sexual thoughts. I believe we'd genuinely found a platonic relationship. At least I had. I got out of bed and stared out across the Mediterranean. The moon's reflection creating a sea of diamonds. I was unsure of the time or how long I stood there. But I was still watching as the light on the horizon brightened with a red hue. To the East, Helios started to poke his head above the dark blue of the sea. I left Affi asleep and prepared myself for the day ahead.

≈≈≈

"Morning, Pete."

"Kalimera Rod. How did last night go? The resurrection test drive."

"Yeah, it was good. More bloody tears, though. On the upside, I think she's finally cottoned on that we can be no more than friends. She called herself my new Giannis."

He burst out laughing. "I wish Giannis was as pleasing to the eye as she is."

"I just wish he was here. I'm concerned about him."

"He will be fine; I have known him for thousands of years. He has always preferred to be on his own."

"That's as maybe. But once I've restarted my phone, you can see who I was talking to last night."

I grabbed my still lifeless phone and sat alongside him. After what seemed like an eternity, it resurrected and pinged endlessly as multiple notifications announced the delayed arrival of messages. I opened the messages folder and scrolled back to the start of the previous night's text conversation. He read the screen one message at a time.

I stopped scrolling at the last of the evening's messages, and we read the remaining messages together:

'No, wait.'

'We will offer guarantees.'

'Tell us what you want.'

'What guarantees you want.'

'Get back to us with your terms.'

"Bloody hell, Rod. Do you know the power that those two represent?"

"Of course, Affi told me all about them. How they set out the laws and enact them. But don't forget. I know that all the deities are phonies."

"Affi? Come on, Rod, what does she know?"

"She has a degree."

"What in mythology? The very stuff you claim is just rumours. No, I meant the number of supporters they have. Across the pantheon, they have more influence than the rest of the Olympians put together. More than Zeus himself."

"That's as maybe, but I have something they want. To keep up their pretence of justice, they can't take the secret from me. They want to negotiate to get it. So, who has all the power now? I just have to figure out how I can meet with them and what guarantees they give for my safety."

"Come on, Rod, you know how you can ensure they don't harm you. You are talking to the keeper of the boxes."

I pondered for a moment. "You mean, you have their amulets."

"No, but you can demand their amulets. In return, you give them your amulet. You can then meet without fear of any of you harming each other."

"One problem. I don't have my amulet. Affi has it. I can ask her for it when she comes in." I could have gone to my apartment and got it but didn't want to remind Pete that Affi stayed the night.

Unfortunately, I hadn't warned Affi of that. "Morning,

guys. Rod, why didn't you wake me?"

I looked at Pete, and he frowned disapprovingly back at me. "Affi, do you have my amulet to hand? I need to borrow it back."

"No, it is at the jeweller's. I am having it made into an item of jewellery. That's the surprise I was going to show you. It will prove we are just friends. Why do you need it?"

"Nemesis and Themis are offering to give me the guarantees I need. I plan to temporarily exchange amulets. You can have it back as soon as I have met with them."

"If you give me the day off, I will go to town and see if I can get the jeweller to hurry up with it."

"Of course, do you want me to come with you."

"No, it's OK. I will be fine. I am immortal, remember?" And she laughed.

"OK, we'll see you later."

Pete and I didn't reply to the texts immediately. We discussed how we could set the meeting up. Pete being my crony, said it was his duty to be the go-between, and they would know he is the keeper of the box.

"Just make sure you refer to me as Petros. We don't want them knowing I am your crony now. They will think I still belong to Apollo."

"That raises another question. Why have they contacted me and not Giannis?"

"They probably tried him first. But even we can't get in touch with him."

"And how did they know my number?"

"These are all questions you can ask them when you meet.

Where do you imagine this meeting taking place?"

"I don't know, where do you suggest? It can't be here; they'll know where I am."

"What about Olympian Dreams."

"NO! Never – I don't want to be beholden to Zeus."

"What about Helios or another of Filipos' hotels?"

"I've got it. I will meet them at Filerimos. It is near Alyss' tomb. There will be nowhere to hide other gods for a surprise ambush."

"Good. Send them a message. Don't forget to refer to me as Petros. Cast your phone to the screen."

I typed the first message:

'I want your amulets.'

They replied instantly – clearly, they had been staring at their phones waiting for something from me.

'OK, and yours in return.'

"They must be desperate to meet you. I expected them to try and negotiate."

'I don't have it now.'

'When will you have it?'

'I should have it before the day is over.'

'Where to meet?'

'Under the cross at Filerimos.'

'When?'

'When to meet?'

'Tomorrow at noon.'

'How can we trust you?'

'How can I trust you?'

'We give you amulets.'

'Use a third party.'

'Do you know Apollo's crony?'

'I know of him.'

'We will contact him. He will have our amulets.'

'He is called Petros.'

'He will be in touch with you.'

'Give him your amulet and come alone.'

'And you. Bye.'

I'd barely typed my last message, and Pete's phone started to ring. I hastily put my phone on silent. Jet jumped onto my lap. Her back arched. I clasped my hand over her mouth before she could start growling. *Bloody hell, she can even detect a god on the phone.*

"I know where they are staying now. They have told me to go to The Nemesis Hotel in town."

"We should have guessed that. It was bound to be close to Trianon café. Nemesis is a server there."

"I better get going. I want them to think I have gone straight there. Try to get hold of Affi. Find out if she has the amulet yet. If she is in town, she might be able to give it straight to me."

"Get theirs first."

"Of course."

And Jet and I were left on our own. I had a nagging feeling. A sense of impending doom. It didn't help that Jet was fretting, pacing around prowling. I tried several times to call Affi. It wasn't like her. She usually picks up my calls or sends a text telling me she is busy. I sent her a text that I'd set to give a delivery report. It would at least let me know when she was within range of a signal.

To fill the time, I loaded up an online game of backgammon. I was always a chess player but took up backgammon after the war. There an endless line of Greeks ready to accept a challenge. Playing online was nowhere near as much fun as playing in an ouzeri or caféneon. There just wasn't the same emotion. But I wanted to be at Pine Trees when Affi got back.

My phone buzzed. I snatched it up, expecting it to be Affi. I was disappointed when it was Pete.

"Have you got the amulets?

"No, Rod, there was traffic. It is Affi, she has been hit by a car. They have taken her to the hospital."

"Shit, if she dies, she will resurrect in front of them."

"No, Rod, this is serious. There is red blood all over the road."

"What? That can't be. I tested her myself. She is immortal. I'm heading to the hospital."

"You get the amulets."

≈≈≈

The medics didn't take much persuading that I was Affi's father, her next of kin. She was still in the emergency room, so I couldn't see her. I paced around for an hour like an expectant father. It gave me plenty of time to reflect. Maybe she would still be running around if I hadn't let her get so close to me. Were the gods involved? They couldn't be. I ran over the last few days. She hadn't been out of my sight since I tested her immortality. How the fuck has she got red blood?

I was brought back to the present as a doctor came out of the emergency room. I was never so thankful that Greeks could speak English. "Mister Koutsos"

"Eh? ... Oh. Yes."

"I am sorry. Your daughter's injuries were too great. She lost too much blood. And we were unable to stabilise her enough that we could try to fix her."

I felt my eyes starting to fill with tears. "No, No... This can't be. You must have the wrong person." I was clutching at straws because deep down, I knew it was going to be Affi.

"I'm afraid the documents on her suggest it was your daughter. My head cleared. This is war. "Can I see her please?"

"Of course. I will get a nurse to collect you when she is ready."

And he went. He left me to my anger and my planning. *I bet that bastard Zeus is behind this.* Suddenly I was filled with anger, with rage. I had someone to blame.

Zeus was going to pay for this. He was going to die. My phone vibrated. I looked at it. A message from Pete. "I have the amulets. How is Affi?"

I could barely see the screen to type through my angry tears. I texted one word, "Dead."

Back came his instant reply. "Shit. You MUST get your amulet from her."

I really couldn't be arsed about the amulet. But I knew he was right. I would need it if I was going to go head-to-head with Zeus. I just texted back, "K." I was broken. I had resorted to the text speak I hated so much.

A nurse appeared, "Mr Koutsos?" I nodded. "Please.

Come with me. I will take you to your daughter."

I remember pleading to myself, *please let it be someone else.* As I approached the bed, I could tell it was Affi. She looked the way I had left her in bed that morning. Her icy pale skin evidence that she had bled out. Her lips were bright red from her lipstick. I began to cry the way she did when she was being immortalised. I was sobbing. I leant forward and kissed her full on the lips. Something she'd always wanted me to do.

The nurse left us alone, and that allowed me to peel the sheet back. I was looking for an item of jewellery that would hold my amulet. A necklace, bracelet, or ring. Nothing. Then I spotted it. Her smooth white skin that was unblemished when I left her naked in bed was now scarred by a navel piercing. Attached to it was my mounted Amulet. At that moment, I could have ended my own life. If only I'd revealed the ultimate secret that she longed for so badly. She wouldn't have had a gold bar fitted. The gold I'd worshipped as my saviour for so long had now become the cause of my saddest day since before the war. *Why the fuck didn't I tell her that gold penetrating her body would mortalise her.* I removed the bar. It still had her red blood on it. I kissed her one last time. She would have liked that.

On my way out, I caught the attention of a nurse and told her that I wasn't Affi's father and that I was her lover. Her parents should be notified. I continued to sob and made my way out of the hospital.

Marmaro

I blamed myself. I didn't think I would ever get over losing Affi. I told myself that it wasn't as if we were lovers, and I hadn't known her for that long. Pete tried his hardest to motivate me, but I'd lost the will to fight.

"Rod, pull yourself together. Do you think Zeus got to where he is by worrying about decisions that had gone wrong? You made your decision to keep the secret for all the right reasons."

"Yes. I made the decision that cost her her life."

"No. You decided to make her immortal. If you hadn't made her immortal, she would still be dead. You cannot blame yourself because she had a gold navel piercing. Imagine if any of the gods had a navel piecing with a gold bar. They would suffer the same fate. Talking of gods, you have a meeting to prepare for. Here are the amulets. You probably don't feel like giving it to me, but I need to ask you for your amulet. I have to get it over to them tonight."

"I know you're right. Take it but remove it from the mount. I don't want them getting their grubby godly hands on that."

He took the amulet and went to his rendezvous with Nemesis and Themis. I went up to my suite and curled up on the bed. I just needed to cuddle the pillow that Affi had slept on and fall asleep while savouring the scent she'd left on it.

It was a fitful night. Most of my dreams were about Zeus and how I was going to kill him. Every time I ended his life, I looked at his lifeless body, and all I saw was my own face. I think a psychiatrist would have had a field day with me, especially if I told them I thought I was immortal.

What would Kam do? Probably slap me around the face for getting upset because another woman had died. Come on, pull yourself together. Affi was a dalliance, a distraction, an ego boost. Platonic, a friend, my new Giannis. That's right, she was an ally against the gods. She would want me to carry on.

By the time Pete arrived for work, I was a different person. As Affi would have said, I was marble. I was hard and cold. I was ready for the meeting. This time there would be no distractions, simply hard talking.

"Morning, Pete. Are you going to be at the meeting?"

"No. They don't want me there, and you don't need me to be there."

"If the meeting goes well, you can return each other's amulets. Otherwise, come back here, and I will do the exchange."

≈≈≈

I arrived a Filerimos a good hour before the meeting time. It gave me a chance to visit the tomb of Alyss's spirit. It always made me sad when I looked at it, more so when I looked at it and thought of Affi. But it did give me strength. Alyss was still immortal, and I needed to focus on making sure she stayed that way. I remained by the pillar of concrete until the peacocks started to pester me for food.

I made my way towards the cross, peacocks shouted loudly in the background. Walking past the stations representing the journey Jesus took on his way to Calvary. His journey towards death and resurrection. Not too different from the trip I was making. I sat on the small wall just short of the cross. It allowed me to observe people coming and going. I knew what Nemesis looked like, and she would be bound to recognise me. At least I didn't have to bring a newspaper and ask her to carry a rose.

I could see them coming as they entered the avenue. When they got closer, I stood ready to greet them. I assumed we would talk from a distance. They wanted a more intimate parley. I got a double cheek kiss from them both.

"Rod, I am so sorry to hear of your loss," said Themis, and she sounded like she really cared.

"You didn't have anything to do with it, did you?"

"God, no. Why would you think that? If you want us to investigate and deliver justice, we will do that for you."

"Humph, why would you do that? You are gods sent to hunt me down."

"You are mistaken. We are not hunting you down. Yes, we are investigating a wrong. But we do not necessarily think you are the guilty party. If you wish to clear your name, we need to know what you know."

"Ok. Talk to me. Do you want to trade secrets? Then tell

me some secrets."

Themis spoke first. "Firstly. Let us clear the air. We can be your closest allies or your worst enemies. We would both rather be the former. We already know how powerful you are, and we would rather work with you than against you." And Nemesis nodded in agreement.

I eyed them both up. The way I was feeling, I didn't trust anyone. Nemesis, save for a white blouse, was dressed in black leather. With her long auburn hair, she carried a sinister look about herself. She almost had an air of arrogance. Her general demeanour was different to when I first met her at Trianon. I'd have put her about the same age as Affi, twenty-five. I gulped and swallowed as I thought about the comparison.

Themis was an ash blonde, and I would have put her about thirty-five years old. Her hair varied between wavy and tight curls. She was more thickset than Nemesis and appeared much less sinister. She was what Lindon would have called a yummy mummy. Her choice of loose white top and sensible length skirt added an edge of secrecy. Her clothes camouflaged the true nature of what was hidden below. Similarly, she carried an air of confidence, trying to disguise her vulnerability. She perfectly balanced the look of the trouser clad Nemesis. It was as if she had tried to be different from her partner.

"Which of you is the chief investigator?"

Themis said. "Oh, please. Don't think like that. It will only slow things down. We are both equal as you are too. We are aware that you already know one secret. You know that we are no more powerful than you."

"Yes, in fact, we think you may be more powerful than us,"

added Nemesis.

"No comment."

Themis held up her hand. "Rod! Stop! This isn't going to work if you are wary of everything you say."

"It isn't going to work anyway. I know that she is the goddess that punishes hubris. If I agree to her statement. I am displaying arrogance before a god." And I nodded towards Nemesis.

Themis smiled. "Oh, Rod. Hubris is displaying foolish pride or arrogance. If you agree with a compliment, that isn't being arrogant."

Then the sinister-looking Nemesis said something that completely disarmed me. "Arrogance is Zeus claiming he is better than all the other gods. Claiming to be king of the gods when in fact there may be fifty other candidates better placed to lead."

Themis stared at Nemesis with a look that was telling her to be silent.

"Rod, let's walk while we talk. Nemesis, please keep your distance and ensure that we don't have any unwanted listeners."

They're playing good cop, bad cop now. They think they're fucking Cagney and Lacey.

"You are plotting a coup."

"No. There may be a coup coming. We are trying to ascertain whether it is a just attempt. Or whether to put a stop to it."

You mean you are trying to figure out which side to be on.

"So why have you been trying to find Apollo and me?

Where do we fit in?"

"We only needed Apollo to be able to locate you."

"Why me?"

"Since your war, you have been the key adviser to Zeus. You probably know him more than anyone. You will have the evidence to prove his weakness or his strength. The secrets we are searching for," said Themis.

"Well, he tells a different story."

"Think about it. You know he will always tell a different story. He has too much to lose, and he has sacrificed you to the gods to silence you. He sees you as the Kingmaker with the power to unseat him. This battle isn't going to be solved by aggression. We will have to use diplomacy, and your crucial facet is your diplomacy. Isn't that right, Rod?

"If you say so."

"You still don't trust us, do you?"

"No, I don't. I only trust one god, and that is Apollo. And even that's in doubt because I guess everything you know about me has come from him."

"You are right. Apollo has told us a lot about you. About you, the man. You should continue to trust him; he is very complimentary about you."

"Something isn't right. If Zeus thinks there is a coup coming. He should keep me close to him, not cast me out."

"You know that, and we know that. But that is the way Zeus works. He thinks that if you feel threatened by those driving the coup, you will destroy them before the coup arrives. He has placed you in extreme danger. Because of his actions, those leading the coup see you as his protector. They perceive that removing you will get them access to the throne."

The more Themis said the more sense it all made. I kept reminding myself that as Goddess of Justice, she was a lawyer. And I knew how good they were at presenting arguments.

She held out her hand and revealed that she was holding my amulet. "Here, take your amulet. And to show you that we mean you no harm. You will keep our amulets."

I reached out and retrieved my amulet. "You realise I could destroy you, now don't you?"

"Yes. But I want to show you how much we trust you. We are putting ourselves at your mercy. We believe you are an honourable man."

I resisted the urge to tell her that I'd already made Nemesis immortal. That would blow any secrets I still held.

"I have a lot to think about. I need time. But tell me… Why did you send Phobos and Deimos?"

This startled Themis. "We didn't send them. How have you encountered them?"

I told Themis the story of how they had broken into Giannis' taverna. She looked puzzled when I named Giannis. I had to explain that Giannis was the name I used for Apollo. I told them how they'd ransacked his apartment looking for something. She signalled Nemesis to join us.

"Nemesis, have you heard anything about Phobos and Deimos being involved with the takeover."

"No. But that is a major development if they are involved."

"Ok, Rod. Go and do your thinking. Mourn your friend, but don't be a stranger. We are happy for you to take the lead in this investigation. But above all, please trust us — we really do want you to be safe. You have my number." And she smiled.

Hugs and double kisses followed. They even waved as they drove away from the car park. I stayed to feed the peacocks. I looked at Alyss's monument. "What do you think, sweetheart? Am I being played?"

I then started to think of Affi. I fought back the tears as I left Filerimos and made my way back to Pine Trees.

≈≈≈

I brought Pete up to speed on the meeting. He was amazed that both Themis and Nemesis had let me keep their amulets. "They must really want your help."

"They made that clear. But they are still not being honest. They say they want to know in the name of justice, which is a lie. They are just trying to figure out which side to land on. They are hedging their bets."

"Of course they are. They carry with them a lot of followers. The direction they choose will have an impact on the eventual results. They obviously value your input."

"Are you saying I should trust them?"

"As Giannis once told you. I trust them, but it is your trust to give. Only you can decide. But they can't do anything to harm you. They suspect you are all-powerful, so long as they think that, then you hold all the cards."

"I feel bad taking them as allies when all the time I know that Nemesis is no longer immortal. I can't resolve that without compromising the amber blood and gold thing."

"There is a much bigger secret than that. Unless Giannis has told them, they won't even know how to bestow immortality."

"Shit."

"That's right. The Olympians are the most powerful gods because of that knowledge. Zeus knows that you share the secret. Throw into the mix that you have power over Zeus. And what comes out is the most powerful god in the pantheon."

"Who is it?"

"You! The only problem is you aren't a god. And that has thrown the whole of the heavens into confusion. Not since the arrival of monotheistic religion has there been so much turmoil. The arrival of Christianity eroded the Olympians power, particularly that of Zeus. He was the only god powerful enough to give others the title of God."

"But we both know that the gods are only gods because they spread rumours about having powers."

"Exactly. Now you come along. A guy called Rod Prince, with the power to blow their rumours out of the water. You have the power to remove their godly status and make them mortal. It's no wonder that Themis wants to be your best friend. She is waiting to see which way you will jump. She will then bring all her supporters with her as she joins you as your ally."

"Why haven't they just come out and said that?"

"I guess that they know you have a hold over Zeus. But they don't know how or why. They don't know you are immortal. Let alone the fact you once made him mortal."

Aletheia

I had another restless night. I'd tried to sedate myself by sharing two whole bottles of Merlot with myself. I'd given up drinking since Affi had died. But as it was the eve of her funeral, I decided it was a tribute to her. I even had pizza ordered and scoffed the lot. It reminded me of our last night together. Unfortunately, the wine didn't sedate me. It acted more like an anaesthetic and knocked me out. I woke in the morning on the marble tiled floor, surrounded by puke and sitting in a puddle of piss. I felt like shit and had a little over an hour to get ready for the funeral. I'd introduced myself to her parents as her employer. I'd offered to pay for the funeral because she was on hotel business when she was killed. Bloody proud Greeks wouldn't hear of it. They asked me if I would give a eulogy. I declined because I thought it would be better done by her friends rather than her sobbing boss. They seemed happy with that.

I was roused from my drunken stupor by Jet. She was at her cat flap hissing and growling. *Shit, there's a god about.* Then I heard the alarm to the cellar beeping. *And they are trying to get to the blood store.*

I scooped Jet up and crept towards the boardroom. She was still growling, but she had learnt to quieten when I placed my hand over her face. The boardroom door was very slightly ajar. I peeked through the gap but was unable to see anyone. I put Jet on the floor to let her loose. She went into full attack mode as I pushed the door open. She launched herself at her target. He didn't stand a chance.

"Aaaargh, get off, you little bitch. It's me. Fuck you, Malaka."

"Giannis! Jet!" I leapt forward to get to the cat.

"Rod, get her off me."

I put my hand over Jets face, and she settled immediately. "Giannis. you're back."

"Put the bloody cat outside."

I did as he suggested and put Jet outside the boardroom. I returned and hugged Giannis. "I've missed you so much, brother." I didn't need to ask where he'd been because I knew he'd spent time with Themis and Nemesis.

"Where is Pete."

"We have a funeral to attend. Affi…"

"I know I heard. Poor kid. If you'd known she was going to get hit by a car, you could have immortalised her first."

"Don't go there. It's a long story, but she was immortalised the day before. Then she had a belly piercing and placed a gold bar into it."

"Damn. That's not good. Why would she do that?"

I just shrugged my shoulders. "We are going to have to catch up later. I'm supposed to be getting set for her funeral.

Will you be coming?"

"No. I am not good at funerals. I was going to give some blood to the store, but it seems you have changed the password."

"Yeah, it's fish and chips." And the door swung open."

"Fees and heeps. Whose bright idea was that?"

I laughed. "I had to find a password that would be hard to pronounce with a Greek accent, making it secure from any gods. Anyway, it's open now. You settle in and give some amber up. Pete and I will see you when we get back. I have to go and get ready."

≈≈≈

After the funeral, it was a long and lonely drive back to Pine Trees. Before even trying to seek out Giannis, I took a moment in the reception. I wanted to sit in Affi's chair and say my last goodbye to her.

I jumped as the main door swung open. "How are you feeling, Rod?"

"Getting there. I can't believe how long the orthodox church gives to a funeral."

"That's nothing, Rod. You need to see their weddings."

"You'll never guess who's in the basement."

"I hope it's someone we can trust."

"It's Giannis. He has come back to us."

We caught up with Giannis in the blood store. We had a lot of catching up to do. He explained why he disappeared so suddenly. Why he decided to help Themis and Nemesis. His thoughts on where they fit in with the threat against us. He told us that when he disappeared, he searched for Themis because she would be on the side of right. She would have been unaware of what was happening if he hadn't gone to her. We filled him in on most of the events at Pine Trees. I held back on the whole Affi 'platonic' thing. There wasn't anything to gain by giving too much detail. I had to tell him that she had found out about Nemesis after the events at Trianon café. He agreed with Pete that Themis and Nemesis would be powerful allies. We all concluded that we were still in danger from potential usurpers. And that Phobos and Deimos were involved in the forthcoming coup.

"What I don't get is that Zeus knew who they were. He also knew we had mortalised one of them. Yet, they are supposed to be part of the coup. Themis and Nemesis didn't know they were even on the island until I told them."

"It seems that it is you that has a decision to make, Rod," said Pete.

"Again? We know what happened the last time you said that to me. This involves more than just me. It involves all three of us. I need to ensure we are all on the same page. One team. What about you, Giannis?"

"I trust your judgement completely."

"Come on, guys, help me out here."

Pete calmed the rising tension in the room. "Let's look at the facts. Just the facts. You have spoken to Themis and Nemesis. Their version of events is different to those that Zeus has claimed. Which we would expect. The coup may already have begun. You are the man in the middle. Both sides concede that you are more powerful than them."

Giannis simplified it. "You are in the driving seat Rod. I say go and see Zeus. He can't harm you."

I still had some concerns. "Let's not forget there are three sides. Zeus, Themis and the coup."

"Themis will jump in any direction you tell her. She has already assured you of that," said Pete.

"And she was quick to come here once I had explained what was going on," added Giannis.

"OK. I'm going to set up a meeting with Zeus. You guys need to decide whether I go alone, or you come with me. By the way, Giannis, I have been using Pete as my crony. I intend to release him from that duty so that he can become your protector again."

"Thanks, Rod. But I would rather he was an equal partner to you and me."

"I was hoping you'd say that. There you go, Pete; you are a free immortal." And I smiled at him.

"Thanks, and I appreciate the gesture. Nothing will change because I am loyal to you guys anyway."

"Just one thing. Do you guys think I am arrogant? Give me the truth."

Giannis didn't pull any punches. "Aletheia? Yes, but I can live with it."

Pete was a bit more diplomatic, "Aletheia? Sometimes you can be quite cold ..." *Don't you dare say like marble.* "... but I think you need to be if you are coming up against the gods. They will expect it. Just try to temper when you are showing your arrogance."

"Thanks for your honesty. What is Aletheia?"

They both chorused, "Truth."

≈≈≈

Before setting up the meeting, I made a call to Themis. I needed to seal the treaty with her as my ally and inform her of my intention to meet with Zeus. She seemed happy enough with that. To test her loyalty, I asked her to provide specific negotiators to accompany me to the meeting. She accepted my challenge and passed my first test.

Within the hour, Themis got back to me. "It is all arranged. They will fly in from Athens tomorrow. Meet them at the airport at 10:00 am, and they will be flying under the names Debbie Webster and Suzanne Jones. They will be expecting you. Hold a card, and they will come to you. Good luck with Zeus."

"Thank you. Zeus' face will be a picture."

"Take care, Rod and speak soon." And she hung up

The guys couldn't believe I'd managed to pull it off.

Giannis said, "How did you manage that. It is so long since I have seen them, I wouldn't have had a clue how to find them. Bring them back here afterwards."

"We can thank Themis. I'll bring them back, and you'll have time to catch up. Book a table at Enigma."

"I'll book it. But I shall not join you. Until we know which direction everyone is jumping, I think it better that I am viewed as a stranger to you." said Pete.

"Book an extra place for Themis."

Giannis interrupted, "How about asking Nemesis."

"You are so bloody obvious. You've got the hots for

Nemesis, haven't you?"

He laughed. "I like an aggressive woman."

"What do you think, Pete? Invite her too."

"Yes. I will contact them. But don't expect me to get involved with any of them. Hopefully, you have learnt your lesson too." And he winked at me.

Giannis spotted the wink. "What's this?"

"Pete will tell you about it. I'm having an early night, and I must clean my apartment. I left it in a mess this morning." And then I reminded myself. *Oh god, dried sick and piss.*

Just before I drifted off to sleep. My phone announced the arrival of a text:

'I am sorry about Affi. – G.'

I pulled Affi's pillow close and inhaled her scent before drifting off.

≈≈≈

I stirred at first light. Before getting myself ready, I sent a text to Zeus:

'Meeting. Your boardroom at 10:15. Alone.'

'What?'

'I want you in the boardroom at Olympian 10:15.'

'What for?'

'Never mind what for – be there, or you are finished.'

'Your threats are incriminating yourself.'

'And who is going to punish me?'

'Who is powerful enough?'

'10:15.'

'OK. But you have lost your mind.'

'Come alone. See you at 10:15.'

Right Rod, get your arse into gear. You've got a date at the airport. I showered and shaved in about 5 minutes and managed to start my journey by nine. It takes the best part of an hour to get to the airport. On my way out, I printed the names Debbie and Suzanne in Times New Roman 150-point font. Landscape orientation centred horizontally and vertically. I even chucked a page border on it. I didn't want a tacky hand-drawn one for my esteemed guests.

≈≈≈

"I believe you are expecting us. I am Debbie, and this is Suzanne."

"Yes. I am Rod Prince. I am pleased to meet you, Debbie and Suzanne."

"Oh, please. We were flying under those names. But please call me Debs."

"And call me Sue."

"OK, I will."

"Thank you for agreeing to come and meet me. Do you have any other luggage?"

"We have known Themis a long time. When she asked us to come, we didn't even have to think before saying yes."

"No, we just have cabin luggage. We will only be staying a day or so."

"Apollo is looking forward to seeing you both again."

"Oh, God. He is such a flirt. I bet he tries to hit on one of us again."

I smiled inside. Knowing that he was planning to hit on

Nemesis. Sue's mobile rang. "Please excuse me. I need to take this call."

She wandered out of earshot, followed by Debs. It allowed me to be a voyeur and check them out. Sue was another beauty. Her strappy top flashing her olive-skinned shoulders. Her brown wavy hair centre-parted and cascaded down her back. It was being made to dance slightly by the breeze. She was wearing a white casual skirt. Her legs were bare the way Affi's always were. I wonder if she has a belly piercing. *Bet it hasn't got a gold bar.* While she was talking on the phone, she looked in my direction and caught me ogling her. She smiled. I just looked down at the piece of paper in my hand, folded it into four and stuffed it in my back pocket. I guessed she was around her late thirties or early forties, give or take three thousand years. Debs was around the same vintage, but she had red hair like Affi. Though, Debs locks were a darker shade of Red. It was clear that they both looked after themselves. Debs looked up and caught me eyeing her up as well. *God, they are going to have me down as a pervert.* From the distance I was looking at them, they both appeared to have jet black eyes. As Sue finished her call and they got closer, I could see they were brown.

"I'm sorry about that, it was a neighbour saying that my cat had got out. She is caring for it while I am away."

"I know the problem; my cat comes and goes as it pleases."

"Oh, you have a cat. I love cats."

"You might not love this one. I will have to explain later. We have a meeting to get to."

From the airport, the journey to Olympian in Kremasti is

only five minutes. But I still felt the need to make conversation. "I take it you know Zeus."

Debs laughed. "Of course, he is my father."

I gulped. *Shit, have I miscalculated?*

"Don't worry. It won't affect our work with you."

"I was pondering about Apollo hitting on you. He is technically your step-brother."

She laughed again. "Rod. You should know that you can't lie to me. You thought that I wouldn't be suitable to be at the meeting. And yes, Apollo is my step-brother, but that wouldn't stop him hitting on me."

"He is more likely to make a pass at me," said Sue.

I laughed. "My wife always said I was a useless liar."

I swung the car into the Olympian car park. Something that I'd done many times before, mostly feeling anxious about meeting with Zeus. This time was different. I felt confident."

Deb and Sue

I entered the boardroom first. My guests had kindly agreed to wait outside until invited in. They knew exactly what I was trying to do to Zeus.

"You have kept me waiting, Rod. I'm a busy man."

"Shut up and listen. I am running this meeting. By the end of it, your fate will be decided. My decision will be made."

His face dropped. The last time I spoke to him like that was at the climax of the war. "What decision? Whether you will stay here or go back to the UK?"

"No, the decision over who will be King of the Gods."

He roared with laughter. "You are the one in trouble. You are showing hubris. You are arrogant before a god. You are breaking a law of Themis. And Nemesis will punish you."

"I don't think so somehow. Before we go on, I would like to introduce my guests to the meeting."

"You said to come alone."

"Yes, I told you to come alone. I didn't say I would come alone."

"You are lying!"

"Well, let's find out, shall we?" And I called out, "Deb and Sue can you come in please?"

Zeus' face was a picture. "Aletheia. Apate. What are you two doing here?"

"Zeus, let me introduce Aletheia Goddess of Truth and her friend Apate Goddess of Fraud and Deception. But I am fairly sure you know that already."

"I know who they are."

"Well, would you like to call me a liar again?"

"I want my lawyer, a representative."

"Who might that be?"

"Themis, I want Themis here. I want to ensure justice."

"Well, now that's the thing. You see, both Aletheia and Apate are here as representatives of Themis."

Zeus looked at his daughter for confirmation. "Is this true?" Aletheia nodded a confirmation.

"All you need to do is convince me that you are worthy of retaining the role of King of the Gods." And I stared directly at Zeus.

"And tell the truth," Said Aletheia.

"I will know if you are trying to commit fraud or deceive us."

If I'd shaved my head, the ensuing interrogation would have been worthy of Telly Savalas as Kojak.

"Let's go through the meeting where you cast me out. Did Demeter leave the underworld to blow the whistle about me?"

"Yes."

"Rod, that is untrue," said Aletheia.

"That is a deception," confirmed Apate. *Bloody hell, I got my own personal lie detectors.*

I looked at Zeus. He knew he had nowhere to run but tell the truth. "OK. Does anyone outside of the Olympian board know I am immortal?"

"No, except you have just told Aletheia and Apate."

Aletheia nodded to confirm he was telling the truth. Then she asked me a question. And Apate looked at me, "Does Themis know you are immortal?"

"I think she might know, but I can't be sure. That's why I asked Zeus the question. We may have to resolve the Themis issue later.

I paused before asking the next question. "Ladies, I'm not asking you to lie. But can I ask you to ignore the next question I am about to put? I need it to stay in this room until I speak to Themis and Nemesis."

Aletheia responded first, "Of course. Unless they ask me to tell them everything that was said. In which case, I will have to tell the truth. Would you rather I left the room?"

"I can hardly lie to you. So, yes, could you leave the room for a moment, please?"

"Of course." And she left the room.

"What about you, Apate? Do you need to leave the room?"

"No, I am not bound by the inability to lie. I am the Goddess of deception. It will be easy for me to lie if anyone asks about your discussion."

The contradiction of trusting someone that claimed to be a mistress of deception stopped me in my tracks. I reassured myself with the thought that every time I went to the ballot box, I was doing just that.

I lowered my voice so that it was almost a whisper. "Is anyone outside of the Olympian gods and my family aware that I know the secret of gold removing immortality?"

Zeus smiled; He knew I was disarmed. He could answer however he wanted, and I had no way to see if he was telling the truth. "As I told you, the whole pantheon knows. That is why you are in danger."

I looked across at Apate. I was looking for a sign that she thought Zeus was deceiving me. She just shrugged her shoulders.

I called out, "Aletheia, can you come back to the meeting, please?"

I looked at Zeus, who was still grinning at me. *Cocky sod.*

I didn't grin back at him. I stared deeply into his eyes. "Tell me, Zeus, did you answer my last question truthfully?"

He looked at his daughter, and he stopped grinning. He sighed then said, "No, I lied."

Aletheia smiled and said, "You are a clever man, Rod. The rumours about you appear to be true."

I continued the questioning of Zeus. "Are you aware of an attempt to overthrow you?"

"Yes"

"That is the truth," confirmed Aletheia.

"Are you aware of who is trying to overthrow you?"

"No."

"Truth."

"Are you aware of anyone that is a direct threat to me?"

He wavered on this answer. He clearly wanted to lie. "Yes."

"Truth."

"Who is a direct threat to me?"

He now waivered even longer than on the previous question. He was squirming in his seat. Then his eyes lit up, and he grinned again as if he found a solution to his dilemma. "Phobos and Deimos. The men that attacked you at Apollos' taverna."

"Who are Phobos and Deimos working for?" *That wiped the bloody smile off your face.*

He sighed. He knew I had him. He still tried to get out of answering it, though. "You know who they work for. You are a threat to me. You are more powerful than I am. There! Is that what you wanted to hear?"

"No, I didn't want to hear that. I have no ambition to overthrow you. I have always been loyal. Whether I have more power than you or not. It has always been used in your service and never against you. Since the war, I have viewed you as a friend. Next question. Are my family in danger?"

"No."

"Truth."

I was now getting mad. I promised myself I wasn't going to ask the next question. I was so angry I broke my promise to myself. I raised my voice. "Were you involved in the death of my hotel manager?"

He looked worried. I could tell by the look on his face he was involved. Even before he answered. "It wasn't me. I didn't tell them to do it. They were acting on their own. They thought it would please me. It was meant to be a small accident. It got out of hand."

I was seething. I banged my hand hard down on the desk

catching his hand as I did so. Aletheia wouldn't have seen it. But Zeus knew. He could tell by the spot of red blood on the back of his hand. He was mortal.

I slid the gold-tipped dart back into my jacket pocket. "You come and see me when you are ready to make amends. King of the Gods. King of Malaka's more like. Meeting over."

I had to fight back the tears as I stormed out of the boardroom. My godly lie detectors followed close behind.

I could hear Zeus shouting after us. "Rod, wait. Come back. Please…"

I used the hour-long journey back to Pine Trees to bring Aletheia and Apate up to date about the Affi saga. I didn't go into all the spicier details, but I think they would have known the truth given who they were. I apologised for getting angry and losing it. Apate understood and suggested I'd shown a lot of restraint. On the plus side, they were looking forward to the sixsome we had planned for the evening. Though Aletheia was still fretting about Giannis hitting on her.

Apokalypsi

Pete had booked one of the round tables in the roof garden. It seated six easily, and it meant there was no 'head' of the table. It provided a beautiful view over the bay, augmented by the aroma of natural oregano mixed with the smell of food cooking. It was always sense heaven when we visited. Giannis had successfully invited Themis and Nemesis. Though we arrived well before they did. It was amusing to see Giannis hanging back to ensure he would be sat alongside Nemesis. Apate and I rode shotgun for Aletheia, with Apate sat to her left and me sat to her right. Giannis sat directly opposite her, with an empty chair on either side of him.

I whispered to Aletheia, "You can relax now. I believe Apollo wants to sit between Themis and Nemesis."

She said, "Poor girls." And giggled.

If only Zeus knew that this meeting was the deliberation on his suitability as King of the Gods.

Giannis was the first to raise the subject of the meeting. "How did the meeting go, Rod?"

"We will talk about it shortly. I don't want to have to repeat myself when the ladies of justice arrive."

The server approached with menus.

As host, it was my role to organise the meal, "What does everyone want to drink?"

"Aletheia?"

"Red wine, please."

"Me too," said Apate.

"Giannis?" And Aletheia looked at me strangely. "Oh, that's Apollos' mortal name. The same way you ladies used the names, Debbie and Suzanne." She smiled to show her understanding.

"Mythos for me, Rod."

I smiled at the server. "I will have Mythos too. We have two more ladies joining us. Can you look out for them and take their drinks order when they arrive? Thank you."

No sooner had the server disappeared and I spotted Themis and Nemesis. I waved to them to signify our location. Giannis' face lit up as he stood and sat the latecomers down. He was impressed that everyone had fallen naturally into his seating plan. It was logistically impractical to give cheek kisses, so everyone reached over the table and made sure they shook everyone else's hand. It reminded me of the number of times I had seen Zeus meet with business partners in eateries throughout the island. Formal yet informal. The fact that all the guys were in jeans, but at the same time wore open-collared white shirts under our suit jackets. The ladies, too, all wore white blouses signifying the formality of the meeting. Three of them wore casual skirts, while Nemesis, like us guys, was dressed in jeans. In her case, they were tight skinny jeans.

I am sure Giannis appreciated them as she squeezed into her chair.

The ladies of justice had also gone for red wine.

I toasted, "Yammas, Chrónia Pollá. May we all have success."

Everyone chorused, "Yammas."

The next few minutes went as one would expect while we all pawed over the menu. Giannis offering various bits of gastronomic advice about the dishes on offer.

Themis said, "There is so much to choose from. Why don't we have it meze?"

"That sounds good," said Apate.

It was becoming clear that Apate was quite a reserved person. I guessed it was because she was always on the lookout for someone deceiving her.

I nodded at the server. "Can we have one each of every starter on the menu, please? A bottle of ouzo and six small glasses, please." I looked at the rest of the table. "Any particular dishes anyone wants?"

Everyone responded either visually or verbally, "No, that is fine for a start."

The server collected the menus, "Thank you."

Themis felt she had to justify her suggestion. "It will be easier to pick and talk rather than having to wait for everyone to finish eating." There was a general agreement that she was right.

Themis took a sip of red wine. "Rod, tell us did you get the answers you wanted from Zeus?"

"Yes, though I could have guessed most of them. But it

was good that Aletheia and Apate were there to tell me when he was telling the truth."

Aletheia and I then fed back to everyone just what had gone on at the meeting. Apate just nodded at crucial points. There were lots of questions thrown in our direction. Apate glanced over at me, raising an eyebrow. She knew I hadn't yet revealed the major revelation.

"There is something else I discussed with him, but Aletheia wasn't present. I thought it inappropriate for her to find out before we had this meeting."

"Go on," said Themis.

Apate knew that what was coming was going to be ground-breaking. She interrupted before I could answer. "I suggest a toast to Rod for risking his life going directly to Zeus over this delicate situation."

Oh god, not ouzo shots. Giannis looked pleased. It meant he might have a chance with Nemesis if she was under the influence of ouzo.

Everyone shouted, "Yammas." I just blushed.

"I think before you all get too carried away. You need to listen to what I have to say." The merriment stopped, and all eyes were on me.

I looked around me as if making sure there was nobody eavesdropping. "The Olympians know how to …"

Giannis and Apate looked at me because they knew what I was about to say. The rest of the ladies all looked at me because they were hanging on to my every word.

"Know how to what?" Said Aletheia. With her sat to my left asking that question, I knew there was no going back. I couldn't lie because she would know.

"They know how to remove immortality." There was stunned silence from everyone. From Giannis because he couldn't believe I had revealed the Olympians greatest secret. The girls were shocked that it was a secret that had been hidden from them for thousands of years.

"Then came the inevitable question. "Do you know how they do it?"

"Of course. And what's more, I have done it often."

"Rod, you do know what you are admitting to, don't you?" Said Themis.

"Yes, and I have more to admit to. But all the problems facing the gods are because of secrets and lies. I want to change all that. Aletheia will be pivotal in bringing that about. That is why I asked her to be present."

"You say there is more."

"Yes. As of the meeting this morning. Zeus is mortal."

Everyone gasped. Giannis choked on his beer.

Giannis said, "I think you ought to tell them that you also know how to make him immortal again." And he grinned.

"Giannis is correct. We have the means to make a mortal immortal."

There was a visible group sigh of relief from the ladies.

I took a deep breath. "Yes, he's probably already arranged to be immortalised again. But, I am sorry to say, there is one of us sat at this table that is mortal."

"Of course there is. You are mortal," said Nemesis.

I just looked at her and slowly shook my head. "I would like to play a game. Please humour me. It will allow you all to regularly test your immortality status."

Everyone was engrossed in what I was saying. Giannis knew it all, but he was amazed that I was baring my soul. More so given that my audience comprised truth, deception, justice, and revenge. He just played ignorant, ensuring that he wouldn't be implicated in any ensuing punishment.

"This test won't make us mortal, will it?" Asked Aletheia.

"No. I promise that it will merely reveal whether you are immortal or not."

She looked at the others, confirming that I was telling the truth. I pulled out a small tube from my pocket. I twisted the top open and let the sewing needles slide into my glass of ouzo. I upended the whole glass onto a serviette on the table. The damp patch of ouzo spread around the glass as the liquid leached into the serviette and tablecloth.

I removed the glass and picked up one of the needles. I held it up until I was sure everyone was looking, then I pricked the tip of my thumb and squeezed it. I saw the amber bubble form. "That, ladies and gentlemen, is amber blood. I am immortal."

I slid the soggy napkin towards Aletheia. She copied my actions and held her thumb up so that we could all see the amber bubble. She must have had thin blood because it didn't stop at a bubble. It trickled a little way down her thumb.

"Immortal," I said.

Aletheia slid the napkin to Apate.

In one swift move, she picked up a needle and stuck it straight into her thumb. She made the thumbs-up sign.

"Immortal," she said and slid the napkin to Themis.

She paused to ask a question before carrying out her test. "As Goddess of Justice, why have I never been told of this phenomenon?"

"You should ask that question of Zeus. The fact he hasn't shared it with anyone is his only claim to power. By being the only god to be able to bestow immortality, he is showing that he is more powerful than any other god."

She pondered on what I'd said for a moment before selecting a needle. She held her thumb up and went for the slow and deliberate method. Her soft skin didn't offer much resistance as the needle penetrated her thumb. She jumped slightly. *I should have warned her quick is better.* She held up her thumb with pride as the amber blood formed its dome on her digit. "Immortal," she squealed. It was a completely uncharacteristic sound from someone that had been so formal to that point. I guessed when you have been immortal for thousands of years, you take it for granted. It must make one anxious when you are waiting for the results of a health status test. I guess it was a bit like waiting for a blood test for some condition you would rather not have. Her squeal was a measure of relief. She slid the napkin to Giannis.

"Before he could pick a needle, I interrupted. "Rest assured, if either of you tests negative for immortality, we can correct it fairly quickly. By tomorrow, you will be immortal again. Carry on, Giannis."

Like Apate, Giannis went for the one-movement quick penetration. He held up his thumb and gave his verdict. "Immortal." He didn't make a big noise about it because he knew that meant that Nemesis was the person I was suggesting had been mortalised."

It must have been a shock for her. She wasn't in tears, but her hand was visibly shaking as she picked up a needle. "I don't have to do it if you know that one of us is mortal."

"I would still like you to carry on. It will illustrate the visible difference we should all look out for. It will allow us all to check our immortality daily. If we carry out regular checks, we will find it easier to correct. Think of it as a disease. We can't treat it if we don't know we have it.

Giannis said, "A quick prick is best. Would you like me to prick it for you?" I looked straight at him and slowly shook my head. *I can't believe you're still flirting with her.*

Without further ado, she thrust the sharp needle into the tip of her thumb. And the crimson red bubble formed immediately.

"And that, ladies, is mortal blood." I was milking it like a magician that had just completed some remarkable feat of magic.

Everyone sat back in their chairs, visibly amazed at what they'd seen. I realised that I had taken a big gamble revealing what I knew. I now had to justify to my audience why I'd taken such a massive gamble. But before I could even start, I was bombarded by questions. Unfortunately, I didn't have a press secretary to speak on my behalf.

"How did you know that I would be mortal?"

"Do you remember when we met at Trianon Café? My cat attacked you."

"Yes. Was it the cat?"

I paused for the slightest of moments. "No, she can only

detect … Never mind. It was me when I retrieved her. I pierced your skin with this." And I pulled my golden tipped dart out of my pocket, making sure not to touch its tip with my pierced thumb.

"Can we look at it?" Asked Themis.

"I'm afraid not. Especially while you have an open wound on your thumb. It is safe for Nemesis to look at." I passed the dart to Nemesis. "Look at it closely and describe to the others what you see."

"I see a dart. It looks like an ordinary dart, but it appears to have a golden tip."

"Yes, that is right. That golden tip touched one of the wounds that Jet, the cat, had inflicted on you at Trianon. That was the cause of your mortality. Until recently, I thought the gold had to penetrate your body. But recent events have shown me the gold merely has to touch the blood from an open wound and a chain reaction starts that will turn your amber blood into mortal red blood. That is why I can't let any of you touch the dart. You each have an open wound."

Sensing the seriousness of what I had revealed, they each removed their gold jewellery, being sure to use the unpricked hand. I held up my hand, showing that the wedding ring that Kam had given me was made of silver.

"And Zeus knows all of this?" Said Aletheia.

"Yes. Like I said, that is where he gets his power from."

Themis added. "And that is where you get your power over Zeus."

"In a way, yes. But he isn't a clever man. He doesn't see that we hold a mutual threat. He only sees the threat that I am to him. And that is why he isn't suitable to be King of the Gods. He is cruel and has no empathy. He is indiscriminate in his use of justice and retribution. Above all, he is dishonest. Because of the present company, I won't even start about his views on incest."

Nemesis, the victim in this magic trick, asked, "You are a threat to us. Why should we not punish you?"

"Because I have been honest with you. I have helped you. If I hadn't conducted tonight's demonstration, Zeus could make you all mortal, and you wouldn't even be aware of it. He would then have the freedom to carry on his reign unchecked. I have only used the power once when it wasn't in self-defence, and that was this morning with Zeus. I used it in anger."

Aletheia contributed to my defence. "I was there, and his use of the power was completely justified. Zeus was involved in the death of his manageress. Aphrodite."

Themis nodded her approval. "OK can you demonstrate how we make Nemesis immortal again; she looks terrified. Poor girl."

Nemesis forced a smile. Giannis put his arm around her and said, "Come back to my office. I will fix you." *For fucks sake, leave it out, Giannis.*

It was too late Nemesis had fallen for his charms. She just smiled meekly at him. "Thank you."

"Before then, let's eat," I said.

The next hour was filled with more questions than prime ministers question time. I just made sure that every answer I gave was open and honest. So different to prime ministers question time. As the food and questions started to peter out, it was appropriate to decant to Pine Trees.

I grabbed the bottle of ouzo and left two hundred euros on the table. "Come, we'll show you our hotel. And fix Nemesis." Giannis looked at me because I guessed he was hoping to get her on her own. When we reached the hotel. I locked the door behind us. I didn't want Jet making an appearance. Not with five gods on the premises.

I summoned Pete to introduce him to those that hadn't met him. Nemesis and Themis were startled to discover how well I knew Pete. After all, to them, he was the neutral box keeper.

Psifos

Everyone looked around the room. I explained the process while Pete readied the draught. I just hoped that Nemesis didn't have a journey like Affi. I didn't want the audience to witness that. It was scary for me; it would terrify them.

"Nemesis, if you would sit in the chair, please." I invited her to sit and relax.

Pete said, "Rod. The jeans."

"Oh, um. I'm sorry, Nemesis, but your skinny jeans are too tight for the procedure. If you go into the changing cubicle, you will find a theatre gown." Giannis adjusted his position so that he could get a better view of the changing booth.

Both Themis and I spoke at the same time. I said, "Giannis."

She said, "Apollo." He skulked back into the centre of the room with the rest of us.

Nemesis returned all gowned up and settled back in the chair. Pete took her blood pressure, describing what he was doing at each stage. "I need the blood pressure because it will dictate the pace at which the procedure can progress."

As he handed Nemesis the draught, he said, "You will all be familiar with this. It is the dream draught we have played with for years. Sweet dreams, Nemesis." And she downed it in one. Like Affi, her eyes didn't close, but she was out.

Pete inserted both catheters himself. Remembering the pig's ear I'd made of trying to insert a catheter into Affi's arm.

Aletheia, Apate and Themis watched with intent concentration.

He fiddled with the valves to get the tubes ready to flow. He adjusted the pump and opened the inlet valve. The familiar sound of blood pouring into the drainage sump started.

"That's it. We must now let her cook for about forty to fifty minutes, and she will be immortal again.

"Mmmmm," moaned Nemesis, who was apparently having a good dream.

Pete busied himself with filling out the records when he motioned for me to join him. He pointed at the figures, and I understood what he was showing me.

I turned to the rest of the group. "OK. Just so that you are aware. There is a cost to this procedure. Every time we do it, we have to use about a gallon of amber blood." Everyone looked at me. "I mean about five litres. And that means that once we have immortalised Nemesis, we will only have enough for one more immortalisation."

"What are you saying, Rod? We can only ever do it once more."

"No. I am saying we need to restock, and the simplest way is for each of us to regularly donate amber blood."

"I think we would all be willing to do that," said Themis.

Everyone looked in horror as I described how Zeus deals with a shortage. "Zeus deals with his supply slightly differently. He uses live human hosts as his blood bank. There is an army of innocent victims that don't know they are immortal. When he needs to complete this procedure, he will take it from a live being. At least, they are alive at the start of the procedure."

"That is disgusting," said Themis.

"I completely agree with you. The horrific thing is, it was probably that method that gave all you folks immortality."

I could see their minds cogitating what I had just said. They knew that for whatever reason, they had been selected and turned into immortals.

"We can't donate tonight; we are full of alcohol. Tomorrow I will ask you all to donate half a litre of your blood ... for the cause."

A buzzer sounded on the pump. 'That's it," said Pete.

I added, "She will come round shortly because the draught has also been flushed out of her system."

Nemesis groaned, "Wow, that was some dream."

"Just stay there for a few moments. We don't want you feeling woozy," said Pete.

"This is an impressive setup you have here, Rod," said Aletheia.

"It's not just mine. It is as much Pete's and Giannis' place. We are equal partners, one team. Nemesis, we'll leave you to get changed. We'll be upstairs in the boardroom." And I ushered Giannis out ahead of me. Giannis tutted.

I wheeled in a couple of chairs from reception and Affi's

office. We sat around the boardroom table, and Nemesis sat in Affi's usual seat, but I didn't dwell on it. My seat was automatically top of the table. Not because of any superiority. It's just where my laptop rose from within the desk.

Aletheia said, "Where is your cat?"

"Don't worry. I've locked her out."

"Awww, I would like to have met her," said Apate.

"Trust me, you wouldn't. Nemesis and Giannis will confirm. Jets main feature is that she doesn't like Gods."

"She can tell the difference?"

"I believe so. Sometimes she is OK with Giannis, but mostly not. I'm not going to risk it. You ladies are my guests. I don't want you to be savaged by a cat."

Themis coughed. "Rod, Apollo and Petros, I know it is your hotel, but would you mind if I chaired the meeting?"

"Of course."

"We have heard what Rod has to say. And we have all figured out Apollo's view of Nemesis. We have seen how technically expert Petros is. But I want to know what you ladies think. Aletheia."

"I can vouch for the honesty of Rod. He has been open with us and spoken nothing but the truth."

"And what do you say, Apate?"

"I say that Zeus has shown that he is full of deceit. And that he has deceived the pantheon for many millennia."

"What about you, Nemesis?"

"At one point when we did the testing, I was frightened by him. But I found his manner reassuring. He showed sympathy for me when I was upset. And he made sure he put right the wrong that his cat had done to me." *Thank god she still blames Jet and not my dart.*

Themis thought for a while. "Rod, when I asked you about the secret. I didn't have any idea how big the secret would turn out to be. Zeus is correct in believing you are a potential threat to the whole pantheon of immortals."

She looked at the others, "I balance that by his desire for honesty and the fact he doesn't use his power maliciously. I further balance that although he can take immortality, he can also restore it. Therefore, by the power of justice, I dismiss the charge of hubris that some have levelled upon him. The balance of justice falls in Rods favour."

"Wait a minute, I didn't know I was on trial."

"You aren't, silly. I was just stating it so that when someone asks why I haven't investigated you. I can tell them truthfully that I did and found you had no charge to answer."

She continued. "On the next matter. It has been proposed that we should support Zeus in the protection of his seat of power. I would like to hear from the two humans before the gods vote on this. Petros, would you start. What is your view of Zeus?"

"I find him arrogant and foolish. He is a selfish god and primarily looks out for himself. He has no sympathy, empathy or sense of care for anyone."

"Thank you. You have been around for as long as we have, and I understand you were crony to Apollo. Is there anyone you have met in all that time that would be worthy of replacing Zeus as King ... or Queen of the Gods?"

Pete looked at me. I slightly shook my head.

Unfortunately, Aletheia spotted him looking at me and my head movement. "Petros, can I remind you that I will know if you aren't telling the truth.

Pete just shrugged his shoulders at me to demonstrate the uselessness of not saying what he wanted to say. He took a deep breath and said, "I know only one person with the power to rule fairly, and that is Rod."

Themis continued, "Thank you for your honesty, Petros. And what about you, Rod? The man of the hour. What are your views on Zeus?"

"You will be surprised to hear what I have to say. He is just misguided. Everything he does is done because he thinks it is right. He hasn't the greatest intellect, and he thinks he has power because of his arrogance. He behaves the way people expect the King of Gods to behave. I have seen him in tears before now sobbing like a baby. I have seen him panicking because he doesn't know what to do. I don't like the way he farms mortals to use them as amber blood storage. But he only does that because he thinks it is the best way of ensuring that all gods remain immortal. Do you understand? He wants to do right, but he doesn't know how. He is stuck in two-thousand BC."

"Thank you, Rod. You have been most benevolent about a man that caused the death of your manageress. I figure she was more than just a manageress to you." I blushed and lowered my head; it was almost a nod.

She continued. "And that same benevolence is why I think Petros may be right. You may be the best candidate to be King of the Gods ..."

I spoke up quickly before she tried to proclaim me as something I don't think I could ever live up to. "I don't wish to interrupt, but could I add something, please?"

"Of course."

"Before you vote on anything. If you choose me, it will create many problems. I am not a god, and some will resent me becoming their king. That would be equivalent to someone from Turkey being installed as a president of Greece. I know Zeus is under threat from a coup. But that is a small proportion of the Gods. What Zeus has got is continuity. You four ladies between you have much more support than anyone leading a takeover. I have already told you that Zeus is misguided. Why not let me give him that guidance? I can add to his power. I can try and make him less of a despot. I'll teach him to be less cruel and oppressive. I would be on hand to help him repel any attempted coup. Besides, without Zeus, there will be a void. This would generate a rush by all and sundry to fill that void. Who knows what type of king you may end up with? All I ask in return is immunity from punishment if defending Zeus results in mortalising and the death of a god."

"Thank you for that, Rod. You do realise that all you have done is make yourself a more suitable candidate to replace Zeus?"

I sighed and shook my head.

Aletheia said, "Face up to it, Rod, Zeus would not speak as highly of you as you are speaking of him."

"No, but he trusts me. He cast me out to battle with the leaders of the coup. He was just dishonest about the way he went about it."

Themis tapped the table with her knuckles. "I think we are ready for the deliberation. I want to put four proposals forward. One: Zeus will be informed that we have adjudged that he is not fit to be King of the Gods in his current manner and that he must change the way he rules. Two: He will retain his seat of power if he has a trusted adviser that will be appointed by myself as the Goddess of Justice. Three: I need your support to appoint Rod as the trusted adviser to Zeus. Four: Rod will be immune from retribution in the event of any god losing immortality and their subsequent death. Off the record, I want Zeus nailed down so tightly that he can't move without Rods say so."

"Do you want me and Pete to leave the room while you vote or discuss it?"

"No, good god, if you hadn't intervened just now, we would be celebrating your coronation as the King." And she laughed.

"OK. I ask the gods in this room. How do you vote on point one?" To which, they all spat at the table. *Fuck, this is going to get messy.*

"Thank you. Sorry about the spitting Rod, but it is the Greek way of sealing the deal. On Point One, I will visit Zeus tomorrow. On points two and three together, how do you vote?" And everyone spat twice on the table." *Shit, so many germs.*

"Thank you. Rod, will you join me when I visit Zeus tomorrow?"

"Of course."

"Point four. This is the big one because we are, in fact, giving Rod a licence to kill gods as he sees fit. You need to ask yourselves the following question: Is Rod the kind of man we can give that power to? How do you vote?"

Giannis spoke before the vote. "Themis, it doesn't need a vote. He already has the power to do all that without punishment. With all due respect to your position, he is more powerful than anyone in this room."

"Thank you, Giannis, but I want it formally stated. Zeus will be told that same thing tomorrow, in case he thinks he can squirm out of any conditions. I ask the room again, on point four, how do you vote?" And they all gobbed onto the table. *That table cost a fortune, and the varnish is going to be ruined.*

"That ends the meeting. Now Rod, where is that bottle of ouzo? I feel like partying."

"Don't worry, there is ample supply of alcohol, and we have plenty of rooms available if you ladies want to stay the night. I will make sure that Jet isn't about."

We started with one celebratory shot. "Yammas. Here is to success and the taming of Zeus."

This led to a second shot. "Yammas. Here is to Rod Prince of Rhodes."

I took the shot but said, "Please, guys, don't refer to me as any kind of Prince. I am just an ordinary bloke that understands your king." At that moment, I wished my surname was Smith or Jones. Anything but Prince.

Everyone broke off into pairs for general chit-chat. I had a heart to heart with Themis. "I really feel uncomfortable about the whole adoration thing."

"You underestimate your role, Rod. You have given hope to every Greek deity."

"Except those planning the coup. Do you need me to report all developments to you?"

"Of course not. If I imposed limits like that, I would be no better than Zeus. You will have complete autonomy. You need to remember; I am not your superior. You could kill me far easier than I could destroy you. I am conceding to you. Anyway, enough shop talk. Now, pour me a drink."

I cast my phone to the screen and selected my Greek Sirtaki playlist. For the next hour, we had sixty minutes of everyone trying to dance the sirtaki. I noticed Giannis slip away with Nemesis, and I was about to stop him when Themis said, "Leave them. She is old enough to make her own decision. And I am sure he will regret it by morning. Nemesis can be quite demanding." And she winked at me.

I laughed to myself quietly as I could hear Jet hissing and wailing in the background accompanied by shrieks from Nemesis and loud swearing from Giannis. *I must sort that bloody cat out.*

Apofasi

We arrived at Olympian Dreams to the sound of Zeus shouting and bawling at his staff. We walked in the direction of the noise, and it was coming from the reception area. Unusually Zeus was in the hub of the hotel. He'd always run the operation from the background. As we entered the reception area, he looked up and spotted us.

He stormed in our direction shouting at Themis. "At last, you are here. I charge this man with hubris. I want him punished."

Themis just said, "Oh really. Can we go somewhere a little less public? I need to talk to you, and I don't think it should be in front of hotel guests."

He led us to the boardroom. The same room that I'd had so many meetings with him in the past. The place where he'd cast me out of the inner circle. The room where the day before he admitted his involvement in Affi's death.

I gently closed the door behind us and locked it. He wasn't going to storm out before we'd finished.

He started his rant again. "I want him charged with hubris."

She raised her voice and said, "Sit!"

"You can't talk to me like that."

"If you want me to help you remain as King of the Gods, you will do as I say."

He sat down as ordered.

"Right. Now keep quiet and listen. I have already investigated the charge of hubris. I have found that there is no case to answer. Furthermore, Aletheia, Nemesis and I have considered the charge that you are not fit to be King of the Gods. We had already selected your replacement. You owe a great deal to Rod because he supported you and spoke out to ask that you be able to retain your seat of power."

Zeus looked at me fleetingly and couldn't bring himself to speak. His lips were pursed tightly together. His olive-skinned complexion was gradually turning redder. *He is going to blow in a minute.*

Themis continued her admonishment, "The way you are currently ruling is unacceptable, and you must change or lose the trust of the pantheon, and that will lose you your crown. To help you change, we are giving you a trusted adviser. You will run every decision past that advisor. That advisor will be Rod, my representative. You shouldn't find that too onerous as I understand he has been advising you since the battle of Rhodes. And in case you plan to harm him, he has been given immunity from prosecution should he mortalise or subsequently kill a god. And that dear Zeus includes you. In effect, Rod will be the power behind your throne. In return, he will be your defence against the coming coup. Do you accept my ultimatum?"

He dithered in answering, so she prompted him with a warning. "Do you accept your punishment, or do you relinquish your throne. You have a straightforward decision to make. Do you want to remain as King of the Gods?"

He boomed the way he usually did when he was stoked by anger, "Of course I do."

"Then accept the conditions."

His tone quietened, and he turned towards me but lowered his eyes, "OK. Welcome home, Rod. I am um … er …"

Themis interrupted him. "I will hand over to you, Rod."

I looked at Zeus. "I think the word you are looking for is sorry. And I take it you are immortal again."

"Of course." And he bloody looked up and smiled.

"Well, things are going to change. The poor mortals you have prepared as donors can retain their immortality, however, instead of draining them completely of their blood and letting them die. You will set up a quarterly donation process. They will continue to live and produce more blood for you. Do you see the wisdom in doing that?"

"What if they refuse to donate."

"Simply give them their mortality back and let them go on their way. They don't need to die at your hands."

"Why didn't you suggest that before."

"I did, but you wouldn't listen because you are the King of the Gods, and you thought you knew best."

"From now on, every decision you make will pass through me for approval. If I don't approve it, you drop it. I am going to micromanage you. Does that sound familiar? It is the same way you managed me throughout the war. If you accept the new order, we might head off the coup and keep you on your throne. If I get a hint of deceit or rebellion on your part, you will be permanently removed from the throne. Do you understand what I am saying?"

"Yes, Rod. I will do everything you ask."

Themis stepped forward again. "In which case, King Zeus, my followers and I will support your continued reign until Rod tells us otherwise. So as well as Rod's power, you now have my legal support, and you can leave the coup to us. And don't forget Rod is my representative!"

≈≈≈

There were several problems with this new alliance. I didn't fancy spending twenty-four hours a day babysitting Zeus. The time to get from Pefkos would be about an hour. I still didn't trust Zeus enough to let him anywhere near Pine Trees. It was Giannis that provided the solution. He would move into Olympian, Zeus was his father after all, so it made sense. I knew that there was enough animosity between them that Giannis would be loyal to me. We had a natural hotline to each other anyway. Pete offered to be the babysitter, but he needed to keep his service to me a secret. Given that he was the keeper of the boxes, and any god could call upon him to hold their amulet.

I contacted Themis. "Is it acceptable for Apollo to take over the day-to-day supervision of Zeus?"

"Of course. I told you that you are in charge. If that is what you want to do, then you just do it. Let me reiterate, you do not need to run every decision past me."

Many times, I would muse to myself I could grow to like this new order.

≈≈≈

"Looks like it's just you and me again, Pete."

"In an empty hotel. Are you going to open it now?"

"No, there is too much chance of getting distracted. What about your family? Could they not come and join us?"

"I've already considered that. Lindon is god knows where with Artemis. Alyss is safely in Athens with Athena, and Kam is with Richard looking after her mum."

"Can you trust Artemis, Athena and Richard?"

The real issue was that I was keeping the knowledge of Kam and Richards relationship secret. I didn't have the slightest idea of how much the kids knew and didn't fancy being the one to explain it to them.

"I think so. Giannis is the link to all three of them. And to the outside world, Zeus is still King of the Gods. My concern is who is planning the coup?"

"I can try and put out feelers. I am assuming that Themis and Nemesis will have information to share too."

"I hope so. I don't like the idea of waiting to be attacked. I would rather be proactive. Talking of proactivity, we will be receiving visitors each day. They are going to donate amber to us to build up a stockpile. We need enough to immortalise ourselves or allies at short notice."

"How many are we expecting?"

"I don't know. Giannis will send over names with appointment times. I have told him we don't want any more than two a day."

"Bloody hell, how many has he immortalised?"

"Your guess is as good as mine, but I reckon it must be at least twelve. One for each Olympian god. And then some spare."

"Storage space is going to be a bit tight."

"Yep, another reason for not opening the hotel. We can use the cold and freezer storage in the kitchen. Potentially we have access to the wine storage area at Olympian Dreams. But that will be the last resort. In the meantime, as much as I hate it, we just have to sit and wait."

I gave Pete a shopping list of things to stockpile. At the very least, we needed another set of golden tipped darts made. We also needed to check the use-by date of the plating solution left from the war.

I gave myself a target. I needed to train Jet. I needed her to be able to recognise a good god from an evil god. I didn't like having to lock her out every time Themis or Nemesis came to Pine Trees. Fortunately, because Giannis was messing with Nemesis, she was at Olympian dreams most of the time. Aletheia and Apate had gone back to Athens to continue their lives as Sue and Debs. But that was near enough that they would be in a position to hear any rumours that may be circulating.

≈≈≈

I spent a straight forty-eight hours interrogating Google. 'How to train a cat'. 'What do cats love', 'what do cats hate'. I watched endless YouTube videos showing me how to train a cat to use its litter tray. I discovered that if you play dead and ignore the scratching and biting, they will lose interest. Somehow, I couldn't imagine Giannis letting Jet attack him until she lost interest. I discovered various things that cats love, like catnip. I considered issuing a catnip supply to good gods. But that wouldn't necessarily stop Jet from having a fit when any gods were nearby. Do I give good gods something that cats love? Or do I give good gods something that cats hate? I was worn out from the pressure of it all. I needed sleep. I hoped that by succumbing to that need, I would get inspiration in my dreams.

I pulled the thin cover over my head to try and block out some daylight. I turned and pulled Affi's pillow towards me. It had become my comfort blanket; I hoped her smell would help me to sleep. I was starting to drift off when I heard the cat flap rattle. Moments later, I felt Jet jump on the bed. She flopped down on my legs and started to purr. I felt secure and drifted off to sleep.

It was still light as I stirred. I was unsure if it was the same daylight or a new day. How long had I been asleep? Jet had commandeered Affi's pillow. "Get off. That's mine." And I snatched the pillow off her. She wasn't happy. I put the pillow near her, and she calmed down again. I lifted it away, and she got snarky. "Oh, you beautiful cat. Thank you."

I grabbed the pillow and sprinted stark naked towards the bedroom door, slamming it shut behind me. I could hear Jet fretting on the other side of it. I placed the pillow at the base of the door and puffed it up a few times. Sure enough, Jet started to purr again. I took the pillow to the opposite side of the lounge, and I could hear Jet scratching at the door. I put the pillow by the door, and she stopped scratching. I opened the door to let her out of the bedroom. I ruffled her fur to show my appreciation. I ran down to the boardroom.

I burst through the door, with Jet following in my wake. "Pete, Pete, I have a job for you."

"Bloody hell Rod. Did you want to put some clothes on first?" I looked down and stuffed Affi's pillow over my embarrassment.

"I need you to find out what the scent is on this pillow."

"You are joking, right?"

"No, whatever the scent is, Jet relaxes when she smells it."

"Well, I'm not going to smell it. Not while you are holding it down there."

"Right. Close your eyes for a minute."

He closed his eyes, and I thrust the pillow into his face. "Do you recognise that smell?"

"Wow. Yeah, that is Aphrodite's scent."

"OK, your new task is to identify the name of that perfume."

He opened his eyes. "Oh, for god's sake, Rod, cover yourself again."

I just turned my back, flashed my bare arse and said, "I'm going to get dressed. See what you can find out."

Jet, of course, followed me because I still had Affi's pillow.

≈≈≈

"Do you have anything else of hers in your suite that carries her scent?

"I don't think so. Why?"

"Because I don't fancy dragging a pillow around the perfume shops in Rhodes. Why don't you ask one of the goddesses if they recognise it."

I called Themis. She answered within one ring. "Rod. How can I help?"

"I need a woman's advice. My hotel manageress…"

"You mean your good friend."

"Yeah, that's the one. She always wore the same perfume. I have an item that has her scent on it. I haven't a clue what it is called. Do you think you or Nemesis might be able to recognise it?"

"We might, but we would have to smell it. Have you thought to ask her parents? Her mother might know."

"I thought of that but didn't want them to think their dead daughters' boss was some kind of weirdo."

"What about her friends?"

"I never met any of her friends."

"OK, take it over to Nemesis. She is at Olympian dreams. If she doesn't recognise it, then bring it over to me. By the way, what is the item?"

"It's a pillowcase."

"In that case, I will have a sniff."

I don't know why but her last statement made me giggle to myself.

≈≈≈

Giannis breathed in the aroma on the pillowcase. "That is Aphrodite's smell. But I wouldn't know the name of the scent."

Nemesis had a quick sniff. "It is a lovely perfume for sure. But I haven't any idea which it is."

"Here, let me have a smell," said Zeus.

I passed the pillowcase to him. He inhaled deeply. "I don't know what it is called, but that is the same smell that Aletheia has about her. I swear it."

I flicked my mobile into life and sent Aletheia a text.

'Debs, it's Rod.'

'Hey, Rod.'

'Do you wear perfume?'

'I do.'

'What is it called?'

'Which one?'

'Whatever you were wearing when we met.'

'When we met with Zeus.'

'It's called Kitten Fur.'

'It smells like a baby cat.'

'OMFG.'

'What?'

'My manageress left it on her pillow.'

'It is the only thing that calms my cat – Jet.'

'It would do. It's all I wear when at home.'

'Because of my cat. Remember I said I had a cat.'

'Where can I get it?'

'My Cat?'

'No, silly, the perfume.'

'Any good perfume shop.'

'You will never guess the name of the company that

makes it.'

'Who makes it?'

'Demeter, lol.'

'Thank you. Life saver.'.

When I told Zeus, he found it amusing that the company bore the same name as the first God I'd banished to the underworld. "Isn't that what you British call irony?"

"Yes, it is." And we smiled at each other. That was the first time I'd heard him speak in a normal tone. There was hope for him yet. Part of me felt terrible for him. For three thousand years, he had grown used to being a control freak and along comes this English bloke, and his power is removed. He was taking it well.

≈≈≈

Instead of putting Pete through the rigours of searching for a supply, I ventured into Rhodes town myself. I stumbled across a perfumery behind the courthouse called Aromaterie. I was served by an extremely helpful lady.

"Do you have Kitten Fur by Demeter?"

"Ah, you are in luck. We don't normally carry it in stock, but it was ordered by a customer that doesn't need it any longer."

I shuddered because, deep down, I knew she could be talking about Affi. "Was the customer's name Aphrodite?"

"Yes, did you know her?"

"She managed my hotel. And it is a great loss to the hotel and me."

"In which case it is free. Aphrodite had already paid for it."

It was all I could do to hold back tears. It was as if Affi had left me a solution from the grave.

"Would you like it to be gift wrapped?"

"No, thank you, it is fine as it is."

I sat in my car on Mandraki, just sniffing the open bottle and hyperventilating from the constant air intake. It was the smell of Affi. I thought to myself, *Jet will be impressed.*

I had invited Giannis to Pine Trees for the evening. I locked Jet in the blood store. When Giannis arrived, I could hear Jet scowling and hissing through the door.

"Giannis, quick come outside with me now."

"I have only just arrived."

"I know, and Jet is going spare downstairs."

"Keep that bloody cat away from me."

"I will. That is what I'm trying to do."

Once we were outside. I passed him the scent bottle. "Put a dab of this on your socks, trousers or legs. Then give me thirty seconds and come back in."

I dashed to the boardroom, "Fish and Chips." And the door swung open. Jet strolled out. She looked indignant that I had locked her in. "Sorry, sweetheart, but I'm experimenting."

I heard the main door open. Jet looked and moved towards the boardroom door. She knew someone was out there. After a while, she started to purr. Giannis opened the door. Jet stood up. *Oh no, here we go.* And then she did it. She figure of eighted between his legs.

"Hey, the bitch likes me. How did you do that?"

"She doesn't like you. She likes the smell."

"Cool. By the way, I asked Nemesis to drop in …"

Before he could finish, I heard the front door open. Jet went into full attack mode, and Nemesis shouted out, "Rod."

Before I could stop her, Jet launched from between Giannis' legs straight onto the approaching Nemesis. *Shit, not again.*

I got to Jet as quickly as I could but not before she had drawn amber blood. I managed to get Jet off the poor woman. Giannis give Nemesis some of the perfume. Put it on her legs or shoes. I had to put my hand over Jets face to calm her. Giannis put the scent on Nemesis' bare legs. The slow massaging suggested that he seemed to be enjoying it too much.

"That'll do, Giannis." And I put Jet on the floor. She was purring as she did the familiar figure of eight between Nemesis' legs. Bingo. *Thank you, Affi.*

We were finally able to enact the new order. We were ready for the coup.

Oceanus

We were still in a position where we were sitting and waiting for the coup to happen. Zeus was getting fretful. Giannis and Pete were bored with the lack of anything happening. I was impatient to get things moving.

"Don't fret, Zeus. We've got this."

"I don't like it. Potentially we could wipe out the entire Pantheon, and I would be left with no realm."

"Relax. We aren't going to wipe anyone out. It's about a show of strength and solidarity."

"But for every god we render mortal. There is a risk they could die."

"Of course. And I am sure there will be victims. But we have the support of Themis, Nemesis, and the Olympians. Together we will be a united and powerful entity. Only a fool would come up against such a formidable foe. And don't forget if we make a god mortal. We can reverse the process."

"I would rather send them to the underworld."

"You don't get it, do you? In this modern era, the underworld cannot exist. It is merely a concept, a location that excludes its inhabitants from all contact with the world. Nowadays, such a place cannot exist."

"I still worry that this is going to go horribly wrong."

"Remember the war. We succeeded then, didn't we? This is no different."

"Yes, it is different. We don't know our enemy."

"I'm sure they will reveal themselves at some point. Meantime we just have to wait."

"But that is my point. Wait for what?"

"For them to reveal themselves. There might not even be a coup. Justice and retribution have thrown their support behind you. That may be enough to scare the enemy away."

"And do I have to keep wearing that bloody scent?"

"Ha-ha, only if you don't want to be savaged by my cat." And I reached down and petted Jet.

My phone vibrated in my pocket. A quick look at the screen told me it was a message from Debs. It was a short, stark message:

'Three deities boarded a flight. Athens to Rhodes. Take off thirty minutes.'

'Thank you so much?'

And there was no reply. I looked at Zeus. "It would appear the wait is over. The coup is coming to us. Do you fancy being a taxi driver again?"

"I will always be a taxi driver at heart." And he smiled, something I'd seen more of. I guessed he was feeling less pressure.

"To the airport then, please, driver."

≈≈≈

We were sat in the airport car park. "God, it's been years since I was in George. I think it was the time that Poseidon nearly polished off the family."

"I think so too. What is the range of that thing?" he said, nodding at Jet.

"Dunno. But I'm going to hold her and go and wait by one of the exits. There is more chance of her detection working if they pass nearby."

They won't let you in the airport with a bloody cat."

"No, but they can't stop me standing outside the exit. I will keep a tight hold on Jet. She will soon let me know if there's a god around."

I checked my aviation app for an update on the location of the incoming aircraft from Athens. "The plane is doing its turn towards the airport. Nine hundred feet and passing Ialyssos."

Zeus looked out of his window towards the East. "There it is."

"OK, I don't want to risk them disembarking quickly. You keep an eye on Jet and me. I will nod when Jet reacts. I want you to see if you can recognise them."

As soon as I'd crossed the road, Jet got skittish. "Settle down, sweetheart. They aren't here yet. The plane is just landing now." She reminded me of a racehorse I'd seen playing up at the start of a race. I guessed she knew she was going to be on duty shortly.

Passengers started to trickle through the door to departures. Then I spotted a group of three twenty-something girls. They clearly knew each other. They were laughing and joking. They could have just been holiday reps, but Jet was getting wound up. She went into full attack mode as she went rigid and started to growl. They approached a couple waiting just inside the door where I was stood. It then became clear why Jet was awry before the trio appeared. They were being greeted by an older couple. The couple had been there all the while I was outside the door. As the group made their exit, it was all I could do to hold onto Jet and nod at Zeus. I put my hand over Jets face. She was starting to draw stares from everyone around us.

I scooted across the road to Zeus and jumped in the car. He craned his neck to reverse out and waited as a red Fiat passed behind us. "There they go. In that Fiat."

"Follow them for as long as we can. Did you recognise any of them?"

"The old couple, yes. The youngsters no."

His taxi took off with a skid as he tried to make up the distance behind the Fiat. "I see your driving hasn't improved," I said, remembering him firing pea grit at my bare shins when I first met him. Out of the airport, they turned right towards Paradisi and away from Rhodes. Judging by Jets mood swings as we dropped back and caught up again, I felt her range was about twenty metres.

"Who are the couple?"

"They are Oceanus and Tethys. They are Titans. I guess the girls were Oceanids, their daughters. They are nymphs.

"Oh, I know all about nymphs."

"Yes, but did you know there are a thousand Oceanids?

"Fuck."

"Exactly."

We trailed them until we reached Soroni. The Fiat turned left towards the mountains and Dimylia. "I can't follow them any further. It will be too obvious. They would spot us following them on the deserted mountain roads."

"No, I agree. Turn around, we can go back to Olympian and try and piece stuff together."

I called Pete and arranged for him to try and assemble the rest of the team to have a meeting at Olympian.

≈≈≈

"Themis sends her apologies, but I can fill her in later," said Nemesis.

"That's OK. There are enough of us to try and make sense of what Zeus and I have just witnessed."

Pete asked, "What's happened, Rod?"

I told the assembled meeting of the text Debs had sent. How we spotted three apparent gods arriving at the airport. That they were greeted by Oceanus and Tethys. Everyone but me already knew they were Titans. I told how we had trailed them to the foot of the mountains. "The point of this meeting is to figure out what is happening. Is it the start of the coup?"

Giannis said, "Don't be concerned that they are Titans. Helios is a Titan, Rhodos his wife was an Oceanid. I have been married to an Oceanid in the dim and distant past. The bigger question is, why would they revolt against Zeus?"

Nemesis added, "Yes, we are all descended from the Titans. They don't pose a particular threat."

"There motivation is obvious. The Olympians overthrew them and seized power. I cast them to the underworld. They shouldn't be here."

I looked at Zeus. "I told you earlier, the underworld is a concept that cannot exist in this age of communication."

He looked back at me. "Either way, they have escaped the underworld. And I think they are looking to get their power back."

"What do you think, Pete? Do they have the power to overthrow Zeus?"

"They must think they do. Otherwise, it would be futile to try."

"Nemesis, can we be sure that they don't know about the whole mortal and immortal thing?"

"Fairly sure. No, I'm certain. Remember, even I didn't know until you told me."

"So where do they get the idea that they can overpower Zeus? They will know he is immortal. I am worried that they have some idea how to make him mortal."

Giannis said, "I would like to know which Oceanids are here."

"OK, we have some unknowns to resolve. Where they are staying, who are they all, what powers they have. Or think they have."

"Pete, even if they recognise you, I guess they wouldn't think you were with us."

"Correct."

"And you Nemesis, are they going to know that you and Themis are supporters of Zeus?"

"I wouldn't be so sure of that."

"OK, thanks."

"Giannis. Are they going to know that you have made up with Zeus?"

"Like Nemesis, we can't be sure."

"In that case, Pete, do you fancy a trip in the mountains with Jet and me?"

"Of course."

"Can the rest of you get your heads together and start to think about battle plans. Zeus, don't do anything other than plan."

With the meeting over, Pete and I looked at the map. The mountain road from Soroni could be taking them anywhere from Soroni to the far side of the island. We needed to plot a route that could take include most of the villages in that direction. We had Jet. But we also knew we were looking for a red Fiat.

We decided that they would be between Soroni and Dimylia. The most obvious places were Dimylia, Eleousa, Archangelos or anywhere on the south coast. If they'd wanted to get to anywhere further southwest, they would have turned into the mountains at Kalavarda. If they had headed anywhere Northeast of Archangelos, they would have gone via the Rhodes to Lindos road. We had our route. We would just head south to Gennadi if we got as far as Archangelos and still not found them. We could stop off at various places on that coast road. Something told me they would be on the road from Soroni to Archangelos. Pete suggested Archangelos to Lindos would be the apparent stretch. He felt they would have a natural draw to water.

"Well, we can pass all of that on the way back to Pine Trees. If we travel via Eleousa, we can check out Archangelos. Spend the night at Pine Trees and in the morning hit all the coastal villages and Gennadi."

"We need to be getting off if we hope to get as far as Pine Trees before it gets dark," suggested Pete.

We arrived at Dimylia, parked the car, and took Jet for a walk around the few streets. There was no reaction from the cat and no red Fiat. We managed to walk the few roads and passed all the houses in the village. Jet didn't give the impression that there were any gods around.

We stopped for a quick Mythos at a taverna called Taverna Mitsos. There were a couple of locals enjoying a drink. Pete introduced himself and asked if any strangers had been around. It turned out we were the only strangers, given that we had a cat in tow.

We downed our drinks and made our way toward Eleousa.

As we closed in on the village, Pete said, "There are two possibilities ahead. There is Agia Eleousa, or there is Campochiaro. It has a deserted sanatorium."

We parked up, and before we'd even opened the doors, Jet went into full attack mode. She crouched on the floor, tail stretched out. She was growling and hissing.

"She is pointing at the sanitorium," said Pete.

"Of course, where better to lie low than in a deserted building."

I picked Jet up and covered her face. She took that as a signal to calm herself. I could still feel the stiffness in her body, but at least it shut her up. And there it was. The red Fiat. I knew we'd located the lair of the Titans. There were five of them and only two of us, so I didn't feel confident in launching an attack.

I threw Jet back into the car, "Sorry, sweetheart, but I don't trust you. Time for another beer, Pete?"

We found a nearby taverna. A few more locals were around, and then I spotted the three twenty-somethings I'd seen at the airport. *Bingo.* They were sat out of the way. Pete and I sat as far from them as possible. "Will they recognise you, Pete?"

"No. Definitely not. The Titans won't even know of my existence. And even if they know of you, they wouldn't recognise you."

Pete asked, "Do you have your dart with you?

"Yes, but I can't see how to use it. There are too many people about."

"Just one little scratch each would mortalise them."

"Yes, but what is there to gain from that. A dose of your sleeping draught would be better. I think we need to get close to them. Do you fancy playing the role of a middle-aged local chatting up a trio of attractive holidaymakers?"

He just smiled. "At least they are talking English."

"Ladies, my friend and I would like to buy you a drink. What would you like?"

And so, the evening began. The three girls were fun-loving. They all went for Mythos large.

Between us, we fired a series of chat-up questions that we already knew the answers to, such as. "Are you girls visiting

Rhodes, or are you local?" "When did you arrive?" "Are you staying locally?"

Then Pete decided to get flirty. "Are you all Greek?

When they all nodded, he came back with, "I thought so. You look like goddesses." *Fucks sake, Pete, that was sailing close to the wind.*

I went for more practical questions. "Do you fancy a visit to Faliraki or Rhodes town? There is a lot more nightlife."

According to their version of the truth, they were cousins. Their parents had sent them to Rhodes under the watchful eye of their Grandparents. They were from Thessaloniki, and their parents thought they were getting unruly. They were forever getting into trouble. They'd been banished to the care of their Yiayia and Pappou. It was almost a punishment because they weren't sticking to Greek ways. They were up for a bit of nightlife.

As this was just a softening exercise and an attempt to build rapport, we played the long game.

We'd introduced ourselves with fictitious names. Pete was Vasilis, and I became Andros. Of course, they returned the favour and lied about their names too. There was Elena, Angela, and Diana. After we had plied them with four drinks each. They were nicely loosened up and readily gave us their phone numbers. More importantly, they agreed to come for a night out. The only condition was we had to bring a friend to make three pairs. This led to lots of flirty chat.

"Which one of you fancies me?" Asked Pete, rather bluntly. They all did.

Only one of them had any interest in me, but that was a

million miles better than none. They all liked our aftershave. We played dumb when they asked what it was called. At least they didn't say we smelled feminine.

Not wanting them to be grounded by their 'grandparents', we suggested getting themselves off before their curfew. We offered to walk them back to where they were staying. They declined.

We left soon after they'd departed. Pete had a laugh with the locals about being lucky to pick up three tourists. I had to make sure I drove safely back to Pine Trees. I could still feel the Mythos coursing through my system. We now had a new problem, finding someone that looked a similar age to me and Pete that could make the sixth member of the night out.

≈≈≈

"We could ask Giannis," Pete suggested.

"Hardly. Have you seen how young and handsome he is? It's OK for you, three of them liked you. Only one liked me. Besides, he is well into Nemesis. We don't know how she might react if he gets off with an Oceanid."

"I get your point."

"It doesn't matter too much because I want them back here before we even go to town."

"What do you have in mind? I'm not entirely sure yet. But I want to have a show of power. I want to send a message that Zeus is still immensely powerful."

"Seems like you have already picked the extra person."

"I suppose he could be the third man. I'll sleep on it. As you're the flirty one of us, arrange for them to come to town with us on Friday night."

"That means you have forty-eight hours to sort something."

"Don't worry so much. If the worst comes to the worse, Zeus can stab them with a dart." And we both laughed.

"Kali Nichta, Rod."

"Night." I took a couple of quick shots of ouzo to make my dreams as vivid as possible.

"Come on, Jet, bedtime."

At least now that I had Affi's perfume, I didn't have to fight Jet for the pillow. She got to have her own scented cushion. As I'd hoped, the ouzo gave me a fretful night, and I woke several times with possible plans. But they all had plot holes. When the sun came up, I was shattered, but I thought I'd discovered a solution. It was all dependent on Zeus being able to act and Pete getting around the Oceanids. I guessed Zeus would be good at acting because he was top of the class at lying.

≈≈≈

"Morning, Rod. You look bloody rough."

"All night planning, too much ouzo before bed. But I think I have a plan. You must get the girls back here on the way to Rhodes."

Easy. I will pick them up from Eleousa in the car. Bring them here under the excuse that we will catch a large taxi to Rhodes."

"Nice. I'm off to spend the day with Zeus; he is going to be the sixth person. I may bring him back here, so he is familiar with the place for Friday."

"What? Zeus here? Is that wise?"

I laughed. "He'll be fine. He is terrified of Themis. I think the days of the old Zeus are long gone. If he so much as farts while he's here, it will be goodbye to being King of the Gods."

"She has definitely got him nailed down, hasn't she?"

"Yep, catch you later. No. Wait. What is the point of traipsing over to Kremasti and coming all the way back? I might as well use my power over him and get him to Pefkos." We both laughed.

I sent a text:

'Zeus, come to Pefkos, Pine Tree House, next to 9 lives cat charity – 90 minutes.'

'Y?'

'Because I want to show you my place and I have a plan'.

'K. On my way M8'

God, I hate bloody text language.

"He'll be here in around an hour. Under no circumstances treat him like the King of the Gods. He is just a team member. Oh, and none of us should access the blood vault while he is here. I don't trust him that much."

"What are the odds he forgets to put the perfume on?" Said Pete, and we both wet ourselves laughing.

"Make sure the CCTV camera is pointing at the main entrance. I want to record this. Jet, come here and get ready to do what you do best." And I petted her and gave her a treat.

Jet announced in plenty of time that Zeus was near. She went on full attack mode. All the usual sounds and a dead rigid body. Her tail pointing in the opposite direction to the approaching god.

"Hello," shouted Zeus as if to announce his arrival. That's all he had a chance to say before Jet pounced on him. Clawing and biting him.

"Get it off me." He screamed.

I leapt forward to rescue his Royal Godliness. I think Jet knew what was coming because she moved her head to stop me from covering her eyes, but I got her in the end. She immediately unlocked her claws, though she was still hissing.

"What the hell?"

"You didn't put the perfume on, did you?"

"No, I didn't think I would need it."

"I guessed you wouldn't have it on, and you became my guinea pig. I needed to know how Jet would react with a god not wearing the scent. It's a lesson to you too. Always wear the perfume."

I passed him a couple of antiseptic wipes and said, "Rub this on the scratches. They'll heal quicker." He gratefully took them and wiped away his amber blood. Zeus was visibly shaking, and I stared at him. I was waiting for a reaction. There was none; I couldn't determine if it was anger or fear.

"Come into the boardroom."

Pete hastily closed the video he was watching on his laptop. I looked at him, and he smiled back at me. I knew that he'd been replaying the CCTV video.

Zeus was amazed when he saw the laptop lower itself into the desk. He looked around the room. "You have done well for yourself, Rod."

I laughed, "My money has all come from the salary you

have been paying since before the war. And don't forget I get other funding via D80 Ltd. And thank you for continuing to pay my salary despite casting me out."

"It is all part of the original contract. The rest of the board insisted we honour it."

"Well, tell them thanks from my family and me."

"So, to business. What did you call me over for? Other than to have your cat savage me."

"I have a plan, but I need to check on some points first."

"Just like old times. You are bringing a plan to me."

"This time, though, I don't need to seek your approval. What I need is information."

"Go on."

"Would the Oceanids know you or recognise you?"

"I don't know. It depends on which Oceanids you are talking about."

"They gave their names as Elena, Angela and Diana. I have a suspicion that they aren't their real names."

"Well, if they are their real names, they aren't Oceanids."

"You saw them at the airport. I guess if you didn't recognise them. Then they wouldn't recognise you."

"That doesn't necessarily follow. I recognise your Queen Elizabeth, but she wouldn't recognise me, would she?"

"It doesn't matter because tomorrow we will have a chance to show how powerful we are. If they think it's you, that's a plus."

"What is the plan?"

"Exactly the same as what just happened?" I then went on to bring him up to speed on the date night with the Oceanids.

The thought of spending time with a nubile woman appealed to him. He had a sparkle in his eyes unless it was his photophobia.

"So, how is that a show of power?"

"Leave that part to me. But I assure you they will leave here with no doubt that they have been done over."

Pete looked disappointed. "Can we not do the show of power at the end of the night?"

I laughed, "You're a randy sod."

"Zeus, I need some more answers. Something is bothering me about the Oceanus and Tethys saga."

"What is bothering you?"

"They're trying to overthrow you. They must know you have allies, even if it's just the Olympian gods, that is a powerful army."

"Yes, it is."

"So surely to overthrow you, they would need to kill you. And possibly the rest of your family."

"Correct."

"But if they don't know about the whole gold makes you a mortal thing. How do they plan to kill you? Think back to the times before Asclepius learnt the secret. How would you have set about killing an immortal? And don't say by a lightning bolt. We both know that's bollocks."

"You need to give them a recurring death. Then when they resurrect, they instantly die again."

"What, something like fire?"

"No, that might kill them over and over until the fire goes out. Then they finish up alive. Naked but alive." And he laughed. *God, did he just crack a joke?*

"My concern is that we need to be on the lookout for them coming for you or any of us. It means their attack won't be based upon mortalising us. It will be to try and give us perpetual death and resurrection."

Suddenly the realisation that he might die hit Zeus. He had a look of sheer panic on his face as he realised he was vulnerable for the first time in 3000 years.

"Depending on how tomorrow goes. You might be safer staying here or even off the island."

He put his King of the Gods head on again. "I will not run or hide."

I banged my hand on the desk. "If I tell you to leave the island or hide here, then Themis will make sure that you do."

He just grunted. "And the plan is, what? I wear ladies' perfume. Your cat savages the Oceanids, and I give them antiseptic wipes to mop up their amber blood."

"Pretty much yes. Do you think you can handle it? The wipes will let us know if they have red or amber blood. Then we know if we are dealing with immortals or mortals. We will know if they are indeed Oceanids or not."

"Suppose they bring Oceanus and Tethys with them?"

"They won't. Pete is collecting them. If there is any danger from Oceanus and Tethys, Pete will be in the firing line at Eleousa. And we needn't worry if they recognise you, because Jet will have already scratched them by then. I just hope she can get all three. By the way, Pete, you will be with them. You won't need the perfume; you aren't a god. I need Jet at her peak. Whatever you do, don't try to get Jet off whoever she lands on. I want the girls to do that."

"I've seen Jet in action. There is no way I would even try to get her off of anyone." And he laughed.

Zeus didn't laugh. "Have you any idea how much cat scratches sting?"

"Brilliant. When you give them the antibacterial wipes, tell them it will help stop the stinging."

"But it doesn't. It still stings."

"I don't care. They must have the wipes."

"Here, put some of this perfume on. I can't keep holding Jet down." And I threw him my phial.

That was more than enough office work for one day. We adjourned to Angel bar for lunch. It was the first time I had ever had a repast with Zeus. It was an opportunity for him to let his hair down because he had no gods to impress. He was alone with humans for the first time in a long time. We ate and had a few beers. The planning faded into the mists of alcohol. The afternoon became evening, and we ate again. We had more beers, and the evening became night. An ouzo filled night. I'd never seen Zeus so relaxed. He was cracking jokes, some of them dated but funny all the same. The highlight of the night was witnessing him dancing to the sirtaki.

At one point, he said, "I didn't realise it was so much fun being human." I smiled because it seemed like he was going to adapt to his new routine. It was decided that Zeus would stay the night at Pine Trees and travel back to Olympian Dreams the following morning.

Adikia

The following morning Zeus learnt about the perils of getting drunk on Ouzo. He looked bloody awful and decided against having breakfast, instead opting for coffee. He was learning fast.

Before Zeus could leave for Kremasti, I received a call from Nemesis. "Hi Nemesis, what's up?"

"Is Zeus still with you? I can't get hold of him."

"Yeah, he is about to come over to Olympian."

"No. Stop him from coming back."

"Why?"

"Oceanus and Tethys visited last night."

"I'll call you back." And I hung up.

"Zeus, that was Nemesis. You cannot go back to Olympian."

"Why? It's where I live."

"Yes, and your enemies know that. They were there last night." That sobered him up pretty quick.

I called Nemesis back and put her on speaker. "Hi. I have managed to stop Zeus from returning. He is with me now.

You are on speaker."

Zeus asked, "How do you know it was them?"

"I recognised them."

"Did they see you? No, the receptionist wouldn't let them through to the office suite. They were aggressive, so she phoned me, and I saw them on CCTV. They smashed some of the ancient relics on your display. Fortunately, she didn't know where you were, so she had nothing to tell them."

"I must come back. I must defend Olympian Dreams."

"No. This isn't about defending your hotel. This is about keeping you as King of the Gods. I've spoken to Themis. She wants me and Apollo to join you in Pefkos and for you to stay safe."

Zeus looked at me. I reassured him it was for the best. "As I said, you are better off staying here. Particularly as I need you this evening. Nemesis, he will stay with me, keep us updated. Speak later." I cut off the call.

"But they will see me as weak."

"No, they won't. After tonight they will see the power you have and think twice before entering Olympian Dreams again."

"What, because your cat has scratched three Oceanids?"

"Trust me, just stick to the script, and they will get the message."

We spent the rest of the morning running over what to say and do. I needed to go to Rhodes town, so I left Zeus in the capable hands of Pete. It was a chance for them to chat about the old days. They sifted through Pete's wardrobe to try and find suitable clothes to replace those that stank of sweat and puke.

I was headed to Aromaterie to pick up my consignment of half a dozen bottles of Kitten Fur. I also took the opportunity to visit the guys at Irene's because I'd discovered that plating solution has a shelf life of 12 months. I needed to restock because I didn't know when it might be required, but it would undoubtedly be inside the next twelve months.

≈≈≈

Final preparations were in an advanced stage. I'd prepared the antibacterial wipes so that they were on the counter in reception. We were all dressed for date night just in case it went ahead. Jet was safely closed in the boardroom; I didn't want her going walkies when she was needed most. I looked at the time, "It's almost six. Pete, you need to be going to Eleousa if you want them back here for eight. Text when you have picked them up."

"I will. And I will try and get back as close to eight as I can."

"Brilliant, just not before seven-forty-five. Don't forget to hang back if you don't want Jet to savage you."

I looked at Zeus. "How does it feel to be on the front line again?"

"I'm frustrated that we aren't doing any more damage than a few cat scratches."

"Be patient, my friend. That time will come soon enough. Tonight will be all about reprisal. Reprisal for what they did at your hotel last night."

I set the timer on my phone for seven-forty, and we started

having a game or two of backgammon or what the Greeks call távli. I whipped his arse several times, and that reminded me why I'd been chosen as the babysitter for Zeus. He just didn't think ahead and had little idea of strategy.

My alarm sounded, so he conceded the third game. I double-checked the antibacterial sheets were where they should be, I ran through the plan one more time. "Do not try to help them remove the cat. I want them all scratched, and you must be the one to offer them the antibacterial wipes. Clear?"

"Yes, of course."

Jet knew there was some action coming. She sat patiently in the doorway to the boardroom, looking at the main entrance. "Don't pounce too soon, sweetheart." She briefly turned and looked at me. I imagined she was saying, "don't tell me how to do my job."

Through the glass frontage, I could see Pete pull onto our forecourt.

"Zeus, Jet, standby." Neither of them looked at me. They were statuesque in their anticipation. Jet was growling and hissing, and she was cocked and ready to fire. Pete pushed the door open and ushered the girls to come in. The last one of the trio entered, and as Pete stepped back, he pulled the door shut behind them. Jet was already in the air and latched on to Diana. I felt sorry for her because she was the most attractive of the Oceanids and the one that had said she liked me. I had to remind myself that she was the enemy.

Elena came to Diana's rescue, but Jet didn't care; she just latched onto Elena. Angela got dragged into the action to try and help her friend. Job done. They all had amber blood on various parts of their body. Mostly the face and hands.

"Girls, I'm so sorry. Bloody cat, stop." And I move forward to recover Jet.

"Zander, see to the girl's wounds." *Shit. Something I'd overlooked. I didn't want to call him Zeus.*

"Of course. Ladies, here are some antibacterial wipes."

Diana was the first to respond, "It is OK. We don't need them."

Zeus said, "Does it sting? Then these will stop the stinging." They each pulled a wipe from the packet and started to dab at their wounds. I quickly gathered the wipes and threw them into the bin by the desk.

"I am so sorry, girls. I don't know what came over her. She isn't normally like that. She is probably jealous of your good looks."

Zeus looked at me as if to say, "Where is my show of strength."

Pete joined us from outside. "What has happened?"

"Jet got vicious with the girls. I am going to have to get her sorted out."

"Damn cat. Hope she hasn't spoiled the evening for you ladies."

Angela, the feline looking one of them, said, "It would take more than a cat to spoil a good night out. Besides, she is so cute." And she pouted at Pete.

Elena nodded in agreement.

"What about you, Diana? Are you still up for it?"

"Of course, you can make it up to me later." And she

pouted at me with her come to bed eyes.

I formally introduced Zeus. I had to so that Pete would know his stage name. "Ladies, this is Alexander. Like Alexander the Great, but we call him Zander. Vasilis, take the girls for a drink, on me." And I gave him a fifty euro note. Zeus looked at me as if to say, *who the hell is Vasilis.*

"Sure, Andy. I will take them to Cavos Bar." Zeus flashed another confused look at me.

As soon as they had gone, Zeus had questions. "What is going on? Why all the pseudonyms?"

"I wasn't going to introduce you as Zeus. And it makes it harder for anyone to try and find our real identities."

"And where is my show of power?"

I reached down and placed my hand into the waste bin to retrieve the wipes that I'd discarded moments before. "Look at the colour of the blood on these wipes."

Zeus inspected the blood-stained wipes. "The blood is red. They are mortals."

"Well, they are now. And who gave them the wipes? You have just removed immortality from three Oceanids. That is your show of power."

"But, how can antibacterial wipes remove immortality?"

I smiled and winked at him, "That's my secret for now."

"Hang on. You gave me wipes when your cat savaged me yesterday. Am I now mortal?"

"Nope. They were different wipes."

He looked down at the red on the wipes. I could almost hear his mind clicking like an ancient abacus trying to calculate how it worked.

"Don't ponder too much about how it works. I will reveal it to you when the time is right. Tonight we enjoy ourselves. We have a victory to celebrate. Come on, we have got a date to keep. Let's get to Cavos."

Zeus had a puzzled look on his face for most of the evening. We gave the girls a good time. I felt we needed to. It was some compensation for stripping them of immortality. We didn't get to Rhodes. Instead, we ended up spending the entire evening in Pefkos by Night. When Pete suggested making a move to Rhodes, the girls decided they were enjoying the music where we were. By eleven, the girls were smashed. I think Pete was hoping they could stay the night at Pine Trees. He was disappointed when I said, "Girls, you must be home by curfew. I will order a taxi."

Diana said, "You are a spoilsport. Can't we stay at your hotel?"

Zeus chipped in his view, "That sounds like a good idea, Rod."

And there we go. You have just shown what an idiot you are.

I tried to quickly move the conversation beyond Zeus using my real name. "No. It isn't. We are honourable men, and these girls are wasted. We can see them again."

By the time the taxi arrived, I was Mister Unpopular with most of the group. I needed to work on Zeus. He was letting the sex appeal of the girls distract him from the real issues. Diana told me she would like to see me again and thanked me for not taking advantage of her drunken state. Little did she realise; I'd taken advantage of her innocence much earlier in the evening. I kissed her on the cheek.

Meanwhile, Zeus had his face stuck to Elena's. At first, I thought it was a bit pervy, a three-thousand-year-old guy with a nubile girl. Then it dawned on me the entire group was the same bloody age, except, of course, for me. Pete was elbow deep in a clinch with Angela. It became clear that moral values were a lot different between immortals three thousand years ago. We each blew kisses at the girls as the taxi sped off.

"Why did you send them home? They were up for spending the night."

"And when we announce to Oceanus and Tethys their loved ones are mortal, they would know where to look. I needed them out of here, going about their normal life for a day or so." I could see the lightbulbs sparkling in their heads as they realised we were still in the middle of the plan.

"You mean you always planned it this way?"

"Yep. What I didn't plan for was you calling me Rod at the end of the evening. If they stayed after making them immortal, then we were open to discovery. I was always looking for a way to ship them back to where they came from. And that brings me to a complaint. You were both distracted because young girls were giving you attention. That cannot happen."

Pete was irritated by my comment. "Oh, like you with Aphrodite?"

"Yes, exactly like that. We all know how badly that ended up." I poured a shot of ouzo. Pete calmed down.

Zeus, who had been puzzled all night, asked, "How did the antibacterial wipes make them immortal?"

"Tell him, Pete."

"I don't know for sure, but I guess that gold plating

solution was involved."

"Yes, the packet was filled with gold plating solution for a couple of hours. As soon as they dabbed it on the scratches, they were immortal."

Zeus looked terrified with my revelation. He didn't need to calculate anything to know that I had also revealed how vulnerable he was. That was the moment I think he came to terms with the fact he was King of the Gods in name only.

Thanks to Affi's death, it was a massive breakthrough in the fight against immortals. There were no traditional weapons needed, and it was executed with minimum contact. Of course, that excluded all the making out at the end of the evening.

"For now, guys, let your hair down, get drunk and tomorrow we prepare for the repercussions that will be upon us before we know it." I poured another shot of ouzo. "Yammas."

≈≈≈

Zeus was sporting another hangover as he arrived for the planning meeting in the boardroom. He sat down and groaned; his olive skin looked green.

I said, "Lightweight."

He looked at me. *God, you look rough.* Which was an appropriate thought given who he was.

"You'll get used to it. Strong coffee all around," I suggested. "Can you manage to remember any of last night?"

"Some," he said.

"What about you, Pete?"

Pete laughed. "I'm OK. I am used to your drinking sessions."

Zeus finally strung more the one word together. "You have poisoned me."

"No, mate. You inflicted it on yourself."

"You could have stopped me."

"I'm not your babysitter …" I stopped as soon I'd said it because we all knew that is exactly what I was.

Zeus just stared blankly at me. He was so out of it; he didn't figure the gaffe I'd just made.

Pete asked. "Are we still in the middle of your plan? Or do we need to develop a new one?"

"Still in the middle. The plan isn't over until we've informed Oceanus and Tethys about the girls being mortal."

"Then?" Said Zeus returning to one-word sentences.

"Then we can expect all hell to break loose. Their visit to Olympian Dreams demonstrated how aggressive they can be."

"But we are immortal, and they won't know how to make us mortal."

"No, I know. I have been thinking about that. If they are planning to overthrow Zeus, they must have some idea how they are going to achieve it."

"Themis and Nemesis have many supporters," said Zeus. Now he was waking up.

"All that does is tell us the Titans won't do it by holding an election or usurping power from Zeus. The only way they can do it is by force. By killing him." I looked at Zeus. "We have to keep you alive."

He managed to force a smile. "Well, stop bloody poisoning

me then."

Ignoring his attempt at humour, I said, "I need you old guys to cast your memories back to when you were very young. To the time of the last battle with the Titans. A time before you knew of the secret about gold. How would you set about killing an immortal?"

Zeus sighed. "I've already told you. I would put them into an eternal cycle of death and resurrection. Like Artemis did with Prometheus. That was one of your plans."

"Yes, but if I recall it correctly, it involved a gold-tipped dagger."

He grunted, which I took as a signal of confirmation.

"What we need to figure out is how we can put an immortal into eternal death and resurrection?"

"But we can take their immortality first. Therefore, we don't need the eternal thingy," said Pete.

"You're missing the point. I know we could kill them, but that would involve getting close to them. I am trying to figure out how they might attempt to kill Zeus. Because, trust me, when they know about their kids being mortal, they will come after Zeus. I want to figure out their options so we can be prepared."

Pete suggested, "Send Zeus to Athens."

"No. I am not running away or hiding."

I added. "Zeus mustn't be seen to leave a power vacuum. They will just walk in and seize power."

"I still think we should just go to Eleousa, make them immortal and kill them," said Zeus.

"And do you know if any other Titans are involved? Who

might step up to avenge their death? Anyway, over to you guys. How would you kill an immortal?"

They just stared blankly at me.

I sighed and looked at them. "You actually know these people. They are going to come and kill one or all of us. Unless we can figure out how it will be a reality. Think guys. I am going for a drive to see what I can come up with. Zeus, do not contact the Titans until I get back."

I had to leave the meeting. I couldn't sit there any longer. I was doing my best not to be condescending with them. They'd both previously accused me of arrogance, but they really didn't get the importance of what I was asking them to do. I just wanted to get out of there and be left to my thoughts. I knew there must be a solution because there is always an answer. I had to redefine the problem. My thoughts wandered back to the doomed relationship with Affi. What if she'd never walked into my office? What if I hadn't succumbed to loneliness? And yet, here I was seeking solitude so that I could think clearly. I headed towards Prasonisi. On the way, I passed what remained of a road traffic accident. In all the time I'd been on Rhodes, I'd learnt that such events are rare. But this was the second one I had seen or heard about in as many weeks. It acted as a trigger, and I spent the rest of my journey once again thinking about Affi and her death. It made me start to think about death in general. I was setting myself up for a gruesome afternoon on the spit of land. I sat on the Mediterranean side, it was less windy, and the sea was more serene and would afford me a relaxing meditation.

I ran through my mind just about every method of death I

could think of, and then I realised I was staring at it all the time. There it was right in front of me. Drowning. Death by drowning. If you are trapped under water, you drown, you die. If you resurrect and you are still trapped under water, you will drown again. An eternal cycle of death and resurrection. Why didn't I figure it before? Oceanus, Oceanids, suddenly it was so obvious. The coup could only happen if they trapped Zeus under water.

I couldn't get back into my car fast enough. It seemed like forever to make the one-hour trip to Pefkos. I dived into the boardroom to find Pete sitting by himself. "Where's Zeus."

"He went for a lie-down. He's trying to clear his hangover."

"Jesus. Did you guys get anywhere with your task?"

"No. We did think about it, though."

"Come on, Pete. You're better than that. I thought you would have figured it out before me."

"Yes, but you didn't have Zeus moaning in your ear about how his head hurts. What did you manage to figure out?"

"Yes, and I could kick myself for missing the obvious. The only way I could kill Zeus without mortalising him first would be to drown him."

"But he would resurrect."

"Yep, but what if he was trapped under water? When he resurrects, he will drown again. Like Zeus told us, it would be eternal death and resurrection. It was obvious given that Oceanus and the Oceanids are leading the coup."

"I get that. But now we know that they want to drown him. How do we stop it from happening? We are on an island surrounded by water."

"We start by keeping Zeus as far away from the sea as we can. I haven't figured the rest of it out yet?"

I called Zeus's mobile. "Get your drunken arse to the boardroom now."

Zeus looked a lot better than he had been in the morning. His hangover had cleared. He apologised for leaving Pete to do the task. I filled him in on my theory, and he agreed it was the most likely scenario. But he still wasn't going to go into hiding.

"Anyway, everywhere on Rhodes is near water." He had a point.

"OK, but wherever you stay, you have to be near protection. Near me! And I will be telling Themis that that is the plan."

"You come and stay at Olympian Dreams."

"No, you will stay here. Nemesis and Giannis are coming here too. The rest of the Olympian board can look after your hotel."

"They're not capable."

"I have thought that for a long time. But they are all we have. I need you surrounded with powerful gods."

"You killed two of the most powerful gods during the war."

"Yes, but on your orders," I snapped. *Take a deep breath, Rod.*

"Back to the matters in hand. Sometime today, either of you should call the girls and carry on as if you plan to meet again. We have to keep those interactions as normal as they can be."

Zeus said, "What about you and Diana? Are you calling her?"

"Nope. I am done with relationships. I am playing it cool. They will expect at least one of us to be blasé about developing a relationship." I looked a Zeus, "Don't forget you are married. I don't think Hera will be too pleased with your shenanigans last night."

He just laughed my warning off. "She wouldn't expect me to behave any differently. She has had three thousand years to get used to it." And he roared with laughter.

"Tomorrow, you will start to spread the rumour that the girls are mortal and that you are responsible. As Zeus, that is, not Alexander. Let it be known that it was punishment for Oceanus and Tethys going to Olympian and kicking off."

Pete said, "They are going to be pissed off."

I laughed. "They are, but I reckon they won't believe it. They have no way of disproving it without killing and reincarnating one of the girls. Then they are going to be really pissed off. That is when they will come looking for us. We must be ready. I nodded at Pete, "You head to Olympian now. Get Giannis and Nemesis and clothes for Zeus. Then all come back here. I want that part sorted before it all kicks off. Kremasti will be a no-go area for any of us after today."

≈≈≈

I wished that Zeus hadn't remained. I wished I was alone again. Solitude was my greatest need at that time, but every decision I'd made hampered that goal. I pondered whether I was too controlling with Zeus. Were people right? Had I become arrogant? My phone rang, it was Pete.

"Pete?"

"We need a change of plan."

"Why?"

"There was a crash on the Lindos to Prasonisi road earlier today …"

I interrupted him. "I know I passed it."

"It was Diana. She is dead."

"How do you know?"

"When I called Angela, she told me."

"Fuck… Hang on. That doesn't change anything. Oceanus will know that Diana wasn't immortal. Zeus's rumour will be validated when he puts it out there. All it means is the enemy will kick off sooner. I will make sure he doesn't light the fuse until you guys are safely back here. See you in a bit."

It appeared some god was watching over me to ensure my fidelity to Kam. Any pretty girl that showed me attention ended up dead. That fact hurt. The thought that by admiring me, two beautiful women had approved their own deaths.

It was a relief when the rest of the team got back from Olympian. With five of us sitting around the boardroom table, things were cramped, to say the least. Fortunately for Nemesis, she had no interest in me.

I opened the meeting by skipping formalities, no introductions were needed, and everyone knew why they were there. "You haven't told anyone about last night, have you?"

"No, the only people that know are all in this room," said Zeus. The others nodded in affirmation."

"Nemesis, what is the best way for Zeus to launch the

rumour?"

"Why a rumour? Why not just contact them directly?"

"We don't have a contact for Oceanus or Tethys."

"We have a contact with the Oceanids," said Pete.

"Let's see how this works. Zeus gets in touch with Elena and comes right out and says he made them all mortal. She will be bound to ask questions. She'll figure out it must have happened last night. She will know of the involvement of Pine Trees. We have the entire Oceanus family bearing down on us. They bring the fight to us."

"But we will be prepared for them and able to defend ourselves. If we just put a rumour out there, we have no way of knowing if, when or where they will come," said Nemesis.

I thought for a moment, and all eyes were on me. "Can you think of a reason that stops us from going to Eleousa and launching a pre-emptive strike? Take the battle to them."

Nemesis looked at everyone in the room. "We would have to consult with Themis. She will only support us if it is justifiable. If she perceives it as justice."

I was already dialling Themis. "Hi Themis, I am at Pine Trees with Zeus. Nemesis, Apollo, and Pete are here too. I'm going to put you on speakerphone."

She spoke to us. "How can I help?"

"Last night, we made three Oceanids mortal."

"That's OK. I assume it was retribution for the event at Olympian Dreams that Nemesis told me about."

"Yes, it was. The plan was to let Oceanus and Tethys know that it was Zeus that did it. It was a show of power."

"Good, that is what we wanted."

"There is a complication, though … One of them was involved in a road traffic incident this morning. She has been killed."

"Were any of you involved in the accident?"

I looked at the others to confirm none of them was involved. "No. So far as I can tell, it was just an unfortunate accident."

"So, what is the problem?"

"Would we be justified in attacking Oceanus and Tethys as part of the original retribution?"

"No, you wouldn't be justified."

"But Zeus's life is under threat."

"Is it? Or do you just think it might be? Now it looks to me like the scales of justice are tipped in their favour. They smashed a few ornaments and created a scene. You created a bit more than a scene. Your retribution has led to the death of one of their family."

I could sense that Themis was getting short. I knew I was getting irate. Nemesis stepped in. "Hi Themis, it's Nemesis. Thank you for taking our call. We have it under control now. Thanks for your help. Bye."

"Good, see you later. Bye and good luck to you all."

Nemesis looked at my phone on the table to ensure the call had ended. She looked up at me. "She was getting angry. She had spoken, and you were about to argue with her. That wouldn't be good. I know how she works."

"I guess that means we can't go to Eleousa."

"Oh, we can. What we can't do is attack Oceanus or Tethys without any provocation. The scales are in their favour. They may just walk away and admit defeat. We must give them that opportunity. If, as you believe, they come for Zeus, then we can defend him. If that harms them, it is fine. I think you humans call it self-defence."

"How do you feel about that, Zeus?" I asked.

"I guessed that would be the case. I understand how these things work."

"I mean. How do you feel about going to Eleousa and personally announcing your involvement? Or would you rather spread the rumour and wait for them to come and get you? It is your life that is at risk. The choice has to be yours."

Knowing how he operated during the last battle. I guessed his one-word answer. "Rumour," he said.

One by one, I looked at the others. "Nemesis?"

"Eleousa."

"Giannis?"

"Eleousa."

At this point, Zeus started to show concern.

"Pete, what is your vote?"

"Rumour. I think it will be better if they come here. We are near the amber blood if we need it. If they come here, that is an act of aggression and gives our justification."

Fuck me, I feel like a reality TV judge. "Well, that's deadlock. I guess I have the casting vote. Pete, that is an excellent argument. Zeus, you have a good argument because you are going to be the target of their revenge. Giannis and Nemesis, what is your thinking behind going to Eleousa."

Nemesis said, "It will force their hand, and they will act on impulse. They will either fight or book a flight. It could all be sorted before the day is out."

"What about you, Giannis?"

"Same as what she said."

"You mean you aren't bothered. You are choosing Eleousa because Nemesis did?"

"No. I want it over and done with, so I can get back to normal quicker. I find it too hot on this side of the island. There is no shade from Helios."

I stroked Jet and put my Simon Cowell-head on. I said, "Right. I have made my decision. The original plan was for rumours, and Zeus has a good reason to support that route. Similarly, Nemesis and Giannis have put forward strong arguments for going straight to Eleousa. Maintaining control of the situation is paramount. Therefore I have decided that tomorrow morning we will travel to Eleousa. Once there, Pete will message Angela and start the rumour. If there is no reaction, we can make them react."

Without warning, Jet went into full alarm mode. I heard a crash from the reception area, followed by shouting and screaming. We all looked at each other with what the fuck expressions. Jet was clawing at the boardroom door. Giannis got to the door first and flung it open.

We were greeted by the sight of a faded red Fiat that had reversed into reception, and there it sat with its engine revving furiously. In the blink of an eye, a masked passer-by jumped through the void that used to be the hotel front. The masked intruder grabbed Giannis and threw him into the open boot of the car. Jet launched at the hooded stranger. This bought time for Giannis to attempt to escape from the boot. I unsheathed the dart in my pocket and threw it at the stranger. He slammed the boot shut, trapping Giannis. Jet was still attached to the attackers' neck. As the car started to pull off, the unknown assailant dived into the back of the vehicle through the still-open door. The same open door allowed Jet to exit the Fiat. Its tyres screeched on the marble floor as it launched through the sea of plaster and glass, with Giannis's fingers trapped outside the closed boot. And the Fiat was gone.

Nemesis spoke. "Now we can exact retribution."

Jet strolled in as if nothing had happened. Her paws and face were covered in amber and red blood. "At least we have mortalised another deity. Shit! Where's my dart?"

We just looked at each other. We were stunned. None of us had any words. We all sensed that we'd just suffered a defeat.

Crowds were gathering outside. In English, I said, "Move on. There is nothing to see here."

Zeus translated. "Metakinitheíte edó den ypárchei típota na deíte edó."

Pete was already on the phone talking to his builder friend to come and make good the hotel front.

"Shit. That is all we want," I said as I saw a police car pull up outside the hotel.

Nemesis said. "I will deal with it. The island is full of jealous people. It could have been anyone."

Anastasi

There was no doubting this was a blow to our plans. We'd aimed to take the first strike. Taking the battle to them was how I'd described it. Instead, they had seen through our scheming and brought the fight to us. We could only guess that they had taken Giannis back to Eleousa. We didn't even know who had taken him. The only link was the red Fiat, which I assumed was the one that Oceanus was driving the day he collected the Oceanids from the airport. As soon as the police were happy that we didn't know who'd wrecked the hotel, we held an impromptu meeting.

The boardroom had taken on a different atmosphere. The cold stone walls seemed to suck all of the life out of the room. The air was heavy with dust caused by the impact at the front of the hotel. I was still stunned. There were so many questions unanswered.

Zeus raised the first question, "What do we do now?"

This was followed by a question from Pete, "Was it the Oceanus clan?"

Nemesis put some context to the discussion. "Surely we

just go ahead with the original plan. All that has changed is that we now have the support of Themis to carry out retribution."

"I am more worried about Giannis. I suspect they may torture him to try and find out where Zeus is."

"Surely they know where I am."

"I don't think so. Otherwise, they would have taken you. I reckon they only came here because of our involvement with Diana's death. Or at least her loss of immortality. I think this was an attack on Pine Trees. They can't be sure that you were involved. To the girls, you are Zander or Alexander." I looked at the rest of the group, hoping they agreed with my summary."

Pete responded, "I think we should assume that one way or another they will get some information from Apollo."

"More to the point. If they have my dart and Giannis tells them the relevance of it."

Nemesis reassured us. "He won't give that secret away. He may let it slip that Zeus is here. He may even give away that Zeus was with one of the girls. In honesty, I think they were after Pete, and they think they have him. It was Pete that collected the girls, and he is the one that contacted them and found out about the dead girl."

"I hope you're right. And like you said, nothing has changed. We proceed with the original plan," I said.

Pete added, "We now have to build in the rescue of Apollo."

We then had discussions about what parts of the plan needed to be changed. How does being a man down might lead to a reallocation of tasks? What kind of danger Giannis might be in? It was fortunate that I had another set of darts made. At least we had three between us. If calculations were correct, and the masked person was Oceanus. Then it meant that Tethys would be the only immortal amongst them. We concluded that it wasn't possible to kill all of them. If dead bodies popped up at Eleousa the day after our hotel was attacked. The police would only look in one direction.

It was getting late, and it had been a long day. I needed a good night's sleep, and I was still using ouzo to get one. My greatest desire was to be alone, just me and a bottle of ouzo. Everyone retired at the same time, which suited me. I waited until I was alone and opened the door to the blood vault. I was going to sleep on the same reclining chair we'd given Affi her transfusion on. Jet joined me, and I locked the door behind us.

≈≈≈

It was a peaceful night. Jet hadn't raised the alarm, so there were no unexpected visitors while we slept. I opened my eyes and looked at the empty ouzo bottle. *At least there were no nightmares about plans failing.*

I was the first to surface. I hadn't shaved, and I was still wearing the clothes from the night before. My stench was masked by the overwhelming aniseed scent of ouzo. I showered and replaced the smell of ouzo with kitten fur. I didn't need it, but it reminded me of what the day was all about. Jet showed her appreciation by rubbing up against my legs. We went to the boardroom, and I put the cafetiere on, ready for when the others surfaced.

"Christ, Rod. You look rough," said Pete as he entered the room.

"It's all part of getting battle-ready. Footballers do it all the time," I replied as if not shaving would make me appear more menacing. I hoped the bloodshot eyes would help too.

One by one, the others surfaced, it was only 7:30, and we were all on our second coffee. We went over the plans one more time. I think that deep down, we were all concerned whether Zeus would remember his role. His commitment wasn't in doubt. It was his capability that was the issue.

It was decided that Zeus would drive. A full taxi speeding in the area would easily blend in. We piled into George. Two gods, two humans, three golden darts, and a hairy black cat. I took the front passenger seat. My hangover would have been more likely to induce projectile vomiting in the back. We pulled onto the main road towards Rhodes, and Zeus put his foot down. As we approached Kolymbia, Zeus took a left turn towards Seven Springs. Just the name reminded me of the visits I had shared with my family. It didn't make me feel melancholy. It fired something within me. The thought of having my family back with me again. Seven Springs disappeared behind us as he took another left at Archipoli.

"Next stop Eleousa," announced Zeus.

I looked at the backseat passengers. "Ready?"

They replied together, "Ready!"

Zeus pulled onto the hard standing alongside the derelict sanatorium. We could see the faded Fiat at the far end of the building. Jet confirmed that gods were in residence. She was already in full attack mode.

"Pete, phone Angela. It is about time they knew that Zeus caused the death of Diana." And I grinned at him.

Zeus added. "Tell them I will come to avenge the kidnap of my son, Apollo."

"I'll put it on speaker."

"Hi, Angela."

Her reaction told us that she had figured out our involvement in her sisters' death. "What the fuck do you want?"

"I know who was involved in Diana's death. I know who made her mortal."

"You did. We know you spiked our drinks with something that did it."

"No. You are wrong. It was the King that did it. It was Zeus,"

She paused. "How do I know that is true."

"I have heard he is coming for you all. You have kidnapped Apollo. Zeus wants his revenge."

And there was silence. The phone squealed, and the voices changed as a clue she'd put her phone on speaker too. "Sorry, can you say that again?"

"Of course. Zeus is coming for you. He wants revenge, and he wants Apollo back."

More silence. I nodded at Zeus.

He put on his commanding voice. "I am coming for you. Before Helios sets one more time. You will have paid your debt to me. You will retire to the underworld."

There appeared to be mayhem on the other end of the

phone. There was a lot of shouting in Greek. Pete shut off the call. "They are going to make a run for it."

"Not before we get Giannis back. I opened the taxi door and let Jet loose." In full attack mode, she launched herself toward an opening into the sanitorium. "Quick, we need to get to the Fiat."

We could hear screaming as Jet did her thing. I ripped open the boot of the car. There was no Giannis. It bought time for us to surround the Fiat. The four of us stood by each of the doors. Zeus was positioned nearest to the sanitorium.

It took moments for the Oceanids to come running out, closely followed by Oceanus and Tethys. It was like a cartoon as they stopped in their tracks. I swear I saw their feet skid on the compacted earth.

Zeus boomed as only he could. "Give me Apollo. Now! Otherwise, you will never see the setting of the sun."

"H-h-he is inside," said Oceanus.

"Fetch him to me."

"We can't. A feral cat is stopping us."

The girls looked confused as Zeus said, "Rod."

I entered the building, and Jet just purred at me. She was sat on top of a metal crate. It was padlocked. I returned to the doorway. "I need the key to the padlock."

"Tethys fumbled in her bag. "Here."

I saw my opportunity. As I reached for the key, I dug my dart into her wrist. She recoiled and shouted, "Ouch." It made her drop the key. As I stooped to retrieve it, I looked up and smiled at Zeus.

"Tethys, as a punishment for locking my son away. I am

declaring you as a mortal. You are now as helpless as the others. If Apollo is harmed in any way. You will all die in retribution."

With the key, I was able to open the metal chest. It was packed to the brim with water. Under the water was Giannis. He was in a foetal position and dead still. He was drowned. *Jesus, he can't be mortal.* The body twitched and made me jump as it lunged to the surface of the water, coughing and spluttering. Giannis gave a loud belch as he expelled water from his lungs. He gasped as he took an intake of breath. Still choking. He managed to say, "Rod."

He took a moment to gather himself. "Where is Oceanus?"

"He is outside. With your dad and the others."

"He looked like a drowned Rat, and he was shivering. "Come on, let's get you into the sunshine."

Zeus looked genuinely relieved as Giannis entered the sunshine. The brightness made him blink. And he was still dripping water everywhere.

"Apollo, my son." And they hugged. "Are you hurt?"

Before he could answer, Oceanus demanded, "You have your son back unharmed, now let us go."

I heard another voice behind me. "It isn't as simple as that. You have broken so many laws. I need to deliberate with Apollo, Zeus, and Nemesis. I need to decide how best justice will be served."

Before I looked around, I guessed who the owner of the voice was. It was Themis.

She spoke to the whole group. "When Nemesis told me of the plan for today. I decided I would join you and solve this once and for all. I have asked Aletheia to come from Athens. In the meantime, the mortals amongst us will be under house arrest at Olympian Dreams." And she looked at The Oceanus family.

Giannis said, "I know how justice will best be served. There is a crate inside with Oceanus' name on it."

"No. You travel back to Pefkos with Rod, Petros. and your father. You will have the opportunity to contribute once Aletheia arrives. Nemesis, you take the Oceanids to Olympic Dreams. I will take Oceanus and Tethys with me."

Giannis wasn't happy. I didn't know if he was irate because he wanted to be with Nemesis or because he wanted instant justice.

≈≈≈

Once back at Pine Trees, we were able to come to terms with how close we'd come to losing Giannis. It reminded us that we needed to carry out daily tests to verify our immortality. We would order some diabetic lancets to solve that problem. We also needed to make sure we were always wearing Kitten Fur. If Giannis had been in running water, it could have removed the scent. Luckily, Jet could still smell the scent in and around the metal crate. We guessed that is why she became protective of it. Giannis described what it was like constantly dying and reincarnating. "It wasn't a pleasant experience. I wouldn't want to be doing it again."

We had no idea if the coup had now ended. Or if others would follow in the footsteps of Oceanus. That needed to wait until Themis had completed her investigation. We concluded that the coup wasn't orchestrated by the Titans as a whole, given that Themis and Nemesis were both Titans.

I received a text from Themis.

'We will meet at Pefkos.'

'Thank you. What time?'

'We are questioning them now and hope to be with you at 6.'

'Thanks. See you then.'

I relayed the update to the guys. "Themis and Aletheia are getting to the bottom of it all now. They are coming here at six o'clock. Let's hope they have answers."

≈≈≈

I thought it appropriate that Themis sat in my chair, as it was her meeting, and she was announcing the results of her investigation.

"Well, gentlemen, you will be pleased to hear that you all acted within your remit and didn't commit any offences."

Giannis angrily responded, "I should think so too. I am the victim here."

Themis nodded at him to acknowledge that she thought so too, and then she continued, "Oceanus, Tethys, Electra, Asia, and Doris are guilty of …"

I interrupted, "Electra, Asia, and Doris?"

"The young girls, the Oceanids. Those are their names. The one that died was called Doris. As I was saying… they are all guilty of usurpation in that they attempted to overthrow Zeus. The general punishment has always been to be struck by lightning. The precedent for this was Salmoneus." And she looked at Zeus.

Zeus nodded. "I remember."

Themis smiled before continuing. "The problem is that Oceanus isn't the leader of the coup. All five of them were just foot soldiers."

I hadn't been giving the meeting my full attention until that point, but that statement made me sit up and listen. "Who is leading the coup? And are there other foot soldiers?"

Themis looked at first at Nemesis and then at Aletheia. "Yes, there are other foot soldiers. The leader of the coup was a surprise to us. And I am sure it will be a surprise to you too."

Zeus spoke before I could, "Who is it that dares to try and take my throne?"

Themis paused and looked at everyone in the room. "It is Helios."

"It can't be. He is an ally. We worked together to save Rhodes. Rod, tell them. He helped you defeat the renegades in the war."

My mind was a swirl as I tried to analyse every interaction I'd ever had with Helios.

"I knew it!" Said Giannis.

Themis looked at me. "Rod. What are you thinking?"

"There is so much wrong with that statement. If Helios is involved with the coup, how come they don't know the golden secret? Have you questioned Helios?"

Aletheia said, "Not yet. We have left a message for him to come here after the sun has set."

"Good because I don't believe it's Helios that is leading the coup."

"When we questioned Oceanus and asked him outright who was leading the attacks, he assured us it was Helios. Aletheia confirmed his honesty."

"Come on, ladies. All that tells us is that Oceanus believes that Helios is the leader. Whoever is the leader would have fed that misinformation to Oceanus to protect themselves or to give value to the coup."

"What makes you say that?" Asked Themis.

"Simple! We have been doing the same thing." And the whole room looked at me puzzled.

"How have we been doing the same thing?"

"We had a meeting in this very room. We decided that every decision Zeus made would pass through me. I am here now because I am the decision-maker. But if you asked Oceanus, who was running the show? Who was defending the throne? He wouldn't say Rod. He would say Zeus. That is why I don't think Helios is involved."

It was like turning on a room full of fluorescent light bulbs as they all flickered their understanding at different times. "I'm afraid that Oceanus won't be able to help because he doesn't know."

"We asked him how he knew that Helios was the leader?" Said Aletheia.

"And I bet he said he received a text message from Helios."

"Pretty much yes."

"It is called…" I paused to try and think of the word I needed, "Catfishing."

Now the room looked even more puzzled. It reminded me of the time I tried to teach Mags that the American general that wanted to borrow money via Facebook wasn't an American general at all.

I took out my phone, "Let me show you." And I tapped a message on the screen.

Themis's phone pinged. She smiled as she read the message that I sent. I think she had started to understand what catfishing is. She typed a message on her phone. Nemesis's phone pinged. She read the text message on it as she too realised what catfishing was. She turned and kissed Zeus full on the lips.

"What did you do that for?" asked Zeus.

"She did it because you commanded her to," I said, answering his question.

"I didn't."

"OK. I sent a message to Themis. It said: Hi Themis, this is Zeus. I command you to order Nemesis to kiss me."

Themis said, "And I sent a message to Nemesis telling her that Zeus commanded that she kiss him."

Nemesis said, "I was just doing what was commanded by the King of the Gods."

It was as if a flash of lightning had gone on inside his head. "Ah, I understand. But how does that relate to a catfish?"

"Not a clue. But that isn't the point. If we weren't in the same room. And I used a different phone. Themis would have thought she was communicating with the real Zeus."

Giannis summed it up. "It is the same as the chat we had when we first met. When I told you about how the gods became all-powerful."

"Yes, that is exactly it. The problem is that it doesn't bring us any closer to the answers we need. All I ask is that the remaining four be kept in custody."

"Custody? They won't be in custody. I have passed my sentence. They have already been struck by lightning or, more precisely, put to the sword. And I can confirm that none of them was immortal."

A shiver ran down my spine as I realised that I had been complicit in their deaths. Four beautiful girls were now dead because I'd meddled.

Arithmos

I struggled to come to terms with the events of the meeting. Some of the most powerful beings of the pantheon in one room, and we hadn't moved any further forward than when I was first cast out.

"We're getting nowhere fast."

"Well, that isn't strictly true, Rod," said Pete.

"I know. It is just the way I'm feeling. Now everyone has gone back to Olympian Dreams. I mean no disrespect to you, Pete. But working with people that are still stuck in a time that is a thousand years before the birth of Christ is a massive challenge. I guess I am just missing interactions with people from today."

"No disrespect back to you, Rod, but your interactions with Aphrodite didn't work out too well, did they?"

"Touché, Pete. I suppose what I mean is I need my family around me."

"As a three-thousand-year-old human, I understand where you are coming from on that point." And we looked at each other and laughed.

Then I brought the discussion back to the brainstorming session. No gods invited. All we can be sure of is the next attack will be from a God."

"Their only advantage is in name only. In the power they hold over each other. And the various realms they are perceived to rule over."

"If we could strip everyone of immortality. We would have all the power.

"That would be far too risky. You would have to get close to every immortal to be able to do that."

I reached down and stroked Jet. "At least I have my god detector."

"What happens once she has used up her nine lives?"

"That's it. Do all cats hate gods or was it just Jet?" I laughed out loud as I imagined sending Giannis into Nine-Lives. "What do you reckon, Pete? Should we send Giannis to the cat charity?"

He laughed. "He would never agree to it."

"What I really need is the contact number of every god."

"That won't happen. Themis wouldn't allow it."

"Circles. We're going in circles. All we can do is sit and wait."

"That's not like you, Rod. You are the initiator. What happened to proactivity?"

"I don't like not having a plan. Being aimless."

And that was the truth of it. I was once again left in a situation where I had no goal. Nothing to work for. Lost ambition. We continued our circular nonsense. Our aimless meandering of meaningless conversation.

"Do you know what I need, Pete?"

"What do you need?"

"I need to get drunk. I do my best thinking when I'm drunk. Come on, Jet, let's go and have a bottle of thinking. Are you coming, Pete?"

"No thanks. I haven't got the same resistance to alcohol as you have. Especially at Eleven in the morning."

It's hardly resistance. I just let it take control. I laughed, "Come on, Jet."

≈≈≈

It felt good leaving the confines of Pine Trees. While it was home, not leaving it was making me stir crazy, and I was spending a small fortune on surplus products from Amazon. It made me see why Giannis had to get out for a while. I headed straight for Angel Bar. It had become a favourite of mine; it was a perfect location for people watching. I'd recently discovered that Pine Trees House used to be a bit of waste land over the road from the bar. This made it perfect for watching the comings and goings at the hotel.

"Hi Zaf, I'll have the usual, please."

"Is that a glass or a bottle?" And he laughed. I think he knew I was planning a heavy session. Zaf was generally OK with me sitting in a corner getting drunk, so long as I didn't bother his customers.

I found my corner and pulled out some playing cards. A good game of solitaire would always stop me fretting on a problem until the ouzo had started to work its magic. I'd long since removed the doom-filled ace of spades from the pack and replaced it with the light-hearted joker. *Better to be a clown than dead.* Jet settled at my feet, and I started to flip cards. A sudden movement and a meow to my right interrupted the click-click of cards being dealt onto the table. It was a black and white cat, and Jet looked up for a second and then settled back down. She'd obviously met the cat before because its presence didn't disturb her. It clearly wasn't a god. It had a peculiar marking of just an island of black under its nose. *Fuck me, it looks like Hitler.* I reached down to stroke it,

Zaf brought my drink to me, along with some salty nibbles. As If I needed any help to accelerate the pace at which I downed the alcohol. "Rod, I thought you played Távli."

"Bit difficult on my own, Zaf. I use the numbers to relax. I look for patterns."

"I see you have met Kitler. Shoo him away if he bothers you."

Kitler. What kind of name is that for a cat?

I drank the ouzo as if I was downing a shot. "He won't bother me."

"Do you want the bottle?"

I just smiled and continued flipping the cards.

Fuck me, the Joker, that was a lucky escape. Haha, Kitler, Hitler, Cat. I get it.

My thoughts were still all over the place. *I wonder if fortune tellers are real. Well, if the gods are genuine, then fortune telling must be real. Athena consulted an Oracle. Perhaps the oracle was just a fortune teller.*

A bottle of ouzo appeared on the table. I just smiled at Zaf again. "Do you know about fortune telling?"

"No, but if you want to know anything about numbers. You need to meet Yiayia Phillis. She will look at your cards and tell you what the future holds for you."

"Is she your grandmother?"

He laughed, "No, she is everyone's grandmother. She has lived in Pefkos since it was a fishing village."

He left me to my musings. *Queen of hearts, what does that mean?*

I poured and downed another ouzo. *Eight of diamonds bet it will be a black card next.*

Kittler got fed up watching me get drunk and wandered off. Jet looked up, sighed, and went back to sleep.

I dealt the next card, *two of diamonds. Well, you got that wrong, Rod.*

I took another shot of ouzo. *That's nice, a couple more and I will be free.* "Hey, Zaf, where can I find Yiayia?"

"She used to live down the road, where Caprice is now. Years ago, she sold up her home and the land. She ran a caféneon, and everyone used to go to her for advice or to have their coffee reading. I don't know where she is now, but I see her around occasionally. I will try and find out for you."

Two of hearts. Whoopee a pair of deuces. The next one must be a black card.

I shot another ouzo. And as I turned the next card, it made me sit up. Two of clubs. *Another two, what are the chances of that?*

I shuffled the cards. I turned the top card. *Fuck me. That's weird. Two of spades.* That was too spooky. I put the cards away and poured another shot of ouzo. I sat back, pulled my hat over my eyes and let my mind do its thing.

In the distance, I could hear my name being called. "Rod!"

I lifted my hat and opened my eyes. It was Zaf. "Rod, Yiayia Phillis. She is coming."

"When?"

"Now!" And he laughed. "You want a coffee?"

I hiccupped an aniseed-flavoured burp and said, "Yes, please. A strong double frappe. No milk and no sugar."

≈≈≈

"At last, I meet the crazy Englishman."

"Hello, I am Rod Prince, and you are?"

"I know who you are. Nothing gets past me in Pefkos. You can call me Yiayia."

So much for keeping a low profile.

"Pleased to meet you. Would you like a coffee or something?"

She looked at the bottle of ouzo on the table and grinned a toothless smile, and nodded towards it. "I want ouzo. I think better when I drink ouzo."

Haha, a kindred spirit.

"Zaf, can I have another shot glass, please?"

I poured us both an ouzo, and before I could even say yammas, she'd finished it. *Shit, that didn't even touch the sides.* She slammed the glass down on the table by the bottle and nodded at it.

"You want more?" There was that toothless grin again. I slid the bottle in front of her so she could help herself.

"You drink," she said. She'd noticed that in my shock, I hadn't touched my last shot. I necked it.

I offered my glass for a top-up. "I think I am going to like you, Yiayia."

"Numbers. You want to know numbers?" And she pulled out a grubby, dog-eared set of playing cards. Nothing extraordinary about them except they looked well used.

"I have a newer pack here," I said, sliding my pack towards her.

"No! These are special. My father gave them to me in 1940 on 23rd March. Ochi Day." She passed the cards to me, and I could smell their age even over the aniseed of the ouzo. "Drink. Then mingle cards."

I downed the ouzo, which she immediately topped up. I shuffled the cards and kept doing so until she said, "Stop now. You will wear my cards out. Take ten cards and hand them to me."

She spread them out in two rows of five, all of them face down. "My row for your situation. Your row for your future. Drink."

God, she can drink more than me.

I looked down at Jet, but at some point, she'd moved on. I downed the ouzo. "So, these cards nearest me are my future."

"Yes. First, I must know you. It is my row first." Without taking her eyes off the table, she said. "Zaf, this doesn't concern you."

I hadn't even noticed him closing in for a look at events. I looked up at him and smiled. He put up his hand and went back to his bar.

I looked back at the table in time to see her turn over the first card. *Shit.* I thought. As she said, "Ace of spades. You have experienced death or a difficult ending. It is holding you back."

Yiayia certainly knew how to get my attention. I immediately thought of Affi.

She revealed the next card. "Five of hearts. You are surrounded by people that bear you ill-will or that are jealous of you."

She moved on and uncovered the third card of my present. "King of diamonds. It represents a grey-haired older man. A man of authority, of high status or influence. Earth will dominate his chart." I immediately thought of Zeus and that awful smell of goat and damp earth he had about him.

Yiayia flipped the fourth card over, and she paused before speaking. "Four of clubs. This card relates to the previous card. The king. The four of clubs tells us that the king is deceitful. And you should not be accepting of him or any of the people from the five of hearts. You are surrounded by death and envy." *Like, I didn't know that already.*

The revelation of the final card summed everything up. She turned it. "Eight of spades. You have recently experienced or are currently experiencing temptation, misfortune, danger and upset."

Christ, if I wasn't depressed when I came to Angel. I will be when I leave. My thoughts reminded me that life was a bit crap at that point. I didn't need to be reminded as I gulped down my latest ouzo and offered my glass for a top-up.

Yiayia asked, "Do those cards reflect you as you are at the moment?"

"Yep, this is my life, unfortunately."

"Well, drink, and we will see what the fates hold for your

future."

I thought fortune-tellers were only supposed to tell you the good stuff.

"Before we go on, what would it mean to draw all four twos together?"

"Why?"

"Because I was playing earlier and drew all of the twos one after the other."

She laughed. "It means you didn't shuffle the cards properly ... no, it just means you are at a crossroads."

Part of me was telling myself that everything was nonsense. But the rest of me wanted to know what the future had in store for Rod Prince.

"Are you going to turn your cards over?"

I didn't answer. I just reached for the leftmost card and turned it over. At least it couldn't be the ace of spades.

"Eight of clubs. This is generally unfavourable. You will be facing more jealousy, particularly in work or business relationships."

That means the shit isn't going to disappear anytime soon.

I moved to the second card and turned it over.

"This is suggesting a change in the business relationships you have, most likely involving splits or breakups. Beware of gossip."

I downed my ouzo and offered my glass for yet another refill. I showed the third card.

She tutted before saying, "Jack of clubs. Do you know someone young and dark-haired? Possible very young. Maybe they are fiery but also playful. They admire you and will be loyal to you. They hold your fate."

Affi? No, this is the future. It must be Jet.

I came to the fourth card. I slid it towards me off the edge of the table, looked at it and then cast it back onto the table.

"Oh. The queen of clubs. All the qualities of the previous card transfer to this one. Except this tells me that the youth is a female. As well as being spirited, this woman will give you good advice. This is a very good pairing of cards."

Suddenly, I felt a lot better about the reading of the cards. But I still downed my ouzo. Yiayia topped up both glasses.

You have a damned good constitution woman, if you can drink like this and still concentrate.

I worried that the last card was going to turn everything on its head. "What would be a bad card to draw now?" I asked her.

She swigged her ouzo and said, "I shouldn't tell you but with the cards that are lying before us. You don't want that last card to be a nine or ten of spades. Now I have told you, do wish to carry on?"

I reached for the last card and turned it over quickly.

Thank god for that.

"Ten of hearts. That is a particularly good card. It signifies good fortune and success. It shows you will have good fortune after a difficulty."

"Do you have a mobile that I can contact you on?"

She laughed. "Why would I want one of them things? If you want to talk to me, just tell Zaf. Then let the gossips do their work."

There wasn't much ouzo left in the bottle, but I let Yiayia take it and settled the bill with Zaf. "I'll see you both. I need to lie down."

I don't recall crossing the road to Pine Trees or seeing Pete, but I do remember looking at the clock as I fell face down on my bed. I had a fitful sleep which had become my new normal. Between sitting up to burp so that I didn't throw up and staggering to the bathroom to throw up, I did manage to get some sleep. Every time I laid back down and put my head on the pillow, the room would spin. The sensation reminded me of the time that I was thrown from Poseidon's boat. By the time I'd woken up fully, it was two in the morning, and I felt rough.

Why do I do it?

I sat up the room lit by the brightness of my mobile. I could barely focus on it.

There was a message from Pete:

'Gone to Olympian'.

That'll be right, all the ancient fogies in one place.

I sent a stark reply.

'Stay there. You have more in common with them.'

He responded, "Don't be like that."

I just ignored him. As I morphed from having an ouzo hangover to a semi-human state, I played on my phone. In what seemed like minutes, I was still on Google as the sun rose.

As the day began its dawn, I had a dawning moment of my own. If the card reading with Yiayia was correct, then my future was already mapped out. I was facing a new normal. I chucked in what Google had taught me and set about making my plans for my new future. I didn't bother responding to

Pete's text message. If he wanted to come back, that was up to him. I'd be happier if he stayed at Olympian. They could all rot together. I didn't need any of them. If anything, they needed me more. I had Yiayia and her cards. For the price of a bottle of ouzo, she would be my oracle.

Stop getting yourself wound up, Rod.

With perfect timing, Jet jumped through her cat flap. And jumped up onto the bed with me. "Looks like it is just you and me against the Titans and Olympians, sweetheart." Of course, my mood and the reading were all based upon suppositions. I had been feeling deceived for a long time. Things weren't ringing true about lots of things. Somewhere in my dreams overnight, I'd decided that Themis and Nemesis were all part of the plot. Google consolidated the idea when it confirmed to me that Themis was a Titan. Not just any Titan, but a significant player type of Titan. She has been setting the rules all along. I had been a fool for not checking before. My first interaction with Nemesis should have told me to be careful. The decision I had was to let on that I'd rumbled them. The alternative would be to keep quiet, but then they'd expect me to follow their every command.

I needed, Yiayia. *Oh God, more ouzo.* Jet jumped off the bed and decided to use the dressing table as a scratching post. *Damn cat, you should save that for the gods.* I left her to it and got myself cleaned up. I needed Zaf to set me up with a date with a lady. I didn't think I should be stinking.

≈≈≈

"Morning, Zaf. A strong black Frappe, please."

"What's the matter. You don't want ouzo?" He laughed, and I just glared at him. Just the thought of ouzo was making me feel sick.

"No ouzo for me today. Just coffee. Can you summon Yiayia for me today, please?",

Yiayia must have been expecting me to get in touch because she was there in minutes. I knew it was going to cost me a bottle of ouzo, but she had something I needed. She knew the cards. I needed her to teach me what each card in a pack meant. I needed to be my own oracle. To be able to make decisions based upon what the cards were telling me. It should be more reliable than using the gods for guidance. And indeed, better than my current odds of a fifty-fifty chance offered by tossing a coin.

She sank her first ouzo and poured her second before the first had even hit her stomach.

Jesus woman, why don't you drink it straight from the bottle?

"The ace of spades you know already."

"Yes, Death."

"Not just death, but misfortune or a difficult ending. If you draw this card, its meaning will be set by the question you pose. If you ask if you should have ouzo, this card is telling you that it won't end well. It doesn't mean you will die."

"Hang on, I need to write this down. Zaf, can I have a menu pad, please?"

The rest of the four-hour session pretty much followed the same pattern. We covered all fifty-two cards in the pack, and she included the joker as well. We were about thirty minutes in and up to the ten of spades when she asked me if I wanted an ouzo. I suggested I would let the cards decide. I shuffled my pack and asked the question, "Should I have a drink of ouzo?"

I flipped the top card, and it was the five of diamonds.

She said, "Five of diamonds. Happiness and success." Then she poured me an ouzo. "Yammas."

I necked it. I had to. Otherwise, I would have thrown up. In moments I felt the warmth hit my stomach. And then I was back on it, gag reflex suppressed. She poured two more shots and proceeded to continue with the ten of spades. "Ten of spades is a worry. It usually signified bad things. If you had drawn that to your question, you would still be drinking coffee."

We went through the same routine with every card. She would name it, tell me its meaning. She would give an example of the range it might cover. I would make her pause while I took notes. It was during these pauses that she would sink an ouzo and replenish her glass. I didn't join her on every round. I didn't dare if I wished to retain everything that she was telling me. And she had given me lots to think about. I now had lots of planning to complete and lots of questions to discover the answers to. She ridiculed me when I told her I had discarded the ace of spades. "You are the King of Dolos. You cannot know your fate unless all destinies are represented. You are a cheat." she said.

Later a quick google search told me that Dolos was the God of Lies, and the Greek word dolos translates to English as deceit. I needed to buy a new pack of cards. I had to have all fifty-two and a joker.

Ouzo

I was alone to my thoughts once again. I didn't know who I could trust. Was I protecting Zeus from a coup or leading the Olympians into a battle with the Titans? Had I been used by Themis and Nemesis to bring Zeus in hand? Once he was in a position of weakness, the Titans could take control without any resistance. They had already made him accept that all decisions had to go through me. This could only serve to delay any decisions that were made. By the time I'd checked the legality of my decision with Themis, it introduced too much of a delay. What if I was wrong and Themis was fighting for the good of Zeus? What would my rejection of her do to the support she offered.

"What do you think, Jet? Am I placing too much reliance on a pack of cards?" She was no help; she just came and lay at my feet. *What if Yiayia is a nut case?*

For the next few hours, Google and I became the best of friends. Is there nothing that the Internet doesn't know? I glanced up from my surfing, and Jet was scratching at the leg of the boardroom table.

Damn cat, that table cost a fortune.

At least I had something to search for with my new buddy. And then we found it, Google and I had done it. We found a kind of false fingernails for cats. They are called claw caps, but I'm sure the feminine side of Jet would love the effect of a bit of nail beauty. My other new buddies Amazon and PayPal took care of the order for me.

Within days my furniture was safe, and Jet loved her new bright red nails. Of course, they had to be removable because of the need to be able to scratch at gods. I wanted her to be furniture friendly, not God friendly. She must have understood my intentions because it didn't upset her at all.

I spent many days or nights just sitting in the boardroom with my new family. Sexy Jet, knowledgeable Google, resourceful Amazon, and rich PayPal. Not forgetting, of course, my absolute best friends, Billy Boredom and Ossie the Open Ouzo. I'd break my days up with visits to most of the drinking establishments in the resort. If one ran out of ouzo, I'd go to another. Sometimes Jet would accompany me, and at other times she could be found flirting with Kitler. I'm not sure he was impressed with her flashy new claws. It probably freaked him out a little. I suspect he preferred his females natural. Every decision I made was ruled by the cards. Simple yes or no questions were the easiest. I read a black card as a no, and diamonds and heart were yes. It was weird every time I asked the cards if I should have an ouzo, I got a red card.

"What do you think, cards? Should I go out for an ouzo?" *Ace of Diamonds. That's a big yes, then.*

On one of these card-supported outings at Karma Bar, I

bumped into Lazaros from Irene's gold.

He was mesmerised by the cat's appearance. "Bright red is an odd choice of colour for a cat."

"I think it looks cute. I've always loved red and black together."

"No, no, it is too much of a contrast. Grey would be good."

I called the owner over, "Rachael, you're a woman, come and give us your opinion on something." I was sure she would take my side because she had dark hair, and I had seen her with bright red nails.

I scooped jet up. "What do you think? Does Jet look good in red claws, or would she look better in grey?"

"Oh no, not grey. Unless, of course, it was silver."

Lazaros laughed, "Let us do business. I could make you some in silver."

I was almost speechless as my mind started to tick over. They both looked at me as time stood still. I continued to formulate a plan.

"Are you OK, Rod?" Asked Rachael.

"That depends on your answer to another manicure question. What would gold nails look like against black fur?"

"I love it. I wish Aris would buy me gold nails. She would be one lucky cat." Then she laughed. "Lucky black cat!" I laughed along with her. Not at the joke but the beauty of the plan. The gods were going to get their karma. And the plan was born at the Karma bar. *Oh, the poetic justice.*

"What do you think Lazaros, could you do them in gold?"

"Of course. You know I can."

"Thanks, Rachael. You don't know how much your

comment has helped me. I will have to have a chat with Aris for you."

"Good luck with that," she said as she wandered off and went about her business.

I looked at the goldsmith. "How long? And how much?"

"You give me the red ones as a pattern, and I will have them for you by tomorrow. I calculate around four to five euros per claw cap. How many claws does she have?"

"Eighteen."

"Five times eighteen, that will be one-hundred euro." His maths was undoubtedly a bit off, but I wasn't bothered. Not when I realised the whole worth to me. It was a weapon I could have only dreamed about.

"You almost have a deal. Make me forty, and I will pay you three hundred euros. How does that sound?"

"Rachael, can we have two ouzos and a glass of water, please?"

"Water? Since when have you been drinking water?"

"It's not for drinking. It is for getting Jets red claws off. I need to soak her paws in water."

Rachael bought the drinks and water to the table. "And she lets you stick her paws in water?"

"Of course. She loves me and trusts me." I wasn't sure that I wasn't going to get scratched, but it progressed well. I was glad that I'd chosen water-soluble adhesive.

"Yammas," said Lazaros.

"Yammas. One last thing, I want the caps to have sharp points."

"Won't she still damage your furniture?"

"Maybe, but it doesn't matter now. Her claws cost more than the furniture." And I winked at him.

≈≈≈

Jet adored her new gold claw caps. She didn't stop scratching at the furniture, but that was good because it kept the claw caps sharp. My excitement was tempered by the fact that the fitting of gold claw caps was an experiment. A gamble based on theory. They needed to be tested. I had limited subjects to choose from. I'd probably burnt my bridges with the Olympian Dreams gang. I pondered which one to pick because I didn't have any other lab rats other than them. I shuffled the deck of cards and flipped the top card over. *Queen of Hearts, that must be Nemesis.* The cards had confirmed my thoughts. If Nemesis still worked at Trianon Café, she would be an easy target, a sitting god. A quick call to Katerina told me that Nemesis was there and would be for a complete shift.

I looked at the cat, "How do you fancy a trip to Rhodes?" She just purred.

Cat, I wish you could talk.

I determined my next drunken interaction with my mate Google would be how to communicate with a cat.

I was able to pull up and park on 25th March Street. Jet was already hissing and ready to attack. She could smell a god. Her reaction also showed me that Nemesis wasn't wearing the Kitten fur. I put my hands over her eyes as I crept past Trianon. This seemed to settle her. I could see Nemesis inside, and fortunately, she was facing the bar. Once I had passed the Lotto retailers outlet, I dropped Jet to the ground and kept walking. I was headed for McDonald's and a Triple Cheeseburger. I could hear the screams and shouting all the way down the street. Jet joined me, and I could see traces of red blood on her claw caps. *Good girl.*

I stuffed her inside my jacket and ordered my meal. Armed with my ready-made cholesterol bomb, I made my way to Amerikis Street. I detoured around the block so that I could reunite with my car without passing Trianon again. I should probably have stayed to watch, but that would have defeated the point of the experiment. I now knew that I could mortalise a god from a distance.

Provided that Jet had picked up the scent, she could launch her attack. It was as good as having a military drone. Perhaps she wouldn't have the 120-mile range of an Exocet missile, but at least I could launch her out of sight of my victim.

Before I even got to the car, my phone was ringing, followed by endless text notifications. Suddenly, I was Mister Popular. I bet every one of my godly contacts wants to be my best friend, but I just ignored them. I had a triple cheeseburger to get my teeth into. There would be plenty of time to read the messages once I was back in Pefkos.

I needed my aniseed anaesthetic before I read any of the messages. There was no way I was going back to the hotel until I had assessed the backlash.

I decided that although the Angel Bar would provide a ready view of the hotel. I needed something that would allow me more anonymity. The Irish Pub was my best bet. It had been a while since I had a bit of banter with Janet or Kosta. Janet was always good for a craic, and Kosta shared my sense of humour. I always saw Janet as a kindred spirit. We both had blue eyes, which was as rare as a frosty morning on Rhodes. I say my eyes were blue, but mostly they were bloodshot from my overindulgence and all-night sessions with Google.

"Alright, J?" What's the craic?" I always tried to put on an Irish accent. Invariably it made Janet wet herself in hysterics.

"Stop doing that when I have a tray of glasses. I'll charge you for any glasses I drop."

"Feck off, I'll pay enough tonight. I'm going to get fluthered." I was never too sure what that meant, but I'd heard some Irish guys say it on a bachelor night.

She put the tray of glasses down on the bar. "Enough now. You want a Guinness?"

"No, no, too heavy for me on a triple Cheeseburger."

"A large ouzo on ice, please." I plonked myself on a barstool. Janet nodded at Kosta.

Jet wandered off, probably in search of Kitler. "Make sure you come back here before closing."

"You treat that cat like a daughter. Let her have a craic. Have you painted her claws gold?"

"I laughed, "No, they are claw caps. Her bling for when she flirts with Kitler."

"We haven't seen you for a while. What you been up to?"

"Getting drunk, mostly. Buying shit online."

Kosta had poured my drink. "Hello, Rod. How are you? Sorry to hear about Affi."

"Thanks. This helps," and I downed the ouzo, nearly choking on a bit of ice. Janet went about her business.

"More?" Asked Kosta.

"Of course. Keep them coming. And keep count, I don't want to be accused of diddling the Irish one." I smiled at Janet to let her know I was joking.

And the cycle began all over again. Wake up with a hangover, cool shower, bake in the sun on the way to a chosen bar. Sit and talk to mortals, drinking endless shots. Stagger home in the dark and collapse fully clothed on the bed. If I was lucky, I would wake up when I needed to pee. Jet was ever-present except when she was on the razzle with Kitler. He was one lucky cat, having my classy Jet interested in him. I don't recall how many days the latest sleep, drink, repeat cycle went on. I did know that I couldn't live like that for an eternity. I'd even considered mortalising myself. Just to be normal again and worry about my health. What I needed, I guessed, was to have Kam back by my side. She would have kept me in check. But Asclepius was the fortunate recipient of that guidance now. People had always told me that living in Rhodes full-time wouldn't be the same as having a holiday. In my case, it was too much like being on holiday. Nothing to do from one day to the next. The gods had seemed to accept the new way of doing things. They left me alone, and I left them alone. I was disappointed that Pete hadn't been near Pine Trees.

"Fuck him," I said with too much volume as I forgot to think to myself.

Ace of Spades

I guessed that eventually, the gods would bring the fight to me. They couldn't let my second attack on Nemesis appear unnoticed or indeed go unpunished. Enough time had passed that I assumed they hadn't realised that it was me or even that Nemesis was mortal. I'd got comfortable in the knowledge that as a body, they weren't that clever. I didn't have to wait too long to see my security blanket disappear.

It was Pete that came and found me at Angel Bar. "Rod. You must pull yourself together. You are in grave danger."

"Hello, stranger. What's the matter? Have you fallen out with your gang of deities?"

"That is unfair, Rod. I have been spying on them. Working for you behind their lines, so to speak."

"Oh yeah. And why should I believe you? You ignored my attempts to contact you."

"Of course I did. I couldn't risk them finding out I was still your friend. I assumed you would know what I was up to. But then I didn't stop to think you would be in a drunken haze all of the time."

"So you didn't want to risk them finding out, and yet, here you are in person. That's a bloody great way to keep it secret. Have you any idea how isolated I've been feeling."

Then I heard him swear for the first time ever. "For fucks sake. Stop with the self-pity and start thinking proactively again like the old Rod. I am your crony. I swore my allegiance to you. And I said I could never work for Zeus. Do you mistrust me that much?"

"I'm sorry, Pete. I should have realised. But you were here one minute and gone the next."

"Perhaps I could have handled it differently. But I needed absolute secrecy."

"Too right, you could have bloody handled it differently. In your own words. Do you mistrust me that much?"

"Touché, Rod. Come, let's get you to Pine Trees and cleaned up. Can you manage to cross the road?" He laughed. I grunted.

≈≈≈

"You have created absolute panic at Olympian. You are public enemy number one."

"I guessed I would be. Did you realise that the coup was Nemesis and Themis?"

He looked puzzled. "No. What makes you say that?"

"I figured it out. They were just doing what the gods do. Using us humans to do their dirty work. They are all contracted to not harm each other. Us poor humans are just pawns in their bloody games."

"Pawns or not. They are out to get you. To punish you."

"I have amulets of the entire board to protect me."

"I'm not talking of the board. I am talking about Nemesis and Themis."

"Since you revealed the secret to them, they are terrified. And then your cat attacked Nemesis again. Did you know that?"

Before answering him, I needed to be sure I could trust him. I thought for a moment. "Of course, I knew. It was me that took Jet to the café."

"Well, it has spooked them."

I laughed. "Did they know that it mortalised Nemesis?"

"No. I don't think they have cottoned on to running checks. How did it mortalise her?"

"I'll show you when Jet gets here." As if on cue, the bloody cat walked in.

I picked her up and held one of her paws so he could see the claws. "Can you see it?"

"Jesus, gold claws. They don't have a clue. Do you realise how much power that gives you?"

"Course I do. I just drop the cat close enough to a god and leave her to do her work. Let's have a drink to celebrate."

"No way. And you stay off the stuff, too, if you want to be prepared for them. You need to know that they have taken the gold secret, and they carry gold weapons. None of these hidden weapon ideas like yours, but they both carry knives."

"I still have an advantage. It is like one country using long-range missiles against another country with bombs. So long as they are dependent on proximity. I have power over them."

"That's all well and good until they attack you while the cat isn't around. You need to be more careful and keep her on a tight rein. The advantage a knife has is that it will mortalise and kill you in one swift thrust."

Unfortunately, the bravado generated by my earlier drinking session allowed me to just shrug my shoulders. Like a spoilt brat, I just said, "I don't care."

Pete just tutted and said, "I won't get through to you until you have the ouzo out of your system. Stay sober, and we can discuss it tomorrow."

I went to my room and cracked open a fresh bottle of ouzo. I pulled the new but tatty pack of cards from my pocket. These were my crutches. The two parts of my life that had become my constant companions. I unfolded the notes I had taken while Yiayia had taught me how to translate the cards. I dealt out ten cards on the coffee table. I discarded the five that I had dealt in the row furthest from me. I wasn't interested in the present or the past. I already knew where I was and how I got here. I wanted to know what was ahead. The five remaining cards were holding my fate. I swigged a big shot of ouzo straight from the bottle.

I turned the first card and let out an audible sigh, even though there was nobody to hear it.

Ace of fucking spades. Shit.

I didn't have to look at my crib sheet to know that it was a bad card to start the reading with. Misfortune, a difficult ending, possibly death. The words bounced around inside my mind. I took another huge swig of ouzo.

I hoped the second card would provide a better omen. I was willing it to be a red card. Something to offer good news.

I flipped the card over. Another bloody spade. I had a solution. The cards hadn't been shuffled while I thought about the question that I wanted the answer to. I scooped up all ten cards and rebuilt the pack. I shuffled while saying out loud, "What does my future hold?" I mixed the collection of cards seven times. Seven is my lucky number.

I took another swig of ouzo and dealt the cards out again. The five cards nearest me were going to reveal my true destiny. I flipped the first card over.

Fuck. Fuck. Fuck.

Once again, the first card was the ace of spades.

I continued hoping for salvation from the next card. I turned it over quickly as if speed would catch it before it changed to something terrible. Another spade, Nine.

What did she say about the nine of spades?

I looked at the scribbled notes on the paper to confirm my worst fears - bad luck. An illness or an accident.

Jesus.

The third card was no better. It was the ten of spades. Bad news and worry. I hurried to get the cards turned over. Hoping that there was going to be some good news among the last two cards. *Please let them be red cards.*

I didn't put enough hope into my internal plea. Eight and seven.

Both fucking spades.

The eight told me of more misfortune, danger, and upsets. The seven didn't provide any better news. Just one word with so many negative synonyms. Loss. If I'd been playing poker, it would have been a winning hand. An ace-high flush. The problem was I wasn't playing poker. I was playing with my destiny. I spent the rest of the night finishing the ouzo and playing online poker. I played hundreds of games and didn't see an ace-high flush once throughout the night.

≈≈≈

"Jesus, Rod. I thought I told you to sober up. You look worse than when I saw you yesterday." Was the only greeting I got from Pete.

"Well, you know me, Pete. I don't do anything I am told to do. I'm my own man. I'm in charge of my destiny." Inside. I knew I was lying to myself because the cards were controlling my destiny.

What did Yiayia call me? The King of Dolos.

"I had hoped you were going to stay sober long enough for me to tell you news from Olympian."

"I'm sober enough. Tell me your news."

"Themis and Nemesis are the coup leaders."

"I already figured that out. They're both Titans. Affi told me, and the cards and Google confirmed it."

"Pfft. The cards told you. Did they also tell you that the coup is over?"

"What do you mean?"

"The whole board at Olympian are mortal. They are controlled by Themis. She and Nemesis are the only immortals left on that side of the island. I got out before anyone realised that I too was immortal."

"Christ. I take it Giannis is no longer enamoured with Nemesis."

"No. That romance is long dead. When it all kicked off, Giannis moved me to Helios to protect me. He said I was to come and warn you if he ever got mortalised."

"Why the fuck didn't anyone tell me any of this sooner?"

"Zeus suspected that you were the secret weapon of the coup. Don't forget when Themis put you in charge of Zeus, he thought you were working with them. When Giannis and Nemesis had a big row, it all came out. They used you to overpower Zeus. By the time any of us realised what was happening, it was too late. The whole board was mortal. With you and me, there are now only four immortals on the island."

"No, there are three, don't forget Jet mortalised Nemesis already."

"OK, three, but there will only be one if they get close enough to us with their golden knives.

"We can make the board immortal again."

"No point while the Titans are in charge. They will mortalise everyone again, and you won't have the resources. Before anyone gets immortality back. We need to overcome the evil bitches."

"I warned the Olympians they would need me long before I needed them."

"You did. And every one of them sends you their apologies and pleads with you for forgiveness and, of course, your help."

"I can sort it inside an hour. Are you coming? You can see Jet in action."

"No, Rod. That isn't the answer. That is why I wanted you completely sober. If you go dashing across the island, you are walking into a trap. You risk everything with your drunken bravado. We need one of your plans."

Deep down, I knew he was right. It wasn't just a case of mortalising Themis. She and Nemesis would remain a threat until they were killed, and the killing wasn't my favourite part of a battle, having only experienced it once with Poseidon. I consoled myself with the thought that he was dying anyway, and I'd just sped up the process. However, Themis was a different prospect altogether. She was a female for a start. I was taught never to raise a hand to a woman, and now I was expected to kill one. I was already aware of the effect that four female deaths had been having on my mental health.

"Are we sure that Themis is the leader of the coup?"

"There is little doubt. She is justice. She is the law. No one else would have the power to do what she has done."

I lightened the conversation by adding, "Or the intelligence. What we don't know is who are her foot soldiers. Her supporters."

"I have been given no clues. But it is probably every Titan that is still around."

"It doesn't matter. She is the bloody coup. But there's a new coup coming. And it will be driven by us. Any foot soldiers will buckle once we have the monsters head. Where do they think you are now?"

"I don't know. I just had to come here and warn you. They believe they will have only one chance to get to you. They are afraid that if that attack fails, you will come for them."

I eyed him suspiciously. I still wasn't sure if he was working as a spy for them. "I have a job for you, Pete. I want you to return to Olympian Dreams. I need you to take Jet with you and engineer an attack on Themis."

"How can I do that? She will attack any of the gods."

"That's fine. Don't worry about it. The Olympians are already mortalised, and they can be fixed later. Do not let on that you know Nemesis is mortal."

"They will expect me to report where you are."

That's ok, tell them you found me drunk in one of the bars. That way, if they check with Aletheia, she will say you are telling the truth. But you can only tell them after you are sure that Jet has attacked Themis. I need her to come here as a mortal."

"I'm not so sure, Rod. If they come after you, they will bring golden weapons. They will try to kill you. And how do I get Jet back to you."

"Don't worry so much. I will know where they are long before they find me. And don't worry about Jet. She will find her own way home."

"I do trust you, Pete. But any more detail than that will put you at risk. If they do head here before Jet has done the deed. I need you to be minutes behind them with Jet."

"Are you just going to sit here and wait for them?"

"Nope. I'm going on a pub crawl; they will expect me to be in one of the bars, and that is where they will find me."

"Please don't get on the ouzo. You need to be sober when they find you."

"Relax, I need to have some Greek courage, and ouzo is my fuel," I smirked at him, and he just did that Greek shrug of the shoulders.

"But…"

"I will see you when it's all over. Look after Jet for me." And I walked out of the hotel.

I sat at Angel Bar with a bottle of unopened ouzo on the table. I watched as Pete loaded Jet into his car. He glanced across at me and shook his head before speeding off in the direction of the main road.

"I'll be back in a bit, Zaf. Here's the bottle back."

"You haven't drunk anything."

"I know. I will drink later. For now, I'm going on a pub crawl. And don't forget that favour."

"You are crazy. I won't forget the favour. See you later, crazy Englishman."

The Joker

I had preparations to make for my godly visitors. I had a few new Amazon presents to pick up from my apartment.

On my pub crawl, I visited Enigma, The Irish Pub, Caprice, Karma Bar and Kavos before ending up back at Pine Trees. I placed a note on the door. 'Back in 1 hour. In an emergency, I am at Enigma.'

Instead of going to Enigma as the note suggested, I went back to Angel bar.

"Any visitors, Zaf.?"

"No, Rod. I would have phoned you as you asked."

"I don't think you will get to do it now I am here."

"You want coffee?"

I looked at him. "You know me better than that. Crack open that bottle of ouzo."

Everything was set. I just had to sit and wait, enjoy the view, the company, and the ouzo.

"Have you put on weight, Rod?"

I looked down at my physique. I laughed at him and said, "That's the body armour." Luckily, he thought I was joking. I didn't want to have to explain why I was wearing an anti-stab vest.

The bloody advert didn't tell me it was going to be so hot wearing it.

I checked my pockets; my other dart was still there and readily accessible. I pulled out my cards. Gave them a good shuffle, turned over the top card, and there was that bloody ace of spades again. And then I saw them. They were coming up the road past the Rock Garden along the side of Pine Trees. In two minutes, they would see the note.

"Zaf, don't make it too obvious, but the two women walking towards the hotel are the ones that will come here looking for me."

"Got it."

I slunk back in my chair and lowered my hat to shade my face. I could see them as they read my note on the door. I became tense as they looked around. They clearly didn't know where Enigma was. They stopped to speak to a couple. I could tell they were tourists because they were both wearing brightly coloured shorts. From the arm waving and pointing, I figured they were getting directions. It wasn't difficult. They only had to walk a few yards. But it meant they had to walk directly past Angel bar. I slunk even lower into my seat. I saw them move towards Enigma.

"They didn't come in," said Zaf. He sounded disappointed.

"Don't worry. They will when they have been to other bars."

The goose chase had begun. I just needed Suzana to remember her script and send them on to the Irish Pub. I knew that once they were there, that Janet would lead them on a merry chase. At least she would if they could understand her Irish accent.

"Right, Zaf, I am off. Remember what to say when they get here. Tell them I am always drunk and most likely sleeping at Pine Trees."

"That's easy to remember because it is true. See you later."

≈≈≈

Within minutes my phone pinged. It was Suzana at Enigma.

'They have gone to Karma.'

'Thanks'

Due to my helpful friends at the different bars, I was able to keep track of where Themis and Nemesis were. I knew that once Zaf, the final link in the chain, sent his text, they would be moments away. The time waiting for his message allowed me to make my final preparations. I sat at my desk. Another text, this time from Rachael at Karma.

'They have gone.'

'Thanks'

I picked up my newly arrived cattle prod. *Five-thousand volts, that's got to hurt*. Its red shaft acted as a visual warning of what was about to hit the victim. I pondered why Amazon didn't sell them, and yet they were freely available on eBay.

Another text. The Titans were headed to The Irish Pub. They were in for a fun time with Janet and Kosta. It was a longer than expected wait for the text from Janet.

'Gone to Angel'

'Thanks'

It was now down to Zaf to let me know when they were coming across the road. I opened the boardroom door to have a clear line of sight to the windows at the front of the hotel. I spotted them approaching at the exact moment that I received Zaf's text. I didn't have time to read it, but I knew what it would say. I retracted the computer screen back into the table and placed the prod on the vacant space. The half-metre red shaft contrasting the light wood of the tabletop.

The front door opened. I looked up and smiled at them. "Ha, ladies. What brings you here?"

"Themis, who was sporting a scratch on her face, replied first, "Your cat!"

Nice one, Jet.

"What do you mean, my cat? I haven't seen her for days. She has a nearby love interest."

"Well, she has been on the other side of the island. And she has attacked both of us."

Nemesis added, "It is the third time that she has attacked me. She came at me while I was at work, a while back."

"Oh, I am so sorry. Why weren't you wearing the perfume I gave you?"

"Because we didn't expect the damned cat to be in Rhodes town or on the other side of the island."

"Well, come in. And you better shut the door behind you just in case Jet comes home." Nemesis couldn't shut the door fast enough. She almost slammed the door in her haste to build a barrier between her and Jet.

Themis sat at the far end of the long boardroom table. Nemesis seated herself next to her in such a way as she could keep an eye on the door. I looked down at the bright red weapon on the table. Neither of them was within grabbing distance of it. They were also out of reach if I wished to prod them with it. That suited me. It meant I was out of reach of their golden knives. They both looked at my long red weapon. Curiosity got to Nemesis first. "What is that?"

"It is a cattle prod. Farmers use it to herd their livestock. It delivers an electric shock of five thousand volts. I use it to keep Jet from attacking me. You can think of it like a lightning bolt. I pulled the trigger on it, and it crackled to show the miniature streaks of lightning."

"The cat attacks you as well?"

"Of course, she is wild and has a will of her own."

The next half-hour was filled with general chit-chat and bullshit. They were buttering me up as if I was the saviour. I was complementing them on how they had successfully squashed the coup. I needed to bring some reality back to the interaction.

"Tell me, why has Zeus not been in touch for help with decisions? And I haven't seen Pete or Giannis for god knows how long."

"Giannis?"

"Yes, Apollo. You've praised me for my help. You've painted me as the Olympian saviour. And yet, I have no evidence they are still alive. Anyone would think the coup had succeeded, and Zeus has been toppled already."

The cheeky bitches looked at each other and smiled. Themis said, "What are you suggesting?"

I leant forward and stared into Themis' eyes. She did that

squinty thing that all gods do when they are trying to figure me out. "Let's cut the bullshit. I'm assuming you are capable of talking without lying. You know, and I know that you two were the coup. It was never just Oceanus and the girls. They were carrying out your orders." I transferred my gaze to Nemesis, who was fidgeting in her seat. I continued to address the pair of them as one. "You have led a Titanic fight back. That is what I am suggesting."

Themis laughed. "The rumours must be true. You have become a drunk with fantastical ideas. If we were leading a coup, the first thing we would have done was destroy you."

I took a deep breath and gulped visibly.

I could do with an ouzo right now.

"And that, ladies, was your greatest mistake. I am still here and still ready to protect the Olympians. I cannot let you ruin Rhodes, or indeed, Greece."

It became clear why Nemesis was fidgeting. She pulled a small knife out of her shorts. I placed my hand on the cattle prod.

Themis leant forward. "You asked why we are here." She nodded towards Nemesis. "We are here to return you to your mortal state."

"What? Like yourselves?"

I might as well have poked them with the cattle prod. They looked stunned. I didn't give them time to process a response. "Yes, you are both mortals. You could die here today. I am immortal, and I intend to stay this way." I leant back in my chair.

Don't gloat. Don't be arrogant, Rod.

They responded in unison, "But …"

"I am not going to reveal how I know. But I will offer you a test if you wish. I have lots of pins." I opened my drawer and slid the diabetic lancets towards them.

They both snatched up a lancet and removed it from its sterile packet. Stabbing their fingers, the red blood they produced presented irrefutable evidence that they were both mortals. I reached into the drawer again and pulled out my latest toy from eBay, a tranquiliser gun. I was shocked at how easy it was to buy ketamine filled darts online. No checks or questions about my intended use. I could have been anyone.

Nemesis picked up her knife. "We can still make you mortal."

"Yes, you can. But where is the gain in that?"

"There are two of us and one of you?"

"Only in this room. You forget that I have the whole Olympian pantheon to call upon. While you have been here, they've been preparing for your return to Olympian Dreams. I am sure they will have a warm welcome for you." I picked up the dart gun and pointed it at Nemesis, "Besides, you could die here today."

The three of us looked at each other. I spoke first, "It would seem we have an impasse."

Themis had clearly been calculating the odds of their success or failure. "What do you want? Can we make a deal?"

Nemesis hadn't calculated the odds, and she stood up, knife in hand. I had no choice. I pulled the trigger. She looked down at the dart sticking out of her midriff. She looked at me and smiled as she realised that she hadn't been instantly killed.

She took one pace towards me, and then I smiled as she stumbled and collapsed on the ground.

"It would seem we no longer have an impasse," I said as I loaded a second dart into the gun.

Themis was stunned at the ease with which I could fight off the threat that Nemesis posed. She put her hand up as I pointed the loaded weapon at her. "Wait. We can come to an arrangement."

"That's funny. You want to have an arrangement now I have the upper hand."

"I have always wanted you to be part of the coup."

"Bullshit. You recruited me to stop the coup as a means of bringing me out into the open. You always planned to overthrow Zeus, but you didn't factor in his human friend."

"Oh, I think you will find I did. And his family."

My amber blood ran cold. "What have my family got to do with anything?"

"Do you know where they are?"

"You have made a big mistake if you are relying on me telling you."

"I don't need you to tell me. But I can promise you that none of them is where you think they are. Or indeed who they are with. If you kill me, you will never learn where they are. My insurance policy is that your wife and children will be killed in the event of my death. They are already mortal."

I felt my pulse quicken and the red mist descend. "That is bullshit." And I pulled the trigger and launched the dart in her direction. It hit her just above her left breast. She winced from the pain. I quickly reloaded a third dart. I wasn't going to risk a rib stopping the ketamine. I pointed the gun at her in readiness, but it wasn't needed because she keeled over the side of the seat, causing it to eject its Titanic load and tip her onto the floor. I had to move quickly because the effect of the drug would wear off within ninety minutes. I stripped the pair of them off completely. I needed to ensure they were free from any more golden weapons. Themis had her knife inside her pants between her butt cheeks. Held in place by her thong. I refrained from doing a full cavity search. Somehow, I didn't think it was appropriate.

I had hours to wait until it was dark enough for me to dump them in the boot of my car. All I could do was sit tight and wait until Helios set in the west.

I had a couple of darts to hand. I needed to keep them anaesthetised. I phoned Pete, "Hey Pete, I need you and Giannis here as quick as you can. I have two unconscious goddesses that I need to get to Olympian. I can't do it on my own."

"I will bring Zeus too. They both need to be immortalised again."

"How many more need immortalising?"

"That's it. The others escaped to our hideout at Monolithos."

"One last thing. Giannis isn't still besotted with Nemesis, is he?"

"No, that relationship is dead and buried. He is more likely to kill her than kiss her."

"OK, just be quick. I am in unknown territory here. I'm pumping them full of drugs. And I don't want to be the one that kills them. Too many bar owners know they are here."

It seemed like an eternity till they all got to Pine Trees. I had to dart both of them twice. I tried putting their clothes back on them, but it seems getting the clothes off a goddess is more straightforward than getting them back on again.

When they finally arrived, I gave Pete a quick induction on the ketamine darts. Told him to keep the ladies nearby and the first sign of life. Give them another dose. He knew how to immortalise Giannis and Zeus.

While they were doing that, it bought me a couple of hours. I needed to visit the bar owners that had been part of the subterfuge. I also needed an ouzo or two. I made an excuse to Giannis and Zeus that I would catch up with them once they were immortal again. I think Pete knew I needed my aniseed fix because he said, "Come back sober, Rod," and he winked at me.

Zaf said, "Did the ladies find you?"

"Yes, and thanks for sending them. Give us an ouzo, mate."

"You didn't say they would be so beautiful."

"Even better than that, they are at Pine Trees naked and asleep." I thought by telling him the truth, he was less likely to believe me.

"Oh yes. I forgot you are a super stud, Rod." We both laughed.

"Give us another," I said, slamming my shot glass down on the bar.

"Are you celebrating the afternoon?" And he gave a wink and a cheeky grin.

"To be honest, I am drinking to forget ha-ha."

I didn't stop for more than the two. I had other bars to visit in the next couple of hours. I told the same story at all of them and got the same disbelieving retort from each of them. I was at Karma when a text arrived from Pete.

'All done.'

I didn't reply. I just staggered back to Pine Trees.

≈≈≈

"Jesus, Rod, you're drunk again."

"I told you I think more clearly when I've had an ouzo."

"Well, think clearly for the next hour. It isn't dark enough yet to load these two into the boot of the car. You can tell us what has gone on."

"And, Zeus and Giannis, you can fill me in on recent events at Olympian Dreams." I slumped into my chair at the head of the boardroom table, which they'd left vacant for me.

The semi-clad Nemesis let out a groan, and Pete said, "Time for a top-up. I have been administering it manually so that we could get them dressed."

"I wouldn't have stripped them, except Nemesis had her dagger stuffed inside her shorts."

"We did wonder about your motive."

"Anyway, what news from Olympian."

Zeus was the first to relate the story. "Right up until yesterday, we thought they were protecting us from the coup. When Apollo and I raised concerns about what they expected us to do, they mortalised us. It then became clear that they had side-lined you. And tried to mortalise the entire board."

"What raised your suspicions?"

"Nemesis started to probe Apollo about the whereabouts of Kam and the kids."

Giannis chipped in, "Don't worry. I didn't give away their locations."

"I know you didn't. I spoke to each of them last week. And told them to move somewhere else. As soon as I realised that the coup had already happened. I took the opportunity to get them all to safety. Minus their chaperones."

"Why without the chaperones?" Asked Zeus.

"I learnt a long time ago that when dealing with deities, it is better to trust no one."

I then relayed all the clues I had picked up that suggested Themis was the force behind the coup. How alarm bells were ringing for a while. I related my interaction with Yiayia. Their reaction was one of incredulity that I had placed so much trust in an elderly eccentric. I told them that my constant drinking started as a means of appearing to be a typical British tourist. Then it became a way of occupying the boredom. Then I realised that it freed up my mind to be able to consider otherwise unimaginable thoughts. This was needed because everything about the gods and immortality was a bizarre notion. It defied reality. My mind needed to be free of conventional thinking.

"And, of course, you were broken by Affi's death," pointed out Pete.

I paused for a moment as I considered what Affi meant to me. "Nah. She was just a casualty of war. I used her to gain knowledge of the gods," I bluffed.

"You are kidding yourself. I saw it from the outside. She was your lover, your nymph." Pete was blunt in his witness statement.

I shrugged my shoulders. "Whatever. Her death was why I needed to get my family to safety. I wasn't going to lose anyone else. We need to remember that the danger is still present." I nodded towards the two sedated goddesses on the boardroom floor.

Zeus said, "We must decide what we do with them. We can't keep them sedated forever."

Giannis joined the conversation, "They need to be killed."

Zeus had to remind him. "We can't kill other gods unless it is in self-defence."

Giannis retorted, "And whose law is that?"

"Underworld?" Suggested Pete.

"Come on, Pete, we all know the underworld doesn't exist. They need to be neutralised. Subjugated."

After a lot of discussions, Zeus proclaimed he had the answer. "We could set them free and tell them where your family are located. When they go to attack your kin, the Olympians would be allowed to kill them in defence of your family."

"No way! There is absolutely no way on earth we are using any of my family as bait. No, no and no. And if you tried that, I would kill you. Forget the self-defence argument. Giannis is right. It's Themis's law. I think we can ignore it if we're killing Themis."

"It looks like you have provided the answer. You kill them. Here and now, just do it."

"No. I can't kill them. I don't have it in me. We just need to have some hold over them, to subjugate them. Have them fear for their lives.

"How? What is your plan?"

"I don't know. I don't have one. Except I'm not going to kill them. And my family aren't going to be worms, dangling on hooks, so that you can kill them."

"We can't keep injecting them with ketamine forever," added Pete.

"I know that. We will have to keep them imprisoned until I can think of something. What happened with Oceanus and co. Weren't they imprisoned?"

"Yes, at first. But we didn't know that Themis was their master in the coup. When she doled out their punishment. She released them."

"For fucks sake. They may still be around. Well, these two can be locked up the same way. But they won't be getting parole until I say so. It's dark outside now. I'll help you get them into the car. Then you can take them to Olympian and secure them."

"And what will you do?" Asked Giannis.

"Me? I am going to try and find a solution."

"You mean to get drunk and play with your cards." Accused Zeus.

Pete made a futile attempt to offer me advice. "You won't find the solution in a bottle of ouzo."

I couldn't see the point of continuing that conversation. I just grunted and picked up Themis' legs. "Come on, let's hide the problem."

I waited until the car, with its godly cargo, had left the hotel. I grabbed my playing cards and headed for the appropriately named Enigma. I planned to develop a solution once and for all. It had to be one that didn't involve being a murderer.

≈≈≈

"Hi Suzana, a bottle of ouzo, please."

"Did the women find you?"

"Yes. Thanks for sending them to me." I smiled at her as I sauntered off to find a dark corner to share a heart to heart with myself and the ouzo.

What was it Zeus said? "Of course, it is OK to kill them. It is a war. People die in wars." Somehow, I didn't think the police would swallow that while they were interrogating me.

At least, I would probably be considered to have diminished responsibilities. No, there must be another way.

I sank another shot of thought fertiliser. *Something will come to me.* I pulled out the cards and did the customary seven-time shuffle. I asked myself the question I wanted to be answered.

How do I destroy someone without killing them? I bet the damned ace of spades comes out first.

I flipped the top card. It was a relief to see it was the queen of diamonds.

No need to shuffle again then.

I placed it on the table in front of me and dealt out four more cards face-down. I imagined that the queen was Themis. *Will this quad of cards reveal the method of dealing with her?*

I broke the internal tension by taking another shot, and I didn't use the shot glass. I swigged it straight from the bottle.

A trick I'd learnt was that a big swig was worth two shots. I had another big swig for good measure.

Before I could unfold the answer to my question, my phone pinged. It was a text from Pete:

'Sad news. Jet is dead.'

I wasn't going to mess around texting back. I called him. "How do you know?"

"We ran her over on the way back here."

"What do you mean? 'We ran over her'. What kind of statement is that? Are you sure it's her?"

"Yes, I am sure. It is Jet. The golden claws prove it. She must have known there were gods in the car, and she tried to attack it while we were moving. There was nothing we could do. I'm so sorry, Rod."

I was stunned. I wanted to scream; I threw my phone down onto the table. As it slid across the slick surface, it dislodged the top card from the remaining 48 cards of the deck. I flicked it over, and though the tears were forming in my eyes, I could see it was that damned Ace of Spades I'd come to hate so much. I loved that blasted cat, and she loved me. She was my crutch, my protector. And now she was gone. I blamed myself. I'd put her in danger too many times, and she'd run out of her arsenal of lives. I knew she would die for me, and she'd finally proved it. I was torn between loss and anger. The way I felt when Affi was killed.

Somehow the cards didn't seem to be relevant anymore. I was about to pack them away when I heard a voice behind me. "Hello, Mister Rod. Let's finish your reading, and you can share your bottle with me." It was Yiayia.

"I'm going to be bad company, I'm afraid."

She looked down at the Ace of Spades. "Why do you have six cards spread across the table?"

I explained the whole phone thing and the death of Jet. "...These are the five cards I dealt first." And I gestured to the red queen and the four cards waiting to be turned.

She picked up the ace. "This card was the cat's destiny. Do not concern yourself with the cat. It was its time. The card says that if she hadn't been hit by the car, she would have died by some other means." And she placed it face-down on the deck.

What she was saying seemed to make sense. I took a swig from the bottle and placed it in front of the chair on the opposite side of the table. She smiled and picked it up as she simultaneously occupied the seat. She took several big mouthfuls of the aniseed nectar. She gulped it the way a kid drinks pop when they are rushing to get back to play.

She let out an aniseed belch and placed the bottle in front of me. "What was the question you asked of these five cards?"

Between the ouzo and Yiayia's reassurance that it was Jet's time, the tide of grief subsided. "I asked how I destroy someone without killing them."

She smiled. "I have seen that question asked many times. And many times, the advice has been ignored. You must heed the cards. They will show you the only way. Any other path will involve you killing someone."

Suddenly my feelings of grief returned. Had I somewhere along the way missed a signal from the cards. I took another swig of ouzo.

Yiayia looked at me. "I told you don't blame yourself for the cat."

Damn, she reads minds too.

I wiped the moisture that was still clouding my vision. "OK, so what does the Queen of Diamonds tell me?"

"You wrote it down on your piece of paper."

"I know, but as you are here, sharing my ouzo, I would like your interpretation."

She reached for the bottle and stuck it in her mouth, let out a burp and said, "This queen is a fair-haired woman. A woman of the earth, she may be a gossip."

She hadn't even put the bottle down while she related the details of the card. She took another healthy swig and offered me the bottle. "Next card."

I took a regular mouthful. No way was I going to try to match Yiayia. I put the bottle down and turned the next card. "Two of diamonds. Wasn't that a change in a business partnership?"

"Yes. But it is a card that carries with it gossip. This is a big confirmation for the queen. Next card."

I turned the next card over. "Nine of Hearts." I looked at Yiayia full of expectation, and she didn't take a swig of ouzo. I wasn't expecting that.

"This is the card associated with wishes. Your wish will come true. We look to the previous cards to find where the answer to your wish lies." She nodded at me to turn over the next card.

I copied her pace and didn't have a drink. "Another two. Two of Clubs."

"Your path is becoming clearer. This card points to obstacles to your success. This may take the form of malicious gossip."

I frowned. I was confused. She was smiling as if she knew the answer to the question. All I could see was that I wasn't going to succeed because of malicious gossip. "I don't understand. I don't see the answer to my question in these cards."

"Then turn the last card." This time she took her customary swig, then offered the bottle to me.

I took a mouthful and flipped the last card. "Two of Spades. I knew there would be a spade in here somewhere. It is bad, isn't it?"

"On its own, I would say yes. It points to break-ups and deceit. If the question involved a lover, it would be warning you of a breakup because they were unfaithful. I assume the person you want to destroy isn't a lover." And she smiled before taking a mouthful of ouzo.

"No, it isn't about a love interest, far from it."

"It doesn't matter anyway. There is a much more powerful message in these cards. Do you remember asking me what it meant if you drew all four of the twos in a reading?"

"Yes. I do remember. It means I am at a crossroads."

"And there is a more powerful drive that comes with a triple of twos. It means the direction of the reading is reversed."

"What? The question is reversed?" In my head, I reversed the question.

How do I kill someone without destroying them?

"No, the question isn't reversed. The person you asked the question of is reversed."

I was still confused. "Someone is asking how they can destroy me without killing me?"

"If you like, yes. That is a way of understanding it. The answer they would get lies in the first four cards. Ask yourself the question, what would destroy Mr Rod without killing him?"

"Shit. I wish I'd thought about the question properly. I was destroyed when my hotel manager was killed. I feel destroyed now that Jet has been killed. But using that answer means I must still kill someone. A loved one of the persons concerned."

She sat back in her chair, hugging the bottle of ouzo. "It is your interpretation that is flawed. Not the question that you asked. Ask yourself this question: What would destroy Mr Rod without anyone dying? Then you will find the answer you seek. And remember, the answer is in the first four cards." She stood up to leave, still hugging my bloody ouzo. I cleared my throat and held out my hand. She smiled and handed me the bottle. I bid her farewell as I settled into the continued lubrication of my thought processes.

I was joined by Kitler. He didn't look his usual self. I guessed he already knew about Jet. I didn't see the point of trying to explain to him. I looked at the bottle.

Bitch. She has only left me a mouthful. I put the cards back in my pocket. Drank the last of the ouzo. Swapped the bottle for my phone and left Enigma. I shouted, "Kali Nichta Suzana." I didn't know if she replied as I staggered out and along the road. I thought of Adel's song Chasing Pavements as each step I took seemed to land on a moving pavement. I tried hard not to stagger, but it was too much effort, so I wobbled all the way back. I'm sure that I had to step back more than once to stop myself from falling over. It reminded me of Alyss when she was 10 months old, trying to walk for the first time. By the time I got back to my apartment, I was crying drunken tears. They say alcohol is a depressant, and it was certainly doing its job on me that night. I was overwhelmed with self-pity. I missed my family.

I drifted off to sleep with tears soaking into my pillow.

Pheme

I had a rough night. I felt total isolation. I could feel the clouds of doom closing in on me. I had nightmare after nightmare. It was still dark, but waking up seemed a relief until my mind wandered back to the previous evenings reading and the lonely walk back to the empty hotel. I stripped off the clothes I'd fallen asleep in. I jumped in the shower. I wanted to wash away the depression that was clouding my thoughts. I shaved hard. I tried to scrape out the negativity that was drawing me down. The razor stung my face with every scrape of its triple blade. My bloodshot eye's stared back at me from the bathroom mirror, and I glanced down at a half-filled glass of ouzo.

What's the matter with you, man? For god's sake, sort yourself out, and pull yourself together.

I answered my own question out loud, "I miss Kam and the kids." I reached down and picked up the glass. I raised it to my nose and inhaled the aniseed aroma. I opened my mouth, ready to slug it and saw someone in the mirror. Someone I didn't recognise. A naked man with scratches all over his face. Amber blood dripping from his chin. He was about to neck an ouzo in the bathroom. What I saw disgusted me.

What the fuck have I become?

I dropped the glass into the scummy water in the sink. It joined the whiskers that I'd scraped from my face.

I stuck bits of toilet tissue on each of the cuts. The amber blood stains on the bog paper telling me that I was still immortal.

An immortal drunkard. Right, pull yourself together. Get dressed and start over.

Suit trousers, shirt, and tie. Clothes I hadn't worn for such a long time. I was travelling back in time; I was returning to my life before shit happened. A time before, the board cast me out. I was blocking out everything that had dragged me down. I sat in the boardroom. Looked at the window overlooking Nine-lives. I'd thought about getting another cat but knew inside that if I was journeying back, I wouldn't have even had Jet. I phoned Pete, "Get the Olympian board together. For a meeting in two hours."

I had an hour to prepare, so I hit Google. Unusually, it provided an answer with the first search... Pheme is the Greek word for a rumour. This gave me time to make a few calls, and I was set for the meeting. I glanced around the boardroom before locking it. I locked the hotel down completely. "Bye, Pine Trees. See you some time."

I walked across to Angel. "Rod, are you going to a wedding?"

"No, Zaf. I am going on an odyssey. I may be gone a while. Keep an eye on Pine Trees for me. You have my number if you need to contact me."

"Are you going to be gone for long?"

"Maybe. I don't know. That's the point of an odyssey."

"It took Odysseus twenty years to complete his journey."

"No. I am sure it won't be that long."

"You want an ouzo before you go?"

"Nope, I can't stand the stuff." Zaf looked at me, puzzled. And I left. I left Pefkos, no looking back, no lump in the throat, no regrets, no fear, and no possessions.

≈≈≈

I sat in the boardroom of Olympian dreams. All my senses stood to attention. They were telling me that what I was about to do was right. I could hear my own pulse, taste my own adrenaline. The wall clock to my right, counting the seconds with an approving tic-tic-tic. I'd sat in the chair usually reserved for Zeus. This meeting was to be on my terms. I played with the komboloi that the board had given me for protection.

Pete was the first to arrive. "Zeus will object to you sitting in his chair."

I just laughed. "Are they all coming?"

"Of course, what is the meeting about?"

"Mostly to decide on what to do next," I said, not wanting to give too much away. The rest of the board started to arrive. And as ever, Zeus was late. When he entered the room, he faltered as he saw me sitting at the head of the table. Not a word was spoken. He just lowered his shoulders and slumped into the chair that used to be mine.

"Welcome, everyone. I have rewound the clock." And every one of them looked at the clock and then at me. I tutted. "Metaphorically, I have turned back the clock." They all smiled, but I don't think they grasped what I meant. "Do you remember the meeting where you gave me this?" And I slid the komboloi across the table. They all nodded.

Zeus looked at me and said, "We do remember, and we are sorry."

"Well, today is that day again. There will be no talk of a coup. You can take your komboloi back because I no longer need it. I don't need your protection. Today we plan how we are to undo everything that has happened." They still looked confused. Poor Helios sat there open-mouthed with a gormless look on his face. He was never going to understand what I was trying to do.

"What do you mean undo everything that has happened?" Asked Giannis.

"We are going to rewrite the last few months. I was never cast out. There was no coup. I never had a hotel manageress, no cat. There was no Phobos, no Deimos, no Oceanus, no Themis and no Nemesis."

"We cannot rewrite history. We cannot make these things disappear," said Zeus.

"We can. You have been doing it for thousands of years. All but one of the gods involved is now mortal. They will know they will die at some point. We are the only ones that can immortalise them again before they die. We have ultimate power over them. The power of life or death. They are going to do whatever we say."

"You want to immortalise them again," said Hades.

"No, but they don't know that. The key is going to be your aunt."

"Which aunt?"

"Your aunt Pheme. The goddess of rumour." Suddenly everyone was paying attention. "Listen. The only people that know of anything that has gone on here are those directly involved."

"What about Aletheia?" Asked Pete.

Damn, I'd forgotten about her.

"Leave that to me." I bluffed.

"Where does Pheme come into it?" Asked Zeus.

"We feed her whatever rumours we want. These rumours should destroy the reputation of all the gods that know what has gone on. What I need the board to do is to figure out what rumours to spread. Particularly what will destroy them in the eyes of the pantheon. You should be able to do it. You did it to me. You isolated me and destroyed me. Now I want you to do it to them. Nobody gets immortalised unless I say so."

Pete looked at Zeus. "Can you get Pheme to go along with Rods plan?"

"Of course. I will contact her immediately." Zeus was about to leave his seat and the meeting.

"Stop. The meeting isn't over yet. I have one more item."

Zeus sat back down. Again, I was the centre of attention.

"I am hoping to bring my family back to the island. I would be grateful if there was no mention of the incident with Aphrodite, at least, until I have had a chance to speak to them first."

Giannis winked and smiled. "Who is Aphrodite?" The rest of the room nodded in assent at my request.

Then the all-seeing idiot spoke out. "Didn't Kam leave you for Asclepius?"

The whole room looked at Helios. Giannis mouthed a shush at him.

I glared at him. "Well, that's your first mistake. Listening to idle gossips and false rumours. I left her."

"Why did you leave her?"

Now he is taunting me.

"Because I knew what was coming. I wanted her kept safe." I lied.

"You knew what was coming?"

"Yep, the cards and my oracle told me."

Pete looked at me. He knew what I was doing. He knew that I didn't have an interest in cartomancy at the time I was cast out. "Yes, didn't you know that Rod consults the cards to map out decisions?"

Nice one Pete, that is the first rumour

Giannis, not wanting to seem as if he didn't understand, joined in. "Let's face it, Helios, You are an idiot, and you always have been. All-seeing pfft, you can't see Jack." And he laughed as he seized the opportunity to bully Helios. I laughed because Giannis used the expression 'Jack'. Helios was just open-mouthed. The fool was amazed and didn't even realise he was being picked on.

"Wow. Can you see the future?"

"Of course. Let me show you." And I pulled my trusty cards out of my pocket. "The card on top of the pack is the

Ace of Spades." I offered him the pack to check for himself.

He turned over the card, and sure enough, it was the Ace of Spades. He was still open-mouthed and couldn't speak.

Close your mouth. It makes you look gormless.

Everyone was amazed at how I had predicted the card. I refrained from telling them that it was the card that Yiayia had placed back on the top of the pack.

All I had to do was figure out how to deal with Aletheia. Knowing she was the goddess of truth reminded me that she could undo any rumours that Pheme could spread. The more pressing problem was how to explain to Kam the events surrounding Affi. After all, my relationship with Affi didn't compare to Kam's relationship with Asclepius.

Except you kicked Kam out of your life.

I wasted no time in contacting my family. I was excited at the prospect of seeing them again. Kam said she couldn't see the point if I was going to row with her again. She took a lot of persuading, but she did agree to visit and talk about our marriage.

≈≈≈

The kids were the first to arrive. I call them kids, but they were both adults with lives of their own. They'd stayed hidden in Greece. Alyss with Athena in Athens, despite me telling her not to tell Athena where she was hiding. Lindon, likewise, had ignored my instructions to shed himself of Artemis, his godly chaperone. As I said, they were adults, but I would have thought they would at least listen to my warning. The fact that they'd ignored me stung my pride like an angry wasp.

I'd arrange with Filipos to have a suite at Helios. Just like old times. We were on the sundeck alongside the private pool. It brought back so many memories and lots of anecdotes. We swapped stories of our lives while we'd been separated.

The pair of them soaked up my edited version of the past few months. Why I hadn't been able to contact them. The ebb and flow of the tide of trust between the gods and me.

Alyss was as chatty as ever, full of her new life with Athena. She didn't appear to have missed the family at all. She had her own tales to tell. I felt a twinge of jealousy that her main love was Athena. Gone were the days that her daddy filled her heart. I consoled myself that it was a different kind of love, and there was room in her heart for both.

Lindon was a lot more pensive and reserved than I'd ever seen him. I'd expected him to be full of the wonders of the natural world that he'd photographed on his tour with Artemis. "What's troubling you, son?"

"It's nothing. Really, it's nothing."

"This is your dad you are talking to. I know something is wrong. You might as well tell me. You know your mum will get it out of you when she gets here."

Lindon and Alyss looked at each other. "I'll leave you guys to it," said Alyss. As subtle as ever, she was signalling something was wrong, and she knew what it was.

Jesus, I hope he doesn't know about Affi. "OK, son, spill. What's the matter?"

He started to get all watery-eyed, and this wasn't the ordinarily nonchalant Lindon. I put my arm around his shoulder. "Come on. Man to man, no judgement offered."

He looked at me through tear-filled eyes. He took a deep breath and blurted out, "I have let you down."

"Oh, son, you could never let me down. I am proud of you and what you have achieved in your life. Do you remember what Filipos always used to say to us? If you believe what you are doing is right, then it must be right. Live life with no regrets. Whatever you have done, it hasn't let me down."

His teary eyes started to overflow, and the salty stream cascaded down his cheeks. "This time, it is a life-changing mistake."

"Jesus, we all make mistakes. We just need to learn from them. You'll never let me down by making a mistake. I just want you to be open with me. To trust that I won't judge you. Don't you remember how your mum and I reacted when Alyss told us she was a lesbian?"

"This is different."

"No, it's not. You're just expecting too much from yourself. None of us is perfect. Don't you remember I used to joke about me being the Prince of Fuck-ups?"

"Well, I've taken your throne on that one."

"We'll never know unless you share."

He took another deep breath. "Artemis is pregnant."

It took all my willpower to stop myself from laughing out loud. I did smile, while inside, I was roaring with laughter. "How is that letting me down? I want to be happy for you. Your mum will be over the moon. We're going to be grandparents."

"It's not the pregnancy that's the problem. It is the lies I have told. I love Artemis, but I promised her it was only platonic. I know you hate liars."

It was my turn to take a deep breath.

Why did he have to say platonic?

My thoughts sprinted back to Affi. And my secrets and lies that would be surfacing when Kam came back.

"See, I told you I had let you down."

"No, you haven't let me down. When you made the promise, it was platonic. That is no lie. Your feelings grew after that. How does Artemis feel about this platonic relationship becoming parenthood?"

"She hasn't said. We've only just found out. She's more worried about what Zeus will say. Don't forget she is a proper daddy's girl."

"Pffft. She needn't worry about him. I have absolute control over him. The first thing you must do is talk with her, find out how she feels about the pregnancy. Just don't worry about your mum and me. It is good news. And you haven't let either of us down."

≈≈≈

It was reassuring that Lindon said he loved Artemis and wanted to be with her. I needed him to find out how she felt about the pregnancy. Potentially this could be the key that would allow me to officially become part of the Zeus dynasty. Instead of controlling him from the shadows. The conversation with Lindon did cause me to examine my own conscience. I had to decide how much I was going to reveal to Kam. And that problem was on the horizon in an Airbus 320, somewhere over Germany. And it was only a few hours away from landing.

It transpired that neither of the kids had seen Kam since before she went to look after her mum. Despite my reassurances, backed by Alyss, Lindon was still concerned about what his mum would say. Alyss was excited to be seeing her mum after so long. Me? I was shitting myself. Would Kam forgive me for kicking her out? How would she take my platonic relationship with Affi? I might get away with it if I don't go into too much detail.

All I knew was that I wanted an ouzo more than anything. I kept thinking back to the card reading and destroyed reputations. Could the cards have been pointing to the destruction of my standing with Kam? A good shot of ouzo would have helped to clarify the way forward. I still hadn't decided how much I should reveal.

Lindon wanted me to go to the airport on my own to collect Kam. I knew what he wanted. He wanted me to tell his mum for him. I was OK with that, but then I wouldn't have a chance to break my news first. Alyss was desperate to see her mum and relate her own news. In the end, I said I would go alone and collect her. They would have plenty of time to talk to her because I hoped Kam was back for good, even if it meant bringing her mum to Rhodes.

≈≈≈

"I'm surprised you didn't get Zeus to pick me up in George," said Kam.

"Don't go there. We are living in a different world now. Come here woman, I need a hug." I pulled her towards me, "I have missed you so much."

"Really? And I thought you kicked me out," she said as she kissed me. This was a different kiss from what I'd anticipated. I expected a full-on snog with tongues and all. This was more like a quick peck as if I was on my way to work.

Shit, I bet she still loves Asclepius.

We both started to speak at the same time, "I've got so much …"

Then I made the mistake of saying "You first,"

"I've got so much to tell you. Rich has been brilliant. I don't know how he did it, but mum is like a new woman. No more aches and pains. She has been so happy these past few months."

Oh, he is still Rich, is he? That's why you stayed there so long?

So much for me giving her my news and bringing her up to speed. She barely stopped talking all the way to Helios. The only gaps in her dialogue were when she came up for air. She kept banging on about how wonderful Richard had been. How he was a godsend. He had done this, and he had done that. She had learnt so much from him. How clever he was. How it was him that developed the transfusions that allowed us to become immortal. How it was him that discovered that gold could turn amber blood back to normal blood. "Did you know the NHS and ambulance service use the staff with a snake wrapped around it? Well, that is because of Rich."

She took a breath, and this gave me a chance to speak."Yes, I did, and not just in the UK." And then, as soon as she had got her breath back, she continued her monologue. We pulled onto the hotel's gravelled car park, and she was still talking.

The kids were there waiting for us.

Fucking great. Now I get to break my news with an audience.

She was out of the car before I could even stop the engine. "My babies…" They got proper hugs and lots of kisses. Lindon was still a bit distant, but the girls were both talking at lightning speed. I don't know how they manage to give each other a turn when talking together. I can never find the gap to say something. I guessed it was a woman thing. Some hidden signal that suggested the talking baton was being passed from one to the other. They managed to tell their different stories simultaneously, yet; it didn't seem like two different tales. I looked at Lindon and nodded my head to the right. He gave an understanding nod.

"Right, girls, you've obviously got a lot of catching up to do. You go and get settled; us boys will be in the bar." Neither of them appeared to hear us. Their conversation just carried on. I guessed they heard us because Alyss picked up her mums' luggage, and they set off towards room 208.

"Come on, son, let's have a drink."

≈≈≈

"Did you get a chance to talk to mum about Artemis?"

I just laughed, sank my second ouzo and said, "You're joking. She hasn't stopped talking since I picked her up. As soon as she and Alyss started, I knew we wouldn't have a chance of getting her attention. That's why I dragged you here. You need her undivided attention."

"I don't want to be alone when I tell her."

"You won't be. Come on, get that ouzo down you. The ice

is melting and watering it down."

I signalled to Tsambikos for two more shots, "No ice this time, please."

He put two clean shot glasses on the bar and left the bottle. I filled up the glasses and pushed one towards Lindon. "Here is to breaking news. Yammas!" and we both swallowed our shots and slammed the glasses down hard onto the bar.

Lindon smiled, "Do you remember that Mexican night we had with the salt and limes?"

"I remember it all right. I was puking all night." We both laughed at the memory.

I signalled to Tsambikos again. He just waved his hand at the bottle. "Unless you want ice or water, help yourself." *God, I love Greek filoxenia.*

"I can't get drunk before I tell mum about Artemis."

"Don't be daft. Of course you can. I think better, and I'm more creative with a few inside me. Besides, it will stop you fretting all the while."

I used the opportunity to tell him what had been going on those past months. At least I had a chance to give my news to someone. I didn't mention Affi, of course. I owed it to Kam that she should be the first to hear about that escapade. I was feeling drunk but not that drunk that I was going to let that secret slip. I told him all about Pine Trees and how beautiful it was.

"When do we get to see this hotel?

"What hotel?" asked Kam, who had suddenly appeared behind us.

"Plenty of time for that. Do you girls want booze?"

"Yuk no. Cola for me," said Alyss.

I looked at Kam. "Beer for you, I guess, sweetheart."

"No, ouzo is fine. I've started drinking it all the time."

"You never liked it."

Don't tell me… Richard.

"I know. You can blame Richard for that." And she giggled like a bloody teenager.

I signalled to Tsambikos, "Cola, please and another shot glass. Thanks." He smiled and slid a shot glass down the bar. Which was spectacular but pointless because he still had to come to us with the cola. The girls didn't bother pulling up a stool. They wandered off towards an empty table. I signalled to Lindon that we should join them. His mood had changed since the girls had arrived. I was nicely lubricated, and there was no mood change for me.

"Have you two stopped talking now? Because Lindon has got something to say… Grandma." I wasn't going to tell her on his behalf, but he looked petrified.

Kam looked at me, then at Lindon. I could see her processing what I'd said. "Oh my god," she squealed. She wasn't at all upset by it. All she wanted were the technicalities. Who was the mum? When was it due? How far gone? Are you still with the mum? Do you know if it's a boy or girl? She poured us each another ouzo. "Here's to another Prince. Yammas."

"See, son, I told you she would be over the moon about it."

"That's not what the problem is."

Kam had a look of concern. "Problem? What's the

problem?"

"I promised Artemis we would just have a platonic relationship. We got carried away, and I didn't want you to think badly of me."

"Don't be silly. We all have platonic relationships. Someone we love and don't intend for it to become sexual. You won't be the first, and you won't be the last."

I nodded in agreement. Then she broke her own bit of news. "Richard and I have a platonic relationship. I love him and confide in him."

I felt a pang of jealousy start to rise, but a shot of ouzo sorted that. Instead, I saw an opportunity to reveal my bit of news. The moment I had previously been dreading. "Yes. Your mum is right. We all have platonic relationships. Mine was with a woman called Aphrodite." Suddenly all eyes were on me.

"Isn't Aphrodite the goddess of love, beauty, pleasure and passion?" Asked Alyss.

Kam was still looking at me open-mouthed. I quickly answered, "Yes, but this wasn't Aphrodite, the goddess. I thought she might have been because she was so beautiful. I even had her checked out. We had a deep relationship where I shared the secrets with her and even made her immortal."

Kams look of shock changed to a frown. The kids were smirking at each other because they'd seen this scenario before. Dad gets a grilling.

I was speechless while I thought to myself. *It's alright for you lot to have platonic relationships but not me.*

When Lindon spoke, I assumed it would take the heat from

me. But I couldn't have been more wrong. "That's my point, I promised platonic, but it so easily became sexual. It made me wonder if I had lusted after her from the start. I felt I had deceived her. I feel I have let you guys down. I just had to be honest with you."

I swallowed hard, took another ouzo. I am pretty sure I blushed.

Kam looked at me. "Come on then, lover-boy. Tell us about your relationship with Aphrodite."

"There's nothing to tell, really. Affi and I were just good friends."

"Oh, it's Affi now, is it?" *Oh shit, now I'm going to get the entire interrogation.*

I knew there was no point in lying to Kam. I just had to go with it and hope she didn't ask the wrong questions.

I looked back at her. I was looking for an escape route. "Perhaps the kids might not want to hear this. We could discuss it later."

"Why? You aren't going to say anything that will embarrass them, are you? Your relationship with Affi was platonic, wasn't it?" She stressed Affi's name.

"No, what I meant was. Oh, it doesn't matter." I gulped down another ouzo.

"Tell us how far this platonic relationship went. I won't be mad," said Kam. She was doing that friendly thing on me. Being pleasant, suggesting that she wasn't upset. It was aimed at getting me to talk. I'd seen it before, and I'd also learnt to shut up. I knew the number of words that came out of my mouth was proportional to the amount of shit I would eventually be in.

Alyss just smirked. She knew how her mum worked.

Bitch, you're bloody enjoying this, aren't you?

"Come on, dad, don't be shy. If it was platonic, there's nothing to hide."

"Awww, bless him. I bet your dad doesn't even know what platonic means."

"I do. It's when a relationship is intimate but not sexual."

"That's good. If it was platonic, then you didn't have sex."

"That's right." At that point, I thought I'd got away with it. Unfortunately, Kam hadn't finished with me yet. "Would you care to tell us how intimate you did get?"

"We didn't get intimate. Well, not in the way you mean. You don't understand." I was reminded that a woman's command of language is so much greater and more precise than a man's. At that moment, I think I would have rather been in an argument with an angry god than my upset wife.

"Well, help us understand what your version of intimate is. You gave her all the secrets. What did she give you to get you to reveal that much?

"It's a long story. I need to go back to the day you left for England."

"We've got all the time in the world. Haven't we kids?" They both nodded and continued to grin at me. I knew she'd won. She'd even got the kids onside.

There was nothing for it. I had to spill everything and leave myself at the mercy of their empathy. "OK, from the start. But no interruptions or questions. Not until I have finished."

The next few hours became a monologue of me relating

the events of the past few months. I was hoping they would be distracted when I told them I had purchased a hotel in Pefkos. They reacted with smiles when I spoke about Jet. They even laughed when I told them that Jet would attack a god just because they were a god. As an audience, they were good. But they still asked difficult questions when I related anything about Affi. They smiled when I spoke about Yiayia and the cards. They looked sympathetic when I talked about my overuse of ouzo. A vice they had unwittingly helped me continue at that moment.

They looked shocked when I described the 'triple date' with the Oceanids. Kam raised her eyebrows at that, and every time I mentioned Affi.

"And that pretty much sums up my life on my own. It wasn't pleasant. It was lonely. I wanted nothing more than to have you all close. Remember, I once said when we are apart, we are not so powerful. Now I've experienced it, I can confirm it is still true. I need you all near me." I had managed to relay almost every event. Of course, I left out the bedroom scenes and the scent on the pillow that had comforted me for so long.

I think I may have succeeded with this.

"Ok, one last question from me," said Kam.

"Go on."

"You still haven't explained why you had to give Affi all the secrets."

Bugger.

"Well, she kept flirting with me. And I said we could only ever be platonic. If she promised to stop flirting, I said I would tell her everything."

"Just for a bit of flirting. How serious was this flirting?"

Even though she'd requested one last question, I wasn't stupid enough to remind her of that. "It doesn't matter how serious the flirting was. I saw an opportunity to evade what she had in mind, and I took it."

"What did she have in mind?"

Jesus.

"I don't know. I'm not a mind reader."

"That's a kop out. Why won't you tell us if it was so innocent."

"I don't know what she had in mind, but she came on pretty strong. I guessed she wanted more than just friendship. So I knocked that on the head straight away. I got her to agree to keep it platonic provided I shared the secrets with her."

"So how did she know there were secrets to tell?"

"She spotted some text messages that came through. They were from Themis."

"So, how far did she go to get these secrets?"

"She went too far; it was almost embarrassing."

"Come on, don't be shy. No one is going to judge you. What did she do that was too far?"

"Nothing. She was just very touchy-feely, and it made me feel uncomfortable. I just said she had to stop it and keep our friendship platonic. That's all. There is nothing else to tell."

"Ok, I believe you. That's pretty much what Pete told me anyway."

"Eh?"

"Did you think I would leave you all alone without me to stop you from making foolish decisions? I got Pete to keep me updated."

I reacted to her question before her statement sank in. "I don't make mistakes."

She just smiled at me, and the implication of her statement finally hit home. "Then, if you knew it all, why the interrogation?"

She giggled and said, "I just wanted to see you squirm. I've missed that."

Bitch.

I was upset. She'd made me denounce Affi just so she could take the piss out of me.

My voice went up an octave and started to quiver as my anger rose. "I take exception to that. I have been making perfect decisions all along the way. I foiled the coup. I saved the Olympians. I identified the ringleaders. Without me, the Olympians would be no more." I started to tremble.

"And now what?"

"What?"

"If you're so wonderful and mister independent. What are you going to do about the mortal Titans currently waiting for your decision on their future?"

"I don't know yet. I haven't decided."

Kam raised her voice. "I thought you were the man that saved the Olympians. So long as the Titans remain here, the Olympians haven't been saved."

"Don't you think I know that?"

"Well. What's your solution?" And she was now frowning.

"They will be destroyed."

"Great plan. Except that it isn't a plan. It's the solution.

How do you intend to destroy them?"

"I haven't figured that bit yet." I was about to say that the cards hadn't told me, but I knew that would allow her to ridicule me further.

My relationship with Affi had clearly upset her. She was sarcastic and cold, not the way I remembered her. "You still haven't told us about your love nest. Oh, sorry, your hotel."

Just as she was about to throw another cross-examination at me, the ouzo effect reached the 'I don't give a shit' level. "I'll tell you what. I am out of here. And if you kids think it's so funny, get your mum to tell you all about her platonic relationship with Richard."

I just looked at her and sighed. I looked at the kids as a way of apologising. Quite what I was apologising for, god only knows. At least they'd stopped smirking by that point.

"You two might as well go and occupy yourselves. You don't want to be here."

They got up to leave but not before Kam gave one more barbed comment. "What's the matter? Don't you want them to hear about your sordid relationship?"

"We'll see you two later," said Lindon.

At that point, I'd had enough.

Who the hell does she think she is? Questioning my judgments over the previous few months. If she'd bloody been here, I wouldn't have had so many decisions to make.

"Was it necessary to involve the kids in your belittling of me?"

"I suppose you want to shirk your responsibility to them too?"

"Jesus, Kam. What's got into you?"

"I don't like being crapped on, that's what."

"Nobody is crapping on you. I've done nothing wrong."

That was the blue touch-paper. "Don't fucking lie to me," she screamed." Tsambikos looked over at us. He tried not to make it obvious.

"Shut the fuck up and listen for once. Everything I have done has been for the safety of you and the kids. Yes, I had to do my best to protect the Olympians, and sometimes my behaviour has been borderline. But it has always been for you and the kids. I've told you everything. I'm not lying. If you don't accept that, then go back to England and Richard. He is good at listening to your problems by all accounts. But if you decide to stay here, you must let it drop and leave me to get on with my job. Without me, the Olympians are nothing. Christ, I'm as good as King of the Gods."

"Yes, that'll be right. You're even turning into Zeus. Pete was right."

"And why shouldn't I. We have the same powers, but I am much more intelligent. And Pete can go and fuck himself. He's supposed to be my crony, not yours. Let's see how he copes when I cast him out."

"Oh yes, he told me about you giving him your amulet. The one you had made for Affi."

"Yes. That's right. At least she knew her place and would never talk to me the way you are. You go and find Pete and tell him he didn't know everything, and neither do you. I'm off. I'll be in Pefkos if you want me. Your friend Pete knows where."

"That's right, run away. Your good at that."

I turned and looked at her. I didn't want to hate her, but at that point, I was sick of the sight of her. "I'm not running away. I'm going where I can get some respect."

The drive to Pine Trees was long and lonely. All I'd wanted was a happy reunion. To be one family again. I just needed to be loved and appreciated. I wanted... the impossible... because she was dead.

Eureka

Back at Pine Trees, I felt secure. I was alone, but not lonely. I had my cards and my bottle of ouzo. My phone kept buzzing, and I guessed who it was. I didn't need to look because I didn't want to talk to any of them.

They were either with me or against me. Every one of them at Helios had turned against me at some point. I had a new reality. I was alone, and I knew I could succeed alone. I didn't need information, knowledge, or company. I didn't need support or treachery from any of them.

I had all I needed. Cards, ouzo and the Internet

They will need me long before I need them.

I had plans to make, and my bottle of ouzo was going to help me. I swallowed straight from the bottle. I had long since passed the stage where the first swig burnt my throat. I took a lancet and stabbed it into my thumb, which oozed amber blood. I picked up the cards and started to shuffle them. I finally understood what the last reading was telling me. It was about destroying someone with gossip. I hadn't guessed it was going to be Pete's gossip. I was going to have the last laugh because it hadn't destroyed me, but it had motivated me to succeed. To show all of them that I didn't need them. For the first time, I was willing the first card to be the Ace of Spades. I stopped shuffling so that I could take another shot from my bottled friend. *Can you take ouzo intravenously?* I thought to myself. *I've got all the right equipment in the basement.*

I continued shuffling the pack. The edges of the cards were becoming stained by the amber blood that was still bubbling from my thumb. If only I still had Affi. I opened my desk drawer and searched among the chaos that was my filing system.

It's here somewhere. I know it is.

And then I found it. My half-used bottle of kitten fur. I squirted it all over the cards. That'll clean the blood off them, and it smells good too. The cards were becoming difficult to shuffle. *They are giving me a signal. Time to stop shuffling.*

I slammed the cards down on the table and neatened the pile so that it formed a perfectly shaped cuboid. I'd already decided which cards I wanted to appear first. I was searching for affirmation that the plan I had in mind was the right plan. I knocked five times on top of the cards. Not for any reason other than Yiayia always did it.

I swallowed more ouzo, and my bloody phone pinged again. I picked it up, and it was a text from Zaf. I opened it.

'The ladies are back.'

Shit. Pete took all the tranquilliser with him.

I jumped up and failed to kill the lights just as I heard hammering on the door. I could hear them Talking to each other. "Of course he is in there. The lights are on."

"He probably thinks we have come here to exact our

retribution."

"No, he will have read our text."

Shit. The ignored messages. I scrolled through the list of senders. There were several from Kam and the kids. A couple from Pete and one from Themis. I tapped the screen and opened the one from Themis.

'We are free. We have a proposition.'

I knew it. Everyone is fucking useless.

The banging on the door continued. "Rod, it is me, Themis. Let us in. We mean you no harm."

I reached over to the table and took a swig from the bottle. *I'm the immortal one, and I'm not hiding from them.* I opened the door and paused for a while. Long enough for them to see me silhouetted by the boardroom lights. At last, they stopped banging the door.

"What do you want?" I shouted through the glass.

"We just want to talk. Please let us in."

"Why should I talk to you? You are mere mortals."

"Here, have these," and Nemesis stooped and slid two coins under the glass door. It was their amulets. I picked them up and inspected them. Sure enough, they were amulets of female deities. As was always the case, the poorly minted features meant I could only tell they were female. But the wording on the back confirmed they were the correct amulets. Nemesis had τιμωρία - retribution on the back of hers and Themis had δικαιοσύνη - justice stamped on hers.

I turned the lock to let them in. The words of Apollo echoed in my head. *When dealing with deities, it is better to trust no one.* I didn't trust this pair. I had no trust left to give. I'd reached a point where I didn't even trust Kam. I latched the door behind them and ushered them towards the brightness of the boardroom.

"Ouzo?" I asked, waving the bottle in the air.

They both shook their heads. I took a swig before sitting down in my chair. They reacted by sitting themselves at the opposite end of the table.

"Don't worry, ladies. I don't have any more tranquiliser. And if you have no weapons, I won't need to strip your clothes off this time." I laughed to myself. *They probably didn't realise it was me that had stripped them.*

They blushed. Themis said, "This visit has a different purpose to the last one."

"We want to make you King of the Gods."

"No, you fucking don't. The coup is over, you lost, and the Olympians want to kill you. You've come to me in desperation to try and save yourselves."

"Yes. What you say is true. But Zeus fears you, and we can offer you the loyalty of all the Titans and Oceanids."

"I don't want loyalty. I can get loyalty anytime by making people fearful of me. That is how Zeus has always worked. All it has done is put a target on his back."

Nemesis joined the conversation. "Everyone is fearful of you anyway. And as you say, you have a target on your back."

"Exactly! This kind of loyalty that you promise me is something I already have."

This shut them up. I could see they were exchanging glances. I guessed they knew that I didn't need them.

Themis took up the negotiations again. "What do you

want? What will buy us our lives?"

"I want believers. You both understand how powerful I am. Otherwise, you wouldn't be here. The Olympians have known for a long time how powerful I am. I want followers that acknowledge how powerful I am and love me for it. I do want to be King of the Gods. But I can do it without your help."

"How?"

I laughed. "You are mistaking me for Zeus if you think I am going to tell you that."

I could smell the fear in the room. I took a couple of mouthfuls of ouzo.

"You can only have that kind of power if all immortals are made mortal."

"I'm afraid you underestimate what is needed. I will only have absolute power once everyone that knows of the power of gold is ..." And I looked at them both as I finished my sentence. "Dead."

I grinned at them.

"We won't tell anyone of your secret. Will we Nemesis?"

Nemesis didn't speak. She just shook her head.

"You see, I have had a lot of time to think. I have used the cards."

"We have heard. And it is clear you are using ouzo to help you too."

"Yes. You are right, but they have both provided me with the answers I need. The secret to being powerful isn't immortality. It is the ability to bestow immortality. That is what provides the power."

I could see understanding wash over them. It took any hope they had of winning me over. It was as if a wave had washed away their sandcastle.

"Please," said Nemesis.

"Trust me. I don't want to kill you. I need you alive. And I also need you immortal."

This piqued their interest. "What did you have in mind?"

"As I've said, I'm not stupid enough to reveal my plans to you."

"But you are going to let us live, aren't you?"

"Yes, with conditions."

I could see their disappointment drain from their faces, but it was their very souls I was after. "What conditions?"

"You will both be my nymphs."

They both sat still, their mouths agape.

"You will worship my being, tend to my every need and serve as protectors to me. Your sole purpose will be to serve me. And in return, I will give you immortality that can't be undone. Thereby rendering the secret of gold useless."

"Is that possible?"

"Yes. Look." I reached into my pocket and pulled out a gold-tipped dart. I prodded it into the end of my thumb, and it stung like crazy. But the look on their faces was perfect as they looked at the bubble of amber blood forming on my fingertip.

"Your blood is still amber. How is that possible?"

"The secret can be yours. But you must both become nymphs and serve me. You will be my apostles. You will tell the pantheon of ancient gods that there is only one god that can control immortality. And it isn't Zeus."

"If you need time to think about it, I can give you time. But I won't be giving you your freedom. You must earn that."

They looked blankly at me. And Nemesis asked, "What do you mean?"

"Until I know I can trust you. You will not go anywhere or speak to anyone without my consent. I will control every part of your life. You are my nymphs. Unless, of course, you decline my offer."

"What if we decline?"

"You will be my prisoner's until your mortality sees the end of you. You will die of natural causes like any human. Then you will get your freedom. If you have any ideas about agreeing then absconding, you won't get the daily medication that keeps you immune to gold."

"I placed a bottle of tablets on the table. What is it to be, ladies?"

Nemesis was the first to agree. "I will be your nymph." She looked at Themis as if for reassurance that she'd made the correct decision.

Themis was clearly thinking about the repercussions of what she had to agree to.

"Themis, what are your thoughts? If you need more time …" I offered before placing one of the protective pills in my mouth and swallowing a large draught of ouzo.

"I am thinking how much I want immortality. But do I need it more than the humiliation of being your nymph?"

"You are overthinking the nymph bit. Try this for a comparison. Immortality compared to ageing and ultimate death. You are a beautiful woman. What will time do to your beauty?"

Her vanity got the better of her as she acknowledged her submission. "OK, Rod, I will be your nymph. When do I get my immortality back?"

"When I see fit. For now, we are going out to eat."

"But we aren't dressed for an evening out."

"You will wear what I say. And I say you are coming out to eat dressed exactly as you are. Or you can stay locked up here and starve. You have a choice."

Nemesis said, "Yes, Your Highness. Whatever pleases you." I wasn't sure if she was taking it too seriously or if it was sarcasm.

"Just Rod will do." And I looked at Themis for her acknowledgement.

"Yes, Rod."

"Tomorrow, we will get you both wardrobes that are fit to be worn by representatives of Pine Trees. To the outside world, you are the ladies that are going to run my hotel. Now drink." And I passed the bottle of ouzo to Nemesis. She took a mighty swig as if trying to prove she was entirely on board. Themis was a little more pensive, but she did eventually take a couple of large mouthfuls. *That's what I like about Greek goddesses. They certainly know how to drink like one of the lads.* I gobbed a mouthful of ouzo flavoured spittle at them, and they spat back. The deal was sealed. I placed the brass-tipped dart into my drawer along with the multi-vitamins.

I informed them that we were headed to Enigma, but first, I wanted to get changed. I made a point of dressing properly for the evening. It added to the embarrassment and shame I intended to put them through. If they'd still wanted to be my nymphs after 24 hours of humiliation, I guessed I'd trust them.

The evening started slow, I was already lubricated, and the ladies soon caught up. Themis remained reserved, but I guessed this was to be expected. In the space of a few hours, she had gone from being a significant deity to being a nymph and, finally, to a mere human. I smiled to myself as I likened it to taming a wolf and turning it into a lapdog.

"Themis, if you intend being my nymph, it is about time you let yourself go and joined the party. Here drink," I said as I slid her untouched glass of wine towards her. Meanwhile, Nemesis was well into the evening, as she swayed to the atmospheric music, humming to herself, eyes closed. I left the nymphs to it; I needed a pee. As I staggered off towards the gents. I passed Suzana and asked her to deliver three surprise cocktails to the table.

"Surprise?"

"Yes, you pick them. I don't need to know what they are."

When I returned to the table, the nymphs were in conversation. It reminded me of a conversation between a mother and daughter. Themis admonishing Nemesis for being frivolous.

"Themis, Nemesis is right. This is your new normal. You may as well relax and enjoy it. For a start, I want you to remove your hair bobble and let your hair down."

"I can't. My hair will look a mess."

"Tough, nymph. Remove your bobble, or I will do it for you. And while you are at it, undo the top two buttons on your blouse."

"But…"

"But nothing, you are here to serve me, and you will do it without question."

She sighed so loud I could hear it above the music. Her embarrassment was complete when Suzana arrived at the table with the drinks. "Which drink is for who?"

"Put them all down in front of my new hotel manager."

Suzana nodded at Themis then looked at me with a look of surprise. Maybe she was surprised because I had a new manageress, or perhaps it was Themis's appearance. As she placed all three cocktails down in front of Themis, she looked at me again. I guessed her surprise was that one woman was going to drink so much. She didn't hang around for the outcome.

"You will now taste each of the cocktails in front of you. You will think about the flavours and then allocate one each to Nemesis and me. The one you allocate will be the one that you think we would like best. Nemesis giggled. "Ooooh, a drinking game."

Themis scowled at her and then proceeded to taste each of the multicoloured drinks in front of her. She tasted each of them more than once.

She slid the red coloured concoction towards me. "This is the one I think you would like best." *At last, she is bloody smiling.*

She slid the amber coloured one towards Nemesis. "You will like this one. It has some fizz in it."

"Nemesis, don't drink it yet. We will each taste the drink in front of us, then rotate them around the table. We can then see how well Themis has judged the drinks. If she has judged correctly, we get to drink. If she is wrong, she must drink them all."

We each sipped the drink in front of us. Nemesis couldn't stop giggling. I knew they were all going to be tasty. I knew that I was going to say Themis was wrong irrespective of what I thought. Themis, of course, was going to say that she had chosen the correct drink for herself. The outcome was always going to be down to Nemesis. I didn't know if she had the intelligence to figure the implications of her decision. But she had the casting vote.

"I like the red one best." And I added to her giggle with a smile.

We both slid our drinks towards Themis. "There you go. In any order you like. But you must drink each of them in one."

"In one?"

"Yes, once you put the straw to your lips and suck, you can't stop until it's finished." The double entendre wasn't wasted on Nemesis, she roared. I smirked, and Themis went for it. She drank all three cocktails in less time than it took me to get my jacket back on.

"Are we going?"

"We are getting a little loud here. We're going to another bar."

Themis was about to eat the cherry from the red drink. "Themis, I want you to give me your cherry." I sniggered, and Nemesis screamed.

Themis licked her lips and held the cherry to her mouth.

Fucking bitch.

"You won't ever lick your lips like that again. Now give me the fucking cherry." She looked shocked.

Nemesis finally stopped giggling. "What's wrong?"

"I don't like the whole licking the lips thing. It makes me feel sick." I laughed to try and hide the pain as memories of Affi came flooding back. I stuffed a fifty euro note into the glass on the table.

Themis proffered the cherry laden cocktail stick to me. I took it and dropped it back into the glass. "Come on. The night is still young."

We visited the Irish pub and Caprice. I had a chance to introduce my manager and assistant manager to Janet and Kosta. We played fuzzy duck. I kept deliberately getting it wrong so that I had to take a shot. I needed lots of ouzo.

We played 'Where's the Water' at Karma. Rachael met Themis and Nemesis. She even remembered them from the night I set up the warning calls. "Ah, the ladies that were looking for you that night."

"Yes. It was an aptitude test to see if they were worthy of the roles."

We tried playing the name game at Cavos, which didn't work so well. But at least Andreas got to meet the girls. It could have been a fun game, but they didn't know enough contemporary people, and I didn't know enough deities. At least by that point, my mood had lifted. My depression was clouded by the fog of ouzo.

Finally, we ended up at Angel. "Hi, Rod. Your odyssey didn't take long, did it?"

I completely ignored the comment about the odyssey. *Twenty years? More like twenty bloody hours.* "Zaf, let me introduce my new management team. Themis and Nemesis."

"Ah, like the goddesses."

"Yes. You can see they're a bit too scruffy and rough around the edges to be goddesses, but they'll do."

The girls had got over my continued attempts to embarrass them. Themis said, "Cheeky."

And Nemesis said, "You made us dress like this, your majesty."

"What will you drink?" Asked Zaf.

"Not sure yet. We'll sit over by the phonebox, and I'll give you a signal when we've decided."

I sat facing the road with the beautiful Pine Trees hotel as the backdrop. I was overlooking my domain. One goddess on either side of me. At that moment, I really did feel like the King of the Gods. Two of my loyal subjects sitting at my right hand and my left.

I must grow a beard. Then I will look the part.

"Do you ladies think a beard would suit me?"

They both had a look of confusion, but Themis verbalised her bewilderment, "What?"

"Doesn't matter. I was just thinking out loud. Have you ever played the yes-no game?" I asked, looking to my left and then my right.

"No. How do you play it?" Asked Nemesis.

"We ask each other questions and have to give an honest answer."

"A bit like truth or dare?"

"No, if it was truth or dare, I would call it truth or dare. With this game, you must take a shot every time you say yes or no. We just talk to each other at the same time, listening out for someone saying yes or no."

"I will win this game," said Themis.

"Did I hear you right? Did you say you will win the game?"

"Yes, that's right."

"Well, you better take a drink then because you just said yes."

"And you, because you said the word too." And she laughed.

I gave the signal to Zaf to fetch a bottle of ouzo and three shot glasses. I wasn't too bothered about the yeses and noes. I just wanted to get to know them a bit more. My idea was they would concentrate on not slipping up, which would make them less guarded about their response to questions. The use of alcohol helped a lot too.

I managed to gain some insight into their motives for launching the coup. The Titans had fought the Titanomachy with the Olympians for ten years before the Olympians seized control. The Titans had never lost their resentment of the younger gods. It had festered for millennia. The Titans heard that a mere human had managed to subdue the Poseidon rebellion. They saw the opportunity to unseat Zeus and the Olympians.

"Why didn't you approach me for support? I don't owe them anything."

"We did approach you, remember? But all you did was try to protect them."

"Only because that is what you asked me to do."

"Yes, I know. But at the time, you were under their spell. It is only recently that you have turned to hate them the way we do."

Nemesis interrupted. "Take a drink. You just said the word."

I laughed as I re-charged Themis's glass.

The evening was also loosening my tongue. "Well, now there is a new King. Do you still want to unseat me?"

They both said, "No."

I poured them both another drink. I took a swig straight from the bottle. Not because I'd said yes or no. But because they kept missing my slip-ups and I wanted a drink. They both took their shots.

Nemesis said, "You didn't say yes or no."

Themis giggled at her. "No, but you did."

I loaded one glass with an extra-large shot for Nemesis and handed Themis her glass again.

"Can we stop playing this game now? I'm feeling a bit woozy," asked Nemesis.

"Yes, I think so, it's getting late, and we've almost finished the bottle. I will keep the rest for myself. Carry on. How do I know that you aren't planning to overthrow me?"

"We are happy that Zeus has lost his power. And you are now in charge."

"What of the rest of the Titans?"

"Like us, they won't have much choice. They will know that you hold the secret to keeping their immortality," said Themis.

"Or taking it away," added Nemesis.

I looked across the road towards Pine Trees. "I now have a dilemma. You have a history of lying to me. And here you are, proclaiming that you want me to be king. I must be sure that you aren't just trying to engineer your reinstatement as immortals. I need you to be immortal so that you can spread the word that I have the means of protecting that immortality. I don't know that you won't take the opportunity to escape my power once I make you immortal."

They both looked saddened. Themis put her hand on my knee. "Then I will prove my loyalty to you."

Nemesis said, "Yes, I will be loyal because I want to stay alive. Don't we all want that?"

"Exactly, I don't want to be king because the gods are fearful of me. I want to be king because the gods have chosen me. Because they want me. Because they believe I am the best person to rule over them."

"As Themis said, we will prove our loyalty to you and do your bidding with the rest of the Titans. We will tell your story. But you mustn't favour the Olympians over us."

I turned my head toward Themis, "Are you telling me what to do?"

"No, I would never tell you what to do. I am suggesting that if the Titans feel the Olympians are favoured, they will still carry their resentment. It will be difficult to convince them that you really are the best person to be the king." And she had started to slur her words.

"I think it is time we hit the road." They both looked at each other, then at me. "Went back to the hotel," I translated. I picked up the bottle and slung my jacket over my shoulder. "Come."

Jack of Clubs

"Nemesis and I have been talking. We have decided that we will alternate which of us sleeps with you. I will sleep with you tonight. Nemesis will serve you tomorrow night."

"How dare you make decisions without my permission. As your master, I get to decide who I sleep with."

"I'm sorry, we thought it would please you. And that it would prove our loyalty."

"Suppose I wanted to have you both at the same time? That is a decision that I make, not you."

They both bowed their heads by way of apology. When they raised their eyes back to mine, I couldn't help but burst out laughing.

"Relax. I have no intention of putting either of you through a drunken orgy. Loyalty isn't about sex. It is about caring and devotion. It is about going out of your way to make someone happy."

"Well, surely that means we have to look after your every need."

"Yes, it does, but I don't need sex. I need you to agree with my decisions. I need you to convince other deities that I am a worthy king. I need you to watch my back and be my protectors."

I guessed that they had been used to seeing nymphs used by the Gods for sexual gratification for thousands of years. They both looked relieved that they weren't going to have some sweaty, drunken Englishman bearing down on them. I was relieved that I wouldn't have to demonstrate my ouzo induced lack of sexual power.

"We will do that for you. Won't we Themis?"

Themis smiled and said, "Yes, we will prove our loyalty to you."

"Good, now get yourselves to bed. There are twin beds in the second bedroom of my suite." I slid the keys across the table to them. "Don't lock it. I will follow you up in a while."

"Can we ask a question?"

"Of course."

"When do you plan to give us back our immortality?"

"Soon. Once I am sure of your devotion. Good night."

Once again, I found myself alone in the boardroom. I pulled out the cards from my pocket and gave them a good shuffle. In one swift movement, I picked up the ouzo bottle and emptied its contents into my mouth.

OK cards, the first one is me. I kept the pack in my hand and dealt the top card face-up in front of myself. It was the King of Spades. *At least it wasn't the bloody joker.* I was satisfied with that card. It described me as an ambitious man.

To my left, I imagined Themis was sat there, and I dealt her card. *King of Clubs. Wow, I didn't imagine that of her.* The card was telling me that Themis had integrity and loyalty. The third card was for Nemesis, and I imagined her sitting to my right. *Shit.* There it was. The Ace of Spades. That doom-laden card I despised so much told me that Nemesis would be involved in my death.

I didn't reshuffle the cards, but I asked another question of them. *How does Nemesis plan to kill me?* I reached for the bottle before I realised it was empty. With the question still repeating in my mind, I turned the top card over. It was the joker. The stupid grin on the face of the character on the card was laughing at me. I remembered Yiayia saying that the joker was telling me it didn't know.

She doesn't know. She doesn't know what? Bloody cards.

My eyelids were getting heavy as the last of the ouzo travelled from my gut into my bloodstream. I attempted to stand, staggered, knocked the empty bottle onto the floor and slumped back into my high-backed office chair. Sleep came to visit me easily.

≈≈≈

I started to stir early as the sun streamed through the window. *Bloody Helios. Don't you ever sleep?* As my consciousness returned, I caught sight of the cards on the table. The joker was still laughing at me, and there was nothing I could do to stop it. The ominous Ace of Spades was still there. I couldn't recall which of the nymphs I'd imagined was sat to my right. But I knew I had to be on my guard. Which of them meant me harm? My ouzo sodden brain drew its own conclusions. I pottered about for a bit, tidying up the mess of the boardroom. I stuffed the cards back in my pocket. That shut the joker up. And staggered up to my suite.

I crept into the suite. I figured that so long as the women were sleeping, they couldn't harm me. I turned the shower on, making sure not to look in the mirror. I hadn't looked in the mirror since the strange monster surprised me that morning weeks before. I didn't want to know if that stranger was there again. I was developing quite a beard by now, so maybe the monster wouldn't recognise me, but I wasn't going to take a chance. But I did lock the door. The shower was my antidote to the excesses of the night before. Bringing me back to consciousness. I needed to keep alert. I had no idea when one or both would strike. I'd shampooed my beard and was just rinsing it out when I heard a light tapping at the door.

"Rod. It's Nemesis. We have no clean clothes to wear."

"You will have to wear yesterday's clothes for now. We will get you some clothes today."

"But we ..."

"Are you questioning me?"

"No, master. It is that we do not have clean underwear."

Bloody hell.

"Well. Umm. You either wear old underwear or no underwear at all."

"Ooooh, That's naughty. Would you like that, Rod?"

"It doesn't bother me what you wear. You do whatever makes you feel comfortable. I'd rather you didn't involve me in your underwear decisions."

I could almost hear her disappointment as the silence signalled that she had moved away from the door. I heard the second bedroom door as it was shut. I quietly unlatched the door lock and peeped through the crack. Then quicker than I could say, "Where or your knickers?" I dashed to my room and locked that door behind me.

Get a bloody grip on yourself, Rod. You're the bleeding master.

I started to think that maybe I should have just killed them anyway, then I wouldn't have to be so alert. Deep down, I knew that murder wasn't an option unless I'd wanted to spend an eternity running from the Police. I couldn't let my paranoia cloud my judgment. I needed to stay alert but not distracted. At that point, I knew I needed ouzo. I dressed quickly, not caring about what I was putting on. I did pause to make sure I had my playing cards and my correct dart with me. Double and treble checking I had transferred them from yesterday clothes.

I shouted loud enough so that everyone could hear. "I'm going to the Angel for breakfast. Join me when you are ready. I glanced towards the second bedroom as if looking for a visual clue that I'd been heard.

Within a nanosecond, I wished I hadn't because Themis was emerging from the room without a stitch of clothing on. She stretched and flicked her hair with her hands. I couldn't deny the image before me was straight out of a google search for 'naked goddess in marble.' She was like a statue I'd seen in the Archaeological Museum in Athens. I got out of there before she could think about turning me to stone. There was something that made me fearful of seeing a real goddess naked. I guessed it stemmed from all the myths I'd been reading about. I had to keep reminding myself that Themis and Nemesis were no longer goddesses, they were nymphs, and I was their master. But, if interrogated, I would've had to admit that they both scared the life out of me.

It was a relief to get to the haven that was Angel Bar. The girls eventually caught up with me. God knows why they took so long. It wasn't as if they had to choose what to wear. As they approached, Zaf said, "I know what you mean about them being a bit scruffy."

They chose not to have breakfast. They just wanted clean clothes.

≈≈≈

In Rhodes new town, I gave them free rein to buy what they wanted for casual wear. I did, however, insist that they kitted themselves out with two changes of business wear. Navy pencil skirts and suit jackets with white blouses. If they were going to be representatives of Pine Trees, they needed to look the part. They both reminded me so much of Affi. Once they'd bought the formal wear, I took the goods and went to Trianon. I left them to buy their casual clothes and underwear. No way was I going to hang about for that. I dumped their bags in the car and walked back up the slope of 23rd March Street.

I sat in Trianon and mused over the events that had happened since that day when Jet had attacked Nemesis. I knew it was going to be a long wait given the time they'd taken to surface that morning. I settled in for the long haul. I ordered lunch for one and started to hit the ouzo. It gave me a chance to catch up with Katerina. She was Kam's friend, which meant

I didn't know whether they'd communicated, and she knew that I'd stormed out. She didn't mention anything either out of ignorance or politeness. I kept my mouth shut about it too.

Time ticked mercilessly on. I was beginning to wonder if my nymphs had decided to do a runner. I could have sent a text if I hadn't confiscated their phones. Inside I could feel my pulse rate quickening. I give them an ounce of freedom, and they take a whole dumper full of piss. I needed to hit the ouzo hard.

Fucks sake, I'm going to have to go looking for them.

I left Trianon, waving to Katrina as I went on my way. *Wait till I get hold of them. Bitches.* I'd only got as far as McDonald's, and I saw them crossing the road. I glared at them and scowled.

Themis was the first to speak. "Hi, Rod. Sorry that we took so long."

I just grunted.

"You know what us girls are like with clothes shopping," added Nemesis.

"Well fuck you. You have one job to do, and that is to serve me. You are my nymphs, and you are mine. You can kiss your immortality goodbye." I was angry. My body was going into overdrive with the rush of adrenaline.

"But …"

"But nothing. How dare you keep me hanging about. Have you any idea how that makes me look? Get to the car now. We're going."

I stormed off towards Mandraki. My fast striding, longer legs meant they had to run to keep up with me. By the time we reached the car, they were both in tears.

"Stop crying. It's too late. You have shown how much you wish to serve me."

Nemesis was in full sob mode. "I'm sorry. I worship you, and I thought it would be OK."

"Well, you thought wrong."

Themis was looking out for her own skin. "I told her we were taking too long and that you would be ang … worried about us."

"You spineless bitch! You're selling your best friend out. You have no loyalty to anyone. I don't even know why I'm still here. Both of you get in the car."

All I could hear was the pulse inside my ears. It was fast and loud, setting a tempo. It was accompanying the intermittent sniff of the goddess trying to suppress their upset. I started the car and just sat there gazing out to sea. *How deep is the water here?* The thump in my ears became deafening. It was drowning out all other noise. The normally blue sky and sea took on a red hue.

I pushed my left foot down hard onto the clutch and forced the gearstick into reverse. The engine screamed as my right foot joined its brother at the bottom of the footwell. Leftie didn't linger, and the tyres screeched in a cloud of smoke with the suddenness of my foot leaving the clutch. My ears barely caught the noise as the girls screamed. I hit the brakes hard, and the car stopped close to the parking meter about thirty metres from the edge of the harbour.

I looked over my shoulder at the girls. "Shut the fuck up. I'm trying to concentrate."

I looked at wide-eyed Themis as she gulped down a mouthful of air. "Rod, don't do this. We made one mistake. Our first mistake. We won't do it again."

I looked at Nemesis, her sobs not letting her speak. Through the rear window, I could see a car pull up, The driver gesticulating. I couldn't hear what he was saying, but I knew he was calling me a Malaka.

I'll show you Malaka.

I faced forward again. The vista was a deeper shade of red, and it had become blood red. In one move, my feet completed the same dance they had previously done. My right hand selected first gear. In the blink of an eye, we hit the high kerb that separated us from the blood-red Aegean. The force caused the car's body to twist and buckle, and the windscreen in front of me shattered as the car somersaulted. When it hit the water, I felt the fragments of tempered glass scratch my face.

The sobs stopped as fear took over, and the girls both screamed. The water gushed into the car. I couldn't release my seatbelt. My body spasmed as I faded in and out of consciousness. Because I'd experienced it before, I knew I was starting the cycle of death and resurrection. In a desperate effort to free myself, I reached for the belt release button. Someone else's hand had beaten me to it. With my right hand, I felt the slender thumb of one of the girls as my seatbelt, slackened and I fell towards the roof of the car.

I had to get out. I glanced into the back of the car. Themis was smiling in her sleep, her hand still on my belt release. Nemesis looked like she was in a deep slumber, still belted into her seat.

I broke the surface of the water quickly. The water wasn't that deep, but it was clogging my lungs. My mind was spinning as my eyelids grew heavy, and I drifted into unconsciousness one more time.

≈≈≈

"You have left us with a fine mess to clear up," said Zeus.

My sense of smell came back to me first, and I could smell the familiar aged leather aroma of George the taxi. It was accompanied by the unmistakable scent of seawater and puke. I shivered as the evaporating moisture from my clothes removed any warmth my clothes could provide. I forced my eyes open and could see the strobe effect of streetlights speeding past the car.

I groaned. "Here is what happened," said Zeus. "You were sleeping off a drunken afternoon at your hotel. While you were asleep, someone stole your car."

"But they didn't."

"In which case, you will be held responsible for the death of two women. The mortal justice system will deal with you. When the Titans discover you have killed two of their kind. They, too, will deal out their justice. Trust me. Someone stole your car while you were drunk and asleep."

"Where are you taking me?"

"You are going straight to Pefkos." And he threw a bundle of clothes at me. "Get changed. I will take your wet clothes back to Olympian. Leave your cash in the wet clothes. There is dry money in the clothes I have given you."

I followed his instructions. It was the first time in a long while that I'd taken instructions from anyone. I made sure I transferred my belongings from my wet pockets to their new dry home.

"Don't take your bloody cards. They will still be wet."

"I'm keeping my dart and the komboloi."

"Keep them. If my plan fails, you will need them." And he laughed.

Yeah. I know why you're laughing. Your bloody plans never work. I was alert enough to realise I had to take control of the plan. "Don't go straight to Pine Trees. Drop me on the edge of Pefkos, go via Lardos. I can mingle with tourists and go straight to Angel."

"You are right, but do something with your hair before you get there."

"It's OK. Zaf is used to seeing me after a rough night." But I tried to tidy my hair anyway, as I used my fingers as a comb.

"You are making a poor showing as King of the Gods."

That comment hit me like a thunderbolt, as if he'd unleashed his infamous streak of lightning. The realisation struck me that I'd usurped him. "Why are you helping me?"

"Everyone believes you are the King of the Gods; you have my amulet. What else can I do? I am mortal. You have all the power."

"I need ouzo."

The car slowed, and I could see the lights of Pefkos ahead of us. He pulled George into a bay at the supermarket by Eclipse.

"I have already thought of that. Here." And he handed me

a quarter bottle of ouzo.

I sank it in one as I got out of the car. Before I slammed the door shut, I asked, "How are Kam and the kids?"

"They are safe, but you have a lot of work to do there. I think you have lost them. And remember, you don't know your car is missing until someone tells you or you need to use it."

I tutted to myself and closed the door quietly. A couple of bronzed tourists came out of the Supermarket as I turned to walk to Angel. I heard George pull away.

"Kalispera, good evening," I said.

She said, "Kalispera."

He said, "Evening." *Good, they're Brits. We can wander into Pefkos as a threesome.*

We journeyed together until we reached Caprice. I was tempted to accept their invitation to join them but decided not to change my plan. Besides, it was now only a short walk to Angel, and enough tourists were mingling around to make me invisible.

"Hi, Zaf."

"Hey, Rod. You look rough."

"I feel it. I fell asleep in my office chair. I was supposed to take my managers to Rhodes and kit them out with uniforms."

"You mean you passed out, and they have gone without you."

"I don't know. I haven't seen them since breakfast this morning."

"You are never going to make a businessman. You want fur of the dog?"

I laughed, "And you are never going to get that right. My tongue has grown fur, and I want the hair of the dog. Ouzo, please. I'll be back in a moment." I visited the tourist shop next door and got myself another pack of playing cards. As I came out, ripping the cellophane off the box, I noticed that Pine Trees was in total darkness as I'd hoped. I also noticed it was obvious my car wasn't visible. I got back to Angel just as Zaf was clearing glasses from my table. "You want your ouzo here?"

"Yeah. I think those bitches have taken my car shopping without me."

He looked across at the hotel and shook his head. "Businessman." He smiled and left me to it.

Sitting in Angel, ouzo at the ready, cards in hand, I felt comfortable and at ease for the first time that summer. I mused to myself about the lengths I had gone to in creating a rumour that gold no longer undid immortality. I'd even got Lazaros to make me a set of brass darts to prove the point to Themis and Nemesis. Now they were both dead, and the rumour was killed along with them.

I began shuffling the pack. Before I could deal a card, I felt something against my legs. I looked down and saw a jet-black bundle of fur. It was a kitten. It was pure black and must have had some Persian history because it was long-haired and had copper coloured eye's which shone like Jets. I scooped it up, and it purred to show its contentment.

I flicked over the top card.

Queen of Hearts.

"Hello, sweetheart. I've got some beautiful gold jewellery that would perfectly match your eyes. Have you ever worn claw caps?"

The End

Appendix - Cartomancy

Although Rod would credit Yiayia with educating him in reading the cards. I have to credit Hugh Fox III and his webpage:

https://foxhugh.com/divination/fortune-telling-with-playing-cards/

Without the help given by Hugh's interpretation of the various playing cards, Rod would not have been able to make any decisions. The information presented on the following pages is taken from Hugh's web page.

Hearts
(Cups – Water – Clergy)

Ace

Love and happiness. The home, a love letter. This card is a particularly favourable card that indicates troubles and problems lifting.

Two

A warm partnership or engagement. This is a very favourable card that indicates strength and support coming from a partner.

Three

Love and happiness when the entire spread is generally favourable. In a difficult spread, this can indicate emotional problems and an inability to decide who to love.

Four

Travel, change of home or business.

Five

Jealousy; some ill-will from people around you.

Six

A sudden wave of good luck. Someone takes care of you, takes a warm interest in you.

Seven

Someone whose interest in you is unreliable; someone with fickle affections for you. This card can indicate lovesickness.

Eight

An unexpected gift or visit; an invitation to a party.

Nine

The card of wishes. A wish/dream fulfilled. Look to the card just preceding this one to determine what the querent desires.

Ten

Good luck, success. This is an important card that suggests good fortune after difficulty.

Jack

A warm-hearted friend. A fair-haired youth; or a young person with Water signs predominating in his or her chart. Often this points to a younger admirer.

Queen

A fair-haired woman with a good nature, or a woman with Water signs predominating in her chart. Kind advice. Affectionate, caring woman. Sometimes, this card can indicate the mother or a mother figure.

King

A fair-haired man with a good nature, or a man with Water signs predominating in his chart. Fair, helpful advice. An affectionate, caring man. This man helps you out without much talk. His actions reveal his kindness and concern.

Clubs
(Wands – Fire – Peasants)

Ace
Wealth, prosperity, unexpected money/gain. However, in a difficult spread, this money may disappear almost as quickly as it appears.

Two
Obstacles to success; malicious gossip.

Three
Love and happiness; successful marriage; a favourable long-term proposition. A second chance, particularly in an economic sense.

Four
Beware of dishonesty or deceit; avoid blind acceptance of others at this time.

Five
New friendships, alliances are made.

Six
Financial aid or success.

Seven
Business success, although there may be problems with the opposite sex. A change in business that may have been expected or earned, such as a promotion.

Eight
Work/business problems that may have to do with jealousy. This is generally thought to be quite unfavourable.

Nine

Achievement; sometimes a wealthy marriage or a sudden windfall.

Ten

Business success. Good luck with money. A trip taken now may result in a new friend or love interest.

Jack

A dark-haired or fiery youth. Popular youth who is good-hearted and playful. It can also indicate an admirer.

Queen

A dark-haired, confident woman, or a woman with Fire predominating in her chart. She may give you good advice.

King

A dark-haired, kind-hearted man, or a man with Fire predominating in his chart. A generous and spirited man.

Spades
(Sword – Air – Knights)

Ace

Misfortune; sometimes associated with death or, more often, a difficult ending.

Two

Breaks in relationships; deceit. A break in an important process in the querent's life. If the question concerns a particular romantic interest, this is considered a warning card – infidelity or separation is quite likely.

Three

Breaks in relationships. Sometimes indicates that a third person is breaking into a relationship somehow.

Four

Small worries, problems. Financial difficulties, personal lows.

Five

Opposition and obstacles that are temporary; a blessing in disguise. Sometimes indicates a negative or depressed person.

Six

Small changes and improvements.

Seven

Advice that is best not taken; loss. There is some obstacle to success, and this indicates that obstacles may be coming from within the querent.

Eight

Temptation, misfortune, danger, upsets.

Nine

Illness, accident, bad luck. The querent is at his/her personal low.

Ten

Worry; bad news.

Jack

A youth who is hostile or jealous.

Queen

Widowed or divorced woman; or a woman with Air predominating in her chart.

King

Dark-haired man, or a man with Air predominating in his chart. An ambitious man, perhaps self-serving.

Diamonds
(Pentacles – Earth – Merchants)

Ace

Change; a message, often about money, and usually good news.

Two

A business partnership; a change in a relationship; gossip.

Three

A legal letter. Be tactful with others in order to avoid disputes.

Four

Financial upswing; an older person may give good advice.

Five

Happiness and success. A change for the better. A birth or good news for a child. This is a good time to start new projects.

Six

Relationship problems, arguments. Separation.

Seven

An argument concerning finances or on the job. Generally expected to be resolved happily.

Eight

New job; change in a job situation. The young or the old may find love on a trip.

Nine

A new business deal; travel; restlessness; a change of residence.

Ten

A change in financial status, often for the better.

Jack

A youth, possibly in uniform or a jealous person who may be unreliable. A person who brings news, generally negative but relatively minor.

Queen

A fair-haired woman; or a woman with Earth predominating in her chart. A gossip.

King

A fair-haired or greying man, or a man with Earth predominating in his chart. A man of authority, status, or influence.

The Joker

The Joker is the only card remaining from the Tarot trumps. He corresponds to The Fool in the Tarot deck and has some of the same meanings in the regular deck of playing cards. His number is zero, and he is truly a "wild card." When the Joker appears in a reading, it means that something unexpected and uncontrolled can occur. If there are two Jokers with your deck of cards, and you choose to use the Joker in your readings, you need to add only one

.

Appendix - Chapter Names

Name Definitions

Istoriko is the Greek word for background or historical. It relates to the Greek word historia which means, finding out, narrative or history. It is probably a better word to use than a prologue.

Monos is the Greek word for alone or one. It is used in English as a prefix. For example, monochrome for one colour.

Pefki is the Greek word for pine tree. The version written as Pefkos translates as pine trees or pine forest.

Aphrodite is the Greek Goddess of love, beauty and passion.

Bastet is the Greek Goddess of cats. When the ancient Greek Gods were revered more than today, the killing of a cat was forbidden.

Phobos and Deimos were respectively the Greek Gods of Fear and Terror. Today we express fear as a phobia. Both Phobos and Deimos are natural satellites of the planet Mars.

Paranoia is the Greek word for paranoia. The Greek language invented the word paranoia. Originally it meant irregular mind. But modern usage takes a key symptom of paranoia and uses the word to represent mistrust. Mistrust existed amongst the Olympian Gods and extends to the current population's distrust of their Government.

Nemesis was the Greek Goddess of retribution.

Harpocrates was the Greek God of silence and secrets.

A **nymph** is a consort and guardian, most usually of natural aspects. Sometimes they would be a consort or guardian of a greater deity. Very few nymphs were thought to be goddesses. One exception is written about. Rhode is considered the Goddess-Nymph of the island of Rhodes.

An **amulet** can be natural or man-made. Believers attribute powers to amulets, and these are the powers of protection and good fortune. One very common amulet is the St Christopher, worn by many travellers as a talisman for safe travel.

Themis is the Greek Goddess of Justice.

Prostasia is the Greek word for protection. The Greek God of Protection was Apollo.

Marmaro is the Greek word for marble. In English, marmoreal means marble-like. Marble is a good conductor of heat, and this is why it feels cold to the touch.

Aletheia is the Greek word for truth. The Greek Goddess of Truth is Aletheia.

Deb and Sue are the contemporary names adopted by The Goddesses Aletheia and Agape. They are each the Goddesses of Truth and Deceit, respectively.

Apokalypsi is the Greek word for revelation. The little-known Greek God of Revelation is Apocalypse, who was the lost twin of Zeus.

Psifos is the Greek word for Vote. It is suggested that the father of democracy was a Greek named Cleisthenes.

Apofasi is the Greek word for decision. The Goddess of Decision is considered to be Klotho. She was one of the three fates that decided the path of everyone's life, from when they would be born to when they would die.

Oceanus was a Titan and is considered the God of Fresh Water. Together with his wife, they had thousands of children. A group of these were known as the Oceanids.

Adikia is the Greek word for injustice. The term derives from the Greek Goddess of Justice, Crime and Wrong-doing.

Anastasi is the Greek word for resurrection. Though there is no defined Greek god of resurrection. It is considered that the first God to be resurrected in mortal form was Asclepius, after his death at the hands of Zeus.

Arithmos is the Greek word for numbers. It is the origin of the English word arithmetic. The Greek Goddess Athena is considered the god of Mathematics.

Ouzo is the national beverage of Greece. While many tourists drink it like a shot, it is better to savour the flavour by adding water and sipping it as you eat. This is considered the correct way to drink ouzo.

The Ace of Spades is considered as the card of doom, predicting death. In cartomancy, doom translates as misfortune, sometimes associated with death or a problematic ending.

The Joker has a cardinal number of zero. Cartomancy tells us that the joker is a wild card. When the Joker appears, it means that something unexpected and uncontrolled can happen.

Pheme is the Greek word for a rumour. The Goddess of Fame and Renown was Pheme. She is often portrayed with wings and a trumpet. She is best known for being a gossip.

Eureka is an ancient Greek word meaning 'I have found'. The most well-known use of the word is attributed to the Greek mathematician Archimedes. He is rumoured to have shouted eureka upon discovering a method to determine if an object is made out of pure gold.

Cartomancy tells us that the **Jack of Clubs** represents a dark-haired or fiery youngster. Someone popular, who is good-hearted and playful. It can also indicate an admirer.

Printed in Great Britain
by Amazon